The Book One

The Cull Book Series

Joanne Roach

Copyright @2024 Joanne Roach
All rights reserved.
ISBN:9798851937590

Prologue

World leaders' summit. Brussels, Belgium. February twentieth, 2050.

"I ask you, ladies and gentlemen, to please indulge me momentarily and ponder this hypothetical scenario. Imagine that you are driving down a meandering country road, music playing quietly from your sound system as you glide past fertile-looking fields filled with wheat and livestock. You are driving at around fifty miles an hour when suddenly, several people appear in the centre of the road, blocking your way. There is no possibility that you can stop in time to miss them all, you are guaranteed to hit someone, and at this speed, their chance of survival is zero. So, I ask you this, whom do you aim for?"

"Is it the pair of adolescent boys with hoods pulled high over their heads and cigarettes dangling from their nicotine-stained fingers? They look like they have been causing trouble, or if they have not yet, they will surely do so soon. Or do you aim for the elderly lady with the loosely permed white-grey hair and hunched back who is slowly pushing her bulging shopping trolley along at a snail's pace? She has lived a full life, reached a good age and would understand you choosing her, would she not?"

"How about the tall, slim man in the too-tight bike shorts? He is a big, healthy-looking chap, no doubt he would be willing to be a hero and sacrifice himself to save the others. Then there is the mother, gripping the hand of her angelic-looking blonde-haired child. A little girl of probably around five years old, who is skipping along slowly, watching her feet as they dance along the tarmac. Surely the child, so young and innocent, deserves to be spared? Doesn't she deserve a chance at life?"

"How do you decide? How do you gauge which life is more important? More worthy of continuing? What if that man in the too-tight shorts is the person who will finally find the cure for cancer and save countless people from needless pain, suffering and even death? What if that little girl grows up to be a murderer? Shattering the lives of several families in the most brutal of ways. How do you guess? How can you tell? Whom do you swerve to hit, and who do you miss and let live another day?"

The Prime Minister of Great Britain pauses for a moment, straightening the stacks of paper stationed on the podium she is standing behind. Grateful that she did not accept her assistant's offer of putting her speech on to a tablet as she now has something to distract her hands with as she surveys the crowd before her. The momentary pause also has the added bonus of creating enough time for the translators to relay her words to their non-English speaking counterparts.

"Now, my fellow heads of state, honoured guests, trusted members of the press, I ask you to multiply that handful of people by a hundred, a thousand, and then try to make that same choice. The time to be complacent has come and gone. Thirty-one years ago, in 2019, a paper was published by the Breakthrough National Centre for Climate Restoration, an independent think tank based in Melbourne, Australia. This paper stated that without significant changes being made to our way of life, climate change posed, and I am quoting directly here, "A near to mid-term existential threat to human civilisation." They suggested that society could collapse as soon as 2050 if serious mitigation actions were not imposed. Sadly, we have now reached this deadline, and it seems that their predictions were indeed correct."

"All of the measures we have attempted to put into place have, at this point, categorically failed. Or, at the very least, have not been as successful as we needed for them to be. Our world now has a population of over ten billion people, which is increasing every moment that we deliberate. Sadly, it is at breaking point. It is time for us to remove the theoretical aspect of my question and come up with some real answers."

"Due to the disruption of food production, brought on by the effects of climate change, food costs have been driven upwards at an alarming rate. It is now estimated that half of the population living in my country, the United Kingdom, are today living in food poverty and often cannot afford to eat more than one meal a day. It is much the same worldwide; America, China, Russia, and many others have all confirmed similar, and in some cases, worse numbers of starvation. Our society, as we know it, is rapidly breaking down, crime continues to rise at an alarming pace, and we can no longer continue as we have been."

"The earth is overpopulated; resources are dwindling. Climate change is causing longer summers, more droughts and, in turn, fewer crops and livestock. Coral reefs are now something we can only read about in the history books, as the last reported reef in the world was pronounced dead late last year. Not to mention the increasingly frequent and dangerous natural disasters like the tsunami that killed over four hundred thousand people in the Pacific last year. Including the entire population of the Aleutian

Islands, which are now wholly submerged as floodwaters have failed to recede."

"Homelessness is at an all-time high as we run out of room to build enough properties to house everyone. There are not enough jobs to go around for people to afford what shelter we can provide. Hospitals are overwhelmed, schools are full to bursting, and the police and fire departments are at their wit's end. The world is full. Someone must get off before it is too late for any of us to be saved. This planet we call home is trying in vain to fight back against the destruction we continue to cause. It is time that we help to save her."

To the Prime Minister's surprise, the room remains eerily silent as she finishes her well prepared speech. Only the low buzz of the electrical equipment powering the translators and the large screen behind her can be heard. A camera zooms in on her slightly sweaty face to ensure that even the people right at the very back of the spacious chamber can catch every expression that flits across her features, and she does her best to keep her face devoid of emotion.

The auditorium is filled with representatives from every single country in the world. Over one hundred and ninety-five heads of state, accompanied by one or two of their closest cabinet members and their translators, fill the seats immediately in front of the stage. Religious leaders of every denomination on earth, from the most significant to the smallest, crowd into the gallery to her right, and a handful of the most trusted press who will be given the task of relaying this information to the public as and when the time is right, fill the pews to her left.

Every single person had to sign a non-disclosure agreement before entering this room, from the highest-ranking officials to the lowliest security guards positioned by the exits. Nothing that is spoken about here is to be made public until the council says so. The members of the various groups present here today are not even permitted to return home and tell their spouses, parents or children what has been discussed. It is of the utmost importance that this situation is handled correctly and discreetly.

She wonders for a moment how it came to this, how she was the one who drew the short straw and ended up having to take responsibility for the barbaric course of action that they are about to recommend. Bile rises in the back of her throat as a trail of sweat trickles down her spine beneath her thin, crisp white shirt and images of historical figures who have dared to suggest similar paths in the past swim in front of her eyes. The Prime

Minister tries to suppress a shudder before continuing, knowing in her heart of hearts that this is the only option left, save for the complete extinction of humanity.

"This is the question that we have been pondering, and the conclusion that we have come to, whilst unfavourable, is the one that we feel has the best possible chance to ensure the survival of not only the human race, but also the hundreds of thousands of animals, plants and marine life species that we share our planet with. This is why I and the other fifty-two countries involved in this proposal, which is a collaboration between the brightest minds from every corner of the globe that we have spent years compiling, passionately believe that we have found an answer. No, let me rephrase that. We believe that countless hours, blood, sweat and tears have led us to what is the *only* possible answer. The only way that we can preserve our species. The only way for us to survive."

"We have come here today to ask you all to sign this document." She pauses again to brandish a thick booklet in her bony fingers and brandish it into the air before her. "The Indiscriminate Agreement. Which you will all find a copy of on your desks. I urge you to read it in detail before you make any final decisions on what is best for you and your country. However, I must advise you that these documents will not be permitted to leave this room. I will outline some of the finer points here now."

"We propose that, on the first Saturday of January 2053, a lottery of sorts will be carried out in every participating nation across the world. Those countries that choose not to sign the agreements will subsequently be abandoned without trade, tourism, or politics. In short, no relationship of any kind will remain between those countries that choose not to try and save this planet and those that do. This lottery will randomly select one male and one female born on the same date, in the same town, in the same year and pair them together. This lottery will be carried out by a computer program which our colleagues are completing in China as we speak. The two people whose names are called for each date will subsequently receive a letter informing them of the time and place of where and when their lives will be terminated."

A chorus of gasps and wheezes echoes around the room, filling the Prime Minister's ears as her words are translated into dozens of different languages. The faces of nearly every person in the crowd turn mutinous as they take in what she has just proposed.

"Please, allow me to finish." The Prime Minister urges, her voice rising for the first time this afternoon as she attempts to draw the crowd's attention back to her and calm some of the dissatisfaction in the arena. Slowly, the room returns to its previous stunned silence as her guests await her next words, although there is a palpable tension in the air now.

"Surely you can't mean every single person in the world will be entered into this lottery. What about the children?" Shouts a young Mediterranean man in heavily accented English, whom the Prime Minister cannot quite recognise from his seat near the back of the room. Several heads nod in agreement with him eagerly.

"We believe that to keep society functioning to the highest degree. The only solution is to remove an equal number of people from each generation. It will not help us if by the end of 2057, when we hope to have completed the culls, we are left with millions of orphaned children who require state care. Therefore, we have decided that every member of the population will be eligible for the lottery provided they have already turned five years old by January 1st, 2053. Certain exemptions will be made for those who are already actively employed in essential services, such as the armed forces, doctors, police and so on, as well as some government officials. We will need to maintain a sense of order during what is sure to be a delicate and trying time."

The atmosphere in the room changes so quickly that the Prime Minister can almost feel the disgust of her peers crawling over her skin like a thousand tiny ants. What was, just moments ago, a quiet auditorium is now a cacophony of hissed insults and outrage as its occupants attempt to digest what she is suggesting.

An utterly unbiased cull of a significant percentage of the world's population. "It's what has to be done." She reassures herself under her breath as several strategically placed security personnel stationed around the auditorium attempt to regain control and quieten the increasingly rowdy crowd. Some of whom have risen from their seats and are brandishing their fists in the direction of her podium, shouting what she can only assume are obscenities in a variety of different languages, most of which she cannot understand. Maybe that is for the best, she admits to herself.

"Please, Ladies and Gentlemen, I assure you that this decision was not taken lightly. Nor were the other provisions set out in the agreement." The Prime Minister says, raising her voice to be heard over the noise and sweeping a stray strand of greying hair that has escaped the tightly wound bun at the base of her neck from her forehead.

"Regrettably, many tough decisions have to be made to ensure the continuation of our species. I can assure you that we have investigated every available avenue in great detail, and we believe that the laws that we have outlined in the agreements are the only way forward. In addition to the lottery, we will end the lives of any currently detained criminals whose crimes have resulted in a sentence of over thirty years or more, regardless of how much time they have left to serve. Specially trained staff will carry these culls out at each prison on or shortly after January 5th, 2053."

"We have also posited that any and all fertility treatments, whether private or state-funded, must stop on this date and subsequently become illegal. It will also be unlawful for anyone to produce more than two children. Once a person has reached this number, they will be required to take medications to ensure that they can no longer reproduce. The state will cover the cost of this. Additionally, we will cease to treat all terminal conditions in an attempt to prolong life. Including but not limited to; terminal cancer, Motor Neurone Disease, some neurological diseases such as Parkinson's and some heart and lung diseases. These will cease to be treated for a period which will last for at least as long as the five-year plan detailed in the indiscriminate agreement. We will also pass a law making euthanasia legal in all participating countries. Giving anyone who wishes to volunteer to end their life the opportunity to do so safely and securely without fear, pain or repercussions."

"At this time, I suggest that we take a short recess for you to digest this information. We will reconvene again in two hours, when I will be more than happy to answer any of your questions with the assistance of my colleagues who have worked so diligently on this document. Thank you."

Scurrying off the stage with as much dignity as she could muster amongst the boos and shouts emitting from the crowd, the Prime Minister blinked back the rapidly forming tears in her eyes. That's it. The hardest part is over. They know what we are proposing. They see what monsters we have become.

Chapter One

"Another price hike Tony? Really? This close to Christmas? The customers aren't going to like that." Stephanie Moore piped up from her spot near the back of the small, rundown restaurant, which has been her place of employment for the last four years. Stretching up on her tiptoes to be seen above the heads of the other staff members crowding around the mismatched tables with their slightly discoloured white linen tablecloths as she speaks to her boss. This will be the fifth price hike in as many months, she realises as she shrinks back down and leans against the crumbling wallpaper behind her, awaiting Anthony's response.
"I know they won't. I don't like it either, but what else can I do? Whenever the suppliers put their prices up, I have no choice but to do the same to cover my costs. Even with these increases, we'll barely be making a profit." Anthony told her, resigned to the inevitable, his thin shoulders sagging slightly under the weight of responsibility that leans heavily on them.
His is one of only a handful of restaurants that have managed to remain in operation on their small high street in Surrey in the southeast of England. Anthony remembers a time when the road was full to bursting with bustling businesses, all competing for the Saturday date night crowd, running special offers every week to try and entice people through their doors instead of someone else's. Now though, with the economy the way it is and the price of food going up astronomically every few weeks, most of them have been forced to close their doors, and for sale signs and boarded-up windows litter the now empty buildings which used to be so full of life. Instead of queues of impatient customers, the doorways are full of homeless people desperately searching out a secluded place to sleep for the night, hoping that they will be somewhat protected from the worst of the freezing December temperatures and the icy cold winds.
Month after month, the government issues statements trying to convince the public that things will improve soon. They reassure the population that they are putting plans into place to return the world to its previous state, something that, at twenty-three years old, Stephanie, along with most of her colleagues, can barely remember. Still, nothing seems to materialise. The government never actually elaborate on these grand plans, or when people might start to see a difference in the ever-greying world around them, they just continue to tell people that they exist. Probably to justify them keeping their jobs more than anything else.

People had spoken of climate change when Anthony, Tony to his friends, was a kid, though it was always portrayed as some far-off problem that wouldn't truly cause issues for the population until his grandchildren's children were born. A few celebrities tried to get the general public's attention about it, and some political parties had sprung up claiming climate change as their main agenda. Still, besides banning plastic straws and charging people for carrier bags in supermarkets, not much was really done at the time. If only they had known then what they knew now, perhaps they would have done something. Maybe they would have tried harder before the cost of a loaf of bread rose to more than the hourly wage he could afford to pay his staff.

"I don't get how anyone will be able to afford to come out for dinner if this carries on." Crystal, one of the other servers, mumbled quietly, not quietly enough so that Tony didn't catch it, though. He looks over at her, and he can see that behind her flippant tone, her mahogany brown eyes are filled with fear. Damned if I do, damned if I don't. Tony thinks to himself. If he doesn't put the prices up, he will not be able to afford to pay his suppliers, and the restaurant will have to close because they'll have no food to serve. Which in turn would put Crystal, Stephanie and the rest of his staff of thirty out of work.

Tony knows full well that with the job market the way it is, they all need their positions, or else they will be lining up to sleep in the doorways themselves soon enough. As it is, he's already had to convert the small attic space above the restaurant into a makeshift dormitory for several of his staff who can't afford their own places. He knows that by putting the prices up again, he will be less likely to entice customers through the door and may end up having to lay people off anyway, but he's doing his best. He already employs more people than he needs, and his wife is always on his back about it. A restaurant this size could be run efficiently with half the number of staff. Still, when a young person comes to his door, dishevelled and hungry and begging him for the chance to earn an honest living, he can rarely bring himself to turn them away.

"I'm sorry, guys, but like it or not, the new prices will go into effect on Monday. The printers we used for the last pricing adjustments on the menus have gone out of business, so I will make the amendments by hand. If anyone complains or has questions, send them to me, and I'll explain." Tony says with a sigh, resigned to this impossible choice. Whatever plans the government has for sorting out this mess, he hopes they put them into practice soon before he loses everything he has worked so hard to build.

Slowly his staff file past him, dragging their feet in scuffed shoes to start their shifts, grumbling quietly to one another as they reach to tighten the frayed strings of the aprons slung around too-slim waists or thrust their hair under nets. Tony settles himself down behind one of the tables with a stack of menus in front of him and pulls a marker pen from his pocket, ready to start altering the prices.

"How bad is it? Really?" a quiet, melodic voice interrupts his melancholy thoughts, and he looks up to see Stephanie's bright hazel eyes staring down at him. He nods at the chair opposite his own, gesturing for her to take a seat and returns his attention to the task at hand as he replies.

"Honestly? It's not good, Steph. I don't know how much longer we can carry on like this before I'll have to start letting people go. You know, last week, my take-home pay was less than any of you made. And with the disruption to the food supplies, the droughts, the reduction in available crops and livestock, I cannot see things changing anytime soon, as much as I might like them to."

"Is there anything I can do? I mean, could we try setting up the garden out the back again? Grow our own vegetables?" Stephanie suggests, hopefully, but Tony just shrugs.

He likes Steph. She is a sweet girl, one of his favourites, even though he knows he should not have favourites at all. He has felt responsible for her since she came to him desperate for work after her parents moved away and left her to fend for herself when she was still little more than a kid. He wishes he had better news for her, an optimistic plan to get them through. The last thing he wants is to be another person in her life that disappoints her and lets her down. Still, there is no point in giving her false hope either, so he decides just to be honest.

"We tried that, remember, nothing will grow out there. The ground will be frozen for the next few months. Then when summer approaches, the grass will all be dead within a few weeks when the heat waves hit, especially with the water restrictions. Not to mention, where would we get seeds from? Can you remember the last time you saw something as simple as a packet of seeds in a shop?" He asks, racking his brain to try and find the answer to his own question.

He can remember when he was a young man, he would spend his Saturday afternoons walking through crowded garden centres, marvelling at all the pretty coloured plants and endless racks of seed packets containing seeds for everything from courgettes to roses. Those garden centres are long gone now, replaced by empty wastelands filled with squatters, grey and dirt-covered, with barely a speck of colour to be seen.

"You'll think of something, I'm sure." Steph pipes up in a forced, cheery tone. "You always do." She finishes quietly, laying her hand lightly on his forearm as she pushes her chair back and pulls out a notepad from the pocket of her apron.

Tony cannot think of an appropriate response. He knows she doesn't believe her words any more than she expects him to. Empty platitudes have become a coping mechanism for everyone, a way to try and forget, a way to try and convince themselves and each other that things will improve and fend off the hopelessness which has settled over them all like a thick layer of dust on an old bookshelf. Yet, at the moment, he cannot muster any hope to offer her in return, empty or otherwise.

Stephanie made her way through the tightly packed, disordered tables and peeling chairs scattered haphazardly around the restaurant's interior. Hissing under her breath as she bumps her hip against the arm of a chair that has not been pushed back properly and pausing here and there to straighten tarnished cutlery or wipe a glass. Not that she even knows why they bother to put wine glasses on the tables now. With the taxes on alcohol being what they are, very few people buy wine with their meals anymore.

"What did the boss man have to say? Reckon we should start looking for new jobs?" Crystal's husky voice asked as she appeared at Stephanie's side and reached out to straighten a stray napkin on the table before them, her ebony skin glinting in the flickering light from the candle Steph had just lit.

"Ha! Look where? The only jobs going round here are for hookers and drug dealers." Steph retorted with a crooked smile.

"Well, I don't know about you, but I think I'd make a fabulous hooker." Crystal winked back. "I mean, have you seen my arse? Seriously, I'm surprised I don't have pimps knocking down my door trying to get them a piece of this booty." She laughs, spinning in a half-circle and sticking out her admittedly well-filled out behind before giving it a hearty smack with her right hand, causing Steph to giggle despite herself.

She is always beyond grateful for Crystal. No matter how dark things get, she knows she can rely on her larger-than-life best friend to put a smile on her face. I wonder if her parents knew she would have such a sparkling personality when they named her Crystal, Steph thinks to herself.

"Please let me know if you start giving out our address to them so that I can make sure I am elsewhere when they come knocking," Steph chuckles back as the pair start to make their way towards the front doors to open the restaurant for the evening.

"Ahh, don't be jealous, babe. I'm sure they'd have a place for a skinny little white girl like you too, especially if I put in a good word for you." Crystal teases.

"I'm alright, but I appreciate the offer. Maybe when you make your millions, you can be my sugar Momma, and I can become a lady of leisure."

"Girl, if I'm getting my lady garden ploughed by every shape and size of spade from here to Brighton, then you sure as hell can manage to keep bringing people plates of slightly questionable meat." Crystal fires back.

"Speaking of, Jose wants us to push the chicken tonight before he has to chuck it out," Steph tells her friend as she pulls open the heavy glass door and gazes at the puddle-covered street outside.

"Oh, does he now? How 'bout you tell Jose from me that he's more than welcome to send any leftover chicken home with us after work rather than putting it in the bin."

"Ha-ha, tell him yourself!" Steph giggles with a wink and heads over to the front desk to check if they have any reservations for tonight.

Whilst she is perusing the diary, Steph catches sight of an elderly couple outside the window from the corner of her eye and watches as they begin to examine the prices on the laminated menu on the wall. The look of shock on the older woman's face as she glances up at her slightly older husband is clear even from this distance as her tired eyes grow wide. Steph sighs as the woman shakes her head in defeat and snuggles up closer under the single umbrella in her husband's hand, linking her arm through his before they continue walking down the street. And that's before we raise the prices again, Steph thinks unhappily.

"It's going to be a long night." She mumbles to herself as she arranges her features into her best and most welcoming smile, hoping they'll have more luck with the next people who walk by.

Chapter two

"Steph, I've just sat a table in your section," Tony called across the barren kitchen halfway through the evening shift, stirring Steph from her daydreaming as she washed dishes to pass the time.

"Thanks, Tony." She replied. Pulling a battered old notepad from the pocket of her apron and retrieving the half-chewed-up pen from behind her ear, Steph twirled it between her fingers as she made her way out into the dining area and towards her assigned section.

She had barely taken three steps when she spotted the familiar face sipping from a glass of ice water in front of him, and her breath caught in her throat. Dammit, Anthony! She cursed her boss internally before squaring her shoulders and stepping forward. I swear he does it on purpose, she thinks to herself, glancing around at the mostly empty restaurant and the other servers who are idling nearby. He could have sat him in anyone's section, but oh no, he has to give him to me, as usual.

"Good evening. Are you ready to order?" Steph asks politely when she reaches the table. She cannot make eye contact with the man seated to her right, knowing full well that her face would instantly turn beet red if she dared to. Instead, she focuses on the person opposite him, flashing them what she hopes is a cheerful smile and immediately wishes that she hadn't.

The man's female companion for the evening is yet another in a seemingly never-ending stream of big-boobed blondes, just like every other time he's entered the restaurant in the last year. The woman's hair is curled perfectly to cascade around her slim shoulders and her makeup has been applied with such precision that Steph cannot even begin to fathom how long it must have taken her.

Self-consciously she tucks a strand of her own dark brown hair behind her ear and wishes she had the money, time or inclination to make more effort with her appearance. It had been years since she bothered with anything as extravagant as foundation or blush, Steph wasn't even sure where someone would buy things like that nowadays and god knows how much they'd afford. Much more than I have to spare, no doubt, Steph tells herself before she can get too carried away and start going on a shopping spree in her head. This afternoon before leaving for work, she coaxed the last dregs out of an ancient bottle of mascara and smeared some Vaseline on her lips in her regular routine, before dragging her hair up into a messy bun and heading out. Usually, she didn't give things like that a second thought. But looking into the bright blue, black eyeliner-framed eyes of the blonde-haired beauty, she cannot help the ball of jealousy that settles in her stomach.

Oh, how the other half live. While the vast majority of the world is scrimping together every penny they can find to keep a roof over their heads and enough food in their bellies to keep them functioning. The more privileged people in society can spend hours ensuring that they look perfect for a date. Knowing daddy's credit card and connections mean they never have to worry about where their next meal comes from. Alright for some.

"Hi Steph, I think we are, yes." The male at the table answers her question, and she is finally forced to look over at him for the first time this evening, her breath catching slightly in her throat as their eyes meet and she is forced to stifle a small cough.

"Hey, Tom. What can I get you?" Steph inquires, tapping her pen against her notepad in agitation and cringing a little at the slight break in her voice when she says his name. Why can't she be as calm and composed as the blonde? Who is leaning forward slightly, her elbows resting on the table, causing her ample cleavage to be displayed more prominently in her low-cut top.

"I think I'll have the chicken. What about you, Tommy?" Blondie says in a tone that almost makes Steph want to laugh. Her voice is as sweet as honey, but from the look in her eyes, it's clear there is nothing sweet about her intentions with Tom this evening.

"Erm, Steak for me, please."

"Medium-rare?" Steph asks, already knowing how *'Tommy'* likes his steak, given that he comes in once or twice a month with a different blonde and orders the exact same dish.

"Please." He confirms, handing her back his menu. His fingertips brush against hers as she reaches out to take it, and Steph cannot control the flush that spreads across her cheeks from the unexpected contact. She quickly busies herself, stowing the menu in her apron and keeping her head lowered, hoping that the flash of colour will dissipate before Tom notices.

"And we'll take a bottle of your finest dry white wine as well," Blondie orders, waving her menu in Steph's general direction without looking at her. With her other hand, she reaches across the table to stroke her perfectly manicured fingernails down the back of Tom's forearm. Steph might have imagined it, or maybe just hoped, but she could have sworn she saw him cringe just a little at the gesture as he subtly moved his arm away.

"Of course. I'll be right back with your wine." She says and quickly spins on her heel and makes her way to the bar.

"Argh!" Steph moans once she is in the relative privacy of the mostly empty and rarely entered wine cellar.

"Another blonde?" Crystal's voice pipes up from behind Steph, making her jump slightly as she wrestles with the cork in the bottle which just does not seem to want to come out.

"Yep. I swear I'll clean the bathroom for the next three months if you take this table." Steph begs her friend as she turns to face her in the dimly lit room.

"Ha! Firstly, you'll clean the bathroom anyways. You always do, neat freak. Secondly, you and I both know that you don't actually want me to take the table. How can you possibly keep your crush on that boy alive if you don't get your fix of staring at him while he eats his steak?" Crystal says sarcastically, giving Steph a conspiratorial wink.

"I do not have a crush on him!" Steph replies indignantly, but both women know full well she is lying.

"You're right, you don't. What you have for that boy out there is far more than a crush." Crystal giggles.

Steph wrestles with the incredibly stubborn cork, trying desperately not to break it. The last thing she needs is Tony asking her to replace the bottle out of her paycheck, it would be at least two shifts earnings with the price of wine what it is. Why can't I just forget about him? She questions herself for the hundredth time.

Thomas Walker had spent the summer before last working behind the restaurant's bar with her. Back when they still needed two staff members on the bar, when people still came out for a drink or two after work and the price of a pint wasn't into double figures, and before he headed off to medical school.

It was only for a few months, but looking back, Steph knew that she had developed a slightly unhealthy infatuation with the dark-haired, green-eyed man who always greeted everyone with a smile. They had bonded over their mutual love of old rock music from the late twentieth century. Challenging each other to guess what song the other was humming the intro to during the quiet periods behind the bar to pass the time. During those months, Tom had been the shining light in her day. The one person could always make her laugh and stop her from focusing on the disasters happening around them as the world grew steadily darker. And then, just as quickly as he had appeared, he was gone.

Thomas's parents weren't exactly what Steph would call wealthy. Still, they were undoubtedly better positioned to cope with the current economic climate than most. Whereas people like Steph had to work unless she wanted to end up on the streets like so many others, Tom was in the lucky position of actually being able to go to school and follow his dreams. He had always talked so passionately about wanting to become a doctor. It was one of the things that Steph liked most about him, so she didn't begrudge his ambitions, but she did miss his company.

Tom had told her that he wanted to open a clinic that exclusively treated the homeless and the poor. When Steph had questioned him on this, asking if he wouldn't rather go and work in one of the more prominent private hospitals in town where he would be guaranteed a hefty pay packet each month and have all the resources he could need at his disposal, Tom had gotten profoundly serious. He had stopped polishing the old wooden surface of the bar and turned to give her his full attention, his shining green eyes feeling as though they were penetrating directly into her soul as he held her gaze so intently that she could not possibly have looked away.

"No, I wouldn't. I'd rather be making a real difference. Those people out there," He had paused to gesture at a small homeless family standing under the awning of the empty shop opposite their restaurant. "They deserve to be cared for too. They deserve to be made to feel like they matter. Like they are valued. That their lives are just as important as someone who lives in a big house and drives a fancy car. I believe that healthcare is one of the fundamental things we all deserve as human beings. A parent should be safe in the knowledge that when their child gets an infection, it isn't a death sentence. I'd rather spend my days putting smiles on people's faces and knowing that I have truly helped them than pumping some rich kid's stomach after he's drunk his way through daddy's liquor cabinet for the third time that month."

Looking back now, Steph is reasonably sure that was the moment when she had first fallen for Thomas. When he stopped being just the guy who sang AC-DC off-key with her and always managed to press the wrong button on the till when he rang up a vodka and coke, and became the kind of man she could see herself building a life with.

Sadly, it had become apparent all too quickly that she was as far away from the type of woman he would date as it was possible to be. About three months after he quit his job, he started turning up at the restaurant every few weeks with a different blonde-haired beauty and Tony always sat him in her section. Steph was sure he'd clocked on to her feelings for Tom and was making a game out of it for his own amusement from the sly looks he threw her way every time Tom arrived. Or maybe Tony was hoping that one of these days, Steph might have the guts to talk to Tom properly, to ask him out herself, or at least manage to come up with something more interesting to say to him other than asking how he wanted his steak cooked.

But here they were, over a year down the line. Tom here with another blonde, and Steph just as timid and mousy as ever.
The rest of the evening dragged on sedately. Tom and his date finished up and made their way outside around nine and Steph is equally grateful and embarrassed by the overly generous tip that they leave her. Unable to decide if it was because of her excellent service, Tom being generous, or just Blondie's way of ensuring Steph knew that she was not even close to being in Tom's league. She sighed, knowing full well that she was too in need of the money to overthink it too much. She was sure that the woman had made a show of touching Tom's arm a little more and laughing a little louder at everything he said when Steph was in earshot. Firmly marking her territory, and she had a feeling that the tip was her parting insult.

Steph had been sorely tempted to make a crass remark about how she would see Tom again in a couple of weeks with the next girl on his arm as the pair had walked past her towards the exit, but thankfully, she managed to restrict herself to just whispering her thoughts to Crystal as they had chatted in the kitchen after he had left instead. Probably for the best.

Chapter Three

It had just gone eleven pm when the two women finally left the restaurant. Armed with their tips from the evening which, paired with last nights, might just allow them to pay their electricity bill this month with a bit of luck and mean they could keep the heater that warmed their tiny studio flat on just a little longer to get them through the worst of the cold weather. Crystal gripped a flimsy foil-wrapped package in her glove covered hand, filled with the slightly iffy chicken they had liberated from Jose in the kitchen on their way out.

Despite the questionable nature of the meat, Steph couldn't stop her mouth from watering when she thought about sinking her teeth into it. It had been weeks since they've been able to afford something as extravagant as meat. The substitutes that the few still-standing supermarkets have been pushing to try and make up for their lack of stock are not exactly awful, the flavour is much the same, something about the texture is wrong though, and Steph can always tell the difference.

They walk arm in arm at a fast pace through the crowded streets, doing their best to stay away from the areas that are notorious for crime at this time of night. Numerous beggars call out to them as they duck their heads against the howling wind, asking for a spare coin or two, or for a scrap of food to soothe the aches in their empty bellies. Steph should be used to it by now. She cannot remember the last time she left her flat without being accosted by a member of the ever growing homeless population. As much as she feels sorry for them, as much as her heart goes out to each and every one of them and she wishes that she could do more, Steph knows that if she isn't careful with the few pounds she has in her pocket, she will be joining them on the streets soon enough. Generosity isn't something she can afford.

A small, high-pitched voice breaks through her carefully constructed barrier, designed to keep their cries at bay, and she cannot help but glance up to seek out its source. Wishing that she hadn't the moment that her eyes locked with those of a tiny little girl, who cannot be more than ten or eleven years old, calling out to her pitifully from next to an overturned rubbish bin which she has clearly just been rummaging through for scraps.

"Do you have any food?" The little girl asks as Steph takes in her appearance. She is wearing what can only be described as a rag instead of a dress, and it's quite a few sizes too big for her, making her tiny frame seem frailer. Her skin is filthy, and the dark circles under her eyes show how little sleep she manages to scrounge out here on the cold, unforgiving streets. The young girl holds herself warily, bouncing on the balls of her feet as though preparing to run at any moment, and Steph's heart goes out to the child. She's far too young to be out here alone.

Steph looks from the package in Crystal's hands to the little girl and shakes her head sadly before digging her hand into her pocket and feeling around for some change.

"Here," she says, handing the child three tarnished two-pound coins, her stomach sinking as she does so. She knows it's not enough, knows it will barely buy this poor, hungry creature a loaf of bread with the cost of food as high as it is, but it is all she can spare. There is no point in giving her raw chicken. She would have no way to cook it and would end up sick.

"Thank you, Miss." The little girl says with a shy smile before scurrying away down a dark alleyway and out of sight. The coins clutched tightly in her small hand.

"You're too soft, you know that? So much for paying the electricity bill." Crystal scolds her.

"I'll make the money back tomorrow, don't worry. Maybe I can ask Tony for an extra shift." Steph tries to defend herself.

"Yeah, right. Have you seen how overstaffed we are? That man is as soft-headed as you are." Crystal fires back, but Steph can hear the sympathy in her voice.

Before managing to land a job at the restaurant and moving in with Steph, Crystal lived on the streets for years. She knows better than most how hard it can be to survive on your own, but she also had to learn to be tough and protect what was hers. She'd never have survived this long if she hadn't.

The women turn the last corner of their route, and in front of them looms the twenty-eight-story tower block they call home. The stark grey building stretches into the night sky, almost disappearing against the blackness due to the lack of lights shining from the windows. Here and there, a candle can be seen flickering against the darkness, showing the only signs of life. Most people have learned to do without electric lights, they cost too much to run.

Steph has lived here for nearly four years now, since her parents decided to move away. They felt that being further away from the big cities would mean a better quality of life and wanted to try their luck in the countryside. Never having been close to them, Steph felt she had no option but to stay behind, rationalising that

if jobs were so hard to come by here, this close to the capital, then they'd be even harder to find in the more rural areas. They had kept in touch for a while, exchanging phone calls now and then. However, those calls gradually faded into the odd email. Now, they pretty much only bothered to communicate around Christmas or someone's birthday. Scratching her head, Steph tries to remember when her mother's birthday was and if she contacted her for it, but try as she might, she cannot recall.
She trudges up the stairs to their small studio flat on the twenty-first floor behind Crystal. Watching idly as her best friends' hips sway from side to side as she climbs and getting lost in the rhythm. It's a handy distraction, a way to forget how many more stairs there are and keep her mind off the dull ache in her feet as they trudge upwards. When they finally reach the landing, Steph pulls the small set of keys from the inside of her bra, where she stores them for safekeeping, opens the front door and shuffles inside.
"Want me to cook?" Steph asks Crystal, hoping against hope that her friend says no. She is desperate to have what will no doubt be a cold bath in an attempt to rid herself of some of the grime from the day.
"Do I hell. We've not had chicken for weeks, and you think I'm gonna leave you in charge of it? Was I born yesterday?" Crystal laughs. She may not know much, but one thing she has learned for sure is that Steph cannot cook at all. She honestly wonders sometimes how Steph managed to survive before she came along. The girl would burn water if she was left to her own devices.
"Har har." Steph sarcastically chuckles back. "I was just trying to be nice!"
"If you want to be nice to me, you can try and leave me some hot water for a change!" Crystal shouts over her shoulder as Steph pushes aside a poorly hung plastic curtain which serves as the divider between their main living space and the bathroom and disappears inside.
The tiny bathroom consists of nothing more than an old greying tub on one side, opposite a sink which only has one working tap and never spurts out anything other than freezing ice-cold water this time of year, and a toilet with a cracked lid. But it is the only place Steph can get a little solitude nowadays.
The tiny studio flat was never designed to have multiple occupants, and there is only enough room for one bed which the young women share. The rest of the space is occupied by an old

wardrobe with a cracked mirror on one of the doors and their small kitchen area. Which is basically just an oven with a hob and a cupboard just about hanging onto the wall above it, with a small fridge down to one side. Which, more often than not, stands empty as they can't afford to buy enough food to fill it.
Steph vaguely thinks back to the days living in her parent's house, with their fully stocked kitchen, decked out with every gadget you could imagine and a few you probably couldn't, thanks to her mother's shopping habits. She sighs unhappily as she turns the tarnished bronze-coloured tap above the bath, watching the water begin to trickle out in a slow but steady stream. She knows that turning the hot tap on is pointless. They have not turned their water heater on for days, so there won't be any warm water. However, she can't seem to break the habit and twists at the metal anyway.
Slipping her clothes off and leaving them in a pile on the cracked tile floor, Steph braces herself for the shock of the icy water. She timidly lowers one foot down into it, feeling a shiver ripple across her bare skin and allowing herself a moment to adjust to the temperature before adding her other foot and slowly lowering her body down into the tub. The water may well be cold, and the tub may well be cracked slightly in places and showing glimmers of silver where the ceramic coating has worn away, but it's still absolute bliss to Steph. The water laps gently at her skin, cleaning away the day's grime, and the simple act of being alone makes this, without a doubt, her favourite part of the day. Laying her back against the tiles, Steph closes her eyes, allowing her mind to drift off to somewhere more pleasant. Which is pretty much anywhere other than here.

Chapter Four

Tugging a thick blue jumper over his soft brown curls in the hope that it would block out some of the bone-chilling wind which he could hear howling outside of his bedroom window as he got ready for another shift at the hospital on a dreary Saturday morning, Thomas Walker's eyes fell briefly on the old framed photograph of his family positioned by his bedside. The dark leather frame made their smiling faces look all the brighter in contrast, and for a moment, Tom wished that he could return to that time, when things were so much simpler.

He had been around eight or nine years old when the photo was taken on a white sandy beach during a family holiday to Greece. Flanked on one side by his younger sister Emily with her pigtails, toothless grin and pretty polka dot dress, and on the other by his mother looking every inch the doctor's wife in her tailored shorts and loose camisole, holding his brother Mark in her arms.

Next to his well-put-together parents and siblings, Tom stuck out like a sore thumb. He was wearing a bright yellow T-shirt and almost neon green shorts that clashed horrifically. He recalled his mother begging him not to wear them together on several occasions, including this one, but they were his favourite at the time, and no amount of bribery or coercion could tempt him to wear anything else, much to his mother's chagrin. Their father stood proudly behind Tom, resting his hands on his son's shoulders as he peered out under a straw sun hat and smiled broadly from ear to ear. They looked like the perfect family, and maybe, back then, they had been. But those days were far behind them now.

Slinging his rucksack over his shoulder, Tom pushed his feet into his slightly worse-for-wear trainers and made his way downstairs. When he caught sight of his father's broad shoulders filling the wooden frame of the kitchen doorway, he braced himself for the conversation he knew was coming, the same conversation they'd had practically every morning when their paths had crossed for the last year. He would be lying if he said he was anything other than supremely bored of it at this point.

"Thomas." His father croaked in a voice still hoarse from sleep and gave him a slight nod in greeting.

"Good morning, darling." His mother almost sang in her sweet silvery tone. "We really should take you shopping and replace those shoes before the weather worsens. Look at all those holes!

The rain will seep straight in. You'll catch your death of cold if you wander around with wet feet all day." She said, from her place by the kettle as she lifted the stainless-steel object and poured torrents of boiling water into two large mugs, causing steam to billow into the air around her.

"Maybe next week, mum. I've signed up for an extra shift on Thursday, so I haven't got any days off till then," Tom told his mother.

"One of these days, you will come to your senses and let me get you a job at my hospital." Mr Walker began. Here we go again, thought Tom. "They work you too hard at that god-awful place. You'll be burnt out by the time you are my age." his dad continued, the disdain in his voice evident.

"I'll just be grateful to live that long," Tom mumbled under his breath before squaring his shoulders and repeating the well-rehearsed speech he had given to his father a thousand times before. "Dad, I know you mean well, but I've told you before that I like my job. I have zero interest in working at a private hospital, listening to rich old ladies complain about their varicose veins, or prescribing Viagra to dirty old men."

"Firstly, I can assure you that my job is much more complex than you like to make out. And secondly, those rich old ladies and dirty old men, as you call them, are my patients, and they keep a roof over your head, son. You might try being more grateful." Mr Walker shot back. "At least I can guarantee that none of my patients will be dragging lice and fleas into my office with them." he followed up in an undertone to his wife, who shot him an unimpressed glare.

One of these days, they would get through a morning without an argument, she thought to herself before turning her back on her son and husband and adding a spoonful of sugar to one of the cups of tea.

"I am grateful, dad." Tom began with a sigh. "Grateful that those ladies have enough money to visit your hospital instead of mine and allow me to continue to help people less fortunate, the people with real problems. Them *and* their fleas." Tom retorted, emphasising his last sentence for effect.

Flicking his eyes to the old-fashioned clock on the wall, he mumbled a curse under his breath. "I've gotta go. Next week mum, OK? I'll be back late tonight." he finished, kissing his mother's cheek quickly and hurrying out the door before his dad could say another word.

A torrent of sideways rain pelted against Tom as he hurried down the street towards the run-down old community hospital where he spent most of his waking hours. He kept his head down and his hood firmly up and tried to shield himself from the worst of the wet weather, occasionally flinching as the ferocious wind smacked against the small patches of exposed skin that he hadn't managed to cover. Tom walked quickly, trying to reach his destination as soon as possible and get out of the rain. He was only a few streets away from work when a loud voice boomed from somewhere to his left, catching his attention and causing him to stop dead in his tracks.

"This is a special news bulletin from Channel Eight. Reports are coming in this morning of yet another severe weather event in the United States. Hurricane Tobias was predicted to bypass mainland America and mostly dissipate over the sea. However, Meteorologists reported its sharp change in direction in the early hours of this morning and issued an evacuation order for some southern states. Sadly, it came too late for most of the population of Louisiana, where the category-five hurricane is thought to have hit hardest. The estimated death toll at this time is around five-hundred-thousand, with entire areas of the state still submerged under eight feet of water, but with wind speeds at still over one hundred and sixty-seven miles per hour and deluges of rain still falling from the skies causing flash flooding in many low-lying areas, this number is expected to rise significantly before Tobias dissipates and rescue efforts can begin. President Scott is due to make an address shortly, and we will, of course, be covering this live."

The crowd of people coming to a standstill in the middle of the street swelled as more and more people stopped, raising an arm to shield their faces from the worst of the rain so that they could watch the bulletin being projected onto the surface of one of the many dilapidated high-rise buildings in the centre of town. This has become the norm over the last few years, as fewer and fewer people have the means to have something as extravagant as a television in their homes.
The number of people who didn't have homes at all had grown to such proportions that it was the easiest way for the television station heads and the government to ensure people saw their bulletins. The reporter's face was slightly distorted as it was stretched beyond all normal proportions to cover at least eight floors of the tired-looking old building. Her flame-red hair shone

brightly against the dull, discoloured brick wall, and the distress in her eyes was visible to all as her voice struggled to rise over the howling wind that tore through the waterlogged street.

As Tom craned his neck to squint up into the grey cloud-filled sky, he felt one of his feet slosh into a deep puddle almost up to his ankle and remembered his mother's words about needing new shoes. Shaking his foot quickly to rid it of the worst of the freezing rainwater, he focused on the screen along with the few dozen other people who had paused to do the same, and his heart sank. Half a million people. And that's just an early estimate.

How many of those people didn't stand a chance in the first place? Tom wondered as he heaved his backpack a little higher on his shoulder and continued his journey to work. The red-headed news anchor faded from the screen, and the building became another nondescript tower in a sea of many on the street. How many of them were homeless, gathered in doorways seeking what little shelter they could find but knowing it was futile? That sooner or later, they would be swept away by the incoming flood waters or dragged off into the swirling wind? How many heard the evacuation order but knew that as they had no transportation and no money for a bus or train ticket, they had no choice but to stay put and try to ride out the incoming storm? With a frustrated sigh, Tom dug his hand into the pocket of his faded black jeans. Pulling out a small handful of change, he offered it to the first vagrant he saw, who thanked him profusely before rushing off to the nearest shop, presumably to buy himself a much-needed meal.

Tom knew that what he had given the older man would not amount to much and would barely allow him to ease the ache in his empty stomach, but it was better than nothing. Giving a cursory glance to his government-mandated wristwatch, Tom kept his head down as his now soggy feet ploughed towards his work, squelching against the cracked tarmac as he walked. Around five years ago, the authorities decided they needed a way to instantly contact the entire country's population in case of a natural disaster or emergency. And so, they decreed that every person over ten years old would be issued with a waterproof watch of sorts which they were required by law to wear at all times. They called them watches, but as their primary purpose wasn't to tell you the time Tom had never really gotten his head around the name. The small rectangular items were no more than a blank black screen most of the time. Occasionally emitting a high-pitched beeping sound loud enough to wake the dead when an announcement needed to be made, before a life-size projected hologram of a government or law enforcement official would spring out of them, standing up tall in front of the wearer and starting to speak.

Tom had experienced several of these announcements over the years, storm and tornado warnings being the most frequent reasons for the watches to go off. On one particularly disconcerting afternoon around eighteen months ago, Tom had been in the shower when the beeping had begun. Before he had managed to turn off the water, a short, pretty brunette had popped up right in the cubicle with him. Even though logically he knew that the woman couldn't see him, he'd still been taken aback and felt the need to quickly grab a towel to wrap around the lower half of his body. Feeling exposed as he looked into the eyes of the stranger while he was half-naked and covered in soap suds as she warned of a tornado which had been sighted a few miles away.

Tom trusted that the watch would soon alert him if the crisis in the US worsened. Usually, when disasters happened in other countries, small web pages would pop up on the two-inch wide screen so that people who had family or friends in those areas could be kept up to date with the latest information available. For now, he needed to put the incident out of his mind. Dwelling on it wouldn't help anyone. If he allowed himself to sink into a pit of depression every time there was a new disaster, he would never find his way out of the darkness again.

Over the past six or seven years, the world around Tom had changed so very much that he could barely stand to watch the news anymore. He could not stomach seeing the lifeless bodies strewn across the pavements in India, where a dam had burst seemingly with little warning. Breaking free from its restraints after fissures had appeared in its walls from the high temperatures, and filling the nearby streets with hundreds of gallons of water in seconds. Drowning everyone in its path.

He could not bear watching the reports of the famine in Africa, which had reached such extreme levels that it was estimated that nearly a third of the population had already died from hunger and another third were still starving.

On top of that, there was the massive Tsunami in the Atlantic that had wiped out entire islands, and then the flooding, droughts, storms and hurricanes which battered the planet. It seemed like barely a week went by without Tom being bombarded with another projected news bulletin on his way to work. As a medical student, he saw first-hand the effects that climate change and overpopulation were reeking every day. Especially as, much to his father's disgust, he had chosen to do his practical work experience in a small, run-down hospital in one of the most deprived areas of town. Tom had no interest in going to work in one of the big private hospitals like Jack Walker. Sure, his father brought home a hefty paycheck each month, which enabled Tom and his two younger siblings to be able to continue their education, keep food on the table, money in their pockets and a roof over their heads. Still, it was not the life that Tom wanted for himself, and it was a constant source of tension between him and his dad.

Being in a comfortable financial position, having been left a large inheritance a few years back when his grandfather passed away, Tom didn't need the money. He had decided that he would prefer to help those who were still relying on the National Health Service to get by than worry about lining his pockets. The NHS had declined enormously in just the few years he had been in school, with hospital closures nearly as frequent as natural disasters. There just weren't enough people who could afford to train to work in the field anymore. Most of his classmates from school had dropped out before they had sat their A-levels. Only a handful of universities were even still operational, as there was no demand for them. With food prices as high as they were, most of his peers had found themselves needing to go and get whatever jobs they could as soon as possible to help support their families instead of continuing their education. Tom knew he was one of the lucky ones, and he planned to give back as much as he could to those less fortunate than himself. No matter what his father had to say about it.

As he turned the last corner and the hospital finally came into view, Tom groaned inwardly, taking in the vast queue of people lined up outside. It was going to be another long day, no doubt about that. People of every race, age and sex stood in disorderly groups outside the large glass double doors, and he knew that at least half of them would not get treated today. They would spend the night out here on the cold, unforgiving concrete pavement, huddled together for warmth in the freezing December temperatures, hoping it would give them a better chance of being seen tomorrow. It was not unusual for people to spend several nights doing this, or for someone in the ever-growing queue to quietly pass away on the hospital's steps before they had even managed to get through the doors.

When he finally reached his office, Tom's first patient of the day was a three-year-old child suffering from acute asthma — one of the many respiratory diseases that had become much more common due to the increase in pollution. When Tom raised her shirt to place his stethoscope on her chest and listened to her struggling lungs, he noticed that he could easily count every one of her ribs through her skin. He placed a hand on her waist to steady her and was shocked to find that it almost went around her entire body. Damn, when did this girl last eat? He wondered to himself as he listened to the wheezing in his ears.

"She needs a course of antibiotics, try and give them to her with food if you can." He told her mother, knowing full well that chances of her being able to do that most days were slim to none, but advising her nonetheless.

The mother's sallow skin was almost grey in places, her lips were dry and cracked, and the bags under her eyes were so prominent that she looked as though she had recently been punched as she gazed up at him from her seat and Tom could not help but wonder how much longer this small child would even have a mother for.

"I'll also give you a prescription for a new inhaler, but I'm afraid they are on backorder at the moment, so it may be a few weeks before you can pick it up." He said solemnly, frustrated that he couldn't do more.

In an ideal world, he would admit the child immediately, start her on a high-dose course of steroids and IV antibiotics, and make sure she got three decent meals daily and a hot bath.

Unfortunately, the children's ward was already full to bursting, and as unwell as she was, she wasn't critical right now, so Tom knew he had no chance of finding a bed for her. As the child's mother heaved her up into her arms with more difficulty than she should have done, given the girl's slender frame, she thanked Tom gratefully. She started to walk out of the small examination room on shaky legs, clutching the green piece of paper with the prescription scrawled on it in her other hand.

The little girl, who had not made a sound during the entire appointment, other than her audible wheezing with every breath, shot him a defeated smile over her mother's shoulder as they walked out of the old wooden door and Tom's heart sank. He knew that chances are, she would be dead within a few months, either from an asthma attack or malnutrition. He took a few moments to try to compose himself, running a hand through his curling brown hair, which desperately needed a good cut, and took a small sip of the cold cup of tea beside him before he nodded to the nurse just outside the door to indicate that she could send in the next patient. It really was going to be a long day.

Chapter Five

At this stage in his medical training, Tom knew he should still be supervised by a senior doctor when examining patients. With the sheer number of people waiting to be seen though, that just wasn't practical. Dr Mahoney, his supervisor, was at least in the next room, no doubt trying his hardest to see as many patients as possible before he became too tired to string a sentence together and gave up for the day. It wasn't unusual for the older doctor to work fifteen or sixteen-hour shifts, stopping only to use the bathroom and often eating a sandwich with one hand whilst his other examined his latest patient. Tom could simply call out to him through the thin walls should he require a more senior doctor's opinion, but as most of the illnesses he treated were the same, day in and day out, he had rarely felt the need to do this. The most common conditions were, of course, malnutrition and respiratory issues, and the occasional bout of extreme food poisoning caused by the patient having to rummage through bins and eat whatever they could find to survive. People with coughs and colds rarely even got through the doors; more commonly, they would be turned away until their conditions had worsened into pneumonia. At this time of year, hypothermia was prevalent. However, as most people with this disease suffered from severe confusion, they rarely made it to the hospitals unless they had a friend or relative to bring them.

Tom's hospital, along with the few others still in operation in the area, had put together a special emergency team of volunteers who ventured out into the streets once or twice a week, depending on how many staff members signed up and attempted to treat people who were either too unwell to get to the hospital, or too disorientated to even realise that they needed to. Tom was not sure exactly how much help they managed to provide, but he would find out for himself in a couple of days. He had signed up to go out on a street shift earlier in the week when Dr Mahoney had told him that the programme might be unable to keep running if more doctors didn't start volunteering. Subsequently, Tom was due to do his first shift on Friday night, no doubt that was going to go down well with his mother. She had already scolded him for how many hours he spent at the hospital and Tom knew that she would absolutely hate the idea of him roaming the streets at night, which was what had stopped him from signing up until now. Still, Tom knew he would not be able to face his reflection in the mirror each day if the emergency team could no longer go out, if he could have helped them but chose not to.

Tom worked six days a week at the hospital, occasionally coming in on his days off to help out as well, as he planned to do this week. On the odd days he did get to relax, he tried to continue the illusion of having a normal life. He saw his friends and spent time with his parents, brother and sister. He went for the odd drink or game of pool with his colleagues. He dated, although fitfully, never managing to find anyone with whom he felt a real connection. Most of his dates ended in a quick kiss on the doorstep and the promise of a phone call which he would never make. Occasionally he went home with one of the women for a night of sordid passion, which he thoroughly enjoyed at the time but always felt empty for the morning after. It was exceedingly rare for him to see the same woman twice.

Most of the women Tom dated were people his parents set him up with. Children of his father's workmates at his posh private hospital, or people they knew through their golf club. In Tom's experience, most of these women carried on with their lives as if nothing were happening in the world. As if everything was still the same as it had been when their parents were in their early twenties like they were now. They were content in their little bubbles of safety, never having to worry about where their next meal was coming from or where they were going to sleep that night. They rarely, if ever, ventured into town. If they did, they turned a blind eye to the homeless beggars on the streets and the rising food prices, preferring to continue to live in ignorance and pretend that everything was okay rather than confront the problems all around them.

Most of them were nice enough, sure, pretty blondes mostly who would happily let him take them for a night out and chat away about clothes and music, their families and friends. Tom just didn't feel that they had any real substance. He was generally bored by the time they ordered dessert and always called them a taxi in advance to ensure he would not have to wait around with them any longer than necessary. He felt that it was important that he at least attempted to have some kind of life outside of the hospital though, if he didn't, he thought he would go mad. Sink into a pit of depression and be of no use to anyone. Besides, it pleased his parents.

Tom's mother loved to hear stories about his romantic evenings at the little Italian restaurant where he used to work behind the bar just ten minutes from their house where he always took his dates. It was his way of trying to show his gratitude to Tony, the manager, who had given him a job fresh out of university when no one else was hiring, his way of putting what money he could back into the tills there to help the struggling business keep its doors open. His mother said that hearing about his dates reminded her of being young again and gushed over the idea of him finding his future wife and her becoming a grandmother someday. His dad, who was always so disappointed in his son's life choices, at least cracked a smile when Tom would occasionally stumble in the morning after a date — wearing the same clothes as the night before. Slapping him on the back cheerfully and making crude comments about him being a dirty stop-out. Tom doubted that his mother would ever get her dream of grandkids, at least not from him. He didn't see how anyone in their right mind could bring a child into a world that was so very broken. Especially when the newspapers were always full of stories of overpopulation and everyone knew that this was one of the main reasons for the many disasters that had befallen the world.

"Tom, code red!" He heard Doctor Mahoney's voice cry out from the room next door. Tom pushed back his chair in a hurry, knocking over his mostly empty cup of tea in the process, the last dregs of which landed on his desk and started dripping slowly onto the floor. He didn't even give it a cursory glance. The bewildered elderly gentleman with a nasty rash that he had been treating looked at him in astonishment as he raced out of the room, almost slipping in his still-soggy trainers as he rounded the corner into Dr Mahoney's office at top speed. Where he found his mentor bent over his desk, pressing his hands firmly up and down on the torso of a young woman, performing CPR.

"Grab the cart, would you!" Dr Mahoney called out, but Tom was already one step ahead of him, dragging the crash cart towards the desk through the mountains of paperwork Mahoney had clearly swept onto the floor to make room to lay his patient down and switching it on for the paddles to start to charge.

"What happened?" Tom asked as he took over chest compressions from the older man.

"Asthma attack. She wasn't too bad when she came in but deteriorated quickly." Mahoney said as he adjusted the dials on the crash cart beside the desk.

"Adrenaline?" Tom asked hopefully before spying the empty needle on the desk beside the woman's lifeless body.

"No use," Mahoney replied as he administered the first shock to the woman. Tom stood back from the desk and watched as the woman's chest lay still, not a single breath of air forcing it to rise. "Again!" Mahoney shouted, reaching forward with the paddles a second time.

They continued to work on the woman for ten minutes before Mahoney finally admitted defeat.

"Dammit!" He cursed, banging his fist on the desk in front of him. "For God's sake, Tom, people shouldn't be dying from something like this! If she had just gotten here a few hours earlier... " His voice trailed off as he slumped into his chair and put his head in his hands in defeat, his shoulders sagging and his greying hair falling into his eyes.

"I know." Was all Tom could think to say in response. He placed a hand on his mentor's shoulder and patted it consolingly. As much as Mahoney was his supervisor and older than his own father, Tom worshipped the man. He had never known anyone as selfless and dedicated as Mahoney was. He felt he had learned more from the year he had spent working beneath the senior doctor than he had during his first two years in medical school.

"I'll call down to the morgue. Have someone come and collect her. Did she come alone?" Tom asked, following the procedure he sadly knew all too well.

"Yes, alone. Thanks, Tom." Mahoney sighed. "I'll use the office across the hall in the meantime." He said and pulled his ageing frame from his chair.

Tom could see the sadness in the older man's eyes and the fatigue lingering in them. His admiration of Mahoney grew further as the doctor walked outside the office and called out, "Next patient, please." before guiding the next poor soul into the opposite room to examine them. Most people, Tom knew, would have needed a few minutes to compose themselves after watching a woman die on their desk, himself included, but Mahoney knew that those few minutes could cost someone else their life. So, he pushed away whatever he was feeling and got straight back to work.

If I'm ever half the man he is, I'll have done well for myself, Tom thought as he covered the patient with a thin plastic sheet from a nearby cupboard and pressed the button on the intercom to contact an orderly to come and remove her lifeless body, before heading back into his own office and following his mentor's example by continuing to treat his patients.

Chapter Six

"I really am sorry, ma'am, but as I am sure you are aware, food prices are rising up and down the country, and we have had no choice but to increase our prices to cover our costs. If you would like, I can ask my manager to come and discuss the matter further with you?" Steph told the customer before her. Holding back the sigh that was trying to force its way through her lips as she repeated the same phrase she had been forced to utter over and over again this evening to the middle-aged woman on table two who was glaring at her from over the top of the faded menu in her hands. Which was dotted here and there with red ink, where Tony had altered the prices earlier that week.
Like so many before her, the customer had taken offence at the new prices. Whilst Steph didn't blame her, she was getting a little tired of people assuming that the menu prices were her responsibility and directing their anger at her. Steph had spent half of the week trying to explain the situation to people and was baffled by how many couldn't grasp it. She'd give just about anything to be able to take a Friday night off work, let alone to be able to go out for dinner in a nice restaurant, and here were these people, dressed in their smart clothes without a single hole in them or a misplaced button, with their hair perfectly styled and their feet slipped into highly polished shoes, kicking up a fuss over a few extra pounds.
It had been a long time since Steph had been on the other side of the table in a restaurant, but she could remember her last dinner out as though it were yesterday. It had been the night her parents had taken her out for dinner to drop the bombshell on her that they were moving away.

"Stephanie, we have something important to discuss with you." Her mum had said as she had moved the spaghetti on her plate around distractedly with her fork.
At the time, Steph had just placed a large morsel of delicious lamb shank into her mouth. God, she missed lamb, and had been able to do no more than raise her eyebrows at her mother questioningly to urge her to continue as the succulent meat had melted away on her tongue.
"The thing is, your mum and I have been talking, and well...
We've decided that with the crime rates rising and the job market

the way it is in the city, we think it would be best for us to move out of town. Into the country. To somewhere with a lower population where we wouldn't be such small fish in a huge pond." Her dad had stuttered, looking down at his steak the entire time and not meeting Steph's incredulous gaze. His words brought to mind images of giant sharks swimming around a large tank in an aquarium, gobbling up every less fortunate fish that dared to cross their paths.

It wasn't like this was the first time her parents had brought up this conversation topic, but Steph had never really thought they would follow through with their threats to move away. She had grown up here, as had her annoying kid brother, who was noisily demolishing a steak beside her at the table. Whilst they weren't exactly well off, her parents had managed to pay off their mortgage when her grandmother had passed away a few years previously, and so, they at least had the security of knowing they had a roof over their heads, which was more than many in this town could boast. Steph took a moment or two longer to chew her food than was strictly necessary, buying herself time to come up with an appropriate response.

"You know there are more opportunities here in the city, dad. Sure, there is more competition, but say you move out to the middle of nowhere. How are you going to find work?" She asked, trying to keep her voice steady as she tried to reason with her father, but it was her mother who decided to chime in and answer her questions.

"You remember your dad's old school friend Paul Taylor? Well, he has a little dairy farm down in Sussex. Nothing fancy, but he's offered to take your dad on there. Since his son passed away in that terrible car accident the summer before last, he needs an extra pair of hands to run things. There is a delightful little cottage on their property that he will let us buy off of him." Her mum said quickly, the tone of her voice rising as it often did when she was excited, causing Steph to have to listen intently to not miss anything she said.

"But Dad knows nothing about working on a farm!" Steph replied incredulously, stifling a laugh at the ridiculous idea. Her father had worked in an office for as long as she could remember, donning a suit and tie each and every morning and heading off with a briefcase tucked under his arm. She just couldn't picture him stumbling around a farm in overalls, knee-deep in cow shit.

"I'm sure I'll be able to pick it up quickly enough. Be nice to get some fresh air. Good for my health." Her dad chimed in again, and this time, Steph couldn't contain the giggle that broke free from her lips, earning her a stern look from her mother.

"Sure, cos breathing in all the pollution floating around in the air and the methane from cow farts all day is really healthy." She chuckled. Taking a moment, she endeavoured to regain control of herself before asking, "You aren't really serious about this, are you?"

"Completely. In fact. We accepted an offer on our house today." Her mum told her matter-of-factly, a sly smile inching across her thin lips. Steph hadn't even known that her childhood home had been on the market until that very moment, and the news hit her like a punch in the stomach.

"The only problem is, you see, the cottage only has two bedrooms." Her father added, and Steph felt as though the food in her mouth had turned to ash as she tried in vain to get it down her dry throat. "And given that you have a job here, friends, we thought maybe you'd rather stay behind. You know, your brother could do with a fresh start, whereas you, well, you're happy here, aren't you?" He asked, but his tone implied that the question was rhetorical.

They didn't want her to go with them. Steph realised as she gulped down nearly all of the glass of water before her in an attempt to wash the ash from her tongue. She had never been particularly close to either of her parents. It wasn't that she disliked them or anything, they just didn't have anything in common. Her mum and dad were straight-laced people who liked things to be done a certain way. In contrast, Steph was freer-spirited. In fact, if she really thought about it, this was probably the longest conversation she'd had with them in years which wasn't solely about her angel of a little brother, who they idolised. Steph was pretty sure they'd never wanted a daughter, had never known quite what to do with their friendly, outgoing little girl who loved nothing more than dressing up in pretty clothes and watching Disney movies on repeat until she could recite them word for word. When her little brother, Max, had come along, some nine years after she was born, after many years of her parents trying, Steph had instantly felt forgotten. Max was the apple of their father's eye, his little mini-me, both with their ginger hair and bright blue eyes, they even walked with the same lopsided gait. Her mother would do absolutely anything for her son, passionately believing that he was the perfect child and could do no wrong.

Allowing her mind to wander for a moment to avoid continuing the conversation with her parents, Steph recalled one particular incident when Max, aged seven at the time, had decided that he was fed up with listening to her old vinyl rock records being played on repeat. The collection had been her pride and joy. Steph had saved and saved for every album she owned and built it up over several years. It might not have been the most comprehensive collection in the world, but it was hers and hers alone, and Steph loved it.

One balmy summer night in the middle of a sweltering August, young Max had snuck into Steph's room whilst she was sleeping and had carefully scraped a sharp carving knife he had liberated from the kitchen around the grooves on each and every single one of her prized possessions. Causing them to refuse to play without jumping and skipping every few seconds and effectively ruining her collection.

When Steph had awoken the following day and tried to play one of the records while she got ready for school, as she did every morning, she was horrified to hear David Bowie's usually sonorous voice jumping all over the place. Hoping that it was just that one record, Steph had tried another, and another, until she had finally collapsed onto her bedroom floor in defeat as tears flowed down her cheeks in rapid succession, surrounded by the sea of albums, all of which were now entirely worthless.

It hadn't been difficult to work out who the cause of her misery was, and she had gone to confront Max, who told her in a cocky tone that only little brothers could truly master what he had done. The smirk on his podgy face still haunted her to this day and made her blood boil whenever she brought it to mind, and, at that moment, she had not been able to restrain herself.

She knew that at sixteen years old, she should have been mature enough to realise that raising a hand to her brother would only do more harm. At that moment, however, Steph had not been able to control her flaring temper. So distraught was she over the loss of her collection, many of which would be near impossible to replace, she had seen red. For the first and only time in her life, Steph had struck another human being. Hitting him around the head and causing him to stumble back into a nearby chest of drawers, catching his elbow on the corner of the hardwood and filling the air with a sickening sound as his bone had cracked.

Instantly, Steph had felt a surge of guilt run through her veins like nothing she had ever experienced before. She had called out in horror for their mother to come quickly and had admitted what she had done as Max wailed and sobbed, clutching his arm tightly to his chest. Steph knew that she shouldn't have hit him, but then he shouldn't have destroyed her records either, they were both in the wrong, and there was plenty of blame to go around. She hadn't meant to hurt him, not really. His broken arm was nothing more than an unfortunate accident.

Sadly, her parents had not seen it that way. They had bundled Max into the car and rushed him to the hospital. Leaving Steph at home alone to think about what she had done. When they returned later that evening, Max's arm was encased in a bright blue cast. After making Steph scribble an apology onto the plaster, her parents had grounded her for a month. Then, she had been forced to watch as her father took a hammer to her beloved record player.

After that day, Steph had resigned herself to the fact that Max would always come first in their eyes, with her a very distant second, watching on from the sidelines as though she were a bystander in her own family. Never again did she raise a hand to him, nor try to tell her parents when he destroyed any more of her possessions, which he did several times over the following years, or upset her in any way, knowing full well that it would do no good. No matter what she said, no matter who was actually at fault, she knew they would always side with their blue-eyed boy.

"When do you plan to leave?" Steph asked her parents in a small voice when she finally managed to swallow the last mouthful of her food, feeling it slide down her throat and settle like a boulder in her stomach.

"Your mum and Max will head down towards the end of next week to get things set up. I'll follow them as soon as the sale here is finalised and I've served out my notice at work." Her dad told her, still refusing to look at her. His bright blue eyes bore into his steak as though his conversation was directed solely at the slab of bloodied meat and had nothing to do with Steph at all.

She had been wondering why her parents had been so insistent on taking her out for dinner. Once a week, the two of them would go on what they called 'date night' to one of the few restaurants around town that still remained operational. They had taken Max along with them on a few occasions, but never Steph. Now, it all made sense. *They thought it would be better to tell me in public, somewhere that I couldn't make a scene,* Steph thought as she drained the last of her water and nodded her head mechanically in response to her dad's answer.

"I guess I better start flat hunting then." Was all that Steph had been able to come up with in reply.

Within three weeks of that dreadful dinner, the sale of the house in which Steph had grown up, and spent countless Christmas, birthdays and other family events in had been completed, and her family had moved away. At nineteen years old, she had walked out of her parent's home for the final time. She had waved a solemn goodbye to her dad as she had climbed into a friend's car with all of her earthly belongings, which sadly amounted to little more than a handful of sturdy brown moving boxes and an old suitcase, and a part of her had prayed that she'd never have to see her family again.

Wiping her hands down her soiled apron, Steph sighed and glanced at the clock. Only another hour to go, she thought to herself as she made her way out to the back of the restaurant to find Tony and ask him to come and explain his new pricing to the disgruntled woman at table two whilst resigning herself to the fact that she had as much chance of getting a tip from them as she did of sprouting wings and being able to fly herself off to the Caribbean to spend the afternoon lounging on a beach under the scorching hot sun. So much for paying off that electricity bill.

Chapter Seven

Tom hurriedly pulled the light green waterproof scrubs over the top of his ripped jeans, struggling to get the thin fabric over the coarse denim. He cursed under his breath as he noticed the time on the old plastic clock which hung on one wall of the staff changing room. He was late. He was supposed to meet the rest of the emergency team for tonight's patrol by the ambulance bay fifteen minutes ago, but his last patient of the day had taken longer to treat than he had anticipated. Now he was rushing to try and pull on the hospital-issued scrubs and hi-vis jacket that the higher-ups insisted that staff wear on these patrols so that it was immediately apparent that they were medical personnel, and get his arse down to meet the others.
Grabbing his backpack off the low wooden bench beside him, Tom threw it over his shoulder and walked quickly out of the room, nearly hitting a disgruntled-looking porter on the way out, who huffed at him in frustration as Tom dodged past him, muttering an apology. Taking the stairs two at a time, he stumbled to a stop, slightly out of breath at the ambulance bay at eight-twenty-two pm.
"Hi, Tom, is it? Glad you could join us." A tall, thin man in an outfit that matched his own said sarcastically with a smile as he extended a hand in Tom's direction.
"Hi, yes, sorry. Got held up with a patient." Tom panted as he tried to catch his breath and shook the man's hand.
"Josh." The tall man introduced himself. "You'll be riding with Mandy and me tonight." He added and gestured towards the front seat of the ambulance behind him. Tom glanced over to where a middle-aged blonde woman with bright red lipstick that clashed horribly with her scrubs sat, drumming her talon-like fingernails against the worn leather on the steering wheel.
Walking round to the back of the ambulance, Josh threw open one of the full-length doors. "Hop in!" He instructed, and Tom clambered into the rear of the van and took a seat on a folding plastic chair attached to one wall. Examining the space, Tom noticed it wasn't as well stocked as most of the ambulances he had seen coming in and out of the hospital. The glass-fronted cabinets above his head were mostly empty, and the trolley bed opposite him was barely clinging on to the wall, held in place by frayed straps which looked like they might give way at any

moment. Its metal bars started to rattle as they tapped against the wall when Mandy started the engine and they began to pick up speed.

"Yeah, I know, not exactly top of the range," Josh said, catching Tom taking in their surroundings. "This ambulance has been out of service for a while. It's one of the older models. The newer ones are needed by the paramedics on shift tonight. So, we make do with this old girl. She may be poorly stocked, but she'll get us where we need to go. Especially with Mandy behind the wheel." He assured Tom, who nodded back at him.

"First time?" Josh asked

"Yes, it is. Anything I should know?" Tom replied, holding onto a nearby shelf to steady himself as Mandy took a sharp right-hand turn a little faster than necessary, and he slid slightly on his plastic seat. Sure, she'll get us where we want to go, Tom thought, but will we get there in one piece?

"It's probably not that much different to the kinds of things you see in the hospital most days." Josh began. "This time of year, it's mostly going to be your standard flu's, coughs and colds, that kind of thing. Probably a fair few with covid or pneumonia. Asthmatics, of course, diabetics, and some elderly people with age-related illnesses. Most of the folk we'll see tonight will be malnourished, no one out here has enough food to stay healthy. We see a lot of dehydration as well, but more so in the summer months."

Tom nodded along as Josh rattled off the list of illnesses, thinking it was pretty much what he'd expected the other man to say and glad there were unlikely to be any real surprises.

"The kids are the hardest ones, as you'd expect. But you can't let yourself get over emotional. We don't have enough people out here as it is. Just diagnose, give them what you can and move on. The worst ones, ones we can't treat out here, Mandy will take back to the hospital, those that will go that is. And we'll call the lads from the CRS if we come across anyone who we're too late to help." Josh finished.

"CRS?" Tom asked, not being familiar with the acronym.

"Corpse removal service. Grim, I know, but with the number of people out on the streets nowadays, they are necessary to stop the spread of more diseases. Normally we'll find one or two bodies a shift. People who couldn't make it to the hospital on their own or those that didn't care enough to bother." There was a hard look in Josh's eyes as he spoke. Tom could tell that although he was trying to be nonchalant, the fact that people were lying dead in the streets clearly bothered him.

"Anyways, we'll be at our patch soon, so do me a favour and fill that backpack you've got there with as many of those medications as you can," Josh instructed, pointing to a battered old cardboard box under the trolley bed. Tom fumbled with the zipper on his bag and started piling in as many boxes of medication as he could manage. Not surprised to see that most of the antibiotics were very nearly out of date and that the few syringes were in packages held together with old masking tape. The ambulance came to an abrupt halt in an area of town that Tom was unfamiliar with, there were some areas that you just didn't venture into nowadays, and this was undoubtedly one of them. The moment Tom stepped out of the vehicle, he could smell it: unwashed, uncared-for bodies, rotting food and human waste. He wrinkled his nose in distaste as he hiked his full backpack a little higher up on his shoulders and took in his surroundings.

The air was thick with smoke from the makeshift fires that battled to stay alight in the drizzling rain, swirling around him in circles and making his eyes sting as he made his way down the street. He watched idly as a man in his fifties threw what looked to be a book into the dwindling flames flickering from inside an old metal barrel and stoked them with a long rod which was charred and twisted from the heat of the fire.

Tom was amazed by the sheer number of people desperately trying to stay warm in their threadbare clothes clustered around the fires, which seemed to be positioned every ten or twelve feet along the road. Young children clung to their mother's legs as they coughed and spluttered in the smoke. An older man stood leaning heavily on a makeshift cane, which appeared to be no more than a sawn-off chair leg, shifting his weight occasionally and positioning a different part of his body closer to the warming flames. A few people scurried away as they approached, giving himself and Josh sidelong glances that made him feel like they did not belong here, nor were they welcome.

It wasn't as though he'd expected them to all start cheering at the sight of their arrival or anything, but Tom had thought they'd at least be a little grateful that someone hadn't forgotten about them. It seemed that many of the men scattered up and down the dimly lit street had no interest in taking their help, whether they needed it or not, and slumped off into the shadows.

"Let's start down here." Josh interrupted Tom's thoughts and gestured towards one end of the street, where Tom could see several tents had been set up close together to protect them from the worst of the elements. Squaring his shoulders, he tried to concentrate on the task at hand and followed behind Josh, squinting his eyes against the smoke.

By the time the bells in some far-away church started to chime at midnight, Tom was already exhausted. His light green scrubs were covered in soot, blood and various other bodily fluids, and his feet were aching with every step he took. How had they only been out here for a few hours? It felt like a lifetime already, Tom wondered to himself as he placed an oxygen mask over the withered face of an elderly lady who was suffering from pneumonia and adjusted the flow rate on the half-empty tank beside him which Mandy had heaved over from the ambulance. So far tonight, he had mostly come up against the ailments that Josh had listed earlier in the van. The most challenging thing for him to deal with was the sheer state that these poor people were living in. Tom had watched sadly as a mother had attempted to coax milk from her breast to feed her wailing newborn, who only looked to be a few days old at most. He had to turn away as she quietly started apologising to the tightly wrapped bundle when there was no milk to be found. As underweight and malnourished as she was, Tom wasn't surprised that she could not produce the milk that her infant craved. Sadly, he also knew that without it, the child was unlikely to live very long.

The number of people living on this long street, flanked by the river on one side and a long row of abandoned warehouses boarded up with thick strips of wood and heavy chains on the other, was astounding to him. There had to be a few hundred at least. It seemed to Tom that the further down the winding road they went, the more pitiful the state of its occupants became. As though those that had more energy, and better resources, stuck to the end of the road closest to town, whilst those that had been here longer, that had lost hope or run out of ways to feed themselves, had migrated into the deeper shadows near the forest at the other end.

"Watch out down here, mate, Needles," Josh said as he deftly hopped over a used syringe which lay on the floor. "Why don't you go see if those guys over there need any help? And I'll head over that way." Josh suggested, pointing at a pair of men who couldn't have been much older than Tom who sat leaning against a nearby wall, sharing an old brown blanket covered in stains and ripped in one corner.

Tom bobbed his head in agreement and started to make his way over to the pair. He'd only taken half a dozen steps away from Josh when he was stopped in his tracks by a sallow-skinned man who had just appeared from behind a nearby tree.

"Alright there, Doc!" The man called out as he made his way towards Tom on unsteady feet. "What you got in there then? Anything I might like?" He asked in a low, gravelly voice, instantly sending a shiver down Tom's spine as he motioned to the bag slung over Tom's shoulder, making him tighten his grip on the strap instinctively.

"Not unless antibiotics or insulin are your thing," Tom replied with a smile, trying his best to keep his voice steady and deter the man from investigating any further.

"Really? Ah, come on, man, you wouldn't hold out on me now, would ya? You've gotta have some painkillers in there I'd reckon. Morphine maybe? I've got this condition, you see, leaves me in all kinds of pain, unbearable it is, pain you'd not want to imagine." The man pushed, moving closer to Tom now and blocking his path.

"Sorry mate, can't help you." He shook his head and risked a quick glance over his shoulder to see if Josh had noticed the exchange. Judging by the track marks he could see poking out under the torn sleeves of the homeless man's jumper, it was clear that he was an addict looking for a fix. Tom wasn't about to give up the very few painkillers he had stashed in the bottom of his bag to someone who didn't really need them when there were so many out here that did.

"Just you and me here, Doc. Don't worry. Why don't you hand over the morphine, and I'll be on my merry little way. Quick as a flash, no one's gotta know." The man whispered conspiratorially, leaning closer to Tom, who caught a strong whiff of alcohol on the man's breath as he spoke.

Unsure of what to do, Tom debated his options. He could try calling out for Josh, but he was uncertain that his colleague would hear him over the noise of the wind and the people around them. Could he try and reason with the man in front of him? Maybe show him the antibiotics which were stacked at the top of his backpack and hope that he didn't delve any further and find the supply of painkillers hiding underneath? He could try and run, but he didn't see himself getting very far on the wet ground with his bag and equipment slowing him down.

Tom could feel the seconds ticking past as he deliberated, and he sensed that the man was getting increasingly impatient. He had started to display some nervous ticks, which Tom was sure resulted from withdrawal. His hands were shaking violently as he twisted them agitatedly in front of his chest, and he was licking his lips incessantly. Before Tom could make a final decision, the man's patience wore out. He lunged towards the backpack, his thin, nicotine-stained fingers narrowly missing their target as Tom instinctively jumped away.

"Don't want any trouble here, Doc." The man tried to reassure him, but the tone of his voice and the look in his glazed eyes had the opposite effect.

"Seriously, mate, I haven't got anything you'd want. Just some basic meds to try and help the people out here, that's all." Tom tried again in vain as he scanned the immediate area around him, looking for an escape route.

The man lunged again, tired of this game, but this time, he balled his hand into a fist and aimed it straight at Tom's nose instead of going for the bag. The crunching noise that followed the impact made Tom's stomach twist. He was reasonably sure that the man hadn't broken any bones, but he was bound to have a bruise or two to explain to his mother tomorrow. That'll be a fun conversation, he thought dryly.

"Hey! What the hell!" Josh's voice suddenly called out from somewhere behind him, and Tom could hear the sound of his colleagues' shoes sloshing through puddles as he raced to reach them, panting under the weight of the equipment he carried.

The homeless man stood stock still, like a deer caught in headlights for a moment. His eyes darted frantically from Tom to Josh and back again before appearing to decide that he didn't fancy his chances two against one, turning on his heel and disappearing back into the shadows.

"You ok?" Josh asked breathlessly as he reached Tom's side, raising a hand to examine his bleeding nose.

"Fine," Tom assured him as he dabbed at his nose with his sleeve. "You couldn't have come back a minute or so sooner?" He tried to joke as he gingerly felt his face to reassure himself that nothing was broken.

"Sorry mate, I lost sight of you for a minute there, won't happen again. What did he want? Drugs?" Josh apologised sincerely, looking genuinely distressed.

"Yeah, painkillers. That happen often?" Tom asked, annoyed that no one had thought to warn him that he might be attacked whilst they were out tonight.

"Not as often as you might think. Only once or twice that I've heard of."

"Lucky me then," Tom replied dryly.

"You want to head back to the van?" Josh asked, concerned.

"No, no, I'll be fine. Come on. We're nearly at the end of the shift anyways." Tom replied. Satisfied that his nose had now stopped bleeding, he wiped the cuff of his sleeve against his already filthy trouser leg in an attempt to remove the worst of the blood and carried on down the street.

The two men managed to get through the rest of their shift without encountering any further trouble, much to Tom's relief. One punch was enough for tonight. He heard the church bells ringing yet again to signal that it was now three am, and he took as deep a breath as he dared in the smoke-filled street as he and Josh made their way back to Mandy and the ambulance. Time to go home.

"Sir! Sir!" A young girl who couldn't have been more than eight or nine years old shouted, as she yanked on the hem of Josh's hi-vis jacket, her tiny hands leaving streaks of dirt across the luminous yellow fabric. "Please, my daddy! He won't wake up!" She exclaimed, tears streaming down her face as she started trying to pull Josh back in the direction that they had just come from.

"Where is he?" Josh asked the little girl, and Tom admired the calmness in the other man's voice. He wasn't sure that his would have come out so steadily.

"Over here!" She shouted again, her voice hoarse with tears. As quickly as she appeared, she started to run off towards a small dark alleyway between two large warehouses. Josh didn't waste a moment and took off after the child. It took Tom's tired brain a second or two longer to catch up, but he, too, was soon splashing through the puddles as he made his way after their retreating figures.

"Daddy! Daddy!" The little girl cried as she clutched the front of her dads' too thin for this weather T-shirt and shook it with all the strength she could muster. "You've got to wake up!" She begged him.

Even in the dim light of the alleyway, with only Josh's torch fluttering over the man's face, Tom could see that it was useless, that they were too late.

The man slumped before him was, he guessed, in his mid-forties or so. He was wearing nothing more than the T-shirt, ripped jeans, and a pair of battered old boots with holes in the toes as he lay propped against the wall behind him. His matted hair was slick against his forehead, allowing small droplets of rain to drip from the ends and trickle down over his skin, leaving tracks in the dirt situated there, through which his pale skin shone in the moonlight. His blue lips were tightly clamped together, and it was clear it had been some time since he'd taken his last breath.

"Sweetheart, what's your name?" Josh asked as he knelt on the floor next to the sobbing little girl, gently prying her hands off her father's dead body he turned her towards him.

"Katie."

"Hi Katie, my name is Josh, and this is my friend Tom. Is your mummy here, Katie?"

"She's in heaven. It's just my daddy and me." The little girl said, and Tom's heart sank. This beautiful little girl was all alone. Orphaned before she had even reached double figures. He swallowed heavily in an attempt to stop the tears from welling up in his own eyes.

"Is there anyone else you know around here?" Josh asked quietly, and the little girl shook her head as she wiped the snot dripping from her nose onto the hem of her dress.

"My daddy's gone to heaven too, hasn't he?" her tiny voice asked in no more than a frightened whisper.

"Yes, sweetheart, I'm sorry, but he has," Josh confirmed, and Tom stood in dumbstruck horror as little Katie crumpled before them, falling to her knees as heart-wrenching sobs racked her tiny chest. Josh caught her as she fell and wrapped his arms tightly around her shaking body, pulling her close to him and holding her as she wept.

And Tom? Tom turned away from the scene before him. He tried to close his ears to the little girl's cries and wipe the image of the shattered look in her eyes from his mind as he walked to the mouth of the small alleyway to radio Mandy and ask her to contact the CRS. Truly understanding, for the first time tonight, why it was so hard to get people to sign up to volunteer to come out on these streets.

Chapter Eight

Saturday, the fourth of January 2053, brought with it a welcome break from the snowstorms that had been plaguing the country for the past few weeks. Many parents took advantage of the clear skies and bundled their children into the warmest clothes they could find in their half-empty wardrobes. Encasing their tiny hands in thick woollen gloves and forcing their feet into plastic wellington boots before heading out to the local parks to build snowmen and ride makeshift sledge's down fluffy white hills.
A couple in their mid-thirties were making the most of their children's momentary distraction during a snowball fight to take a sip of the warm tea they had bought out with them to fight off the bitter winter cold. Perching on the edge of a snow-covered bench, their coats tucked underneath them to keep their threadbare trousers from getting wet, they sipped gratefully at the warming liquid as they looked down the hill and over the city of London spread out beneath them.
Without warning, the sounds of children playing, teenagers laughing, and adults deep in conversation were interrupted by the all-too-familiar beeps emitting from their government-mandated watches. On edge, the couple looked from each other to their children in fear. Should they leave? Try and get away quickly before the beeping ceased, and the inevitable announcement followed. What would it be this time? Another disaster? Were they in danger? They seemed to have a silent conversation using only their facial expressions to ask each other these questions, but before either had reached a conclusion, the beeping stopped. The world around them suddenly became a flickering sea of lights and a cacophony of deep booming voices in a variety of different languages as life-size projections sprang from not only their own wrists, but those of every person in the vicinity who was old enough to be required to wear a watch. The same tall figure of a smartly dressed black man with salt and pepper hair and a severe countenance sprung up every few feet like some kind of strange multiplying bacteria and began to speak.
"Please stay calm and remain in place. There is no emergency. You are safe." The voices said in calm but authoritative tones, and the couple breathed a sigh of relief. The watches automatically translated the hologram's words into whichever preferred language its owner had set. The couple could pick out a few languages that they were familiar with echoing over the park, but many were totally new to them. If anything, this only

added to their unease. Several people who had begun running whilst the couple debated their options took a few moments to listen to the message, which was being repeated on a loop, before finally trusting its words and coming to a standstill. Their projections halted with them and flickered gently in the afternoon sunshine.

"My name is Professor Peter Jones, and I am the head of the cull Enforcement agency or C.E.A in Great Britain. An acronym that I know will mean little to you now but in the coming weeks will become quite familiar, I assure you. As you know, in the past decade, the world around us has become almost unrecognisable. As the climate crisis has worsened and overpopulation has increased, the world's governments have not been idle. Three years ago, leaders from every one of the one hundred and ninety-five countries on earth gathered in Brussels to listen to a proposal from The British Prime Minister and a team of experts from around the globe. A vote was held, and the proposal passed with an overwhelming majority. With the exception of those countries who have chosen to abstain, this announcement is being made by the heads of the C.E.A's sister organisations all over the world right at this very moment."

The couple looked at each other in a mixture of relief and astonishment. They were pleased that there was no imminent danger to themselves or their young children but concerned about what sort of announcement would need to be made on such a grand scale, all over the world, at the same time.

Professor Jones took a deep breath, composing himself one last time before he began to recite the speech that had been written and rewritten by some of the country's brightest minds over the past few months. He was still unsure as to how this rather unpleasant task had fallen to him and not the Prime Minister, but he was determined to see it through without getting emotional or overwhelmed when his entire country was focused on him.

"It has been decided that our world's population has reached such large numbers that we can no longer accommodate everyone. We have therefore decided that at five pm this evening, a lottery will be carried out across the country." he began, speaking clearly but quickly so as to not leave his audience time to debate if the lottery would have a positive outcome. This news would be hard enough without giving them false hope. He continued, "This lottery will include every member of the population who is a registered citizen of the United Kingdom over the age of five years old. It will randomly pick two people, one male and one female, born on the same date, in the same county, in the same year, to be paired together. These two people will receive a letter summoning them to a government facility on a particular date, where their lives will be terminated. We are calling this process 'The culls."

There was an audible intake of breath from the crowds gathered in the park on Hampstead Heath, London, as they all struggled to take in this shocking news. Wondering if, somehow, they could have misheard the well-spoken professor whose image was being projected all around them and whose voice seemed to be emitting from the very depths of the ground beneath their feet as it swarmed into their ears from every possible angle. Slowly the sound of whispering reached the couple as they stood mute, in complete shock, staring over at their small children. Melissa, aged three, and Graham, six, had stopped their games to stare up in awe at the face of the professor projected all around them. Melissa, having always been a curious child, was not used to the sight of these life-size projections, having only ever seen one or two in her short life, reached out one of her tiny, gloved hands and tried to poke the man in the stomach, giggling loudly as her hand passed through the particles of light.

Professor Jones paused momentarily to let his words sink in before he bowed his head slightly and continued reading from the tablet in his shaking hands. He hoped that people would choose to believe that the vibrations were simply the result of a bad connection or maybe a gust of wind disrupting his projected likeness. He did not wish to portray the image of being frightened. This was just the start of a very long and hard road that he had to walk, and ensuring his authority was recognised from day one was imperative.

"We intend to commence the culls immediately, starting with those currently held in prisons nationwide. Any prisoner currently held at his Majesty's pleasure whose sentence exceeded thirty years in total will be put to death in the next three days. Regardless of how much time remains to be served on their sentence. I suggest that those of you with relatives currently incarcerated make plans to say your goodbyes to them as soon as you are able to do so."

The couple watched in horror as a young man sitting on a mound of snow nearby sprung to his feet and began running. Faster than they could remember seeing anyone run before, leaving deep divots in the snow as it was crushed beneath his trainer-clad feet. The couple could have sworn that they heard the distressed young man calling out a single word as he whipped past them with tears streaming down his pale face. "Dad."

"The lottery results will be sent directly to your watches. They will not be televised. However, a full list of every name called will be available to be read by the public on our website. Whilst the lottery is being drawn, a special program will be aired on every channel starting at four pm, providing more in-depth information about the process and the subsequent culls. Whilst this measure may seem extreme to many of you, I can assure you that the greatest scientific minds on our planet have decreed that it is the only way to ensure the survival of our species. At this time, I would like to pass the floor to the head of the police force in your respective counties. Please do not attempt to disable this projection before the announcement has finished. Thank you. And good luck to you all."

The hologram of the professor was replaced by a small message in bold red lettering, which shone like a thousand tiny fires against the backdrop of the crisp white snow on the heath. The couple stood dumbstruck as their young children raced over to them, stumbling slightly in their boots as they tried to make their way through the thick snow. As Melissa reached her mother, she stretched out her arms to be picked up. Her mother did this gladly, longing for the comfort of her child's warm body against her own. Cradling her daughter, she looked around at the people scattered across the heath and took in their reactions.

Many, like herself and her husband, stood paralysed, looking around themselves in fear and confusion, unable to take in what they had been told, some opened their mouths as if to speak, but no sound came out of them. Others were starting to make their way back to the car park or down towards the footpath leading to the main road, the gleaming messages emitting from their wrists bobbing ahead of them as they went. A few people had pulled mobile phones from their pockets and were trying to place calls home. Melissa's mother wondered why they were even trying. Didn't everyone know that all mobile towers were shut down when announcements were made to ensure people's full attention?

Her gaze was caught by a young couple in their late teens or early twenties, she guessed. Who stood with their arms wrapped tightly around each other. The young woman's entire body was vibrating as she sobbed into her boyfriend's shoulder, who buried his face in her soft blonde hair as if hiding himself from the world would somehow change what he had just heard. An older man sitting on a bench nearby sighed profoundly. He straightened the bowler hat perched on top of his head before reaching down to pet the fur of a huge German shepherd at his feet and saying in a low voice, "Let's hope they call me up, eh old girl? Give the young ones a chance."

Tears sprang into the mothers eyes as she looked down at her son, who was happily building what appeared to be a snow dinosaur by her feet without a care in the world. *"All citizens over the age of five years old",* the words echoed in her head. She could have sworn she felt her heart skip a beat at the thought of her perfect baby, with his whole life ahead of him, being marched into some god-awful government facility to be murdered. They could jazz it up with fancy words any way they liked, but that's what it was when you boiled it down, murder.

Mass murder on a scale she could not even comprehend and did not wish to. Before her emotions could overwhelm her, a shout echoed across the open space. It seemed to reverberate all around her, and she wondered if, in her distracted state, she had missed the start of the next announcement. However, a quick glance in front of her showed the red lettering still shimmering mid-air. She soon realised that it was actually the sound of many voices, all shouting indignantly as one in horror. "What gives them the right?" "Five years old? They're going to murder children and call it necessary?" "I tell you what, my name gets called, and I'm going on the run!" The shouts and cries around her were soon drowned out by the return of the all too familiar beeps from hundreds of watches. Slowly but surely, the screams dimmed as people realised their words could not be heard anymore. They turned their attention to the projection in front of them, now of a middle-aged man in a police uniform covered in medals.

"Good afternoon. I am the commissioner of Police of the Metropolis and the head of London's Metropolitan Police Service. I will not keep you long. I understand everyone is anxious to return to their homes and families. Still, I ask you to give me just a few moments of your time and attention. Our city's population will be reduced by approximately five million during the coming culls. Whilst this number may seem extreme, given that our latest census data estimates a total population of over fifteen million people living in the city limits, for most people, day-to-day life will not be affected. I must remind you that all of the country's laws must be obeyed during this time. Anyone found to be breaking the law will be dealt with swiftly and extremely. Keeping this in mind, as of Monday the sixth of January 2053, the government will reinstate the death penalty for certain, more extreme crimes whose sentences would result in imprisonment of thirty years or more. To keep the peace, my officers will patrol the streets, and you will most likely see an increased police presence across the capital."

"Please remember that these officers are there for your safety and co-operate with any and all instructions that they give you. cull Enforcement Agency members will also become a familiar sight on our streets. We ask that you do not attempt to interfere with their work in any way and warn you that the penalties for doing so will be severe. I would also like to take this time to remind all foreign nationals currently residing in or visiting our country that if their homeland has chosen to take part in the culls, they will be subject to their own countries' lottery, rules and regulations."

"The C.E.A and the police forces, as well as the army across the country, will be assisting in returning people whose names are called in the lottery to their country of birth. We will be doing so without exception. No asylum will be granted, and as of today, we will not be issuing British citizenship to any person who does not already have it. I ask you now to please, return to your homes in an orderly fashion and await further details of the culls, which will be televised on all channels across the country from four pm this afternoon. Thank you for your time and understanding. And good luck to you all."

As the last of the projections flickered out, the bright sunshine that had shone across the heath just a moment ago was wiped out by a sudden band of clouds, casting eerie shadows across the snow-covered hills, almost as though mother nature herself was mourning the announcement.

"Can we go home now, mummy?" Melissa asked, peering up from her mother's chest, against which she had been dozing whilst the police commissioner spoke and emitting a giant yawn.
"Sure baby, let's go home." She muttered. She watched as her husband scooped their son into his arms. Graham protested loudly, but his cries fell on deaf ears as his father seemed in his own little world as he reached out and took his wife's hand, squeezing it gently in a pitiful attempt at reassurance whilst silently praying to God that his own family would be spared the pain of their names being called and slowly forcing himself to put one foot in front of the other and join the crowds of people heading for their homes.

Chapter Nine

The sunlight shimmering through the threadbare curtains that hung somewhat loosely over the two small windows in the sparsely decorated studio flat seemed strangely bright all of a sudden. The birds outside the window appeared to increase the volume of their songs. Even their own breathing appeared abnormally loud as Crystal and Steph sat beside each other on the double bed they shared, snuggled under a blanket. It was as if everything in the world had suddenly been magnified after the last lights of the flickering holograms had sputtered out and for a moment, Steph wondered if she was dreaming..
Neither of the women knew what to say, think, or feel. A total numbness seemed to envelop them as they stared wide eyed at the place before them where just a moment ago, the police commissioner had been projected in front of their fridge. Hoping against hope that another announcement was going to be made, that there had been some kind of mistake. Because surely, the world's governments had to have been able to come up with a better plan than this? The brightest, most influential minds on the planet couldn't have been reduced to mass murder to solve the earth's problems. Could they?
Reaching a trembling hand across the bedspread, Crystal entwined her fingers with Steph's and squeezed lightly, finally turning her gaze to her friend and noticing the shocking white pallor of her face, which she was sure was reflected in her own dark skin. The first thought that went through her mind was to thank God she didn't have children. The pain and horror Crystal felt now would have been multiplied tenfold if she knew there was a possibility that something she had created, cared for, bought up and nourished could have its bright light snuffed out just because some computer algorithm picked their name from amongst all the rest.
Her second thought, though, was more selfish. What if they called her name? Would she have the strength to walk into some government facility and be murdered? How would they do it? She wondered. Firing squad? Lethal injection? Would they all be marched into gas chambers like Hitler used over a hundred years ago in World War II to try and wipe out the Jewish population in one of the worst atrocities ever committed by man? A shiver ran down Crystal's spine, and she felt beads of sweat break out on her forehead as Steph finally broke the silence.
"They can't be serious?" she asked incredulously, her innocent

brown eyes widening and staring into her friends, begging her to refute the government's claims, to tell her that it wasn't true. That it was just a bad dream that they'd wake up from at any moment and that their broken world would return to normal. Crystal would have given anything at that moment to have the power to make everything okay again for her best friend. The woman who had taken her off the streets, put a roof over her head, shared her bed with her and what little food she had. Steph had even got her a job and Crystal would have done anything to take away the look in Steph's eyes. If only she could.

"Preposterous!" Thomas's mother shouted. "They cannot be seriously implying that everyone in the population is eligible for this so-called lottery? Surely the more sensible course of action would be to take those poor souls off the streets, the ones already dying in horrific and tragic ways, and put them out of their misery? How will this help the world if, in the end, all we are left with are a bunch of homeless people with no money to their names?" She continued, and Tom felt his jaw fall slack in shock at her unkind words.

He had been enjoying a rare, peaceful day off at home with his family. They'd had a delicious roast dinner of real pork, a rare treat, thanks to his mum and sister slaving away in the kitchen for what seemed like half the day. They had watched a movie afterwards, all curled up on the sofa together with full bellies, and even managed to converse without any arguments breaking out for once.

But that was before. In the time that Tom knew would now become referred to as 'before the culls'. A time when, despite the global hardships, things were simpler. Everyone on earth would remember exactly where they were when they heard the announcement. What they were wearing, who they were with, and ever-exaggerated versions of these events would be passed on for generations to come and be recorded in the history books for posterity.

"Mum!" He scolded her in a tone he generally reserved for his dad. "How can you say that? Those people are still PEOPLE, and they have as much right to live as we do!"

His mum, to her credit, had the decency to look ashamed of her harsh words. Deep down, he knew that she was just lashing out in anger, that she hadn't had time to really think through what she was saying, and that she was a good person at heart. But it still bothered him immensely that her first thought after hearing such horrible news was so very self-centred.

"Your mother's right, Thomas. I know you have a soft spot for these down and outs, but be realistic. How can the country, no, the world, be expected to prosper if all those people of means, of education, are wiped out in this so-called cull? I would imagine that the government will exempt some people from the lottery. For one thing, they aren't likely to allow themselves to be entered into it, now, are they?"

"I can't believe you'd be so fucking selfish!" Thomas shouted, springing up from the sofa and starting to pace around the living room, trying to calm himself down before saying something he'd regret. He loved his parents dearly, no matter how different their political views were, they had brought him into this world and given him everything he had ever needed, but there were times when he just couldn't work out how on earth they were related.

"Watch your mouth in front of your mother and sister." his father admonished him, glancing over at Thomas's younger siblings sitting silently on the opposite sofa, not having moved an inch while the announcement was being made or since. As Tom looked closer, he saw unshed tears sparkling in his sisters' eyes, and he rushed to her side. Sitting on the arm of the sofa, he drew her to his chest and tried to comfort her, feeling his shirt dampen as her tears finally began to flow.

"Ssssh Em, it'll be alright." He consoled her, hearing the emptiness in his own words as he said them.

How could he possibly know that? Anyone of their names could be called in this lottery. What would he do if Emily got called up? Or Mark? A thousand thoughts ran through Tom's head so quickly that he could barely make sense of them. He wondered if it would be possible for a friend or family member to replace someone unlucky enough to have their name drawn out of the proverbial hat. Maybe if Emily's name were drawn, he could offer to relinquish his life for hers? Was his father right? Would there be exceptions made for those people who had means? Or from certain professions, maybe? Surely the armed forces and Police, at the very least, would still need to be functional during this time? More so than usual, probably.

A long line of faces swam through his head as he cradled his little sister in his arms, trying to block out the conversation his parents were continuing on the other side of the room. It seemed like the image of every person he'd ever known flashed through Tom's mind. Childhood friends, teachers, family, girls he'd dated, children he'd seen playing in the local park on his way home from work, patients at the hospital, colleagues. How many of those people would still be alive after all this? He wondered despairingly.

"Put the television on, dear," His mother's voice interrupted his thoughts as she instructed Mark, who was closest to the remote, to switch on the large flat screen on the wall. "All this speculation is getting us nowhere. The programme they spoke about in the announcement will start shortly, and they will undoubtedly answer all these questions." She finished, clearly trying to ease some of the tension in the room with her light tone.

Thomas shifted slightly until he was squeezed into the small space next to Emily on the sofa and, keeping a protective arm around her slim shoulders, turned his attention to the TV, equally scared and intrigued by what this programme would tell them.

Chapter Ten

Steph tried in vain to get comfortable on the hard-backed chair in the restaurant as she and her colleagues waited for the TV programme to begin. As televisions are expensive to purchase, not to mention the cost of electricity to run them, herself and Crystal, like most of their workmates, didn't have one at home. Tony, knowing this, had called everyone an hour or so ago, shortly after the announcement and told them that he wasn't going to bother opening the restaurant this evening, as no doubt, everyone would be at home watching the programme. But he also told them that he would be there with his wife to watch it and that anyone who wished was welcome to come and join them. Steph had been relieved to hear that he wasn't planning on having them work tonight. She wasn't sure that she could have mustered a cheerful, smiling face for any customers that did decide to venture out after the announcement. She was grateful for the opportunity to watch the show surrounded by people she knew and cared about rather than having to stand outside in the freezing cold flurries of snow that were falling from the darkening sky and watch a distorted version of it projected onto the side of one of the abandoned buildings in town. She didn't fancy trying to take in such shocking and upsetting news in front of a bunch of strangers and she was almost certain that the streets would not be a safe place to be tonight. People were bound to be scared after the programme, scared and probably angry, and liable to lash out at anyone who so much as looked at them the wrong way.

Next to her, Crystal straightened her shoulders and attempted to exude an aura of calm. Of course, the announcement had shaken her to her very core, as it undoubtedly had the rest of the world. Still, she was determined not to show that to the people around her, especially not Steph. She knew that her best friend was taking this even harder than she was, being so kind-hearted and always wanting the best for everyone, and so Crystal was trying her best to remain strong for her.

"Good evening, and welcome to the BBC. This special broadcast is being shown on all channels simultaneously at the government's request. Please be aware that as the government themselves produced this programme and it is being streamed live, we cannot give you any warnings about what it may contain. Still, from the announcement earlier today, we can safely say that

it will undoubtedly be difficult for us all to watch. We here at the BBC will be on hand to discuss the contents after the show has ended and would welcome your thoughts. The programme will start promptly at four pm."

The anxious-looking newscaster on the screen disappeared suddenly, his smart suit, fear-filled eyes, and large desk fading from the screen and being replaced by a large clock which started counting down solemnly.

Sixty seconds. The group of twenty or so who had gathered in the small restaurant bar looked up at the out-of-date television suspended in one corner. You could have heard a pin drop as the entire group seemed to hold their breath collectively, watching the clock countdown.

Fifty seconds. A few people reached out to take the hand of the person next to them for comfort, whilst others sat at a distance, as isolated as they could be in the cramped space.

Forty seconds. Jose, the head chef, ventured out from the kitchen for once. He poured himself a pint of beer, which probably cost him most of his morning's wages, and leaned against the ageing wooden surface of the bar. Refusing to meet anyone's eye, even as Steph tried to give him a reassuring smile.

Thirty seconds. Tony raised a glass of ice-cold water to his lips, trying to keep it as steady as he could in his trembling hands but failing miserably and cursing under his breath as a few droplets landed in his lap. The ice cubes tinkled against the edges of the glass as it shook.

Twenty seconds. Crystal shifted nervously in her seat, a trickle of sweat making its way down her spine and an uneasy feeling swirled uncomfortably in her stomach.

Ten seconds. Steph felt her breath coming faster as her heart rate increased in nervous anticipation. In an attempt to force herself to relax, she took a deep breath - in through her nose and out through her mouth, remembering the technique from a long-ago taken yoga class and attempting to use it now to calm herself.

Five
Four
Three
Two
One.

The numbers were replaced by a pitch-black screen. For a moment, Tony wondered if something had gone wrong with the broadcast and debated changing the channel. Still, thankfully within a few seconds, the now familiar face of Professor Jones appeared and began speaking.

"Good evening, and welcome to tonight's special broadcast. In this programme, I will be giving you more information about the upcoming culls and how they will affect those living in Great Britain. Whilst I am sure that many of the things I am about to tell you will seem shocking, I want to reassure you once again that a great deal of thought has been put into this proposal. It was deliberated over for several years by a committee of members from over fifty countries, including Government officials, members of the World Health Organisation, scientists from around the world and some of our brightest citizens. It has been put together for the good of the entire planet. Without bias or racism. Without considering anyone's social status, religion, education, gender or sexual orientation. As you watch this, a carefully constructed computer programme is being booted up, ready to begin the lottery. The drawings will be made entirely at random and will begin promptly at six o'clock this evening."

Tom shifted uncomfortably in his seat, unable to sit still as the professor began speaking on the large screen before him. A substantial part of him wanted to get up and run. He didn't know where on earth to go, given that this was happening all over the world, but run nonetheless. He wasn't sure that he could cope with hearing the intricate details of how these mass killings would be carried out. Still, one thing that Tom knew for sure was that he'd much rather watch this programme alone. Somewhere where he could make notes, and most importantly, somewhere where he could scream and shout at the television without fear of upsetting his family or causing an argument. Where he could let his emotions run wild. Sadly, though, he knew that his dad would chastise him if he even attempted to go upstairs to the second smaller television in his parent's bedroom to watch the show in peace and no matter how tempted he was, he couldn't leave his younger brother and sister.

Tom had switched seats with Emily as they watched the clock countdown on the screen. Positioning himself between his two younger siblings, a comforting arm slung around Emily and a reassuring hand resting on his brother's knee. Their parents were seated on the smaller two-seater sofa opposite them, both turned to face the screen. His mother reached one of her delicate hands behind her, as she watched, absent-mindedly twisted her husband's wedding ring with her index finger and thumb. Tom smiled at the gesture. His parents rarely displayed much physical affection in front of him, and something in the movement warmed his heart.

"I wish to reassure all of you that the culls will be carried out as quickly and humanely as possible. Each person whose name is called in the lottery will be given a minimum of thirty days to set their affairs in order before their summons date. We will be carrying out the culls in numerical order. Therefore, those people whose birthdays fall on the 1st of January can expect to be the first to be summoned. The chosen method of execution in England, Scotland and Wales is lethal injection.

In contrast, Northern Ireland has opted to utilise the services of their firing squads. Each county will designate their own centres for the executions, which will be run by government officials. However, the injections themselves will be carried out by licensed medical personnel. Now, down to the rules."

Professor Jones continued, his expression turning serious. He stood next to a large screen which flashed to life as he spoke. "If any person called passes away of natural or unnatural causes before their execution date is set, they will not be replaced in the culls. There is no option available for anyone to offer to take the place of a family member or friend in the cull unless they are the same age and gender as the designated subject, as it is imperative that an even number of people are removed from each generation for society to continue to function. For this reason, parents cannot take the place of children. Siblings, except for twins of the same gender, cannot replace one another and so on. The executions of all children under the age of fourteen will be carried out at specially designated private buildings. One parent or guardian may stay with any child under the age of fourteen whilst they are being put to death. After execution, to not overwhelm funeral directors, the state will cremate all bodies. Funerals may be arranged with religious leaders at the cost of the deceased's family members. Still, no bodies will be released to the public. Therefore, these will be more symbolic."

Steph couldn't hold in the gasp that left her lungs as she thought of children as young as five years old being taken into bleak, rundown buildings and strapped down to hospital beds, needles being forced into their tiny arms as they cried. She swallowed down the bile quickly rising in her throat and turned her attention back to the professor.

"As I mentioned earlier in the announcement. The first step in the culls in the United Kingdom will be the immediate execution of all peoples currently held at His Majesty's pleasure whose sentences exceeded thirty years at the time they were handed down. This will be a total of approximately three hundred people. These executions will be carried out at prisons with suitable facilities already in place. They will be carried out in three days without exception."

Professor Jones took a sip of water as the camera panned to focus on a large screen to his left, which displayed prisoner numbers throughout the UK and the prisons which would be carrying out the culls. He held little to no sympathy for these men and women, feeling they had bought their fate upon themselves. Back in the old days, and even now in many other countries around the world, they would have been sentenced to death for the horrific crimes that they had committed, and the professor felt no pity for them. As the camera focused back on him, he began to outline some of the more delicate aspects of the culls, the parts he was sure would cause outrage.

"From Saturday 11th January 2053, I regret to inform you that it will become illegal for any hospital, whether NHS or private, to carry out fertility treatments. It will also become illegal for anyone to conceive more than two children. Women already pregnant with their third or more child are exempt from this law. But anyone who already has two children and is found to have fallen pregnant after this date will be given a non-optional medical abortion. Subsequently, over the coming months, anyone who already has two children will receive a letter from their general practitioner advising them that they are required to take a dose of a new drug by the name of 'AC1', which has been developed by some of the best pharmaceutical minds in the world. This drug will render the patient infertile. This process is irreversible and mandatory. Any person, male or female, who refuses their prescription or does not take the medication as directed will be charged under the new Crimes Against Humanity laws."

"These laws cover many new crimes, all of which are listed in full on the government's website. Please make yourself familiar with them, as ignorance of the laws will not prevent you from being charged if you are found to be breaking one or more of them. Additionally, from the same date, all NHS and private hospitals will be prohibited from treating terminal conditions in an attempt to prolong life, including but not limited to terminal cancer, Motor

Neurone disease, some neurological diseases such as Parkinson's, and some heart and lung diseases. A full list of all illnesses which will no longer be treated is again available on the government's website. Patients diagnosed with any of these will be contacted by their primary care physician and given medication to ensure they are not in pain. We will also offer them the option to self-terminate if they wish."

Tom glanced over to his father, catching his eye and raising an eyebrow questioningly. Two years ago, his mother had gone into remission following a bout of breast cancer. She had had a mastectomy and, for now, was tumour free. However, there was always a concern that the cancer would return to another part of her body. His dad shook his head almost imperceptibly to not draw the attention of the rest of the family. Tom took this as reassurance. The professor had said only terminal conditions wouldn't be treated anymore. His mother was never diagnosed as such and hopefully would never be. But Tom couldn't help thinking about his patients. At the hospital he worked at alone, hundreds of people were being given chemo and radiotherapy daily to try to shrink their tumours and prolong their lives. How many lives would be ended prematurely because of this new law alone? He wondered as he turned his attention back to the television.

"Emergency care for those who suffer accidents, heart attacks, or similar medical emergencies will still be given as usual. However, we will be initiating a do not resuscitate law countrywide." Professor Jones finished up. Once again, the camera panned to the screen to his left, now displaying their website address and the list of conditions he had just mentioned. "These laws will stay in place for a minimum of five years, which is the length of time we expect it to take for us to complete the cull in its entirety in the United Kingdom. After which time the situation will be reassessed."

"Now, back to the lottery itself. It is my duty to inform you that any person whose name is called in the draw who subsequently fails to appear at their designated execution destination on the date and time set will also be guilty of Crimes Against The Human Race. My job and the job of the cull Enforcement Agency will be to locate any persons who do not present themselves for execution. Please be assured that my team and I will do this without prejudice. We believe wholeheartedly in this cull and take our jobs incredibly seriously. We will, without fail, apprehend any and all persons who fail to appear and take them into custody. Let me be completely clear on this. If your name is called in the lottery, your life is forfeit. If you choose to try and run, then anyone found to be assisting you in any way or hiding your whereabouts from the authorities will also be guilty of Crimes Against The Human Race and subject to harsh penalties. The culls have been agreed upon by over three-quarters of the world's countries. We in the United Kingdom will not disappoint our fellow men and women around the world by failing to carry out our duties."

Chapter Eleven

A shiver ran down Steph's spine at the professor's words, so cold, so clinical. She did not doubt his sincerity when he said he believed in what he had been asked to do and would do everything in his power to ensure the culls were successful, it was clear from the look in his cold eyes that he would show no mercy. Steph couldn't help but let her mind wander as the professor continued talking, wondering what she would do if her name were called? Would she have the courage to walk into one of these centres and willingly surrender her life to help to preserve the human race? She knew that she would run into a burning building to save someone she loved, but to have the backbone to allow herself to be strapped to a table in some random building surrounded by strangers and not fight back as they plunged a needle into her skin? That she wasn't convinced she could do.
She just had to hope that her name wasn't called. And really, what were the odds that it would be? As a list of statistics flashed up on the screen in front of her eyes, detailing how many people were expected to be culled in each participating country around the world, Steph quickly did the maths. One in four. Those were her odds. One person out of every four would receive an alert over the next seven days to inform them that their name had been called. All she could do now was hope that hers wasn't one of them.

"As I am sure many of you have already surmised, there will be some exceptions to the cull. Some people whose names will not be entered into the lottery for various self-explanatory reasons. These groups include all current serving members of the British Armed Forces, The Police Force, the Fire Brigade and some medical personnel. The Prime Minister and a select number of her cabinet. His Majesty the King and other members of the Royal Family. Members of the cull Enforcement Agency, including myself, are also exempt. All those whose names will not be entered into the lottery will receive an alert to their watches within the next hour. Please be advised that these exemptions only cover British Citizens. Each participating country will be responsible for deciding who is exempt from their lottery, and any foreign nationals living in the United Kingdom will need to contact their country of birth for further details. Any foreign nationals whose names are called in their countries' lotteries must surrender themselves to their local Embassy, who will arrange for them to be transported to the execution centres in their country of origin."

Tom felt a surge of hope rush through his veins at the professor's words, 'Some medical personnel'. Did that mean that he didn't have to worry? Sure, he wasn't a fully trained doctor yet, but he was a good halfway through his degree and had been working at the hospital for a year now. A familiar high-pitched beeping sound tore through the air in the large living room, drowning out the professor's voice as he continued to discuss the policies for immigrants and pulling Tom's attention away from the screen.

"Dad?" Emily's small voice croaked hopefully as their father raised his wrist and tapped the screen of his watch, silencing the continuous beeping.

"I'm exempt." their father replied, exhaling a long breath of air and squeezing his wife's tiny hand as Emily burst into tears of relief.

"Thank god." Tom's mum said quietly, raising her husband's hand to her lips, kissing it fiercely. Tom couldn't help but glance down at his wrist, willing the small black rectangular object situated there to start beeping. To alert him that he was also exempt. He stared down at the screen for several seconds, but nothing happened.

"They'll probably alert the higher-ups first." Emily tried to reassure him through her tears. "I'm sure you'll get a message soon." Tom tried to be comforted by his little sister's words, but he didn't hold out much hope. His father was a well-respected surgeon who had worked at one of the most prestigious hospitals in the country for the last twenty-five years. In contrast, Tom was nothing more than a second-year resident.

"Well, I am glad they're using some common sense." Thomas's dad said loudly, "I am surprised that other professions haven't been included though, academics, scientists and the like. I suppose ultimately, having working emergency services is more important than keeping the universities open, though." He finished. There was a newfound confidence in his tone, a conviction that only a person who knew they were exempt could exude at that moment. Unsure what to say, Tom turned his attention back to the screen. Whilst he was pleased that his father's name would not be entered into the lottery, he couldn't help but think about all the millions of people worldwide who would not be so lucky.

"And finally," Professor Jones continued, "Parliament passed a law earlier this week, which allows anyone who wishes to do so the opportunity to take their own life in a safe and pain-free manner in the comfort of their own home. Anyone who wishes to contribute to the culling and the preservation of humanity by surrendering their life may request an 'Ending' package from their primary care physician. This box will include medication and detailed instructions on how a person may set their affairs in order and end their life without fear." Professor Jones informed his audience as the camera zoomed in on him for one last close-up before the end of the programme.

Overall, he was pleased, feeling that he had displayed his authority whilst ensuring that the population had all the facts. All that was left for him to do now was wait. As a lifelong bachelor, his only family member was his frail, elderly mother. Although he did not want her name to be called, he knew that if it were, she would go gracefully, with dignity and obey the law. He was not convinced that the same could be said for everyone. And so, he would wait. See how many people thought they could outrun the cull if their names were called. Wait to see how the population as a whole would deal with the executions. Wait and see how difficult his job would become.

Chapter Twelve

Monday morning saw the return of the snowstorms that had plagued the south of England for weeks. Coating every surface in a dense cloud of sparkling white crystals as far as the eye could see. As Tom navigated his commute to work, humming along to the classic rock album he had playing in his headphones, he made sure to step carefully on the compacted snow on the roads beneath his feet, which had turned into treacherously slippery ice. One wrong misstep could easily land him with a nasty sprain or worse, and the last thing that he needed was for his first patient of the day to be himself. Thankfully Tom had at least found time to pop out and get some new shoes with his mother last week, meaning that he didn't have to worry about having soaking-wet feet by the time he reached the hospital, but that didn't make the journey much more comfortable.

Everywhere Tom looked as he made his way down the half-empty main roads on his usual route towards the hospital, what he supposed were meant to be motivational posters seemed to stare back at him. *"Britons! Your country needs you. Don't be the person who lets us down. If your name is called, step up bravely!"* One such sign urged in black ink on a patriotic background of the union jack. Yeah, cos it's that simple, he thought to himself wryly. It's one thing to conscript people into the army and send them off to war. At least then, they had a chance. They may send you off to unfamiliar lands, rip you away from your friends and family, but they also put a gun in your hands and train you to use it. Show you how to fight back and try to give you the best chance of survival possible.

But this? This isn't war. This isn't nobly stepping into battle to try and defeat the enemy. The enemy was humanity itself, and no amount of Churchill-esq posters at every bus stop and in the windows of the abandoned buildings around town could change that fact.

Tom was dreading his shift at the hospital today. He hadn't been at work since the announcement on Saturday afternoon, having had a rare weekend off and he was not eager to be confronted with angry and confused patients today. The news was still so fresh that he knew people were bound to have a lot of questions, and no doubt, at least some of the patients he saw today would be looking to him for answers. Yet, he had no more information than anyone else, short of an email he'd received the night before which instructed him that the hospital now had a full stock of at-home euthanasia kits, which they were to hand out without prejudice to anyone who requested one. The idea made him sick to his stomach. He had decided to pursue a career in medicine so that he could help people, to save lives! Not to assist people in killing themselves. However, now it seemed that Tom was expected to be a willing participant in mass murder, and he appeared to have no say in the matter at all.

As much as he was dreading the long ten-hour day ahead of him and had been trying to prepare himself for the worst, the sight that confronted him as he approached the hospital was unlike anything Tom had expected. It made him stop dead in his tracks on the snow-covered ground and pull his headphones from his ears in shock as he rounded the last corner and the hospital came into view. Tom had become accustomed to seeing large crowds gathered outside the main entrance of the building most days when he arrived, but not like this, never like this.

In front of the glass automatic doors that led into the accident and emergency ward, where Tom spent most of his working hours, were at least fifty people holding placards high into the air above their heads. As Tom edged closer to the crowd, trying to remain inconspicuous and blend in with the scores of patients waiting to be seen, he could make out the few signs closest to him and a chill ran down his spine as he read the words emblazoned on them.

"Doctors are trained to CURE, not CULL!" stated one in dark black ink. *"My children deserve a future just as much as people in lab coats!"* proclaimed another. A final sign had just one word scrawled across it in vivid red paint, *"Murderers."*

Tom bowed his head and, changing tact, walked around the crowd as quickly as possible and headed into the hospital. Why are they protesting here? He wondered. It's not like we signed off on this cull, or that everyone in this building is exempt from the lottery, he thought unhappily. Tom had waited in vain for an alert to come through to his watch on Saturday night, just like it had his father's. Irritatingly, the small device stayed silent against his skin for once. His dad had spoken to a few of his colleagues yesterday and the general consensus was that only high-level physicians who would be too difficult to replace had been exempt from the lottery. It seemed that unless you were a senior doctor or higher, your name went into the computer programme along with the rest of the population. So, Tom, along with probably three-quarters of his colleagues at the hospital, maybe more, were just as likely to get called up as any one of the people protesting outside.

Tom could understand their desire to take their frustrations out on someone, to scream and shout that it wasn't fair. He even agreed with them on some things. But ultimately, this cull had been decided upon by the government and other heads of state across the world. The doctors, nurses, porters, cleaners, radiologists, paediatricians and cafeteria workers at the hospital had no more say than the protestors had. It seemed cruel to Tom to make them feel guilty about something they could not control.

"Morning, Tom."

"Dr Mahoney, good morning." Tom greeted his mentor as cheerfully as he could manage, forcing a smile onto his face, which he knew did not meet his eyes.

"Going to be a tough day today. You might want to take a few minutes to prepare yourself." Dr Mahoney suggested soberly, placing a well-meaning hand on Tom's shoulder. "I'm afraid we've already started seeing people come in whose names have been drawn in the lottery. Scared, confused people who don't know who else to turn to for advice, so have come here." he continued. "If you find yourself unsure of what to say to them, then give me a call, and I will come and talk to them." He told Tom.

"I must admit I have no idea what I would say." Tom shrugged. "How do you comfort a perfectly healthy person who has been told they must die for the good of the world? A world most of them will never see more than our tiny corner of?" he asked his mentor, genuinely hoping that the older man had some words of wisdom to impart and feeling his shoulders slump under the weight of his questions.

"Carefully and with compassion, my boy." Doctor Mahoney said and started leading the way from the locker rooms down to the treatment area where he and Tom would be working today.

"Doctor Mahoney? Can I ask... I mean, I don't want to pry or anything, but I was just wondering if, if maybe..." Taking pity on his young charge stuttering over his words, Mahoney cut him off mid-sentence.

"Yes, Tom, I am exempt from the lottery. Not by choice, of course. I'm an old man. I've seen plenty of the world. I'd have happily given up my last few years in it so that someone else could have had a chance at a full and plentiful life. But sadly, that was not my decision to make." Doctor Mahoney said sadly, and Tom could tell that the ageing Doctor meant every word he said.

"God give me the grace to accept with serenity the things that cannot be changed." He added, quoting the long-ago written Serenity prayer, which he had brought up often, but never in a situation where it carried as much meaning as this.

"And the courage to change the things that should be changed?" Tom continued the verse. "Are those people outside, right Doctor? Should we be out there protesting this insanity too?" He questioned.

"Thomas, you are but a young man still, so let me give you some advice. There are some things in this world that are certain. The sun will rise, the rain will fall, and the earth will continue to turn on its axis. And, no matter how much people protest, the governments of this world will do what they deem to be right. For today, all you and I can do is our jobs. We can try and keep as many people healthy as possible and hope against hope that those who find themselves left after these atrocities have been carried out will be fortunate enough to live long and happy lives. So, let's get to work, shall we?" He finished and headed into his office, flashing Tom a slight smile as he reached his desk and took a seat on the lone leather chair positioned behind it. Resigning himself to the fact that his mentor was right and that for today at least, all they could do was their jobs, Tom followed suit and headed into his own treatment room, ready to start the day.

Chapter Thirteen

"Nooo!" The wail that seemed to explode unbidden out of the customer at table three shook Steph to her very core and her heart rate increased at the terrible sound.

Steph had heard the beeping of course, everyone in the restaurant had, and everyone's heads had turned sharply toward the table in the corner from which the sound was emanating. As much as Steph had not wanted to intrude on such a heartbreaking moment for the mother who was sitting at the table sipping at a glass of water whilst her two young children nibbled at a pizza between them and sucked heavily on two straws positioned in their single glass of milk, she couldn't help but hover at a nearby table and watch the moment unfold. It was like driving past a car accident, Steph thought to herself. Every decent bone in your body is willing you to look away, but you can't help it. As you reach the scene, you just have to take a look. Your brain demands it. And this was exactly the same.

Since the announcement on Saturday, Steph had heard that a few people she was acquainted with had received notifications to inform them that their names had unfortunately been called in the lottery. One of the younger waiters, Jimmy, who had only been working in the restaurant for a few weeks and whom Steph did not know well, had apparently received his alert early on Sunday morning and hadn't returned to work since. She didn't blame him. What was the point in continuing to work when you knew you would be put to death in the coming months? It wasn't as though you had to worry about overdue rent or bills going unpaid when you weren't going to be here for much longer anyways. Steph was pretty sure that she'd never set foot in the restaurant again if she received an alert.

The woman at table three began to sob uncontrollably as she jumped to her feet, knocking the glass of water before her flying across the table with a loud crash. Her two startled children, whom Steph estimated to be around four and seven years old, stared dumbstruck at their mother, not knowing what to do. Within a few moments, the younger of the two children also began to cry adding to the cacophony of noise filling the restaurant. Before Steph could think twice about her actions, she felt her feet carrying her across the small space between the tables and over to the woman's side. She reached out a hand and lightly touched the woman on the arm, trying to get her attention and maybe help her in some way, although she had no idea how.

"Ma'am, is there someone I can call for you?" She asked the woman quietly as she gently eased her back onto her seat and handed her a napkin.

"My... my parents..." The woman spluttered between great heaving sobs that seemed to rack her entire frame as tears spilt over her cheeks.

"Mummy, what's wrong?" The older of the two children asked in a timid voice, gazing up at her distraught mother in confusion.

"Hi there, what's your name?" Steph asked the little boy.

"Andrew."

"Well, hi Andrew, my name is Stephanie." She said as cheerfully as she could manage. "You see that man over there?" She asked, pointing towards Jose, who was peering over the kitchen counter, trying to see what the commotion was all about. "If you go over there and ask him nicely, he'll take you into the kitchen and show you where we make the pizzas! Would you like to see that?" She asked the little boy, raising her voice until she was confident that Jose could hear her. When the chef raised an unhappy eyebrow in her direction, she knew she'd got the volume right.

"Yes! That'd be awesome! Come on, Amy!" The little boy shouted enthusiastically, and, grabbing his sisters' hand, he hopped off his chair and made his way over to the kitchen door, where a very disgruntled-looking Jose was now standing.

"I'm more than happy to call your parents for you, Miss. Do you have the number? What's your name?"

"C-C-Claire." the woman stuttered. She pulled her handbag onto the table in front of her, plopping it right smack bang in the middle of the puddle of water from the drink she'd spilt and fished out a mobile phone. Quickly unlocking the device, she tapped the screen several times and handed the phone wordlessly up to Steph, who saw that it was already ringing a contact labelled 'mum and dad home.'

"Erm, hi there, my name is Stephanie. I work at Tony's on Broad Street? Anyways sorry, I'm with your daughter, erm, Claire, is it? And her children." She paused for a moment as a confused gentleman on the other end of the line caught up with her words and responded in a hoarse voice.

"Is everything alright?" He asked her

"I'm afraid that Claire's had some bad news, an alert came through to her watch not long ago, and well, I think that you might want to come and pick her up," Steph told the man, realising as she spoke that she had just inadvertently informed him that his daughter was going to die, a shudder ran down her spine.

"Shit. I'll be there in ten minutes. Stephanie, was it? Can you please stay with her until I arrive? Are the children okay?" The man asked after a moment of silence. His voice was much steadier than Steph thought hers would be if the situation were reversed.

"Of course I will. The children are fine. We're giving them a tour of our kitchens. I will take Claire in the back, and we'll wait there for you. Just ask for me when you arrive." Steph told the man, thinking that the best thing she could do for Claire and the rest of the customers right now was to let the woman have some privacy to try and digest this awful news.

"Thank you. And thank you for calling me. I will be there as soon as I can." The man said quickly, his voice catching in his throat slightly as the news started to hit home. Steph ended the call and returned the phone to Claire, who had now stopped sobbing and was sitting quietly on the chair next to her, staring vacantly into space. Tears still rolled over her cheeks, and a small wet patch had formed in the centre of the woman's light khaki green skirt from where they had fallen from her face and collected on the thin fabric.

"Why me? I'm a good person." Claire mumbled quietly, and Steph wasn't sure if the woman was actually asking her directly, expecting a response, or just putting the sad question out into the universe in general.

"How about we go out the back, huh? It's more private there. We can find your kids and wait for your dad." Steph suggested. Claire nodded almost automatically as if she hadn't really heard Steph's words but was willing to just follow along and do whatever she was told and slowly started to ease herself up from her seat. Steph quickly grabbed the children's coats and scarves, which had been discarded on their chairs when they had hurried off to the kitchen, and then taking Claire by the elbow, started to lead her out the back of the restaurant to the staff room.

The two women had not taken more than half a dozen steps when the high-pitched beeping noise sounded again. Seriously! How many alerts does this poor woman need? Surely one is enough. Steph thought to herself and began lightly rubbing Claire's upper arm in a show of reassurance.

"It'll be alright. It's probably just a malfunction." She tried to soothe her, wishing that the bloody beeping would stop. Claire was already traumatised enough.

"I...I... don't think that's me." the young mother whispered, her eyes wide with fear as she glanced pointedly at Steph's wrist. As Steph followed her gaze, time seemed to slow and almost stop entirely. Her brain felt unable to process what was happening and was attempting to shut down in order to protect her from reality as the edges of her vision darkened. When her eyes finally met the shining black surface of the device on her wrist, Steph had to blink several times to clear her vision and read the stark white writing shining back at her.

Stephanie Moore.
DOB: 10/03/2029
Your name has been drawn in the lottery.
You will receive your end-of-life date within one month.

Chapter Fourteen

The words floated before her eyes, but Steph couldn't seem to make sense of them. It couldn't be... She couldn't be... There had to have been a mistake.

Hurriedly she tapped her fingers against the screen to acknowledge the message and silence the beeping without really taking in the information and fixed her eyes back on Claire's. The two women had come to a complete standstill smack bang in the centre of the restaurant and she could feel the eyes of the other customers on them again. All sitting silently, the food before them seemingly forgotten. Some with their forks raised halfway to their mouths as they watched the scene unfold in front of them, waiting to see how Steph would react. Others frantically checked their own watches, raising their wrists to their faces and peering intently into the small screens with looks of pure fear on their faces as they checked to see if they had received a message too. An older gentleman, who Steph recognised as one of her regulars, dabbed at the corner of his eye with a napkin. "Too young." He mumbled in a voice laced with sadness. "Far too young."

A wave of all consuming numbness swept over Steph as she tried to process the situation. She had no idea how on earth she was supposed to react to such earth-shattering news, so she did the only thing she could think to do at that moment. She pushed her own thoughts and emotions down, way down into the very pit of her stomach where she could feel a hard ball of tension forming, and focused on the young mother she was supposed to be helping.

"Let's go find your kids," Steph said, flashing the traumatised woman beside her what she hoped was a cheerful smile even though the movement felt foreign, utterly contradicting how she was really feeling at that moment. Steph forced her feet to start moving again and half accompanied, half dragged the still quietly sobbing Claire through the side door to the kitchen and away from the prying eyes of the other diners.

Steph could not quite work out how she got through the rest of her lunchtime shift. She could barely remember greeting Claire's father or helping him take his distraught daughter and grandchildren out to his car, but she knew she had done it. She couldn't recall a single customer's face clearly from the entire afternoon, couldn't remember how busy they'd been, or even how much she'd made in tips, something she usually kept a close eye on throughout each shift.

She had stumbled through the motions like a zombie. Take order, serve food, clear table, get check. The mantra had echoed through Steph's head on repeat and she just kept putting one foot in front of the other. Maybe, just maybe, if she behaved as if nothing had changed, then it wouldn't have? Perhaps she could just carry on living her life the same way that she had done for the last few years. Maybe if she did that, nothing would change.

"Look what the cat dragged in," Crystal said sarcastically as Steph made her way through their front door and put her bag down on the frayed carpet. "Jesus, you look like a drowned rat! What did you do? Decide to take a shortcut through a river on your way home?" she asked her friend in alarm as she took in Steph's soaking wet form. Water droplets dripped from the split ends of her mousy brown hair, her once light blue jeans looked almost black from the amount of water they were saturated with and her hands seemed to be trembling uncontrollably.

"I... no, nothing. It's raining." Steph managed to stutter out through chattering teeth. She stumbled across the room on unsteady feet, leaving wet footprints in her wake, and perched herself on the edge of the bed without thinking to remove her sodden layers first.

"Hey! You're getting the sheets all wet!" Crystal exclaimed, gently pushing against her friend's back in an attempt to entice her to get back up, but Steph didn't seem to notice the encouragement, in fact she didn't react at all. She sat stock-still on the slightly yellowed-from-age bed sheets, seemingly off in her own world. "Steph? What's going on?" Crystal asked, her voice betraying some of the apprehension that she felt. Steph never behaved like this. Sure, she wasn't the most extroverted of people, especially compared to Crystal herself. Typically when Steph got home from work, she would regale Crystal with stories from the day and fill her in on anything she'd missed when they weren't working the same shift. Today though, something was different. Something was wrong.

After a few minutes, Steph raised her gaze from the floor and looked up at Crystal, turning herself slightly on the bed so that she could make eye contact with her friend. The moment their eyes met, and Steph saw the concern reflected back at her, all the emotions that she had been working so hard to keep in check that afternoon suddenly came pouring out of her in a rush. She couldn't control the torrent of salty tears that spilled from her eyes and cascaded down her frozen cheeks. She felt as though she were trying to breathe underwater, and she heaved in great gulps of air in between sobs.

"Oh my god Steph what's wrong?!" Crystal asked, wrapping her long arms around her friend's slim frame and pulling her close to her side. Steph couldn't find the words to reply at that moment. It was taking every bit of energy that she had to keep herself together. She felt as though if she dared to speak, the last piece of thread which was holding her in one piece would snap, and she'd start screaming and never stop. Laying her head on her friend's lap, Steph continued to sob uncontrollably, her tears adding to the growing wet patch on the bed from her clothes. Worried and confused, Crystal didn't know what to do. So, she settled on simply stroking the wet strands of hair off Steph's face and whispered consoling sshing noises, trying to reassure her friend that it would be okay, whatever it was.

They remained this way for what seemed like an eternity to both women until finally feeling that she should try and articulate to Crystal what was wrong, Steph attempted to speak.

"I....I..." It was all she could manage before a fresh wave of sobs overwhelmed her, and she buried her face back in Crystal's lap. Trying to fight through the fog of hopelessness in her brain, Steph raised her wrist to her face and clicked at the watch lying against her frozen skin. Tapping it a few times, she recalled the alert she had received earlier today and held her arm up so that Crystal could read the message. She let her sorrow overtake her again, but somewhere deep in the distance, Steph could just about register the sound of Crystal screaming.

Chapter Fifteen

As he predicted, Tom's day at work was both more challenging and more prolonged than he'd have liked. The never-ending stream of patients continued to pour through his door just as they did every other day. Strangely, he didn't encounter anyone wanting advice or to be consoled over the cull announcement. Though secretly, he wondered if Dr Mahoney, having seen Tom's reaction to the idea of discussing the matter with patients, had asked the receptionist to direct anyone who wished to talk about it into his room instead of into Toms. As grateful as he was for his mentor's thoughtfulness, Tom couldn't help but think that he was just delaying the inevitable. Mahoney couldn't protect him forever. The government had told them all that they expected it to take several years to complete the cull, and there was no way Tom could avoid the subject for even half that long.

He had been home for about an hour when his mother called from the kitchen to let him and his siblings know that dinner was ready. Begrudgingly, Tom forced his tired body off his bed, where he had been lying since he got back, and made his way downstairs to join his family around the dining table.

"It was horrible, mum; the poor woman was completely inconsolable." Tom's brother Mark said to their mother as he carefully laid the table.

"My goodness, imagine getting an alert when you're out in public and with little ones around too. How terribly sad." Tom's mother replied, seeming genuinely concerned. It was a sharp turnaround from her attitude over the weekend when they'd been watching the TV special.

"I don't think I want to imagine it, to be honest. The worst bit, though, was that one of the waitresses was trying to help this poor woman. I was only sitting a couple of tables away, and I heard her calling the ladies' dad and asking him to come to pick her up. Then, when the waitress was leading the lady out the back of the restaurant, out of nowhere, her watch started beeping too, and she received an alert too!"

"She didn't!" Tom's mother exclaimed, clearly gripped by her youngest son's story. Tom had to admit that he was getting curious himself now. So far, he'd not witnessed anyone receiving an alert, and he wasn't in a hurry to, but he couldn't help but wonder what it would be like to see.

"What did she do? The waitress?" Tom's dad asked, joining the

conversation and pausing halfway through carving a roast chicken, holding the oversized fork he was using to steady it aloft like some kind of mini trident as he waited for Mark's reply.
"Nothing! It was the weirdest thing. She glanced down at her watch and silenced the alert, then she just carried on as though nothing had happened! She was back out working again in time to get me my check. Didn't even look like she'd been crying." Mark finished his tale with a flourish, clearly enamoured by this mystery waitress.
"Did you hear that, Tom? This all happened at that place you used to work at." Tom's mother told him, and his stomach somersaulted in fear.
Who had gotten the alert? Which one of the waitresses? Was it someone he knew, someone that he'd worked with? He had been trying to come to terms with the fact that a large number of the people that he had grown up with, played with as a child, studied with or worked with would receive alerts from the lottery but now that it had seemingly happened, he realised that he hadn't sufficiently prepared himself at all.
"Which waitress?" He asked in a monotone, all his attention now fixed on Mark, who was busy piling mashed potatoes onto his plate.
"Erm, Steph, I think her name is? The shortish one with the brown hair, kinda pretty? It's a shame. She seems nice, and she's been working there for as long as I have been going." Mark answered him.
Shit. Tom thought to himself, suddenly losing his appetite for the roast dinner that his mum had no doubt spent half the day preparing for them, not to mention spent a small fortune on. He liked Steph. He had fond memories of working behind the bar with her, she'd trained him when he first started working there. He remembered passing the time on dreary shifts by singing old rock songs with her and quizzing each other about bands that most people had long ago forgotten. Sure, they weren't close now. Their only interactions since he'd left the restaurant had been when she'd been his waitress. Still, the idea of her smiling face not being there to take his order anymore felt like a punch to the gut.
Staring down at his dinner, Tom pushed his peas around his plate with his fork as his family continued chatting away around him about some inconsequential topic, the weather or some crap, Tom didn't care enough to pay attention. His little brother was shovelling food into his mouth without a care in the world in

between speaking and Tom wondered idly for a moment if he should prepare to perform the Heimlich manoeuvre as he was sure the kid would start choking soon if he didn't slow down. Their mum cut up small pieces of chicken to daintily place into her mouth while Emily slurped at her glass of water noisily. Their dad stared down at his mobile phone, which was sitting on the table next to his plate and scrolled through some article he was reading. Not paying any attention to the rest of his family seated at the table as per usual now that Mark had finished his tale.

Tom couldn't stomach a single forkful. All he could think about was Steph. About the customer she'd been trying to help whose name he didn't know. About the protestors outside of the hospital and about every single other nameless, faceless person all over the planet who had received their death sentence already or would in the coming weeks. Gazing down at the fork in his hand, Tom seriously debated stabbing it into his thigh for a moment. Perhaps the shock and pain of such an action would awaken him from the dark and depressing nightmare in which he was stuck, but he knew it was useless. This was no nightmare. There was just no way his imagination was callous enough, corrupt enough, to come up with something as horrible as the cull.

"Thomas, did you hear me?" His mother interrupted his thoughts, and he forced himself to look up from his plate and meet her eyes. "I was asking how your day at work was, dear." She finished when she knew she had his attention.

Tom opened his mouth to give her some watered-down version of his day in response as usual. He never told her the full stories of the horrors he saw each and every day, knowing that they would only upset her, which wouldn't do either of them any good. Before he could utter a single word though, every thought in his head was drowned out by a loud, high-pitched beeping noise emitting from his wrist.

Thomas Walker.
DOB: 10/03/2029
Your name has been drawn in the lottery.
You will receive your end-of-life date within one month.

"Thomas? What is that?" he heard his mother ask, but her fearful voice seemed a million miles away to Tom as he stared down at the text on his wrist in horror. No. This couldn't be happening, not to him. He'd worked too hard on his studies, pushed himself to breaking point to try and get on the right path to fulfil his dream, and pretty much ruined his relationship with his father in the process. He was a good person. Sure, he had his faults like anyone else, but at his core, Tom knew that he was a decent and caring man, and that he deserved to live.

"Tom?" Mark's shocked voice piped up from across the table, and Tom could hear the tears catching in his brother's throat, but he couldn't think of a single thing to say.

He sat frozen, unable to move even enough to silence the unending beeping, which was still emitting from his wrist until he felt a strong, steadying hand on his shoulder.

"It'll be alright, son. Let's turn this off, shall we?" His father's voice suggested as he lifted his eldest sons' wrist from where it lay against the table and tapped his large finger against the screen, silencing the device.

"Dad?" Tom managed to squeak out, finally taking his eyes off his wrist and raising them to look up at his father, who was still standing over him.

"Don't worry about it. I'll call Henry Peterson tomorrow and talk to him. Get this straightened out." Mr Walker said confidently, trying to reassure his son and squeezing his shoulder slightly as he lowered the boy's wrist again.

Henry Peterson was their local MP, a balding man who Tom's father had gone to university with, and would surely be able to do something. Henry wouldn't let his Tom be put to death. Surely politicians must have some sway, Mr Walker thought to himself, must be able to do something to protect bright young minds like Tom's from being snuffed out unnecessarily. Yes, he'd call Henry first thing in the morning and get this whole mess straightened out. It'd be like it never happened, he reassured himself as he looked down into his son's broken, tear-filled eyes.

"Yes! Henry, of course! Why didn't I think of that? Jack, you really are such a clever man. See Tom? There's nothing to worry about." Mrs Walker said confidently, seeming to honestly believe that it would be that simple. That her husband could just make a single phone call, and that would be that. Tom's name would be removed from the list, and another unsuspecting person would be called up in his place.

"But, even if Henry could... then wouldn't someone else have to die instead of me?" Tom asked quietly, surprised at how hoarse his voice sounded as it cracked over the words.

"Yes, well, that's regrettable, of course, but..." Jack began, but Tom cut him off. Abruptly pushing his chair back from the table and rising to his feet, almost knocking his father over in the process.

"But what? What dad? It doesn't matter because at least it won't be me? Christ, you're a fucking doctor! How can you think like that? How can you decide that my life is worth more than someone else's? Than *anyone* else's?" Tom screamed in fury. He could feel his face growing red as he stared down at his father, realising, for the first time, that he had now become taller than the older man.

"Thomas, don't worry about that now. The important thing is that we keep you safe." His mother tried to console him, but it was no good. Tom was past the point of being comforted by anyone. He spared a quick glance at Emily, who hadn't uttered a word since his alert went off, and saw the tears flowing down her cheeks before turning on his heel and rushing out of the dining room and into the hallway. As he paused for a moment to put on his jacket, his father appeared beside him once more.

"Tom, we're your parents. Of course, your well-being is our top priority. Come back inside so we can talk about this," Jack said sternly, but Tom wasn't in the mood to listen.

"No. Dad look, I know you mean well, but just don't, okay? Don't call Henry. I wouldn't be able to live with myself if I knew that someone else had to die because my daddy has powerful friends. Please. I need some air, Alright?" Tom said quickly, trying to keep the anger out of his voice, knowing that it was fruitless as the trembling in his shaking hands as he attempted to do up his coat gave him away regardless.

He had to get out of here. He couldn't breathe in the too-tight hallway, and he needed to think. Reaching out his hand, Tom grabbed the front door handle and wrenched the door open as his other hand stuffed his keys into his pocket and then stepped outside. Before his dad could say another word, Tom slammed the door shut behind him and started to make his way down the dark, deserted street. He'd barely gone more than a few roads when he saw it, one of the posters that he'd walked past this morning on his way to work.

"Britons! Your country needs you. Don't be the person who lets us down. If your name is called, step up bravely!" And at that moment, with the heavy snow crunching under his feet and cold icy droplets settling in his hair on the barely lit suburban street, Tom knew what he had to do.

Chapter Sixteen

Steph sat completely still, watching on in silence as Crystal bustled around their tiny kitchen area, making herself a sandwich. Trying to force herself to focus on the familiar domesticity of the scene and not let her mind wander and dwell on the events of the day, but it was no use. Crystal had offered to make a sandwich for Steph too, but the mere idea of putting food in her mouth made Steph's insides feel like a washing machine on a spin cycle, so she had declined, but at least she'd managed to stop crying in the couple of hours since she had got home.

Sitting in the dry clothes that Crystal had helped her into, Steph tried to quiet the incessant voices in her mind, telling her all the things she needed to do. She had always been a practical person, and it seemed that even now, when she was staring death in the face, her mind couldn't help but make lists and plans for what little future she had left.

She would have to call her parents, Steph thought to herself. They had a right to know. God, what if someone else in her family had received an alert today? She fretted, bile rising at the back of her throat at the very thought. No, they couldn't have, Steph reassured herself, taking a deep breath and forcing herself to think logically. The one thing she had deduced about the lottery was that the alerts were being sent out in date order. Both she and Claire, the customer at the restaurant earlier today, had been born in March. Jimmy, the waiter, had received his alert before her, and his birthday was in February from what Tony had told her. All of Steph's family member's birthdays were later in the year, so logically, they wouldn't have received an alert, or at least not yet.

Glancing around the cramped flat, Steph took stock of her meagre belongings and mentally started calculating who she would leave what to. Most of it would go to Crystal, all the household stuff for certain and anything else she thought that her best friend could either make use of, or perhaps sell to help keep her afloat after Steph was gone. The two girls weren't the same size, so Steph's few items of clothing would be useless to her friend. Maybe she should see about taking them down to one of the local homeless shelters, she thought to herself. Perhaps someone could make use of them there. She should find a couple of keepsakes to send to her family, she had an old necklace that had once been her grandmother's, and Steph knew that she should definitely make sure that that made its way back

to her mum. There were just so many things to think about. So much to figure out. Steph barely knew where to start and the weight of her current situation sat heavily in her chest.
The television programme the government had aired on Saturday night after the announcement had said that anyone called up would receive 'arrangement kits' in the mail, which would give them instructions on how best to set their affairs in order before their end-of-life date, maybe that would help. *End of life date.* The words echoed in Steph's mind. She was going to be executed. Someone she had never seen before, who she had never done anything to and who had no reason to dislike her, was going to stick a needle into her veins and pump poison into her until she was dead. Because the government told them to. Because some computer programme had spit out her name and decreed that she had to die.
Steph jumped off the bed as though she'd been electrocuted, crashing into a small cabinet and sending the discarded coffee mug on top of it clattering to the floor with a smash as the realisation hit her like a ton of bricks. Heart racing, Steph suddenly felt claustrophobic and her throat began to tighten, as though there wasn't enough air in the room, as though the very walls were somehow closing in on her. Grabbing her coat from its hook by the window, Steph threw it around her shoulders and started towards the door.
"Steph! Where are you going?" Crystal called out after her, alarmed by her abrupt actions.
"I just need some air. I can't breathe in here." Steph replied quickly as she pulled open the front door, gasping for breath.
"Wait up, I'll come with you," Crystal replied, putting down her half-made sandwich and starting towards Steph, who shook her head vehemently.
"Thank you, but I just need to be alone for a bit. Is that okay?"
"Of course it is, but are you sure you'll be alright?" Crystal asked, concerned.
"Yes, I'll be fine, I promise. I'm just going to walk around the block. I'll be back before you know it." Steph tried to reassure her, flashing Crystal what she hoped was a convincing smile as she stepped out of the door and pulled it shut behind her.

The sense of panic she had felt in the flat soon began to alleviate as she made her way down their long road and steadily drew in lungfuls of cold, refreshing air. Ever since she was a little girl, Steph had always liked being outside. Whenever her parents had told her off as a child, she had run across the street from their house to the vast playing fields and walked around the soft grass until her dad came and found her and dragged her back home. There was something about being outside in the fresh air, with nothing to confine her, which comforted Steph in a way that being cooped up inside could not.

Strolling through the dark streets, Steph carefully avoided the patches of slippery ice which had formed on the pathways beneath her feet. Thankfully, it had at least stopped raining. Steph felt an overwhelming urge to pay special attention to her surroundings as she sloshed through the puddles on the street. She had walked these streets a thousand times, but now... She guessed it was only natural when you've been told that your time is coming to an end to want to take everything in and experience as much of the world as you possibly can before it is too late. Every tree suddenly felt worth pausing to admire, every building held people with their own lives, their own worries, their own stories, none of which she would ever know, but for some reason, tonight, she wanted to. Steph was so lost in taking in every tree, every house, every car that she made her way past, that she didn't notice the person coming towards her until it was too late and she accidentally bumped her shoulder against theirs.

"Sorry." She mumbled, backing away slightly and looking to see who she'd hit, hoping that it wasn't some little old lady who she might have hurt.

"Steph?" a familiar voice called in the semi-darkness and Steph tilted her head slightly until she could make out the person's features under the glow of the street lamps.

"Tom!" She said in surprise, caught totally off guard by his presence. "What are you doing here?" She asked almost rudely. She was so used to only seeing him in the restaurant, smartly dressed in his shirts and perfectly creased jeans without a single hole in them, that seeing him out in the real world was startling. Especially tonight.

"Steph! It is you. I'm so sorry. I heard about your alert." Tom stammered, forgetting his own worries at that moment now that he was confronted with another person who was facing their imminent demise. Someone he knew, someone he had laughed with, sang with.

"Oh, yeah, erm, thanks, I guess," Steph murmured, suddenly wishing she'd stayed home. The last person that she wanted to console her was Tom. The man she'd daydreamed of maybe someday having a future with. Now she wouldn't have a future with anyone. "Well, erm, it was nice to see you." She stuttered quickly, turning to make her way back towards home and away from this awkward encounter.

"Steph, wait. I got one too." Tom whispered so quietly that Steph could almost convince herself that she had heard him wrong, or at least she hoped that she had.

"What?" she replied, turning on her heel to face him again and almost slipping on a patch of water beneath her boots.

"An alert," Tom said quietly and tapped against his watch, pulling up his information and showing it to her.

"We have the same birthday." was the only thing Steph could think of to say as she stared down at his wrist in shock. Of all the people in town who must have been born on March 10th, 2029, why did the man who was picked to die opposite her have to be him? The one man she would have wanted to live. The one man she knew who really deserved to?

"Oh," Tom said dumbly, annoyed at his lack of eloquence. He didn't know why he had called her back, didn't know why he had wanted to tell her, but he hadn't been able to stop himself. Something inside Tom had urged him to open up to Steph, to try and make her feel less alone perhaps? So that she'd know that she wasn't the only one going through this.

Why am I so awkward? Steph cursed herself inwardly as she scrambled around the dark recesses of her brain trying to come up with something to say. A large part of her wanted to throw her arms around Tom and console him. Another part of her wanted to take his hand and just start running. Running until their legs gave out and they couldn't go another step. Running as far away as they possibly could. So far away that no one could find them. Not the police, not the cull Enforcement Agency or whoever else was responsible for ensuring that those called in the lottery turned up for their execution dates.

Instead, she just stood there silently, staring into the eyes of the kind man that she had spent so many hours singing off-key with behind the bar. Who she had bought medium-rare steaks to every couple of weeks for the last god knows how many months, and who's dates she'd bitched about in the kitchen at work with Crystal.

"I'm really sorry, Tom." Steph finally managed to say. "I thought that doctors were exempt?" She added as an afterthought.

"Only high-level ones," Tom told her with a shrug of his shoulders. "My dad was. So that's something."

"Yes, that's something. The alerts seem to have gone out in date order, and my friend, Crystal, well, her birthday is in January, and she didn't get an alert, so I guess that means she's safe too."

"Really? My little sister's birthday is in January as well. That's a relief." Tom said, feeling a weight being lifted from his shoulders. Maybe, just maybe, if he looked at the cull as though it was something he was doing for Emily, so that she could grow up and have a family, then maybe he could find the strength to walk into the execution centre and submit to his fate.

"I don't know for sure," Steph said quickly, not wanting to give him false hope. "But it seems that way."

"I don't think anyone knows anything for sure anymore. So, what are you doing out here so late by yourself?" Tom asked Steph, then, quickly realising the answer to his own question, continued, "Same thing I am, I guess, had to get out of the house?"

"Yes, something like that. How about you? Shouldn't you be with your family?" Steph asked him as they slowly fell into step together and continued walking down the road without ever agreeing to do so.

"I had to get out of there. My dad, he's friends with our MP Henry. Anyways he was going on and on about how he could call him and get this 'straightened out' – his words, not mine, and I just couldn't listen to it anymore. He didn't seem to understand that someone else would have to take my place if he did that. I couldn't live with that." Tom told her quickly, unsure as to why he was confiding in a woman he'd exchanged no more than a handful of pleasantries with in the last year but compelled to talk to her all the same.

"Maybe you should let him? I mean... you're a Doctor Tom. You help people. God knows the world could use all the help it can get right now. If your dad can save your life, maybe you should give that some serious thought." Steph said, conflicted. Of course, she didn't want anyone to die, and she didn't want some nameless, faceless stranger having to take Tom's place. Still, at the same time, she desperately didn't want *him* to have to die. For reasons she didn't want to examine too closely right now.

"I know he's just trying to do what he thinks is right. He's my dad. Of course, he doesn't want me to die. But I couldn't bear it knowing that someone else had lost their life because I was too cowardly to answer the call." said Tom

"You sound like one of those stupid posters that have appeared all over town," Steph said, surprising herself by needing to suppress a slight giggle that caught in her throat and caused her to cough.

"Ahh, yes. 'Your country needs YOU!'" Tom said, chuckling, emphasising the 'YOU' by pointing his index finger into Steph's face. She batted it away like it was a wayward fly and let out a soft laugh. As Tom looked down at her in the moonlight, he was suddenly reminded of his brothers' words from earlier, *'Brown hair, kinda pretty.'* Mark had been right; Steph was pretty. Why hadn't he noticed that before? Her olive skin shone in the dim light, contrasting against her dark hair and eyes, and her small mouth pouted slightly as she shivered against a fresh gust of icy wind. Excellent, Tom thought to himself as he felt a warmth in his palms, and his heart started to beat a little faster. Finally, find a girl you might like, a girl who's been under your nose for years, just as you receive your death sentence. Great timing, Walker. Shaking his head, Tom cleared his mind of such thoughts.

"It's freezing out here. You should get home. Where do you live? I'll walk you back?" Tom offered, not liking the idea of her walking the streets alone at this time of night, especially after his recent night out working with the homeless. He knew what kind of people prowled the streets just a few roads away from here and wouldn't feel right letting Steph walk back on her own.

"Erm, thanks. I'm just down that way, on Maple." Steph replied, pointing back the way they had come. She was slightly surprised by his offer. It had been a long time since a man had offered to walk her anywhere, but then Tom was a good person. Of course, he wouldn't want her walking home alone.

They turned back quickly, both bowing their heads slightly against the rising wind, and started to make their way back towards Steph's flat in silence. Both brooding over the day's shocking events.

Chapter Seventeen

"Steph, what are you doing here?" Tony asked incredulously as he noticed the young waitress setting out cutlery on the restaurant's freshly laid tables. Having just returned from visiting his ailing mother-in-law in Newcastle, Tony had only found out that the poor girl had received an alert a few days ago, whilst at work of all places, and honestly, he hadn't expected to see her again. Jimmy, another staff member who had been unlucky enough to have had his name drawn in the lottery, hadn't returned to work since he'd received his alert. Tony didn't blame him, and had resigned himself to the fact that he would sadly be missing a few familiar faces around here as more and more people's names were drawn in the lottery. So far, he and his family have been lucky. None of their names had been called, and whilst he was incredibly grateful for that, his heart bled for the poor men, women and children up and down the country and around the world whose lives were soon to come to an end and the families that would be left behind to mourn them.
"It's Friday night, Tony. Where else would I be?" Steph asked him in the most casual tone she could muster as she picked up a glass from one of the tables in her section and began to rub a napkin against a watermark on the stem.
"But Steph, you, I mean, you don't have to... You shouldn't be here." Tony stuttered, struggling to find the words to convey what he wanted to say to her. As he followed Steph around her usual section, watching as she busied herself shuffling cutlery a centimetre to the left or right until she was satisfied it was correctly positioned, and rubbed at spots he couldn't see on the already sparkling wine glasses, Tony noticed the dark purple smudges under her eyes, the pallor of her skin, to his eyes it even looked as though Steph had lost a little weight in just the few days he had been away. Her uniform definitely hung more loosely on her small frame than he remembered it doing previously.
"It's fine, Tony, honestly. I don't want to talk about it. Right now, I just want to work." Steph tried to reassure her boss, who was looking at her as though he was scared she might break in two at any moment.
Before getting her alert, Steph had been sure she wouldn't set foot in the restaurant again if she were unlucky enough to be called in the lottery. And for the first couple of days afterwards, she didn't. She called her parents and broke the news to them.

That had been a fun phone call. She had been unsurprised to find that whilst they were unhappy that her name had been called, they wholeheartedly agreed with the cull. They had always been the kind of people who put their faith in the government, and were just happy that something was finally being done to try and improve the world around them. Whether it was the right thing for a large portion of the population or not. Her father had even uttered the phrase *'It's for the good of the many'* as he had commiserated with her over her upcoming death.

They had tried to convince her to go and visit them, but Steph had declined. She hadn't seen them in a couple of years now, and she felt things were best left that way. That way at least, they could remember her as the child she had been, not the forlorn woman she had become. Besides, she couldn't afford the train fare. After that horrible phone call was done, Steph had realised that she had extraordinarily little to do with her time other than sit around and fret over what was to come. She couldn't settle to anything for longer than a few minutes before images flashed before her eyes of rows of seemingly endless mass graves scattering the countryside. Crystal and Steph didn't have a TV, so watching movies to pass the time was out, and whenever she tried to read one of the few battered old books they owned, all the words just blurred together on the page as her mind wandered.

So, she'd decided the best, most productive thing she could do right now was return to work. To carry on her days as usual, put a smile on her drawn, washed-out face and try to save up as much money as she could to help Crystal when she was gone. Steph knew that her friend was going to struggle without her. They barely managed to make enough money between them to cover their bills and put food in their bellies, and the guilt she felt about leaving her alone was almost more than Steph could bear. At least this way, she could try and earn enough to tide Crystal over for a few weeks, give her time to get back on her feet after... No, Steph couldn't finish that thought.

In all honesty, the distraction of work helped.

Thankfully, no other customers or staff had had the misfortune to receive an alert whilst at the restaurant, so Steph hadn't had to relive that experience. Most of the time, she could go about her usual routine and manage to forget, just for a few hours, the awful fate that awaited her. Crystal, predictably, had told her not to be so stupid, that she wasn't worried about how she'd cope financially once Steph was gone. She was worried about how

she would cope without her best friend. But Steph had been adamant this was the best place for her right now. She didn't even know how long it would be until her execution date. Her alert said she would receive it within one month, but for all Steph knew, the date could be a year or more away. What was she supposed to do until then? Sit at home, acting like she was already dead?
"Look, Steph, if you need anything, if you want to leave early or, well, if there is anything I can do, just let me know, ok?" Tony told her, placing a reassuring hand on her thin shoulder. Of all of his staff, why did it have to be Stephanie? He wondered to himself as he entered his office to take care of the paperwork that had accumulated whilst he'd been away, a heavy weight pressing against his thin shoulders.

Chapter Eighteen

As Tom sat in an uncomfortably hard chair in the hospital staff cafeteria, trying to coax a dry ham sandwich down his throat, his attention was caught by a tall, dark-skinned woman he didn't recognise who was pinning some kind of notice to the staff information board. He couldn't make out what it said from here. The one and only thing Tom could see perfectly clearly were the letters C.E.A emblazoned in gold across the black briefcase that the woman carried. cull Enforcement Agency. Tom realised. What are they doing here? He waited until the woman had moved away to talk to one of the senior doctors at another table before he got up to investigate. Dumping the remains of his sandwich in a nearby bin, he approached the noticeboard along with two other members of equally intrigued staff.
"Volunteers needed." read the headline. As Tom read on, his stomach churned, and he momentarily worried that what little of the lunch he'd managed to consume was about to make a reappearance.

The C.E.A. is looking for medical staff volunteers who are trained in administering injections and monitoring vital signs to work at a government execution facility which will be located opposite this hospital.

Anyone who wishes to volunteer will be recompensed financially for their time and should make themselves known to the C.E.A. Agents at the facility as soon as possible.

We regret that those persons whose names have been called in the lottery are not eligible to apply.

The printed notice had been hand signed in bright blue ink at the bottom by none other than Professor Peter Jones, head of the cull Enforcement Agency and the very man who had first announced the culls to the British population.
"Seriously? Not only do they want to kill half of us off, but now they expect those of us whose names aren't called to actually administer the injections?" A disgruntled red-headed nurse who was reading the notice from somewhere behind Tom's shoulder cried out indignantly.
"It could be worse." a second voice answered her. "I heard that they totally botched it at the prisons. There weren't enough

medically trained personnel available at each location to administer the drugs and a fair few of the ones who were trained simply refused. Apparently, one man in Edinburgh was given an incorrect dosage, started convulsing, vomiting, it was a complete shambles."

"I heard that they had resorted to shooting some prisoners," a third person chimed in. "Cos they didn't have enough medication on site to dispense with them all."

Not wanting to stand and listen to any more unsubstantiated rumours, Tom quickly backed away from the growing crowd of people and quickly made his way out of the cafeteria. Not slowing until he reached the double doors which led to the staff gardens. Or at least what was left of the gardens at any rate, a small outside space which basically consisted of a circular path surrounding a tiny patch of grass and a few trees. Tom pushed at the doors with all his might, letting out a little of his frustration, and as the heavy glass flew open, a gust of icy cold wind barrelled into his exposed skin. Dressed only in scrubs, Tom shivered as he made his way out into the rows of planters which had been empty of any actual plants for as long as he could remember and took a seat on the single bench that sat in the centre of the grassed area, sheltered by an old birch tree.

How could they be so insensitive? Tom asked himself as he sat on the cold, damp wood and buried his head in his hands. *"Those persons whose names have been called in the lottery are not eligible to apply."* As if we'd want to! As if any self-respecting doctor would choose to sign up to commit mass murder whether their name had been called or not! He thought to himself angrily, bringing one of his hands away from his face and banging his fist onto the wood beneath him, which shuddered at the impact. But before the bench had finished vibrating from the force of his blow, Tom realised that some doctors would be happy to sign up. He had heard whispers around the hospital already of certain members of staff who were one hundred per cent in favour of the culls and he knew that others would volunteer for the positions simply to put a few extra pounds in their pockets to help feed their families.

Tom hoped that a few of the more kind-hearted members of staff might sign up simply so that those people, like himself, who would be the ones being strapped down to the beds, having the poisons injected forcefully into their bloodstreams, might at least have a friendly face to look at as their lives came to an end. A compassionate person to hold their hand and sit with them in their final moments instead of some unfeeling bureaucrat. Tom brushed a tear away from the corner of his eye as he heard the doors swing open behind him. He hadn't told any of his colleagues about his alert. Not even Doctor Mahoney, and he did not want to draw unnecessary attention to himself by letting any of them see his tear-stained cheeks.

Tom wasn't sure why he hadn't managed to confide in his mentor, to whom he told most things. When he had returned to work the day after receiving his alert, and the older man had greeted him and asked how he was, Tom hadn't been able to bring himself to say the words out loud. It felt as though the more people that knew, the more times he had to verbalise what was going to happen to him, the more real it became. And for now, at least, all Tom wanted to do was try and forget. To go about his days as best he could, doing the job that he loved, that he had trained so hard for and had planned to dedicate his entire life to. He didn't want to waste what little time remained to him focusing on the inevitable. He certainly didn't want to spend his remaining weeks or months on this planet with everyone he knew looking at him like they looked at their terminally ill patients. The pity in the eyes of his colleagues as they spoke in hushed voices to patients who weren't long for this world was not something Tom wanted to be aimed at him. He had seen that look too many times, even felt it on his own features on several occasions. The last thing he wanted was to be on the receiving end of it, and so he kept the news to himself.

The day passed by, just like so many others had before it. It was strange. Tom felt as though, in some ways, his entire life had been turned upside down, yet in others, nothing at all had changed. Why hadn't it? Why weren't people screaming from the rooftops about the injustices? Sure, there were still a group of protestors outside the hospital doors, but even their numbers were dwindling. Mostly, people carried on with their lives as though nothing had changed. As though a third of their friends, families, and neighbours weren't soon to be executed indiscriminately.

As a general rule, Tom wasn't the kind of person to get particularly mad about things he couldn't change. Preferring to focus his energy on the things that he might be able to improve. To spend his time helping those he could and trying to make the world just a little bit nicer, a little more bearable. But this? This government scheme that had been cooked up in board rooms and laboratories behind closed doors by people who knew they would be exempt made him exceptionally angry.

By the time Tom finished his shift, night had fallen, and it was raining steadily as he exited the building. With his head down to protect himself from the worst of the weather and music playing in his ears, Tom crossed the road quickly to get away from the still-shouting protestors and his eyes flitted to the usually abandoned building he had walked past daily for the past year and paid little attention to.

For as long as Tom could remember, there had been a ten-story apartment block opposite the hospital which had fallen into disrepair. Doctor Mahoney had told him that it had once been used to house some of the staff members and trainees at the hospital. But as staff numbers fell and funding grew tighter, it had been sold on to some company or another who had decided against actually doing much with it other than fastening some plywood boards over the windows to stop the multitudes of homeless on the city streets from getting inside.

Tonight, however, the building was bustling with activity. Workers in hi-vis jackets pulled at the plywood, exposing old glass windows covered in dirt from years of neglect. Others, working tirelessly with torches affixed to their hard hats to light their way, carried row after row of what Tom could see were old metal framed beds from a large van parked in the building's unused car park, through the front doors. This is it, he thought to himself, this is where I am going to die.

This must be the building that the notice he had read earlier today referred to, the one being set up as a government execution centre. Tom did his best not to focus on that thought and continued his walk home. He hadn't gone more than a few steps when he heard someone calling out to him.

"Tom? Hey Tom!"

Tom spun around to try and locate the person calling his name and was surprised to see Josh, the volunteer that he had gone out on the night shift with what felt like a lifetime ago now, standing a few feet away, calling his name. Josh was huddled in an oversized black coat and gloves with a hat pulled so far down over his face that Tom barely recognised him at first.

"Josh, Hi." He said by way of greeting, slowing down slightly but not stopping, he didn't fancy getting caught up in a conversation out here in the rain, nor did he want to spend any more time in the shadow of this building than was completely necessary.

"Joining the queue?" Josh asked, gesturing to the handful of people behind him. "Cut in here with me. I'm sure these people won't mind." He added, looking at the man closest to him in the queue, who shook his head and smiled slightly.

"Erm, no, actually, I'm just on my way home." Tom corrected him. Was Josh signing up? That surprised him. Granted, he didn't know the guy well, but during the few hours they had spent together that night patrolling the streets, Tom had gotten the impression that Josh was like him and wanted to help people, not kill them.

"Oh well, you should think about it, buddy. I know it's not the most glamorous job, but, well, someone's gotta do it, and I've heard the money's good. Twice what you'd earn for the same number of hours at the hospital." Josh informed Tom with a smile on his face.

How can he be so heartless? Tom wondered to himself as he tried to formulate a reply. He wasn't really sure what prompted him to tell Josh the truth. Even hours later, when he sat back and went over the conversation in his head, Tom couldn't decide why, of all people, he had chosen to tell a near-stranger about his alert, but he had.

"I can't. I got an alert four days ago. I'm ineligible." Tom heard himself saying and Josh's smile faded instantly.

"Mate, I'm... I'm sorry, I had no idea." Josh stuttered, his face turning a deep shade of crimson in embarrassment.

"Never mind, eh? As long as they're paying you well! You never know. Maybe you'll be the person who gets the pleasure of killing me?" Tom snapped. He waited for just long enough to watch all the colour drain from Josh's face under the glow of the streetlamp as the other man stumbled to find something to say in response, before turning away and continuing his walk home. Pushing his earbuds back into his ears as he went and turning up the volume until he could feel the bass of the rock song that was playing vibrating in his chest. Fuelling his anger and frustration with each pounding step he took along the pavement.

Chapter Nineteen

Jack Walker perched awkwardly on the very edge of the chair behind his desk in his office on the thirty-third floor of the private hospital where he worked on the outskirts of central London, entirely unable to settle or stop his mind from replaying the events of the last few days. The sun was setting outside the window, which reached from floor to ceiling behind him, casting an eerie glow across the room as the rain tapped rhythmically against the glass. Jack sipped at the tumbler of whisky he had just poured himself and drummed his fingers against the dark wood of his desk in agitation. The amber liquid seared his throat as he swallowed, it was an inferior brand with none of the smoothness that he remembered from the varieties he used to purchase back when alcohol was more readily available and didn't cost quite so much, but tonight, it would have to do. These days even a bottle like this was an extravagance, costing nearly as much to purchase as an old used car had back when Jack first learned to drive. It was something Jack had hidden away on his bookshelf behind the volumes about anatomy and various surgical techniques, which he only allowed himself to dip into rarely. Despite that, the bottle was almost half empty. Jack knew his wife would be angry if she found out about it, and he'd have to brush his teeth several times before going home to rid himself of the smell, but tonight, of all nights, Jack needed a stiff drink.

Tonight, against his eldest son's wishes, Jack planned to contact his friend and local member of parliament, Henry, and beg him for help. Despite Tom's protests, Jack felt that he had to ask the man that he had known since childhood to intervene to somehow save his son from being put to death, even though he knew it would mean that another unsuspecting person would have to take Tom's place. That thought, more than anything else, was what had caused Jack to crack open his Whiskey after he had finished surgery for the day.

Jack didn't know who the person would be exactly, but he knew they'd be male and twenty-four years of age, born on March tenth, 2029. Just like Tom. Because that was how they had been told the lottery worked. One male and one female from each date and year, born in the same town at the same hospital. Another young man who was just starting out in life, who had dreams and aspirations just like his own boy, would receive an alert and have to die if Henry was able to remove Thomas's name from the list.

Another father, someone who was perhaps less connected than Jack was, would have to say goodbye to his son, to the man who he had hoped would become a better version of himself, someone who he could be proud of. After all, wasn't that what all fathers wanted for their sons?

All of this had to happen just so Jack didn't have to watch his own boy walk into one of those god-awful government execution facilities that he had seen springing up all over town. Maybe Tom was right in what he'd been telling him for years. Jack was a selfish man.

He downed the last of the whisky in one large gulp and buzzed his secretary on his intercom.

"Mandy? Can you get Henry Peterson on the line for me?" He asked

"Of course, Doctor Walker, right away." Came the timid voice of his secretary. She was the fourth one Jack had employed in the last two years, and he wasn't convinced she liked him very much. None of them did. But then he wasn't here to make friends. He was here to work.

A few moments later, his telephone rang, and he picked up the receiver with a shaking hand.

"Henry? Jack Walker here. How are you? How's the family? All well, I hope?" Jack asked. Engaging in the small talk which was the polite prelude to asking anyone for a favour.

"Jack! It's been a long time. All well here, yes, thank you, and yours?" Henry asked cheerfully, seeming to not mind the unexpected interruption to his evening from his old friend.

"They are well, thank you. I won't keep you long. No doubt you're run off your feet at the moment with all this cull business." Jack added, gently bringing up the subject that he was so desperate to discuss.

"Oh yes, and I don't mind telling you, I wouldn't have minded a bit of a heads up about this whole mess before it was announced. Did you know we weren't even told first? No warning at all. They were concerned about leaks apparently. We had to find out in line with everyone else in the world. But of course, we're the ones who are expected to keep our constituencies in order whilst it's all happening. I tell you, Jack, it's been a complete nightmare." Henry said.

"I'm sorry to hear that, Henry. I must admit I assumed that someone such as yourself would have been given advance notice. But at least you were exempt from the lottery, right? "Jack said, edging closer to his point.

"Were we hell," Henry said, his voice sharper now. "It seems that MPs such as me were deemed easily replaceable, and our names went into the proverbial hat with everyone else's. The MP for Brighton got her alert just yesterday in fact. Now I can't say I was particularly fond of how she ran things down there, but even so."

Henry was speaking about the woman in the past tense already, Jack noticed. It seemed that anyone who received an alert was perceived as already dead by the people around them. Is that how people would be looking at Tom? Like a lost cause that was already six feet under? Not worthy of their time or concern?

"Anyways, forgive my rambling. To what do I owe the pleasure of your call?" Henry questioned in a more amiable tone.

"Right, yes, well, you see, the thing is. You remember my boy, Thomas?" Jack stuttered

"Thomas, your eldest, right? Doesn't he work at the hospital over on Bleecker Avenue?" Henry asked

"Yes, yes, he does. The thing is, he received an alert. His name was called in the lottery." Jack said solemnly, trying to keep the torrents of emotion he felt bubbling up in his chest from colouring his voice. Besides his immediate family, Henry was the first person he had discussed Thomas' fate with, and saying the words out loud made them seem all the more real.

The line was silent for a few moments, and all Jack could hear was a faint buzzing that told him Henry was still connected to the call for what felt like a lifetime before the other man eventually responded.

"Jack, I don't know what to say. I am sorry, truly." Henry finally replied.

"Thank you, it's come as quite a shock to us all, as you can imagine, and well, that was the reason I was calling. I wondered, perhaps, if there was anything that you could do?" Jack asked, finally getting to the crux of the matter.

"I wish that there were. I'm sorry, Jack, but even if my own wife got called up, I wouldn't be able to do anything about it. Not even if I was myself. I have absolutely no influence whatsoever regarding the lottery or the culls. It's all being done far above my pay grade." Henry told his old friend, wishing that there was something more that he could do. The whole idea of the cull was abhorrent to him. That the governments of this world could come up with no better solution to the crises they were facing other than to murder a large part of the population was unfathomable.

If Henry had his way, he'd save as many as possible. Sadly, his hands were tied.

"There's no one you know higher up that you could call? Someone who might have some influence?" Jack pressed, a lump rising in his throat, which he tried in vain to swallow back down with another hearty glug of the amber liquid. He was near begging now but knew he had to try. Knew he would never forgive himself if he didn't.

"I'm sorry, Jack, but I'm afraid there isn't. The only people with the power to put anyone on the exemption list are presidents and prime ministers... and even then, those people could only be exempted for a good reason. From what I have heard, this Peter guy, the head of the enforcement agency? He takes his job very seriously and ensured that as many people's names were entered into the lottery as possible. I heard that he didn't even add his own mother to the exemption list and that he tried to stop some of the essential service personnel from being excluded as well," Henry explained.

"I wish he had," Jack muttered. One of the hardest things for Jack was to know that whilst any of his family members could receive an alert at any given moment, that his wife or younger children potentially still could and that he could be facing losing more than one child, he personally was exempt. That no matter what happened, Jack would live through this. Whether he wanted to or not.

"I take it you were exempt?" Henry asked,

"I was. There's really nothing you can do? Could you even point me in the direction of someone who might be able to...?"

"I'm sorry, Jack, I can't," Henry interrupted before Jack could finish his latest plea. "It's more than my life's worth. I could be found guilty of crimes against humanity under these new laws they've bought in if I am caught interfering. Then I would be up for execution myself, regardless of the lottery. There's really nothing that I can do. But, if you need anything else, any advice, any further information about the executions, or just someone to talk to, please, feel free to call. I'm afraid I have another call waiting. Good luck to you, Jack." Henry finished, and with that, before Jack could reply, the line went dead.

Jack sat holding the telephone receiver for several minutes, listening to the static on the other end of the line, but somehow unable to bring himself to put it down. Once he lowered the handset, that was it, the last chance he had of saving Thomas was gone. Jack wasn't sure that he was ready for that reality to hit him just yet. Reaching across his desk with his free hand, he poured himself another glass of whisky and continued to listen to the empty crackling on his phone as he drank deeply.

Chapter Twenty

After his run-in with Josh, Tom had taken the long route home, stretching out the journey as long as possible despite the rain. He felt the need to try and work off some of his anger before facing his mother, who was still in complete denial about the fact that her eldest son was soon to be executed. It seemed that she had decided that some magical solution was going to present itself and save him, even though Tom had expressly forbidden his dad from calling his MP friend and there really weren't any other options available to them. Tom wasn't so naïve, or perhaps not as hopeful as his mother, and he was doing his best to accept his fate as much as he could.

Sure, Tom was angry as hell. He spent most of his waking hours alternating between wanting to curl up in a ball and sob and wanting to destroy every inanimate object he came across. He'd gotten so frustrated with a pen that refused to work today that he'd snapped it in half with his bare hands. Mostly though, Tom was also absolutely terrified. Scared that he wouldn't have the strength to walk himself into the execution centre and that he'd do something downright embarrassing like pass out and have to be carried in. The last thing Tom wanted was for that to be his last act on this earth, what he'd be remembered for. However, he wasn't living in false hope either. He knew that no miracle was going to happen and change the fact that his name had been drawn in the lottery. Knew that there was no white knight racing on their noble steed to come and save him. Tom had decided that if it helped his mother to live in hope, if it was easier for her to pretend nothing was going to happen than to live in reality, then so be it. She'd have to deal with the truth soon enough. She'd have to mourn for him. Clear out his belongings, and comfort his siblings. There was no point in forcing her to start now.

By the time he arrived home, Tom was soaked, his supposedly waterproof coat having done little to stop the rainwater from seeping through to his skin. His boots squelched with every step that he took, and standing dripping in the hallway of his home, Tom decided he was better off removing as many of his layers there and then as possible rather than splashing water all over the house which his mum took so much care to keep clean. As he started to peel off his clothing, the sounds of hushed voices emanating from the living room to his right filled Tom's ears. The door was closed, which was unusual enough in itself, but it was the tone of the voices that caught his attention and caused him to prick up his ears.

As much as he and his father often butted heads, Tom honestly couldn't remember the last time he'd heard his parents arguing with one another. Regardless of the fact that both of them were obviously trying to keep their voices down, the anger in his parents' whispers was clear enough for Tom to hear. Slipping off his boots, Tom tip-toed to the door in his bare feet and leaned his head towards the polished wood. He knew he shouldn't be listening in to what was no doubt a private conversation, but what were they going to do? Punish him? Even his father, who had always been imaginative with his punishments when Tom was growing up, couldn't come up with a worse fate than the one Tom was already facing.

"I just can't believe there is nothing he can do! Are you sure you really tried Jack? Really pushed him?" Tom's mum whispered in disbelief.

"I swear to you, Mary, I did! Do you honestly think for one minute that I want to see my eldest son dead? That I want to mourn him? Henry said he wouldn't be able to do anything if he himself was called up, that he has no influence." Jack tried to defend himself. After his call with Henry, Jack had put off returning home for as long he reasonably could. Sitting in his office in the semi-darkness until he finished most of the whisky bottle. He had subsequently stumbled in the door only half an hour ago, quite drunk and in no fit state for this conversation, but Mary had ambushed him, and he'd had no option but to admit the truth.

"What you're telling me is, that's it? My son is going to die?" Mary said aghast, her voice breaking over the words.

"*Our* son Mary, he's my boy too, remember." Jack bit back, raising his voice slightly now. He was reasonably confident that Emily was fast asleep and knew nothing short of an earthquake would likely wake her. When he had checked on Mark when he got home, he'd had his earphones firmly in his ears, blasting the god-awful rap music that Jack had forbidden him to play without headphones because the language was so foul. Thomas, it seemed, had yet to return from work yet as the raincoat Jack knew his son had worn to work this morning had not been hanging on the hook by the front door when he had, with some difficulty, placed his own there when he had stumbled in..

"Your boy. Yes, we all know he's *your* boy, Jack. God knows you've spent enough years trying to mould him into a younger version of yourself! Never satisfied! Never willing to let him be his own man! You'll be happy when he's gone. You won't have to be disappointed in him anymore!" Mary said, shouting now, the need to keep her voice down entirely forgotten as her anger got the better of her. Mary knew that she would regret her harsh words and wouldn't have uttered them if she had taken just a moment to think about what she was saying. She knew that what she was saying was wrong, that she didn't truly mean it, and that her words would haunt her for many years to come, but at that moment, she couldn't seem to control herself. Obviously, Jack would be devastated when Tom was gone. No, not when, *if*. She refused to give up hope. Mary wouldn't accept that there was no way out for her firstborn until he took his last breath.

Tom had heard more than enough. Before his father had the chance to try and defend himself, Tom threw open the living room door and stepped inside, slamming it shut forcefully behind him as he shook in anger.

"You called Henry?" Tom asked, desperately trying to control the rage he felt bubbling up inside him. He wanted to scream and cuss his father out for, as usual, completely ignoring what Tom wanted and thinking that he knew best. But for his mother's sake, Tom tried to keep his composure.

"Tom, Son, I didn't know you were home," Jack said quietly, slightly slurring his words. His eyes were red, and he looked unsteady on his feet. The smell of whisky permeated the air between them as Jack spoke, and Tom realised that his father was drunk.

"Dad, I asked you not to. No! I told you! Unequivocally that I didn't want you to try and get me out of this! I don't want someone else to have to die for me!" Tom yelled, losing his fragile grip on his temper. How dare his father go behind his back like this? And then get drunk? Seriously! It was Tom that was going to die, not his dad and he wasn't drowning himself in booze. Jack had no right!

"What did you expect us to do? Just sit here and do nothing? Not even try to save you? You're our son Tom!" Mary cried, tears welling in her blue-grey eyes, and for the first time, Tom truly saw how tired she looked and how much of a toll this was all taking on her.

"I expected you to respect my wishes. Christ, mum, it was practically a deathbed request!" Tom shouted.

"Don't use that tone with your mother," Jack ordered.

"Who are you to tell me what to do? Look at the state of you, dad. You're drunk! How much did that whisky cost, eh? A terms tuition for me, Mark or Em? More?" Tom spat back, "Mum's right. My whole damn life, you've tried to mould me into the man you want me to be. Can't you, just for once actually trust me to know what's best for me? I'm not a child anymore, dad! You can't use your connections to clear up my messes. Or your money, your friends! They can't save me this time."

The room was silent for a few moments, and Tom's words hung in the thick air between them. He could see in his dad's eyes that he was trying to take in his son's words through the haze of alcohol clouding his thoughts. Tom briefly considered writing them down so that Jack could read them in the morning when he was sober. The silence was broken suddenly by a noise so awful that Tom had to fight the desire to throw his hands up and cover his ears to block it out. It was the sound of a heart breaking.

His mother had been standing shell-shocked beside his dad, tears sparkling in her eyes as the two men stood up to one another, right up until it had all become too much for her. When reality had finally set in, and she had collapsed to her knees on the carpeted floor with her head in her hands, wailing like a frightened child as she clawed at the flooring with her long nails. As he looked down at her, a part of Tom wished he was already dead so that he wouldn't have to witness this moment. No child ever wanted to see one of their parents in so much pain. Especially not when they were the cause of it.

"Mum, I'm sorry!" Tom said suddenly, all the anger rushing out of him in an instant at the sight of his mother on the floor.

Scrambling to her side, he crouched on the floor beside her, and she fell into his arms, clinging to him tightly and sobbing profusely.

"They can't! I can't! Please don't make me!" She said incoherently, seeming unable to finish a single thought before another took over.

Jack stood looking down at his wife and son, curled on the floor of their living room, tears pouring down both their faces, and he realised it was the first time he'd really seen Tom cry since he was a little boy. It had been a long time since his son had broken down in front of him. Unsure how to help, feeling useless and ashamed that he couldn't fix this horrible situation, Jack gingerly lowered himself to the floor, feeling completely sober all of a sudden, and wrapped his long arms around his wife and son and joined them in their grief.

Chapter Twenty-one

"I just want to see it, that's all." Steph protested feebly, the tone of her voice making her sound more like a young child pleading for just one more sweet than that of a fully grown adult. She knew that she wasn't exactly making the most eloquent argument. It wasn't a good explanation, Steph was well aware of that, but it was the only one that she had for Crystal right now as the two women stood in the sparse surroundings of their high-rise studio flat. Steph couldn't quite put her finger on exactly why she was so desperate to go and see the population control centre on Bleecker Avenue, the very last building that she would ever enter. Morbid curiosity, perhaps? Or maybe it was so that she could at least insert an accurate picture of the place in her nightmares instead of letting her imagination run wild.

Ever since Steph had received her alert, her mind had become consumed with images of tall, barbed wire fences surrounding a weathered government structure with not an ounce of soul or character. A building that would be replicated up and down the country and become somewhere the locals would walk past in fear and children would cross the street to avoid. Perhaps it would be something like the prisons she remembered seeing on television when she was growing up, with security guards patrolling the perimeter, machine guns strapped to their chests, ready to take down anyone who tried to make a run for it. Whatever the reason was, for weeks now, Steph had had an overwhelming desire to walk to the outskirts of town and see the centre for herself and today she had decided, was the day.

"I don't see how it can possibly be healthy, Steph," Crystal countered. "But if you're that bloody desperate. I'll come with you. You aren't going alone."

"Thank you, I'd like that," Steph admitted as she grabbed her shoes and pulled them onto her feet. Having Crystal by her side always made Steph feel stronger. Not to mention that it would be nice for the two friends to spend some time together outside of home or work, something it felt like they never had the time to do anymore.

The distance between them had been growing more pronounced for a couple of weeks now, and despite her best efforts, the gulf between them only seemed to be getting bigger. Steph was practically positive that she only had herself to blame. No matter how hard she tried, she had been struggling to open up to the woman who she thought of more as a sister than a friend. Steph just felt so emotional all the time. She was so frustrated at her bad luck that every time she opened her mouth, it took all her self-control not to scream and she couldn't find the words to articulate to Crystal how she was feeling. Steph was so sad that it took all her willpower not to burst into tears every five minutes, and utterly full of despair that her life was being torn out from underneath her when it had barely had a chance to begin and that there was nothing at all that she could do about it. How could she possibly make Crystal understand all that? And, did Steph even want to? The burden her friend had to carry was heavy enough, knowing that in a few weeks, Steph would be gone. The last thing she wanted to do was to put more stress and worry on Crystal's shoulders.

Steph had dreams and plans for the future like everyone else. Sure, they might not have been particularly grand or world-altering, but still, they were hers, and they were precious to her. What had she done to deserve to have those ripped away? It wasn't fair. The last thing she wanted to do was leave Crystal with endless memories of her in self-pitying tears though, which would do nothing to change her situation. She wanted to be strong for her. God knows, Crystal had lost enough, suffered enough already, she didn't deserve to have to go through this either, and so Steph spent most of her days desperately trying to hide her true feelings from the one person she'd always been able to be entirely honest with, in order to protect her.

Crystal undid the zipper on her faded hoodie, hoping to cool off a little. Unable to decide if it was the bright yellow sun beaming down on her ebony skin, which was making her sweat, or if it was just nerves. The women walked at a sedate pace down the street, neither of them in a hurry to reach their destination. Personally, Crystal was struggling to think of anything worse than being faced with the building into which she would surrender her best friend in a few short weeks, never to be seen again. She would have preferred them to spend their one day off together in weeks doing something more fun. Making memories together before it was too late, memories that she could hold on to after Steph was gone and remember fondly. But she had seen the look that had flitted across Steph's face when she had admitted where she wanted to go today. It was a look Crystal had only seen a handful of times over the years she had known Steph, a look which meant business and that there was no use arguing with her. When Steph set her mind to something, there was rarely any way to dissuade her. Either Crystal could go with her and at least be there if it all proved to be a bad idea and too much for Steph to cope with, or she could let her friend go alone. It hadn't been a choice she had to think about for long.

The two women managed to keep the conversation light on their walk, gossiping about inconsequential matters, mostly discussing work, their colleagues and a particularly colourful couple who had decided to have a blazing row in the middle of the restaurant last night.

Thankfully the heavy snowfall and torrential rain had dispersed, and spring was in full bloom, which made the trip easier. Both Crystal and

Steph had gotten used to the fact that the seasons seemed to start earlier and earlier each year as they got older. Whereas when they were children, it was perfectly normal to have snowfall into February, now, in early March, the sun was shining brightly above their heads. The wildflowers in the abandoned fields they passed were in full bloom and danced happily in the breeze, a sea of colours as far as the eye could see.

It was just over forty minutes walk from their flat to the centre, the location of which Crystal only knew because she'd spent endless hours queuing up outside the hospital opposite when she was a child and her mother was sick, waiting to see if they'd have time to treat her that day. Turning the final corner, the hospital came into view first, the tall, stark white building with the large glass doors standing out brightly against the afternoon sun. The memories came flooding back without Crystal's permission, causing her to close her eyes for a moment to try and pull herself together as she remembered the painful, seemingly never ending days and nights trying to look after her ailing mother on the hard, unforgiving concrete.

As they began walking down the street, Steph let her eyes linger on the hospital for a few moments, preparing herself to turn her attention to the other side of the road and hoping that what she was about to see there wouldn't send her running in the opposite direction as fast as her legs would carry her.

"Oh, my god. Steph... look." Crystal whispered, her voice coming out as little more than a squeak which Steph found herself having to strain to hear.

Turning her head slowly, Steph finally allowed her gaze to fall onto the population control centre. She couldn't imagine that the sight of the building had been what had upset Crystal. The centre itself was, thankfully, nothing like Steph had imagined. It looked almost identical to all the other high-rise buildings in town, except in slightly better shape due to the fresh coat of sparkling white paint that had been slathered onto the outer walls. The windows had been blacked out on the lower floors to stop people from peering inside, but other than that, it was just a building. It even had a small courtyard out front with freshly mown grass and even a few plants scattered around making it appear almost inviting. There was no barbed wire, no guns that she could see. Only a handful of people in dark brown jackets with the acronym C.E.A emblazoned on their backs in bright yellow were milling around at the entrance with electronic tablets in their hands. As Steph continued to scan the surrounding area, though, she finally saw what had Crystal so on edge.

Children. A long, snaking orderly queue of frightened and confused looking children.

Chapter Twenty-Two

It took a few moments for Steph to process the scene before her. Why on earth would there be so many children here, of all places? It couldn't be a school trip, the children varied too much in age, and all seemed to have at least one parent with them, clutching tightly on to their hands. As her gaze ran over the crowd, Steph noticed that some of the adults were crying, quickly wiping their tears on their sleeves and turning their heads away from the children beside them in the hope that they wouldn't notice their distress. Without warning, the words rang clearly in Steph's ears as if Professor Jones himself were standing directly beside her.

> *"All persons over the age of five years old will be eligible for the lottery."*

Steph's stomach lurched and she threw a hand over her mouth in horror as Crystal pulled on her arm, trying to drag her away, but Steph couldn't move. She was paralysed by the sight in front of her. She could see children of all ages lining the street, some so small that she couldn't possibly believe that they were at least five. They barely looked old enough to be standing on their own two feet. Still, the terror in the eyes of the adults accompanying them told the two women all they needed to know. These children were lining up to be culled.
"Please, her father can take care of her. She won't be a burden to anyone. Please, let me take her place." A frightened-looking woman at the very front of the queue begged the agent in front of her in a distressed voice.
"Name and cull card." the agent replied, barely bothering to look up from the small tablet in his hand.
There was no point in listening to her pleas, he thought to himself as the woman held out a shaking hand and begrudgingly handed over her child's card. There was nothing that the agent could do for her or anyone else lined up out here on this dingy street. He'd been at his post since six o'clock this morning, when the first of the damned for today had started to arrive just as the sun rose, and already he had heard every entreaty he could imagine and a few that would never have occurred to him in his wildest dreams. One man had even turned up with a suitcase full of crisp banknotes, telling the agent to take as many as he liked in exchange for his child's life.
Didn't they get it? Couldn't they see? He had no more say in who was on the list than they did. In his everyday life, he was an office assistant, a lowly paper pusher who had been strong-armed into taking this

position by his boss, who had made it clear that if his staff didn't do their part, they'd be looking for another job before the culls were completed. He had sat through three days of vigorous training before his first shift just a few days ago, and whilst it was mostly pretty straightforward stuff, the one thing that had stuck firmly in his mind was the warning he and the other new recruits had been given over and over again,

'Any attempt by staff members to help those whose names have been called in the lottery will be seen as a crime against humanity and will immediately result in the staff members' arrest. I warn you that the punishment for this particular crime is severe, as it must be to ensure that our staff are not tempted by the bribes you will no doubt be offered. Anyone found guilty of helping people to escape their execution date will be sentenced to death.'

At the time, the warnings had seemed extreme to the agent, the trainers had repeated the exact same phrase in stern voices so many times that he and the other trainees could all recite the warning by heart by the time their course was complete. Yet, after today, after witnessing the lengths people would go to for himself, he was beginning to understand.
"Amy Barnes, age six?" He asked, finally raising his head to verify that the picture on the card matched the child standing before him.
"Yes. But please, we have money..." The woman begged again as tears began tumbling down her cheeks.
"I'm Amy!" The little girl chirped, and as she smiled, the agent noticed that she was missing one of her front teeth. He swallowed heavily and wrenched his eyes away from the child's, composing himself the best that he could.
"Report to floor four for processing. Next!" The C.E.A agent stated clearly, trying to ensure that he could be heard over the woman's crying. As she was ushered towards the doors, the two women standing transfixed at the end of the road could still hear her sobbing long after the little girls' ringlets had disappeared out of sight.
Crystal could not believe the scene in front of her. She couldn't remember ever seeing so many kids in one place before, outside of a school or a playground maybe, let alone so many of differing ages, ethnicities and classes all clustered together on the same patch of cracked pavement. She wondered how many of them truly understood the gravity of the situation that they were in. What had their parents told them? Had they tried to explain as they left their homes this morning that it would be the last time they'd ever set foot in them? Or had they pretended that their sons and daughters were just going to the hospital

for a check-up and that it was nothing untoward so that they weren't so scared walking into the centre?

As Crystal's eyes roamed over the line flowing down the street, she noticed that most of the children were decked out in what her mother would have called their 'Sunday best'. Little girls in pretty dresses, boys in smart shirts and trousers, all with perfectly styled hair and not a speck of dirt to be seen on their small shining faces. A shudder ran down Crystal's spine as her eyes locked with those of a woman who couldn't have been more than thirty, who was standing silently in the queue a few pairs back from the front, her hand tightly clasping that of a young girl who was a carbon copy of her. The pain in the woman's eyes was palpable even from this distance, and try as she might, Crystal could not tear her gaze away. She tugged again on Steph's arm, trying to pull her friend away from the scene in front of them. She still couldn't get her head around why Steph had wanted to come here.The one thing she knew for sure though, was that this was the last thing that either of them had expected to be confronted by.

"Even though I walk through the valley of the shadow of death, I will fear no evil, for you are with me." A nearby priest began intoning loudly over the tears of the devastated parents and shouts of the angry mob of protestors on the opposite side of the street who were surrounded by more agents in brown jackets. The priest made the sign of the cross in the air above the heads of the frightened children as he made his way down the line, some of whom were now starting to sense that something was amiss and were fidgeting uncomfortably in their parent's tight grips, trying to get away.

Steph watched in amazement as a teenager, a boy of probably thirteen or so, with long greasy hair, pulled back into a ponytail and holes in his jeans, finally managed to wrestle his hand free from the grip of the man next to him, who she assumed was his father. The boy spun on the tarmac, his trainers squeaking slightly in protest at the sudden movement and before his father had a chance to protest, the boy started to run. The older man cried out after him in fear, but the teen didn't so much as glance over his shoulder.

"We've got a runner!" One of the C.E.A agents called, and out of nowhere, a sea of security guards appeared and began dashing down the street after the boy, who found another gear from somewhere when he saw the group of agents who had sprung from their posts and were starting to chase him, his legs seeming to move at an impossible speed beneath him.

"Stop!" called one of the security guards as he planted his feet and pulled a gun from the holster around his waist. Levelling it at the boys retreating form. "Stop, or we will shoot."

"Oh, my god." Crystal's shocked voice joined the rest of the crowds as they watched on in horror. She was sure that every single person there not employed by the C.E.A was silently willing the boy to hurry up, to make it to the corner and disappear out of sight. Maybe, just maybe, if he got away, there would be hope for the rest of them? The boy didn't slow down at the guard's warning. He didn't even seem to register it as his feet kept pounding rhythmically against the pavement. Pushing at any people who got in his way and screaming at others in his path to move.

Finally reaching the end of the road, the boy hesitated, seeming unable to decide which direction he should go, and Steph's heart sank. What are you doing? Don't stop! She screamed internally as she watched him, his head darting from side to side as he contemplated his choices and tried to decide which way to turn.

"ON YOUR KNEES! This is your final warning!". The guard holding the gun called again.

The boy turned his head and looked into the eyes of the man who had once again levelled his gun at him and gave him a defiant look as he started moving again.The young boy didn't manage to take more than two steps before a deafening crack echoed through the street. Several screams rang out in the seconds that followed. The young girl Crystal had spotted before, the one who was so very like her mother, fell to the ground in a dead faint. The tired-looking old priest stumbled forward, falling to his knees and reaching his hands into the air in the international sign of prayer, mouthing something unintelligible as tears fell down his cheeks. And the boy? The boy lay unmoving on the ground, a dark puddle of blood seeping from beneath his still body, staining the pavement.

Chapter Twenty-Three

An ear-splitting pop sliced through the air in Tom's office so suddenly and without warning that both he and the gentleman he was in the middle of examining flinched in their seats and stared at one another wide-eyed as the sound reverberated around them.
"Was that a gunshot?" The man asked Tom as he turned his head to look out of the small window which looked out across the street, squinting into the afternoon sunshine to try and see what all the commotion was about.
Tom had never heard a gunshot before, or at least not outside of movies or in the old crime television shows that his dad liked to watch reruns of on his rare evenings off anyway. So he couldn't say for sure either way and simply shrugged at the older man in front of him as the sound rang in his ears.
"I'm not sure." He mumbled to his patient. Wondering whether he should go and investigate the disturbing noise or continue examining the man in front of him.
"Believe me, doc, it was. I've heard enough of 'em before." The man said, stretching out his arm to reveal a slightly faded tattoo which even Tom knew depicted a somewhat distorted version of the British army's logo. Ex-military, Tom realised, he would certainly know more about gunshots than I ever will then, he thought to himself.
Frowning down at the symbol, Tom felt a knot tightening in his gut. Gunshots were rare in Britain, almost unheard of, in fact, as guns themselves are illegal, with the exception of properly licensed riddles and shotguns which were mostly used for hunting. The only people that really carried guns were special members of the armed police force, and even they were few and far between. As far as he could remember, Tom had never so much as seen a gun in his life and he was in no hurry to.
Standing from his chair, Tom walked slowly towards the window and craned his neck as he peered out of the single panel of discoloured glass to see what was happening on the street. Regretting the action almost as soon as he made it and wishing he had stayed at his desk.
The long queue of parents and children who had been standing outside the population control centre opposite the hospital all day was now in complete chaos. People were clearly incredibly upset about something, what exactly, Tom could not make out from his office. All he could see were the gesticulations and frantically moving mouths of the many people in the queue, some of whom were wiping tears from their eyes, and who all seemed to be staring in the same direction towards the end of the street, which Tom could not see from his position no matter how

awkwardly he craned his neck and pressed his nose to the glass,
"I'll be right back," Tom told his patient and made his way out of his office, leaving the confused man staring after him as he hastily dashed out of the door, his white coat whipping behind him.

Tom had only just stepped into the corridor when Doctor Mahoney appeared, having also vacated his office next door to try and find out what was going on. Out in the hallway with the automatic double doors that led out onto the street held open by the sea of protestors crowding the steps, the voices of the frantic people in line across the road were much more audible. Although Tom couldn't work out their words, he could sense from the tones of their voices and the panicked tension in the air that something had gone very wrong.

"I thought they were using injections?" a small, frightened-looking boy of about nine or ten years old asked. The boy was perched awkwardly on his mother's lap in the waiting room, sharing her seat as there weren't enough to go around in the packed space as usual.

"So did I." His mother replied in a low voice, her pale face betraying the fear she felt as she stared at the commotion outside.

"What happened?" Tom asked Mahoney, pulling the door to his office shut behind him with a click.

"I don't know, but I would hazard a guess that it was nothing good." His mentor replied and started making his way quickly into the foyer.

Tom followed Mahoney towards the hospital entrance, dodging around the waiting patients who seemed to take up every spare inch of space and doing his best not to accidentally tread on anyone. The two men didn't get more than halfway across the room before a pair of tall, well-built men in brown jackets with the acronym C.E.A stamped over their hearts walked through the doors. Seeing what one of them had slung over his shoulder stopped Tom dead in his tracks, but thankfully, Doctor Mahoney was more in control of himself..

"Trolley! Someone get me a trolley now!" Doctor Mahoney shouted to no one in particular. Continuing forwards through the throngs of people with much less care now, causing them to scramble quickly out of his way.

A skinny orderly who had been standing dumbstruck taking in the scene seemed to come back to himself and ran off to get a trolley as Mahoney started firing questions at the two cull Enforcement Agents before them.

"What happened?" Mahoney asked, and Tom could tell that the older doctor was trying to keep his voice level, but knowing his mentor as well as he did, he could sense the rage undercutting his words.

"He tried to run." Was all the guard carrying the boy said in response in a voice utterly devoid of emotion. He unceremoniously tossed the bundle he carried down onto the trolley, which had appeared by his side, as though it weighed no more than a bag of flour, not sparing it a second glance.

When Tom looked down at the small, frail body on the bed before him, he instantly knew they were too late. That there was nothing they could do. There was an exit wound the size of a small coin in the boy's chest, positioned directly over his heart. The boy would have died instantly.

"See folks? Let this be a lesson to you all, eh? This right here? This is what happens if you try to sidestep your responsibilities. This is what we will do to you if you try to run. There is no escaping the cull. You'd all do well to remember that." The guard said, raising his voice and speaking to the room at large.

"You shot this poor child because he was afraid to be killed and attempted to run from you?" Doctor Mahoney asked the guard incredulously, his thick grey eyebrows shooting up as he spoke, unable to believe what he was hearing.

"Yep. That's right. I did." The second guard said proudly, puffing his chest out like a peacock, his voice full of unearned authority.

"And why, may I ask, did you then bring him here? Surely even someone with no medical training can see that the poor child is deceased. There is nothing that we can do for him. You have your own mortuary in your centre, do you not? Should you not take him there?" Doctor Mahoney questioned.

"We do, yeah. And I could have. But our boss thought this was a better idea. A good teaching experience, he said." The second guard continued.

"Teaching experience?" Tom echoed dumbly,

"Yep. To show you, them, everyone," The first man began, gesturing to the people around them, "That no one escapes the cull."

Before Tom or Doctor Mahoney could say another word, the two cull Enforcement Agents strode back out of the building with their heads held high, appearing to be incredibly pleased with their day's work, leaving Tom and his mentor to deal with the blood-soaked young boy before them. Tom stood shell-shocked, wondering what their next step should be. Should they call the police? Standard procedure decreed that they were to contact the authorities if anyone was bought into the hospital with a gunshot or knife wound. Yet Tom honestly didn't know who had the higher jurisdiction anymore, the C.E.A or the police force? Should they send someone to the population control centre to find a higher-up staff member and ask them? Or to at least try and find out the poor boy's name so that he could be processed and his death recorded correctly? Or would the C.E.A take care of all that? Tom wondered as the voices around him began murmuring again, having been utterly silent whilst the guards had been present, too afraid to utter a word.

"My boy! Where's my boy?!" A loud, traumatised voice rang out as a man in a misshapen bowler hat and black trousers with holes in the knees ran through the doors.

"Tom, take the boy out of sight. Now." Doctor Mahoney ordered Tom in a whisper, but he was too late. The man was only a step or two away from them now, tripping over his own feet in his haste as he made his way towards the gurney, his tear-filled eyes locked on the unmoving body of his son.

The wail that left the man's mouth as he threw his arms around his child and pulled his body towards his chest, cradling him tightly in his arms was a sound that Tom didn't think he would ever be able to get out of his head. It was a similar noise to the one his mother had made on their living room floor a few weeks ago when she'd finally accepted that he was going to die. It shook Tom to his very core to hear it again, even from another source, a stranger.

How many parents have made comparable sounds today alone? He wondered. Thinking back to the length of the queue he had seen on his way to work this morning. Hundreds? Thousands? Up and down the country, Tom was sure that similar scenes were taking place at every population control centre in the land. Goodness knows how many had been put to death today alone.

It had been announced shortly after the culls began that the government had decided to commence the culling of all the children under the age of fourteen first. So that if their parents were also called up, the children were not left to fend for themselves in the interim or become a burden to the state. It was also suggested this was for the best so that they would have someone to accompany them to the centres, a parent or guardian to hold their hand as their young lives were ended prematurely. The culling of the children had started around three weeks previously and was expected to take another month to complete in total. The grim sight of long lines of children, some as young as five years old, had become all too familiar to Tom now. It was what greeted him each and every single morning when he arrived at work, except on Sundays. Apparently, even government-mandated death facilities closed on Sundays. Perhaps so that the murderers who worked there could go to church to confess their sins, Tom thought wryly.

"Sir, please. Let us take you somewhere more private where you can say a proper goodbye." Doctor Mahoney said gently, placing a hand on the man's shoulder and prying him carefully away from his son.

"He was just scared. He's only a boy." The child's father mumbled, turning his head to face Mahoney as he stood up and stuttered out the words in disbelief. "I was supposed to be with him. We were meant to have time to say goodbye. Before, before they..." The man was

seemingly unable to finish his sentence and gave up as a fresh wave of sobs racked his body and he began to shake from the sheer force of his grief.
Doctor Mahoney caught the attention of the orderly who had brought the trolley out to them just a few minutes ago and quietly instructed him to move the boy into an unused side room, which was little more than a closet really, but was the closest empty space available in which his father could say goodbye.
"The least we can do is afford the man that right after it was ripped away from him." The older doctor said quietly before turning to address the room at large.
"Ladies and gentlemen, I apologise for any distress that this unforeseen situation has caused you. If you would all calmly remain in your seats, we will begin seeing patients again shortly." He reassured the crowd in a steady voice, offering them a weak smile before turning back to Tom and gesturing that his young charge should follow him as he made his way towards his office.
Tom was surprised to find Doctor Mahoney's office empty when they stepped inside. His mentor must have been taking one of his few and far-between breaks between patients when the commotion broke out he surmised as he took a seat opposite the desk and tried to make sense of what he had just seen.
So that's what happens if you run. He thought to himself as Doctor Mahoney made them both a cup of tea. Wondering for what seemed to be the hundredth time whether he would have the strength to walk into that god-forsaken building when his time came to surrender his life or if he would end up being shot in the back like that poor boy as he tried in vain to get away.
"Are you alright, Tom?" Doctor Mahoney asked, placing a cup of steaming hot tea on the desk.
"Animals. They're treating us as though we're animals." Tom said, his voice laced with fury as he forced the words out through his tightly gritted teeth. "Surely there was a better way than shooting him in the street? In full view of all those other children? Should the last thing they see on this earth really be a murder? That's what it was. That's what they did. They murdered a kid. Shot him in the back because he was scared."
"Yes, Tom, they can pretty it up with whatever flowery language they choose, but ultimately this is nothing more than murder, cold and calculated. And I fear that it won't be the last." Doctor Mahoney said.
"And bringing him in here like that? To make an example of him! To scare those poor people out there even more. It's sick." Tom added, feeling his stomach churn and lowering his head into his hands as he pictured the wide vacant eyes of the young boy on the trolley.

"I'm afraid that this is more than likely only the beginning, Thomas." Doctor Mahoney replied, and Tom raised his head to meet his mentor's gaze. "We are only a few short weeks into a process that the government predicts will take several years. The more time that passes, the more people will have time to think about this whole sorry situation, and the more people will run. I don't doubt that many whose names have been called have already started making plans. Fleeing the country if they can, or perhaps going on the lamb in less populated areas and trying to live off the land. I believe that it will only get worse as time goes on."

The two men sat silently for a moment while Tom tried to compose himself. He sipped at the too-hot cup of tea clutched in his trembling hands and attempted to push the image of the dead boy from his mind to no avail.

"Thomas. I have to ask you, have you considered any such actions?" Doctor Mahoney questioned, and Tom's eyebrows shot up in recognition of what his mentor was saying.

Despite receiving his alert some weeks ago now, he still hadn't managed to find the words to tell the man who had been like a second father to him that he was to be culled, and hadn't been aware that Doctor Mahoney had somehow figured it out until that very moment.

"How did you know?" Tom asked quietly.

"Call it an old man's intuition. This is important, Tom. Tell me, have you made any plans to escape your fate?" Mahoney asked again.

"No. I haven't." Tom finally responded after a few minutes of contemplative silence. "Honestly, the thought of running never really crossed my mind. Surely no one will be able to get away. They'll make sure of that. Just like they did with that kid. So, what's the point?" He asked.

"The point, Tom, is that sometimes the only way to stand up and fight is to run away from immediate danger and return only when you are in a strong enough position to win the battle." The older man said sagely.

"You think I should run?" Tom asked, aghast, his voice rising an octave or two in shock.

"I think that a bright young man such as yourself, a man who is resourceful, talented, clever, should consider all his options extremely carefully."

"You saw what they just did to that boy. Shot him in the back in broad daylight! And you think that I have options?" Tom asked incredulously, not understanding what his mentor was getting at.

"I do, Thomas. I do. And I want to assure you here and now that should you decide to follow a different path than the one they have set out for you, that you can always come to me for any assistance. I am not afraid to die. I am not scared of their laws. I am a doctor; it is all I've ever wanted to be. Like you, for as long as I can remember, all I have wanted to do is help people. And so, if there is anything that I can ever do to help you, I want you to know that I will be there. In whatever capacity that I can. And that you must not be afraid to come to me."

Chapter Twenty-Four

The weary, heart-sick priest made his way slowly down the seemingly never-ending line of people that littered the pavement as he had done every day for weeks now. He was certain that the lines were getting longer, positive that the population control centres were expanding their capacity daily. Perhaps that was natural as they perfected the process of mass murder and became more efficient at their unforgivable task, he thought to himself as he raised his hand to form the sign of the cross above the head of the next poor soul in line.

At least they have finished with the children, he thought, taking a moment to pray for the tiny souls of the children whom he had watched walk into the building over the last few weeks and were now safe in the kingdom of heaven. Those early days had been the hardest. It had taken all the strength the priest possessed and a little extra that he borrowed from his lord and saviour to convince him to keep making the trip from the outdated parsonage that he called home just a few streets away and try to offer what little comfort he could to those whose names had been called, despite knowing that it was not enough. It could never be enough.

Every single day for the first nine weeks of the cullings, weeks which had felt more like a lifetime to the priest, he had come to the centre and borne witness to the queues of the frightened tiny faces of those under the age of fourteen who had been summoned to their deaths.

He had begged and pleaded with the stone-faced guards to let him take the place of just one of them. One single young soul could so easily be exchanged for that of his own. His old, withered body creaked and protested with every step he took as he made his way down the street. His pained feet felt every rock, every divot in the ground through the thin soles of his worn shoes, and he knew that cull or not, he was not long for this world. He would soon be drawn into his fathers welcoming arms. So why not sooner rather than later? Why not allow one of those poor souls who were only a few short years into their lives to have a chance?

Much to the priest's frustration, his pleas fell on deaf ears. Even when he fell to his knees on the hard concrete and clasped his hands together in earnest, with tears dripping down his cheeks, begging the guards to take him instead, he was all but entirely ignored. Did they have no compassion? No empathy for their fellow man? He had wondered.

Deep down, he knew the truth. The men and women working here had no more control than he did. They were paper pushers, nothing more than that, and if he were sensing the government's mood correctly, they would more than likely be forfeiting their own lives if they tried to interfere with the culling process. That hadn't stopped him from trying, though. A small piece of his heart went out to those working at the godforsaken place as he watched them avoid eye contact with the children, and bow their heads in shame when hysterical parents were dragged into the centre by burly security guards.

After what seemed like an eternity, the young children who lined the streets each day got older, and the sight of parents leading their babies by the hand to their deaths became nothing more than a horrific memory. Although it was still incredibly difficult for the priest to grasp that all of these people's bright lights were soon to be snuffed out, it was at least slightly easier to deal with than the sight of the children.

And so, he kept coming back. Day after day. Sometimes arriving early in the morning before the sun had risen and not returning home until long after dark. The centres, in theory, only carried out cullings between the hours of seven am and seven pm, but often the queues of people took much longer than that to process and the priest spent long hours praying with the faithful and non-religious alike, trying to ease their upcoming passing and help them to come to terms with their lots.

He knew little of what went on behind the tall mahogany doors to the centre, and if he was being honest, he didn't want to know. Better to live in ignorance he deduced than to carry that pain around with him. When the announcements had first been made, he had wondered if perhaps members of the clergy, such as himself, and representatives from other faiths might be invited to pray with those poor unfortunate souls in their final moments, but the government had quickly shut down any such speculation. They claimed that a lack of space in the facilities made accommodating each and every denomination was impossible.

However, the priest wasn't convinced that this was the only reason they had been banned from comforting the dying.

He was reasonably confident that a large part of the decision had been made in order to minimise the number of people who bore witness to what transpired in the centres and then lived to tell the tales. He knew, of course, that every child under fourteen had been permitted to have a parent or guardian with them as they were put to death, but that, he was sure, had been to stop riots from breaking out in every city across the world as they surely would have done had parents been told that they could not be with their children in their last moments. The priest felt sure that If the government had felt they had a choice, they wouldn't have allowed that either.

They didn't want to risk people going to the press or selling their stories, telling the rest of the country and, subsequently, the world how things were being run in their respective little corner of it. They had learned back in January when they completed the culls in the prisons how quickly things could go wrong. How many horror stories could be flashed on to the front pages of every internet tabloid and news site from the most reputable to the least, and how badly that damaged Britain's reputation. Particularly as she, and her leaders were one of the first countries to suggest the idea of a mass cull and had been instrumental in putting their ideas into practice around the globe. They had to be seen as perfect or as near to as possible. To be sticking to all the rules and regulations which had no doubt been set in stone across the world in the indiscriminate agreements. They could not risk the kind of negative publicity that had already caused considerable issues in other parts of the world.

Just that morning, whilst sipping at a cup of strong black tea, trying to fortify himself for the day ahead, the priest had been skimming through news articles on his battered old laptop, reading about the shocking scenes in Sao Paulo, Brazil, where things had started to fall apart already.

It seemed that instead of carrying out the cullings by use of lethal injection as they had initially stated that they would, the Brazilian C.E.A had resorted to hangings when their supply of the toxic drug cocktail needed to put a human to death humanly had been washed away by an unruly tsunami off their coast which had destroyed the ships carrying their stock of pharmaceuticals.

Instead of asking other countries for help, or confessing that they had a problem, the Brazilian government decided to deal with the matter in-house. Within two weeks of the culls starting, scaffolding had been erected in every town square in the country. People were being hung by the dozen in public, in full view of terrified crowds. Something which had not been seen for over a century. That alone was bad enough, but when Sao Paulo had spent twenty-four hours hanging children as young as five in a public park, the population had rioted.

The reports he had seen showed once busy and bustling streets of shops, cafes, and bars turned into blackened piles of ash from the fires that had been deliberately set there in protest. The police soon became overwhelmed as the population fought back and soon found that heading out into the public was tantamount to committing suicide. The moment an authority figure was spotted, the crowds would descend upon them in an angry mob, often leaving little behind but a pile of blood and a mutilated body.

The last straw came when someone had gotten hold of a list of people working locally for the C.E.A. in any capacity and had started to systematically hunt them down. Breaking into their houses and slaughtering not only them but any family members who also happened to live there in their beds.

The priest was sure that other countries around the world were now terrified that their own citizens would take a leaf out of the Brazilian's book and start fighting back as well, and were now, no doubt, even more determined to keep whatever happened in the centres a secret. If word got out that even one culling had been poorly handled in Britain, they could be facing the same kind of violence here with the population already so fractured and angry.

Squinting his eyes into the last rays of the setting sun, the priest looked down the street and tried to figure out where today's line ended, but he could not see. It was too far away. Without dwelling on the matter, he moved along to the next poor person in line and began to pray for their soul.

Chapter Twenty-Five

You'd think that they would have learned by now, idiots. I wonder if they ever will. Captain Jonathan Williams mused to himself as his armoured vehicle careened down the streets through the dim light of the few still working street lamps on its way to his fourth destination of the night.

There were no sirens, no flashing lights or markings on the sleek black sedans to alert any of the people still crowding on the streets despite the strict curfews that had been put in place a week ago to the fact that the men inside the car were C.E.A agents. Still, from the way that people scurried into shadow-filled doorways or, on occasion, even turned and ran when they saw the line of cars approaching, he was pretty sure the public had gotten the message.

Break the rules, and we will come for you. It was as simple as that. No one escaped the cull. That message had been made crystal clear to every single member of the British population since this whole thing started a little over three months ago. Bills had been drafted; laws had been passed. Entire agencies like his own had been established purely to ensure that those whose names were called in the lottery could not back out of their responsibilities to their fellow man. All over the world, in more countries than he knew the names of, similar processes were being followed.

So why, he wondered, did so many citizens still think they could get away with not turning up at their appointed centre on their end-of-life date as instructed? Why did so many still believe that they would go unnoticed if they stayed home and hid away quietly with their families? Why did they think there was anywhere far enough that they could run where they would not be found?

The security at the exit points around the country was more stringent now than it had ever been. Even when terror alerts had caused them to rise to a whole new level back in the early 2000s, after the attacks on the World Trade Centre buildings in New York, never had there been more thorough checks in place to confirm that those leaving the country were permitted by law to do so than there are now. If your name had been called in the lottery, your passport automatically flagged as invalid the moment you attempted to board a plane or get on any form of transport that was crossing an international border. Even travelling from England into its sister countries, Wales, Scotland and Northern Ireland was forbidden if you were an English citizen who was due to be culled. If your birthdate was later in the year and the cull candidates for that month had not yet been announced, and you wished to leave your country of origin, then you had to provide the full address of where you were going to be staying, have a return ticket booked, and check in with the local embassy on a bi-weekly basis the entire time you were outside of the country.

Failure to do this would result in the perpetrator being rounded up, arrested and bought straight home. The moment they touched back down on British soil, they were taken to one of the many detention centres which had been hastily assembled up and down the country and held there until the lottery had been called for their date of birth. If they were lucky enough to not receive an alert, they were then released, but those whose names were called rarely ever saw their homes again.

It wasn't a perfect system. Williams knew that. He was sure some perfectly innocent people ended up being incarcerated for reasons which were outside of their control. In fact, just last week, a friend who worked at a detention centre told him about a man who had recently been imprisoned there because he had failed to check in with the British Embassy whilst on a business trip to France. He had become unwell and had fallen asleep and failed to appear for his appointment, after having spent two nights in a local hospital running a fever, an innocent mistake that could happen to anyone. Still, the man in question was now looking at having to spend the best part of the next six months in a run-down, overcrowded detention centre in central London. Surrounded by real criminals and unable to see his family or friends whilst he waited for the lottery to be called for his birth month of October and discover whether his life could continue. For now though, this system was all that they had.

Passport fraud had also become rife throughout the country, causing yet another issue for the C.E.A. You were just as likely to see people exchanging the small pamphlets in back alleys as you were to see an illegal drug deal nowadays. Thankfully, most of the forgeries were easy enough to spot and, as far as Williams knew, no one, as yet, had managed to flee the country to escape their date.

Many people had gone on the run, disappearing into the depths of densely packed forests or the open countryside and trying to live off the land now that the weather was warmer. That was one of the many reasons why the curfews had been initiated in the first place. Anyone found to be on the streets between the hours of midnight and seven in the morning was subject to arrest unless they could prove that they were commuting to or from their place of work or had a legitimate reason to be outside of their homes.

Of course, with the amount of homeless that sought refuge on the streets night after night, a number that seemed to grow by the day from what Williams had seen, it wasn't easy to know who might be on the run and who just didn't have anywhere else to go. Despite that the police were doing their best to round up and question as many people as they could, as were the C.E.A, and Williams doubted that many, if any, people who went on the run would stay at liberty for long.

Initially, it had been easy to spot those who were not genuinely homeless and might have another reason for trying their luck on the streets instead of returning to their homes once the curfew set in as they were supposed to do. Their clothes were just a little too nice, their shoes fit too well, their hair had been cut too recently. But it didn't take long for the *Cudo's* - a poor amalgamation of the words 'cull and dodgers' - which they had been colloquially nicknamed by the press and subsequently the public at large, to wise up to this and start purposefully dishevelling themselves to blend in, making law enforcements jobs much harder. Thankfully though, walking the stinking, smoke-filled streets night after night trying to distinguish junkies from Cudo's wasn't Williams's problem.

Captain Williams was part of the C.E.A's special task force assigned to visit the homes of anyone who failed to turn up on their designated date to be culled. He was proud that at just thirty-two years old, he had been chosen for the elite team, which consisted of military veterans who had all seen at least some action overseas as part of the British Armed Forces. Like many other decorated veterans, he had been exempt from the lottery itself and was drafted early in the process to help maintain law and order during the duration of the culls. It was a position that he took great pride in being offered and one he carried out to the best of his ability. Believing wholeheartedly as he did, that the culls were the only chance to save the country he had fought so hard to protect since he was a spotty-nosed eighteen-year-old fresh out of high school and, ultimately, the world at large.

Tonight, for the fourth time, Williams, part of a team of eight, was on his way to the address of one of the Cudos who had failed to appear at their designated population control centre this morning. Williams, having served in the army on deployment in some of the harshest wartorn countries on the planet, was deaf to the pleas and excuses that greeted his team when they forced their way into a property. Searching for the person, or people in some cases, cowering in a basement or attic, having heard them in various languages a hundred times before from people in much more dire situations, the pleas of those who were due to be culled did not stir much empathy in him.

On one occasion, they'd entered a property only to find a family of six all sitting around the dining table enjoying a large bowl of rice without a care in the world. As though it were any other day. When the team had arrested the father, a Cudo who had been due to be culled that very afternoon, who had been sat at the head of the table surrounded by his wife and four children, the wife had fainted almost instantly, falling off of her chair and landing on the floor with a heavy thud at their feet. It had transpired that her husband had never even told her about his alert. He had just ignored it and tried to carry on as though nothing had changed. It was the last time she ever saw him alive.

The line of three vehicles pulled up and killed their engines a few houses down from their target address on a suburban street in a small town in south-east England. The team quickly stepped out as one. Dressed head to toe in black bulletproof jumpsuits, the men and women did one final weapons check before stealthily approaching the home of one Cassandra Jones, twenty-six, who had failed to surrender herself to be culled as directed this morning.

Chapter Twenty-Six

None of Williams' team bothered to knock on the stark white PVC door with the gaudy brass knocker when they reached it. There was no point. They knew from experience that no one would answer. The new crimes against humanity laws had given them licence to enter any property without so much as announcing themselves if they believed a Cudo to be hiding inside. It gave the criminals less opportunity to run or attempt to evade their fate for a second time if they were given no warning before the C.E.A entered their homes.

They barely so much as paused to take a breath as two of the team members used their sturdy three-foot-long metal battering ram to tear the door from its hinges and clamber over it into the property. The crash and clang of the metal hinges detaching from the thin wooden door frame soon announced their presence and a high-pitched scream rang out in the air around them as they made their way down the empty hallway.

"C.E.A. Do not attempt to run. Cassandra Jones? Come out with your hands where I can see them. You are under arrest." Their most senior officer, Lieutenant Colonel Todd Armitage, shouted in a clear voice as they made their way deeper inside the house, not yet having come across any of its occupants despite hearing their screams.

Williams watched as his lieutenant and three other team members veered off and started to climb the stairs to the second story of the semi-detached family home, taking them two at a time, their semi-automatic firearms held out before them. So far on these missions, they had yet to come up against any Cudos who were armed or even many who attempted to fight back when cornered. Still, it was better to be safe than sorry.

Continuing down the hallway, he picked up his lieutenant's chant, echoing the same words as he reached a closed door which he assumed led into the kitchen from the house's layout. Pricking up his ears, he listened carefully, trying to make out any sound he could and get an idea of whether or not there was anyone inside.

"Cassandra Jones? Come out with your hands where I can see them!" He shouted, but there was no response.

Nodding back to his team, Williams pointed at the door, and, without a word, everyone took their positions, well-practised at this point, they did not need verbal instructions to know their places. Stepping back, Williams raised his right leg and reared up before kicking the door hard with all his might. It swung open instantly, barely protesting against his intrusion.

Inside, cowering in the far corner of the room, stood three people. A woman with long blonde hair in her mid-twenties was clinging to a small whimpering toddler in her arms. That's where the sniffling was coming from, Williams realised as his gaze fell on a heavily built man who was well over six feet tall standing next to the pair. Raising his eyebrows questioningly, Williams kept his gun aimed at the woman as he spoke. She was the one he was here for.

"Cassandra Jones?" The woman nodded minutely in response. "You are under arrest for breaking the recently agreed upon crimes against humanity laws. You have been sentenced to be culled and have failed to appear at your designated centre for this process to take place in accordance with the law. We will escort you to a detention centre where you will be held until a new cull date can be arranged for you." Williams finished as the woman began to cry, globs of liquid pouring from her terrified eyes as her shoulders shook from the force of her sobs.

Stepping forwards, Williams made sure that his team had him covered before handing his gun over to one of them and pulling a pair of shining silver handcuffs from his belt as the man next to Cassandra reached out and prised the still whimpering bundle from her arms, his head hung low in shame as he whispered: "I'm sorry. I love you."

Williams almost felt for the woman then, as her child was torn from her arms without her even having a moment to say a proper goodbye. Almost. Right up until she started to move. As quick as a cat on a hot tin roof, she spun on her slippered feet, stretching out a shaking hand to the house's rear door positioned just a few feet behind her. Grasping the handle, she flung it open so hard that it bounced off the tiled kitchen wall behind her, the sound echoing loudly all around them as she charged out into the night.

"Stop! Stop, or we will shoot!" Williams shouted, chasing after the woman into the darkness. His heavy boots sunk into the springy, uncut grass as he pounded down the garden with his team following close behind. It was then that he remembered that he didn't have his gun.

"Shit." He murmured to himself as he closed the distance between himself and the woman whose blonde hair was bobbing up and down in front of him, illuminated only by the light of the moon.

Williams knew she didn't stand a chance. He would catch her long before she could escape into the alleyways that he knew ran along the back of these houses, which were no doubt her intended destination. He ran six miles every morning before he had so much as had a cup of coffee. There was no way a suburban housewife was going to outrun him.

"Cassandra Jones! Stop!" He called again as she reached the fence at the end of the lawn. He didn't much fancy the paperwork that would follow if one of his team were forced to shoot the woman or the bloody mess it would leave behind for that matter. So he zig-zagged slightly, blocking his team's ability to get a clear shot as he ran across the final few feet that remained between him and the woman.

Grabbing hold of the low wooden fence, Cassandra attempted to heave her tired body over it and escape into the darkened alley, but her slipper-covered feet lost purchase on the ground beneath her, and she tumbled, crashing to the floor and letting out a small cry. Whether in frustration, defeat or pain, Williams did not know, and he didn't much care at this point either.

"GET UP!" Williams shouted as he reached her side, looking down at the pathetic woman on the floor and losing any sympathy he might have had for her just a few minutes ago. What did she think she was going to achieve by running? By not turning up to her appointment in the first damn place? Did she really think she could escape her fate? No one escapes the cull. Better for her to have had the chance to say a proper goodbye to her partner and child and surrender herself to the population control centre this morning as she had been instructed to do, rather than their last memory of her being a frightened woman running down their garden.

Cassandra lay on the floor sobbing into the now dewy grass beneath her face. It had been worth a try, she thought to herself as the last remnants of fight slipped from her body. She had tried to be brave. Really, she had. She had gotten up this morning and got dressed as usual. She had played with her two-year-old boy, fed him his breakfast, and kissed her husband before heading out of the home they shared for the last time and started the long walk to the population control centre to surrender her life. Only the moment she had seen the building in person, seen the long queues of terrified people awaiting their fate, she had felt a surge of fury run through her veins. Why her? Why did she deserve to die when so many others did not? Why couldn't they just pull the people from the streets into these centres, the ones who did nothing to contribute to society? She had a job and paid her taxes. She had a family, a home. She was a good person and didn't deserve to die like that. She deserved to see her son grow up, get married, and have a family of his own. She deserved to die old and grey in her bed. Not with someone sticking poison into her veins, alone in a strange place without a single person she loved to comfort her.

And so, she had turned away from the centre. Turned away from the fate that waited behind the boarded-up windows and headed back home to the family she loved. She had told herself that if the government wanted her that badly, they would just have to come and get her. It seems that someone had heard her stubborn thoughts, though. Because here they were.

Fed up with waiting now, Williams bent over, grabbed a handful of the blonde hair sprawled across the ground in a tight fist, and began to heave the sobbing mess of a woman off the ground. Deaf to her screams as she tried to gain some purchase with her feet to relieve some of the pressure on her scalp as he dragged her upright.

"Please! Let me go!" Cassandra whimpered.

"There's only one place left for you to go," Williams told her unkindly as he fastened his handcuffs around her wrists. "It would have been easier for everyone if you had just gone there this morning like you were supposed to." He added and began leading her back to the house.

"You going to cause us any trouble, big man?" He asked her partner as they re-entered the kitchen. The well-built man had barely moved since Cassandra had run out the door and still stood in the corner of the room, holding the kid in his arms, looking just as terrified as the toddler did.

"No, sir." The man said quietly.

"At least one of you has some sense then," Williams said.

It's the right choice. It's what I would do too. He thought to himself. Picturing his own two children at home with his wife as they led Cassandra out of the building and down the road to where they had left the sedans. The mother had to die. That much had already been decided and could not be changed. But the man? He did not. By stepping back and allowing Williams and his team to carry out their work, the man ensured his child didn't grow up as an orphan. He couldn't save the woman, but in letting her go, he gave himself and their child the best chance at a long and happy life. What more could a mother want?

"Watch your head." He intoned as he helped Cassandra into the back seat of the armoured car he had arrived in.

Four down, and it's only one in the morning. Williams realised, checking his watch. He wondered how many more he'd arrest before his shift ended at six am.

Chapter Twenty-Seven

The paperwork, when it arrived, was smaller than Tom had expected it to be. He had been waiting for it to slip quietly through the door since the day he had gotten his alert, building it up in his mind and dreading the morning when it would arrive. Tom wasn't entirely sure what he had been expecting, honestly. Still, something about the plain manilla envelope, barely bigger than the green and white notepads he used at work to write prescriptions on, just didn't seem grand enough or important enough to contain the documents that would tell him when his life was to end.

More by luck than judgement, he had been the first person to venture downstairs this morning, having had enough of lying in bed staring at the ceiling, unable to sleep as thoughts of his impending future, or lack thereof, swam through his mind. He had therefore been able to grab the few pieces of post which had been thrust through the letterbox haphazardly before any of his family awoke.

Tom had piled the other mail onto the kitchen table as was his family's routine, spending more time than he needed to arrange it into a neat stack as though he were trying to cover up something. It wasn't that he wouldn't tell his parents about his letter; of course, he would, just not today. Today he needed a moment or two to prepare himself to even open the envelope, let alone inspect its contents and digest them.

Tom knew he would be better off reading it in private rather than around the kitchen table with his parents and siblings. No doubt his dad wouldn't even let him read it himself if he saw it. Jack would insist on being the first one to go through it to try to locate any potential loopholes they could exploit to try and get Tom out of this, no matter how much Tom asked him not to or told him it was pointless. Tom was sure that the government, or the Cull Enforcement Agency or whoever it was that sent out these letters, would have ensured that there was no way that they could be challenged, that anyone who received one was left in no doubt as to what was going to happen to them and when. Any attempts to escape his fate were futile. Tom knew that. He'd seen it with his own eyes. He could still hear the screams of the dead boy's father reverberating in his ears whenever he remembered that day at the hospital, and he was certain that the sight of the warm blood coating the teenager's frail body would linger in his mind right up until Tom himself was killed. A stark reminder that there was no getting out of his situation. More than anything, he could remember the C.E.A security guard's words as though they had been etched onto his skin. "No one escapes the cull."

Hearing a creak on the staircase, Tom hurriedly shoved the envelope into the pocket of his jeans, scrunching it up as he did so and hoping there was nothing in there that shouldn't be bent before quickly turning to the kettle and busying himself making a cup of tea.

"Morning, son." Jack Walker said, clearing his throat as he joined Tom in the kitchen, already dressed for work in a smart blue suit.

"Hi, dad," Tom replied awkwardly, trying not to look too guilty about the secret he was hiding in his pocket. The envelope felt as though it weighed as much as a brick as it sat heavily on his thigh.

Since Tom had received his alert, his father had ceased his morning lectures about Tom's choice to continue working at the local NHS hospital, and, as much as Tom was grateful to not have to start his working days with the same tired old argument, he wasn't quite used to this new version of his dad. The one who insisted on calling him 'son' as though he were laying some kind of claim to him and trying to take him back from the government who had called his name in the lottery as if it would somehow change things. This man who didn't berate him for every decision he made and didn't feel the need to explain why he knew better and why Tom should follow his path instead of his own was nicer, sure. Easier to deal with? Perhaps. But truthfully, he made Tom a bit uncomfortable. Tom didn't want things to change because of his alert, didn't want people treating him differently or walking on eggshells around him. That was precisely why he had barely told anyone he knew he had received one. Yet here was his own father, suddenly acting as though Tom were the best son a man could ask for, all because he was going to die soon. It wasn't exactly comfortable.

"I was thinking I'd walk to work with you this morning if that's alright?" Jack said, placing a slice of bread in the toaster and pulling down the plunger on the slightly rusted appliance.

"Erm, sure, if you want. Aren't you working today?" Tom asked, confused. His dad never walked to work with him. In fact, his dad rarely went anywhere with him, truth be told, at least not just the two of them. Tom couldn't remember the last time they had been alone together. Another change, he thought to himself as he sipped at his too hot tea.

"Not until later, no," Jack said ambiguously, not giving Tom much to go on to understand why Jack wanted to walk him to work.

Probably to try and convince me to let him talk to Henry again, Tom reasoned, or to try and talk me into going on the run or something stupid like that. Well, whatever, Tom thought to himself, his dad could say what he liked. Tom was already resolved to follow the letter in his pocket exactly and not put anyone else in jeopardy by trying to bend or break the rules.

"I'll go get my stuff. We'll need to leave in about ten minutes." Tom told his father, standing from the table and taking his cup to the sink to rinse it. His dad nodded in response, his mouth full of toast, and Tom headed out of the kitchen to retrieve his bag. Still conscious of the letter in his pocket. He had planned to open it on his walk to work, perhaps find a quiet corner in the park on his route to sit and read it in peace. It looked like that wasn't going to happen now, though. Never mind, he thought to himself, putting a fresh pair of clean scrubs into his backpack. It's not like I'm in any real hurry to know how many days I have left to live. The letter isn't going anywhere.

The sun beat down heavily on the heads of the two men and an eerie orange glow filled the air as they made their way down the long high street which would eventually lead them to the hospital. Tom wiped a few beads of sweat from his forehead with the back of his hand as he walked, sneaking the odd glance at his father, who had been mostly silent since they had left the house, and noticing that he looked tired. No, tired wasn't the right word. Exhausted was more fitting, Tom realised, averting his eyes when Jack turned in his direction so as to not be caught staring at him.

The lines that had been growing deeper in the skin around his dad's eyes for the past few years as he teetered over the edge of middle age and nearer to retirement had become even more pronounced in the past couple of months. He had dark purple circles under his eyes and looked as though he hadn't gotten a decent night's sleep in weeks. Tom was pretty sure that the bags under his own eyes could probably contain a week or more worth of grocery shopping, given how little sleep he'd been managing to scrounge lately. Still, it pained him to see it reflected back at him on the older man's features.

Between the constant, relentless nightmares that had been plaguing Tom ever since he'd received his alert and the extra shifts he'd been putting in at the hospital, he was rarely managing to grab more than a few hours of rest each night, and he knew it was starting to show.

Tom didn't mind working the extra hours, it kept him busy and stopped him from dwelling too much on what was to come, and it meant getting home long after his family had all gone to bed for the night, which was a bonus. Before heading to his room, Tom would stand awkwardly in the kitchen and force down a few mouthfuls of whatever leftovers his mother had put out for him. This way he got to spend less time looking into his mum's sorrow-filled eyes across the dining table over dinner, or trying to cope with his sister Emily, who still hadn't managed to come to terms with what was to happen and burst into tears pretty much every time she saw him.

The nightmares were another matter entirely, though. Those Tom would do just about anything to get rid of. They were exactly the same, night after night. He would wake in a cold sweat, his blankets sticking to his skin as he stifled the screams he couldn't control into his pillow, with images of having to be dragged into the population centre, kicking and screaming, after his courage failed him running through his mind as the dream continued to plague him even after he had awoken. Each and every single night for weeks now, it had been the very same security guard who had shot that boy and brought him into the hospital that half dragged, half carried Tom into the centre. Before he was secured to a bed so that they could administer the lethal injection into his thin arm. Tom had read somewhere that you couldn't die in a dream, although he wasn't sure if there was any truth to it or not. If he was remembering correctly, the article he had read said that if you were to die in a dream, you would die in reality as well as your brain could not distinguish between the two, and so, your brain would always wake you up before you did as a form of protection before the dream reached that final point. Tom guessed, if it were true, that explained why he always awoke at the same part of the dream, night after night. Watching the bright blue fluid from the syringe disappear into his veins.

"Son? There was a reason why I wanted to walk in with you this morning." Jack began nervously. He'd spent the last fifteen minutes trudging along the pavement next to Tom in near silence, stretching his slightly shorter legs to try and keep up with his son and cursing the bad night's sleep he'd gotten the night before, which was making him drag his feet.

He hadn't been sleeping well at all since that god-awful night around his dining table when Tom's watch had gone off and his alert had come through. Tossing and turning into the small hours no matter how tired he was, alternating between feeling a bone-deep torturous pain because he couldn't do anything to change his eldest son's fate and crippling guilt that Jack himself had been exempt from the lottery and would live on long after his son had taken his final breaths.

Last night had been particularly dreadful, though, even by Jack's standards, as he knew he had to talk to Tom this morning and come clean before he found out what Jack had done on his own, which would be much worse. He had spent most of the night racking his brains, trying to figure out the best way to go about telling him.

For weeks now, Jack had been trying desperately to come up with something, anything that he could do that might just make this process a little easier for his son. He had just about come to terms with the fact that he couldn't change what would happen to his boy. He couldn't take his place or have one of his friends or colleagues step in and somehow get Tom out of what was to come. However, he had to do *something* to try and make it easier, and last week, he finally came up with an idea.

When he'd seen it, Jack had been at work, taking a break between patients to grab a coffee from the staff room a few doors down from his office. The yellow piece of paper covered in stark black lettering attached to the notice board had seemed innocuous enough at first, but as Jack had approached it, he had realised what it was. A call for medical professionals to sign up to work at the local population control centres administering injections to the damned and declaring them deceased after the fact.

That was when it hit him. Jack might be unable to stop this from happening, might be entirely powerless in this situation and unable to save his precious son, but he could be at Tom's side as he took his last breaths. He could try and keep him calm, reassure him, hold his hand perhaps. He had to pull a few strings to ensure he would be assigned to the population control centre opposite Tom's hospital on Bleecker Avenue, which he was pretty sure would be the one his son was summoned to. Yet he had managed it, and in around two hours, Jack would start his very first shift.

Chapter Twenty-Eight

"Okay, dad, what's going on?" Tom prompted his father after he'd been quiet for a moment or two. A quizzical furrowing his brow. His father rarely had trouble articulating his thoughts, if anything Jack was a bit too open and honest about his opinions than Tom would like for him to be, it was unusual to see his dad struggling to get his words out.

"Well, you see. The thing is... " Jack stumbled, instantly forgetting the well-rehearsed speech he'd spent most of the night perfecting now that the moment of truth was upon him and feeling his mouth going dry. "I've been thinking, for the past few weeks, of what I could do to, you know, help you through all of this."

"Dad, we've talked about this. I don't want your help. I'm going to face this like an adult and accept what I cannot change. I don't want you trying to interfere. It'll only mean that someone else has to take my place, and I wouldn't be able to live with that!" Tom interrupted angrily, frustrated that they were having this conversation yet again. He knew it had been too good to be true, that his father couldn't have possibly just wanted to spend time with him whilst he still could, that he had to have an ulterior motive for insisting on accompanying Tom on his walk to work this morning.

"No, no, son, you don't understand! That isn't what I was getting at. Please just let me try and explain?" Jack pleaded, stopping in the street and turning to face his son to get his full attention. "I know that you don't want me to interfere, and honestly, I don't think there is anything more that I can possibly do, as much as it pains me to say that. But I can't just sit at home and watch you walk out the door for the last time alone. *I* wouldn't be able to live with *that*." Jack continued, echoing his son's own words back to him with as much emphasis as he could manage to try and get his point across.

Taking a deep breath, Jack squared his sagging shoulders and mustered all the courage that he could before speaking again.

"I wanted to tell you that I have taken a position at the population control centre opposite your hospital Thomas. So that I can be there when... Well, so you won't have to be alone." He managed to finish with a gulp.

"You've done what?! Dad! How could you?! You cannot be serious! You're going to spend months, maybe even years killing innocent people? Participating in mass murder? Why?" Tom shouted, his voice raising way above what was considered polite in public, but he couldn't seem to control himself.

He could not even begin to get his head around what his father was telling him. He couldn't understand it at all. Why would anyone in their

right mind agree to work somewhere like that? Especially when one of their own children had been called up in the lottery? How could his dad even consider it? How would he be able to look at his own reflection in the mirror each day? The thoughts raced through Tom's mind as he began to pace in agitation, running his hands through his hair.
"Thomas. Calm down. Please try and understand! I am your father! The day you came into this world, I was there. I cut the cord. I cried when you wrapped your tiny fist around my index finger and squeezed it with all your might. I changed your nappies and wiped away your tears. I fed you, clothed you, and sang to you in the small hours of the morning when you wouldn't sleep. I have been there through every step of your life. From your first day at school, the day you learned to drive, your first girlfriend, your first heartbreak. Every school exam, every sports day, I was there. I know I haven't been the best father to you. I know that I haven't always agreed with the choices that you have made or perhaps expressed my objections in the best manner. I haven't supported you the way that I should have. But I was there when you took your very first breath in this world. And I'll be damned if anyone is going to tell me I cannot be there when you take your last." Jack replied, his words coming out so thick and fast that Tom could barely take them in.
Tom blinked away the tears he could feel pricking at the backs of his eyes and watched in amazement as his father allowed his to stream freely down his cheeks without an inch of shame, despite the eyes he could feel boring into them from passers by as they stood facing each other on the cracked pavement. Tom couldn't remember the last time he'd seen so much emotion from his father. He couldn't recall them ever talking to one another this way in his life. It stunned him momentarily as he tried to take it all in.
Jack was willing to put himself through unimaginable heartache, to help the government to murder countless amounts of innocent people, to carry that pain with him for the rest of his life, remembering their faces, their screams, and the sounds of them begging him for help. Just so that he could be there when Tom's life came to an end. Just so that he could hold his son's hand and help him through what would be the hardest thing he'd ever have to endure in his too-short life.
Tom had always thought of his dad as an unsentimental man, but he could see from the expression on Jack's face that he had been entirely wrong about that. All the little moments throughout his life that he had taken for granted, all of the times when his dad had just been there without him ever having to ask flashed through his mind. For the first time, he realised how much they had meant to the man who had brought him into this world, and a wave of pain came crashing down around him

as they stood facing one another in the street.

Chapter Twenty-Nine

Six weeks and three days. How is that all that I have left? Steph wondered as she read the stark black ink on the folded piece of paper which had arrived in a plain brown envelope that morning, trying to take it all in. It's not as though she hadn't known this was coming, but Steph still had to make a concerted effort to swallow down the bile she could feel rising in the back of her throat. Steph had been doing her best to save every spare penny she could since she received her alert to put aside to help Crystal when she was gone, the last thing she could afford to do was start throwing up what little food she permitted herself to eat today. Turning her attention back to the pieces of paper in her hands, she sat on the edge of her bed. She tried to make herself focus on the letter, even as the words on the page before her swam and merged before her eyes.

Stephanie Moore, this letter serves as your formal notice that you are hereby summoned to appear at the Cull Enforcement Agency Population Control Centre at 3 Bleeker Avenue at 9:00 am on 20th July 2053. The full address of your designated centre can be found at the top of this letter.

Please find enclosed details of what you are required to bring with you on this date, prohibited items and a list of items which you may bring if you choose to provide you with comfort in your final hours.

Whilst we endeavour to ensure that all persons summoned are culled on their end-of-life date as stated above, we must inform you that you may be housed at the centre for up to three days before your life is terminated. We request that you bring enough clothing to keep you comfortable for this amount of time. We will provide any and all toiletries and personal hygiene items that you may need.

You must bring with you:

Your laminated cull card, which has been sent with this letter and shows your name, date of birth and end-of-life date.
Formal identification in the form of a passport, driving licence or citizenship card.
Your government issued smart watch.
The name, full address and telephone number of the person whom you have allocated to collect your personal belongings and remains after your death. *Please note that these will not be ready for

collection until five working days after your end-of-life date.
Clothing as specified above.
Any medications you require to keep you of sound mind and body until your life is terminated.

Personal items:

You are permitted to bring with you, should you wish:

A religious or spiritual book of your choosing.
Up to three personal photographs or mementoes.
A pen and paper.
Jewellery of a religious or spiritual nature.
Glasses/contact lenses if required.

Prohibited items:

Weapons/sharps/needles or any item which could be used to cause injury to yourself or others.
Non-prescription medication, illicit drugs or their paraphernalia.
Alcohol.
Food or drink of any kind – these will be provided for you.
Personal hygiene items; make-up, creams, lotions, or anything not considered essential to your health.
Mobile phones/tablets/laptops/electronic devices of any kind with the exception of your government issued smart watch.
Jewellery not of a religious or spiritual nature. Please remove any piercings before surrendering yourself to the centre.

Please note that you will be subjected to a thorough search on your arrival, and any prohibited items found on your person will be confiscated and disposed of. These will not be returned to your allocated collector with your permitted belongings.

The Cull Enforcement Agency, the United Kingdom government and the population of the world at large would like to take this opportunity to thank you for your sacrifice. In forfeiting your life, you give humanity the best chance at long-term survival. We will forever owe you a debt of gratitude.

Any noncompliance with this letter, failure to appear at your designated Population control centre at the appointed time or attempt to interfere in the cull process in any way are crimes

punishable by law. Should you break any of these laws, you will be subject to execution.

Sincerely

Professor Peter Jones
Head of the cull Enforcement Agency in the United Kingdom

Six weeks and three days. That would make her twenty-four years, four months and ten days old exactly when her life ended. Steph quickly did the calculations in her addled brain, amazed that she could, given her current state of mind. It felt as though a thick black fog had descended on her the moment she had torn open the envelope, clouding her thoughts and making it difficult for her to focus or even read the words staring back at her from the paperwork in her hands.
Was that really all the life she was going to be allowed to lead? It seemed like such a short amount of time, the blink of an eye. Even now, her mother was twice the age that Steph herself would ever reach. She had been given opportunities that Steph could now only dream about, only read about in books or see in movies. She'd never even been in love. Instantly, as though summoned there by some invisible force, Tom's handsome face sprung into her mind's eye, forcing its way around the fog and shining back at her through the darkness. Did he get his letter today too? Steph wondered. Is he sitting on his bed, in his home, surrounded by the family that loves him and would do anything to get him out of this, reading the same few words on the crisp white paper that she was?
Steph wasn't in love with Tom, that much she knew. She cared for him, sure. She was attracted to him, but love? Love was an emotion she had yet to experience outside of the way she felt for her friends and family. Romantic love was a notion she had only read about in books. Something that she felt sure that she would feel at some point, later down the line, when she had more time to worry about such things and the world wasn't fractured into so many broken pieces. Perhaps given time and different circumstances, she could have allowed herself to fall in love with the trainee doctor with the big heart and the soulful sea-green eyes. However, time was not a luxury she had been permitted. Now she could count the weeks she had to live on her hands. Now she'd never have the chance to discover what might have been.
Shaking her head to clear it of the thoughts of things she could never have, Steph turned her attention back to the letter in her hands, realising for the first time that she was trembling. The pieces of paper vibrated against her fingertips as she tried to hold them steady so that she could

go back over the lists of permitted and prohibited items and decide what she was going to take with her. A religious or spiritual book, she wondered if one of the classic romance novels she had read and re-read throughout her short life would count. They might not be spiritual in a traditional sense, but, she drew comfort and solace from the words contained within the battered and yellowed pages of the decades-old copies that she had managed to procure in second-hand stores when she'd had a few extra pounds to spare, something which didn't happen often and so her collection was sparse. Surely if she were faced with the possibility of sitting in the centre for up to three days as the letter threatened, waiting for her name to be called, they wouldn't argue over her taking a simple book with her to occupy her time? No matter if it was considered religious or not?

The rest of the lists were all pretty obvious to her; of course, they weren't permitted to take any form of weaponry into the centre. God forbid one of them snapped and decided to use said weapon on their would-be murderers before they could fulfil their duties, she thought. Picturing herself trying to walk in there with one of the oversized kitchen knives Jose used in the restaurant to carve the meat, the blade glinting in the sun as she tried to fight her way out through the throngs of armed C.E.A agents. I wouldn't stand a chance, she realised, knowing she couldn't fight her way out of a wet paper bag.

No drugs or alcohol also seemed like fairly obvious exclusions. It's not as if many people could afford such things anyway, she thought as she made her way down the list. Although a few stiff drinks might be the only thing that would give her the courage to walk into the centre in the first place. Perhaps she should ask Tony if he would give her one of the dusty old bottles of wine in the cellar that no one could afford to buy as a parting gift.

Steph almost caught herself laughing out loud as she re-read the sentence about bringing any medications required to 'keep you of sound mind and body'. Yeah, because we wouldn't want anyone getting deathly ill before they're murdered, now would we? She thought dryly, amused that even the voice in her head could sound full of disdain and sarcasm.

The audacity of these people to try and sugarcoat what they were going to do to her bothered Steph more than she had expected it to. After all, hadn't she walked past a hundred posters in the past few weeks, all proclaiming the same thing? That those whose names were called in the lottery were doing a great service to humankind? She should be used to it by now, really. No matter what fancy terminology they used or how many times they thanked her, no matter how grateful they were, they were going to kill her. Was she supposed to be proud of the grand sacrifice that she would be making to save people whom she would never meet? Who would live on happily long after she was reduced to nothing more than ash?

The only thing that gave Steph pause for a moment as she scanned over the letter was that she had to provide the name and contact details of the person responsible for collecting what was left of her after her death. The obvious person to ask was Crystal, but could she do that to the woman she considered to be more of a sister than a friend? Ask her to walk into that horrible, soulless building, the building in which Steph would be put to death, and collect her few meagre belongings after she was gone?

Steph wondered for a moment if she should ask her parents. Would they be offended if she didn't? Would they want to scatter her ashes somewhere as a family and mourn her? Or would they be pleased not to have to make the two-hour trip from the countryside where they now resided and be happy that someone else was taking care of such a morbid task on their behalf? Maybe she could ask Tony? He would be happy to do it, she was sure, well no, not happy, but he would if she asked him, that much she knew.

No, Steph would ask Crystal. It would be an unpleasant conversation that would no doubt leave both women in the regular floods of tears that seemed to plague them more often than not nowadays, but it was the best solution for everyone. Crystal knew Steph better than her family ever had. If the only final resting place she was ever to have was in a nondescript container provided by the government, Steph would rather it be put into her best friends' hands than anyone else's.

It troubled her that she didn't have a partner to do this for her, someone to share the burden of what she was about to go through with, to hold her tightly in their strong arms the night before she had to present herself at the centre and whisper that everything was going to be alright, even though they both knew that it wouldn't be. However, at the same time, perhaps that was for the best. Her social circle was remarkably small, which had to be a good thing, right? The fewer people that cared for her, the fewer people there would be that would be hurt by her passing.

As if on cue, Steph heard the familiar heavy tread of her roommate making her way down the hallway to their tiny flat. She couldn't quite put her finger on how exactly she always knew when it was Crystal walking through the building and not one of her many neighbours, perhaps they had just become attuned to one and other in the time that they had lived together, but she always did. A few minutes later, her intuition proved accurate as she heard the jangle of keys in the door before it swung open to reveal her best friend, looking hot and sweaty after her long walk home from the restaurant.

Before Steph had the presence of mind to hide the letter from Crystal, to find a way to gently bring up the subject instead of ambushing her with it the moment she stepped through the door after a lengthy day at work, Crystal's eyes fell on the sheets of paper in Steph's hand. Lingering there for a moment or two before they veered off to the envelope on the bed, on top of which sat the laminated cull card that Steph had to take with her to the population control centre, which had an out-of-date photo on it from when she'd gotten her citizenship card over five years ago at the local town hall, a compulsory requirement for all citizens. Now that having a car was a luxury, few people bothered to learn to drive or get licences, and passports were even less common, the government had decided they needed to provide each member of the population with photographic identification, and thus, the obligatory citizenship card was created.

"Is that what I think it is?" Crystal asked. Nodding towards the envelope as she made her way into the flat and pushed the door closed behind her. She didn't even bother to remove her shoes or put down her bag as she walked over to Steph's side, too entranced by the paperwork in her friends' hand.

"If what you think it is, is my letter from our friendly head of the C.E.A, Professor Jones, informing me when they will kill me, then yes, it is." Steph quipped, trying to keep her voice light and not betray the real emotions bubbling up just under the surface of her carefully in place façade, threatening to spill over.

"When?" Was all Crystal could manage to ask, her bottom lip trembling as she did so. She quickly drew it between her teeth in an attempt to stop Steph from noticing her distress, but she could see from the look in her best friend's eyes that it wasn't quick enough.

"July 20th. Six weeks." Steph replied, keeping her gaze focused on the bedsheet beneath her. She could see the sadness written all over Crystal's face, her bottom lip trembling, and she couldn't bear it. Hold it together. She instructed herself, taking a deep, steadying breath.

"So soon?" Crystal gasped. "I thought these culls were meant to last for years. How is it possible that your date is so soon?" she asked frantically, her voice rising as emotion overtook her.

"That's what happens when you're born early in the year, I guess. It doesn't take that long to get through the candidates from January to March, I'm afraid." Steph told her. "It's better this way anyway. Can you imagine sitting about for months, Christ, even years? Waiting for your date to arrive? Constantly feeling like you're living on borrowed time and jumping at every bit of post that comes through the letterbox? No, this is better. At least now I know. I can start making plans." She finished, brandishing a smaller envelope which had been inside the first, which she had not yet opened, which had the words 'End of life preparation kit' printed on the front.

"But, Steph..." Crystal began, her voice thick with unshed tears, but Steph cut her off.

"Nope. Don't start that. There's no use in crying. It won't change anything. And besides, I need to ask you an important favour. Consider it my last request." Steph said, forcing a giggle from her tightening throat.

"Anything. I'd do anything for you, Steph, you know that." Crystal reassured her honestly, knowing that there was nothing in this world that she would refuse the woman sat across from her who had pulled her from the streets, given her a home, found her a job and ultimately saved her life.

"I need to allocate someone to collect my belongings and my, well, what's left of me after... after I'm gone. And I was hoping that you would agree to be that person?" Steph asked in a small voice, unable to say the words 'after I am dead' or hide her emotions this time as they started to overwhelm her again.

Crystal could almost feel her heart breaking as she took in Steph's request and the physical pain in her chest nearly made her double over. She clutched at the thin fabric of her work shirt in agitation, forcing herself to remain upright. She couldn't imagine how horrible it would be to walk into the population control centre, the same building that Steph would enter a few days before. But instead of leaving with her best friend, all Crystal would have left of Steph would be a pile of ashes and a few nick-nacks. Crystal honestly didn't know how she would manage it, didn't know if she was strong enough and if she would be able to keep herself together and not embarrass herself or Steph's memory. But she wasn't about to tell Steph that.

Her roommate had more than enough on her plate as it was, and Crystal already knew that Steph was worrying way more than she should about how she would cope alone after Steph was gone. She wasn't about to add anything else to her plate.

"Of course. I would be honoured." She said, and closing the last few feet between them, she sat on the bed and wrapped her arms around Steph's trembling body, biting back her tears as she stroked her hair.

"I'll take care of you, Steph. I promise." She whispered. Knowing that her best friend would know exactly what she meant.

Chapter Thirty

Crawling along in second gear down the swarming city streets in the heavily armoured truck which had been assigned to him and his team Williams squinted through the tinted windscreen, trying desperately to see through the dense plumes of thick black smoke which seemed to be wafting towards him from every direction and not hit any of the scores of people who had descended onto the streets en-masse this evening.
It's starting to fall apart. Williams sensed, flinching as a tower of flames erupted in his peripheral vision, shooting a cascade of red and orange sparks high into the night sky as something exploded on a bonfire outside one of the few grocery stores that were still in operation. Or at least it had been before tonight, Williams realised, seeing the shards of glass littering the pavement from the stores' blown-out windows.
They're destroying the few meagre supplies this town has left, he thought to himself as he coaxed the car forwards at a steady pace.
Williams wasn't unfamiliar with civil unrest; he'd seen it before in half a dozen of the war-ravaged countries in which he had served in the past ten years, but something about this was different. These people weren't fighting back against a regime or a callous dictator. They weren't smashing shop windows and looting the half-empty stores searching for food, although he was sure some of them would take advantage of the distraction to fill their empty bellies. These people were fighting for their very survival and their right to exist.
Williams would be lying if he said that he hadn't expected some kind of resistance to spring up sooner rather than later, but the 'Right to Life' group, as they called themselves, had appeared much more quickly than he had anticipated and even worse, they were well organised. Too well organised, he thought, they had to have someone with experience leading them to be causing this much chaos in so many different places at once, in what felt like a coordinated attack on the C.E.A. and the very city itself. Right to Life, that was a joke. Didn't they understand that the whole point of the culls was to give humanity the chance to live on? In order for that to happen, the population had to be decreased by any means necessary. They're fighting against the very thing they claim to want to protect, he thought to himself.
When he had arrived at work tonight, bang on six o'clock, already dressed in his black jumpsuit with his gun cleaned and loaded in his holster, Williams had expected to be sent out on another night of home raids, just like he had been on every shift for weeks now. However, one quick glance at Lieutenant Colonel Armitage had quickly dispelled any such notions. Williams had already known about the unrest. Obviously, he had. He wasn't blind. Anyone who had stepped outside their homes

in the past few days, turned on a television, or a computer had heard of the R.T.L by now. They had made damn sure that their presence was being felt in every corner of town. The news stations were lapping it up, broadcasting the chaos on the streets onto every other high rise in the city in twelve-foot-high technicolour to ensure no one missed out on a minute of the action. Vultures thriving on the destruction to boost their ratings.

Those law-abiding citizens that could had barricaded themselves in their homes in an effort to keep themselves and their families safe, but Williams knew from experience that it was only a matter of time before the hundreds of people littering the streets in their dark clothes and with their hoods pulled up high over their heads in an attempt to hide their faces, would soon run out of commercial properties to ransack and would no doubt make their way into the more affluent areas of town. Wanting to take their frustrations out on the elected officials, city workers, doctors, police and even agents like him, who they either blamed for the culls or who they felt deserved to suffer because their chosen occupations had made them exempt from the lottery. As if we could have known when we decided what career path to follow, he thought sarcastically.

"Shit!" Williams cursed. Dragging himself back to the present and slamming his foot on the brake as hard as he could with lightning-fast reflexes just in time to miss the kid who had just darted into the road ahead of him. The sound of screeching rubber filled the air as the car's tyres protested the sudden restriction to their movement and Williams gripped the steering wheel with all his might to keep the vehicle steady. The car came skidding to a halt in a haze of gravel just a foot or two away from a skinny teenager who didn't so much as glance in their direction as he made his way across the street, a man on a mission, his arms laden down with what looked to Williams in the darkness to be planks of wood.

"Should we do something? That's kindling he's got there." Cathy, one of William's assigned team for the night, called out from her place in the back seat, leaning forwards between the two front chairs and digging her fingernails into the leather headrests as she tried to get a better view of the scene out of the windscreen.

"No. We have our orders. Someone else will have to clean up this mess." Williams told her, shaking his head before putting the car into gear and continuing down the street.

Their lieutenant had been clear about their duties tonight, and Williams didn't intend to deviate from them for a moment. He and the two other vehicles bringing up the rear of the cavalcade were to head straight to Bleecker Avenue, to the population control centre. It seemed that a small contingent of the R.T.L had split off from the main group, who seemed content enough to set fires and destroy public property and headed directly for the centre. To what end, Williams didn't know, but one thing he was sure of, whatever they wanted there, he was going to make sure they didn't get it.

Williams took a deep breath as the vehicle rounded the final corner on their journey. Small contingent, my arse. He thought to himself crudely as he caught sight of the crowd of people lurking in the shadows opposite the hospital. Scanning the area, it only took a moment for him to realise that he and his team were sorely outnumbered, and there was no way they could take care of this on their own.

"Lieutenant, this is Williams." He spoke directly into the watch on his wrist, which doubled as a communications device for all law enforcement personnel, opening the channel so that his words would be heard by the vehicles following him as well as his superior.

"Go ahead, Williams." The voice came back loud and clear.

"Arrived at destination. Numbers more prolific than anticipated. Additional backup required." Williams said clearly, keeping his sentences short and to the point, not wanting to waste any more time than necessary. His fingers were already twitching to wrap around his gun as it was. All he wanted to do was get out there and show these degenerates who was in charge around here.

"Understood. Sending more units to your location. Estimated number of rebels?" Lieutenant Colonel Armitage asked.

"A hundred. Maybe a hundred and fifty." Williams told his superior, hoping he had his numbers right. It was almost impossible to make out individuals in the sea of black-clothed bodies in front of him, and for all he knew, there were more hiding in the shadows or on their way.

"Shit. Alright, Williams, back-ups on their way." Armitage confirmed, and Williams hoped they wouldn't take long to arrive.

"What do we do now? Wait?" Cathy piped up from the backseat, not sounding at all happy with that idea.

"God, no, they'll tear that place apart if we let them." Martin, another of the team, answered her before William's had the chance to respond.

Cathy looked at Williams questioningly, raising a perfectly shaped eyebrow in his direction and ignoring their other colleague entirely. Williams didn't blame her, Martin held the lowest rank in their team, and he wasn't in a position to be making decisions, but still, the guy had a point.

Even from this distance, thirty metres or so back from the centre, pulled over to the side of the road under a broken street lamp trying to go unnoticed, Williams could see the handful of security guards who worked in the building huddling together in the doorway, their hi-vis jackets making them stand out against the night sky. They might as well have printed targets on their chests. They'll be overrun in minutes, he thought to himself, trying to come up with a plan.

"Alright, this is what we're going to do," Williams said, raising his watch and opening the comms channel as he started to outline his plan to the team.

Chapter Thirty-one

Under cover of darkness, the team crept slowly towards the freshly painted facade of the building which houses the population control centre. They kept their backs tight up against the rear of the row of buildings between them and their target, and tried to remain invisible to the seemingly ever-expanding group of rebels who were becoming clearer with each carefully placed step that they took. If this plan had any chance of success, it was imperative that they weren't spotted, Williams thought to himself as he led his team past the row of abandoned buildings littering the street.

Allowing his mind to wander, Williams pictured them suddenly occupied again, as he knew they once had been back when he was a kid, with florists, card shops, grocery stores and those weird little corner shops that seemed to sell everything from pints of milk to toy cars and everything in between that he remembered buying sweets in with his meagre pocket money after school. That's what we're fighting for, Williams reminded himself. For a better future. For the remaining population to have a chance at living long and happy lives. For the return of civilisation, when the sight of rundown buildings became a half-forgotten memory, and the world returned to some semblance of normality. Where a loaf of bread didn't cost as much as an hour's wages, where there was enough food, drink and shelter to go around. Williams held on to that thought as he crept along, his steel-toe-capped boots making no sound against the pavement as he stealthily made his way forwards. A trickle of sweat dripped down his spine, but he ignored it; nervous anticipation was to be expected. He wouldn't give it any more attention than it deserved by dwelling on it right now. He needed to focus.

Arriving behind the building next to the population control centre, an abandoned four-story monstrosity covered in graffiti and half hidden by overgrown trees and vegetation, Williams came to a halt and held up a hand to signal to his team that they should do the same before peering around the corner and assessing the situation once more.

Directly opposite the population control centre stood a group of maybe seventy people, primarily men, Williams thought, judging by their heights and builds, but he couldn't be sure. One thing that was clear even in the darkness though was that each of them held some kind of crude weapon. From baseball bats to planks of wood and tools to flaming torches, each rebel was armed and ready for a fight.

Silently, Williams reached down towards his belt and detached a tear gas grenade, grasping the small metal object tightly in his fist. Disperse as many as possible. He thought to himself. That was the goal here. If they could keep them away from the centre for long enough for backup to arrive, perhaps the rebels would realise that they couldn't win this. That they were only risking their own lives by trying to what? Storm the centre? Free the people inside? If there were even any still alive. Williams knew that a lack of volunteers to carry out the lethal injections and doctors to declare the dead meant that the centres often didn't manage to get through their daily cull quotas and that many people were forced to wait there for a night or two before their names were called. It was Saturday evening though, the end of the week. And Williams would bet a week's wages on it that the workers here would have done their damndest not to have to come in on a Sunday because they still had candidates housed there. Given the nature of their jobs, they'd want their solitary day off, maybe more than most people would, so he imagined the number of living people inside would be low, if there were any at all.

Are these people really willing to risk their lives to liberate some corpses? He wondered, trying to block out the sounds of the rebels shouting. He couldn't quite make out their individual demands, too many of them were screaming at once, but that didn't matter. It didn't matter what they wanted or how well thought out their arguments were. All that mattered was that they were breaking the law. Multiple laws actually, they were breaking curfew for one thing, not to mention trying to interfere with the cull process, a crime now punishable by death. Willaims realised he'd be perfectly within his rights to open fire on the lot of them, but he didn't relish the thought. He hadn't taken this job so that he could harm people. He wanted to help save the human race. That was the entire point.

Taking a deep breath, Williams closed his eyes for a moment to steady himself before darting out into the small clearing between the two buildings, forcing his way through the tall grass and weeds poking up from the ground and yanking the pin from his grenade. Thrusting his arm over his shoulder, he tossed it in a high arc over the pavement and into the tarmac-covered road, where the Right to Life rebels had congregated between the centre and the hospital, and watched with satisfaction as it landed smack bang in front of them.

The toxic gas cloud exploded almost instantly, spreading through the air at top speed. Picked up by the slight gusts of wind flowing down the street, wispy tendrils of grey smoke soon filled the air and obscured William's view of the rebels. The cacophony of voices that had been unintelligible to him just moments ago quickly became a chorus of coughs and gags as his targets inhaled the poison and struggled to catch their breath.

Williams started forwards into the crowd without a word, his standard issue mask tightly secured to his face protecting him from the gas. Multiple hands grasped at him as he moved, trying to use his sturdy frame as leverage to keep them upright as their coughing fits overtook them and they doubled over, gasping for air. Williams stumbled over what he was pretty sure was a fallen body, although he didn't stop long enough to check its status. Behind him, his team followed, and he could hear Cathy's voice rising above the din.

"C.E.A. You're all under arrest for breaking curfew and attempting to interfere with the cull process." She called out, and the crowd began to scatter like rats fleeing a sinking ship.

As Williams reached the end of the tear gas cloud, he pulled another grenade from his pocket. He tossed it just a few feet into the scampering masses, watching as they yanked their clothes over their mouths and tried to breathe through their ragged shirt sleeves in an attempt to not inhale the gas whilst tears streamed from their eyes, blurring their vision and making escape almost impossible. Through the haze, Williams saw the fuzzy outline of a fist heading directly for his face and years of training kicked in, muscle memory forcing his body to react before his brain had even registered what was happening. The fist was mere centimetres from his jaw when he caught it, twisting it harshly in a tight grip and feeling something snap as he tore it away from its intended target. Its owner attempted to scream but managed to do nothing more than take a deep inhale of the toxic fumes and keel over, gagging and choking as Williams slapped a pair of handcuffs around his wrists.

The sound of his teammates doing the same was audible all around him over the few remaining coughs and wheezes and Williams breathed a sigh of relief. He knew that the majority of the rebels had already dispersed, that most of them had still been lurking in the shadows when the grenades had gone off and hadn't been affected by them at all and had chosen to make a break for it rather than help their supposed friends, but that was fine with him. Their objective here wasn't to try and arrest every single one of them. It was to protect the centre, and he was sure that with a show of force like this one, they had achieved that. The sound of sirens in the distance calmed his racing heart as he secured another prisoner and shoved him roughly toward one of the other teams who had now reached them, coming up behind the rebels and effectively boxing them in. The agent nodded at Williams once before leading the new prisoner and one he had already secured back down the street towards the line of black armoured trucks emitting piercing sirens into the night air as they tore down the road towards Williams and his team.

When the smoke finally started to clear, and the last of the rebels had been secured, Williams took stock of the scene around him. The centre hadn't been breached. That much he was grateful for, but the crowd of people who perpetually littered the steps in front of the hospital on the opposite side of the road had taken some damage by the looks of things. He couldn't be sure how many of them had been injured before the rebels had arrived and had already been waiting outside the hospital seeking treatment or if any of them had actually been with the Right to Life group themselves, but he could see blood-streaked faces and tear-filled eyes even from his position on the other side of the road. So he squared his shoulders once more, removed his mask and made his way over to them to see if he could help and to try and gather a few witness statements before he headed back to headquarters to receive his next mission for the night.

Chapter Thirty-Two

Through the floor to ceiling windows that flanked the exterior of the restaurant, Steph could see the last rays of the setting sun beginning to dip out of sight behind the tall buildings on the opposite side of the street, a myriad of reds, oranges and yellows disappearing behind the brick and mortar as the darkness of the evening swept in. I should make an effort to watch the sunset tomorrow, she thought to herself. It's not something she'd ever considered taking the time to do previously. Now though, with only three chances in her life to, she felt like she should make an effort. Isn't that what people did in the movies? When they know their time is coming to an end? Find an abandoned hilltop somewhere, look out over the city they have lived in and loved all their lives, and watch as the sun sets on the horizon?

Melancholy thoughts like this had become Steph's constant companions in the last couple of weeks. She tried in vain to commit everything she did to memory in the minutest detail, wondering if it would be the last time she would experience it and not wanting to miss a moment of this wonderfully perplexing world. Every street that Steph walked down, every tree that she saw, she tried to commit to memory. Each person that she spoke to, each interaction that she had, no matter how seemingly mundane or insignificant, Steph tried to make meaningful. Determined to try and convey to everyone in her life just how much they meant to her before it was too late. She wanted to leave them with happy memories of her rather than the sight of the despondent look that she knew perpetually covered her features nowadays. Steph wanted the people around her, those she had worked with for years, spent her days and nights laughing and joking with, to remember her with a smile. Not pity her for her rough deal or lament the fact that she was gone.

That was partially why, even though she had little over seventy-two hours left to live, Steph had still come in to work tonight. Just like she had done nearly every Friday night for as long as she could remember. She had donned her threadbare and stained grey apron, tried to smooth out as many of the creases in her slightly discoloured white shirt as she could, popped a pencil behind her ear, a notebook in her pocket, and carried on as though nothing had changed. As though this wasn't the last shift that she would ever work, as though she wasn't a dead woman walking.

Tony had tried his best to convince Steph that she should stop coming in weeks ago when she first got her end-of-life date and officially knew how long she had left on this earth. Telling her that she should be spending her time doing things that mattered, things that she would regret not having taken the time to do later, but Steph had been deaf to

his suggestions. Determined to continue working and saving as much money as she could right up until the last. Determined not to sit at home dwelling on what was to come and to keep as busy as she could.
What would have been the point of finishing work sooner? She supposed she could have made the trip to see her family. They had not shown any inclination that they were interested in seeing her before her life ended though. She had called her mother once or twice in the last few weeks, trying to ask her all the questions that she wanted answers to before it was too late. Making one last-ditch attempt at fixing their fractured relationship so that her mother wouldn't have to live with the knowledge that the daughter she had abandoned was gone, without her ever having had the chance to really get to know her, but their conversations had been stilted and uncomfortable. Too much time had passed since they had really talked to one another, and it seemed that no amount of phone calls, questions or attempts at conversation would be enough to close the gulf between them.
The only thing that Steph wanted to do before she had to trudge her too young to be as weary and worn out as it was body to the population control centre on Monday morning was to spend time with Crystal, and seeing as her best friend and roommate was working, it only made sense for Steph to continue to as well. Tony, whether by design or not, Steph did not know for sure, but she had an inkling he had done it on purpose, had not scheduled either of the girls to work tomorrow or Sunday, for which she was grateful. At least they could have a couple of days together, curled up in their cramped studio flat, talking and comforting each other before Monday morning arrived, and they had to say goodbye.
At least the restaurant was busy tonight, Steph thought to herself as she scraped the few crumbs of cake that remained from the plates that she had just collected from table nineteen into the oversized food bin next to the washing up station. Whilst she was content to be at work, the last thing she wanted to be doing was wasting her few precious evenings, and so the sight of the full booths and tables and the sounds of the happy customers chattering around her managed to make her feel valuable and like her time was being well spent, as well as giving her hope for the future of the restaurant, and for her friends that worked in it. Perhaps the world was already beginning to change for the better.
I'll catch the sunset tomorrow night, she thought to herself as she placed the dishes in the washer and snuck one more glance out of the small old window at the back of the kitchen. Resolving to take herself off to the local park, the one with the cracked wooden bench under the tall oak tree, which looked down on half the town, and live out one of those movie moments.

"Steph, can I speak to you in my office for a moment?" Tony's voice called from over her shoulder.

"Erm, sure," Steph replied, wiping her hands on her apron and following her boss through the two-way swinging door which led into the small room that he called his office, which was little more than an oversized closet really, with just enough room for a thin desk to be pressed against one wall with an out-of-date computer propped on top and a battered old leather chair which had seen better days in-front of it.

"What's up?" Steph asked as cheerfully as she could manage. Forcing a smile onto her face.

"I just wanted to give you this," Tony said, pressing a foil package into her hands. "It's just some fish that we're going to have to throw out tomorrow if it doesn't get eaten, and I thought perhaps, it might be nice for you to have one last decent meal before... before." He cut off, eyes flitting around the room and focusing on anything other than Steph's face as he spoke.

"Thanks, Tony." She murmured back, grateful for his kind gesture but hoping that he wouldn't try to drag this conversation out for too long. There were few people in her world that Steph was dreading having to say goodbye to, but Tony was undoubtedly high up on that list. He had been like a father figure to her since her family had moved away, and she had become very fond of the older man.

"I just wanted to tell you, Stephanie, how very proud of you I am." Tony began, his voice thick with tears. "Few people could have handled themselves through all of this with as much dignity and grace as you have. Even those twice your age would have struggled to comport themselves in the same way that you have during this time. You have become a remarkable young woman in the years that I have known you, Steph, and I couldn't be prouder of you if you were my own child." He said, and Steph felt a lump rising in her throat.

At that moment, she wished, not for the first time, that she was one of those people who knew what to say in situations such as this. Who was eloquent, well-spoken, and able to conjure up just the right words to tell the man in front of her how much he meant to her too, but Steph knew that wasn't her, that it never would be now. It was one of the many character flaws she had run out of time to try and improve. So she flashed Tony a watery smile and shrugged with embarrassment as she felt her cheeks heat up at his kind words.

"And there is this as well," Tony added, saving her from having to try and respond and thrusting an envelope towards her. "It's not much. Certainly not enough to repay you for everything that you've done here, for the restaurant, and for me since you came to work with us. But I wanted to at least give you something, and I hope this might give you a little peace." He finished, and this time Steph could clearly make out the tears sparkling in his dark brown eyes.

Reaching out a trembling hand, Steph took the envelope from Tony, and she could have sworn that she felt his thumb rub across the back of her hand as she did so, lingering there for just a moment and caressing her skin. Flipping open the unsealed envelope, Steph could see a thin wad of crisp banknotes staring back at her, and instantly a wave of relief washed over her entire body.

"Thank you, Tony. For the fish, the money, everything. You've been like a father to me, and I... I don't even know that there are words to tell you how much your support has meant to me. I would have ended up on the streets long ago if it weren't for you. So many of us would have." Steph finally spat out, gesturing at the building around her to indicate that she was referring to her colleagues as well as herself.

Tucking the envelope safely into the pocket of her apron, Steph turned back towards the office door and started towards it with the foil packet of fish in her hand. She paused as she reached it and began to turn the handle, spinning back to face her boss.

"Tony? Can I ask you just one more favour?" She asked, feeling as though she had no right to request anything more of the man before her. He had already given her so much more than she deserved, but knowing that she'd kick herself tomorrow if she didn't take this opportunity.

"Of course," Tony replied.

"Please take care of Crystal for me? She's going to be hurting after, well, after it's all over. It's going to be hard for her to come to terms with. Keep her busy? Try and make sure she eats and takes care of herself and doesn't mourn me too much. She's the one that's got the harder end of the deal here I think, and she's going to need all the help she can get." Steph said in a rush.

"Ahh, Stephanie, see, that's what I mean. Only you would be more worried about your friend right now than you are about yourself. Please don't be, I will look after her. I promise." Tony reassured Steph.

"Thank you, Tony. Goodbye."

"Goodbye, Stephanie. And good luck." Tony said to her, retreating back as she stepped over the threshold with one last smile and exited his office, closing the door behind her and permitting him the quiet and solitude he needed to allow his feelings to overtake him.

Sliding down into his damaged old desk chair, Tony put his head in his hands and allowed the tears he had tried so hard to keep hidden in her presence to slide across his face at will. Mourning the young life that he had tried so hard to protect for years, only to watch it be snatched away from him, from her, from all of them, and there being nothing at all that he could do about it.

Chapter Thirty-Three

"I don't think you should come to the centre with me on Monday morning." Steph blurted out to Crystal's back as her friend stood at the old stove which only had one working hob in their tiny flat the following afternoon.

Crystal had been slaving away for the past half an hour cooking their lunch, which consisted of a couple of fillets of fish which Tony had given to Steph before she left the restaurant for the last time yesterday evening, and a few misshapen vegetables that they had managed to pick up at the local grocery store.

"What?" Crystal bellowed in surprise, nearly upsetting the pan in front of her as she spun and faced Steph, brandishing a spatula in her raised fist.

"Okay, okay, take it easy. Put the weapon down, please." Steph quipped, trying to lighten the moment. "I just don't see that there is any point in you coming and standing in that queue of the damned with me for God knows how long. It'll only upset us both. I think that this is just something that I need to do alone. I am not sure that I'll have the strength to walk in there and leave you outside the doors. It'll just make it harder for me." Steph admitted, unable to meet her friend's eye and she finally allowed Crystal to see, just for a moment, how very scared she was.

"Are you sure? I mean, I know it won't be easy. I'm not stupid. But if it makes it even a little bit better for you if I am there, if it'll give you just a tiny bit more strength, then you know I will do it. I'd stay with you right up until the very end if they'd let me. I hate the idea of you going through all this alone." Crystal said, meaning every word.

As much as she could understand the logic behind what Steph was saying, Crystal wasn't willing to give in that easily. She wanted to make sure that Steph was making the right choice for *her*, not just insisting on doing what she thought was right for Crystal. Trying to protect her, as always. Right up until her last moment.

Crystal had been trying to come to terms with the fact that in just thirty-six hours time, Steph would have to present herself at the centre and join that horrible line of people all awaiting the same fate. She had assumed that she would accompany her. That she would stay with her best friend right up until the very last moment that she could. The moment when they closed the doors on her, and Crystal had no choice but to let her go. To come home alone to their shared flat, which despite barely being big enough for one person let alone two, Crystal knew was going to feel terribly empty after Steph was gone. She had no idea how she was going to cope eating here alone or not having anyone to greet her and talk to about her working day after a rubbish shift at the restaurant. Just the thought of having to crawl into the uncomfortable bed with the lumpy mattress and try to sleep without the steading sounds of Steph's even breathing beside her already constricted Crystal's chest and she was dreading every minute she'd have to spend here without her friend after she was gone. .

After spending so much time preparing for it, fortifying herself for the inevitable pain it would cause her and how difficult it would be not to fight and scratch like a rabid animal to stop them from taking Steph into that place, Crystal wasn't sure she was able to agree to Steph's request now.

"I'm sure. Really. I've spent a lot of time thinking about this over the past few weeks, and I think it would be better for us both this way. We can say our final goodbyes here, in the comfort of our own home. I would much prefer that to be your last memory of me than of a sobbing mess trying to force myself through the doors of that place." Steph insisted.

She didn't want to be unkind or upset Crystal, but she knew this was the best course of action for them both. Since Steph was a little girl, she had always been stronger alone. She would fall and scrape her knee or topple from her bike and pick herself up and dust herself off and carry on as though nothing had happened. Unless one of her parents or even, on occasion, her brother spotted her and came over to ask if she was okay, at which point Steph would fall apart. Dissolving into an inconsolable mess of tears the moment any of them attempted to comfort her. She would cope better with this whole horrible mess of a situation if she was alone.

This was the best thing. For her and for Crystal. Steph was sure of it.

"If that is what you really want, Steph, then I'll do it. But if you change your mind at any point, even if it's the moment you're walking out the door or when you've already gotten outside the building, all you have to do is tell me, and I'll be right there, okay?" Crystal said. She could see from the look in Steph's eyes that her friend's mind was already made up, and the last thing that she wanted to do was to push her. After all it was Steph that was about to relinquish her young life, not Crystal, what right did she have to argue with her? It was practically Steph's last request.

"I will, I promise," Steph said solemnly as she watched Crystal's shoulders slump as she turned back to the stove, slid the spatula underneath the now probably over-cooked fish in the pan, and placed the fillets onto the cracked plates beside her.

Chapter Thirty-Four

For the first time in a long time, perched on the edge of a slightly moss-covered bench in the shadow of a giant oak tree, Steph found herself grateful for the too-warm weather that clung to the air around her like a blanket. Making it feel challenging to inhale a full breath as the humidity made the air feel more like a liquid than the mixture of gases it actually was, and causing sweat to trickle down her overheated skin.
It wasn't that Steph had suddenly developed a liking for the blistering heat which she had despised since she was a child, always preferring to be cold and snuggling up in layers of warm clothing under soft blankets rather than being too hot. No, it was that she was pleased to be having the experience of watching the sunset over the horizon without worrying about her frozen arse getting stuck to the bench beneath her or catching hypothermia.
Not that it would matter if I did now, she thought to herself. Perhaps it would actually be a blessing to come down with some kind of flu or cold. The kind that would make me slightly delirious before I have to walk into that centre in thirty hours. Maybe that would make it easier, if she was out of her mind with fever and unable to comprehend what was happening to her. .
Thirty hours. How has it gone so fast? Steph wondered, tapping her foot against the dried dirt underneath the bench and watching as tiny puffs of soil blew into the still air, falling almost instantly back to the ground. It felt to her like it had been just moments ago that the culls had been announced when she and Crystal had been interrupted in the middle of a snowy afternoon by Professor Jones springing out of their wrists and informing them that something like a third of the world's population was going to be disposed of by its governments. Steph couldn't quite wrap her head around the fact that half a year had passed since that day. She didn't even want to think about how many other people, just like her, had sat on this very bench watching the sun dip behind the hills in the far distance in the evenings before their end of life date came around, contemplating their lives and all that they were leaving behind. .
How had she been so unlucky? Steph asked herself for the hundredth time, feeling the weight of the depression which had become her closest companion settling on her shoulders once again. So far, the only other person she knew who had been called up in the cull's was the waiter from work. He was more of an acquaintance than an actual friend, and whilst she knew that hundreds of thousands of people worldwide had been handed the same fate as her, it seemed unfathomable that she was the only one in her social circle who had been received an alert, not that her circle was particularly big, she could count her friends on one hand.

Steph was glad that the people she cared about weren't having to face the same fate as she was of course, still, it was hard to know that everyone else's lives would just continue as normal when hers was about to be snuffed out. Except for Tom's. Not that she could really count him among her nearest and dearest, as much as she might once have hoped to have done, one day. One day in a future which no longer existed. Where the possibilities were endless and Steph could allow herself to dream about all kinds of unlikely scenarios coming true. Kind, caring, sweet and considerate Tom. The man who wanted nothing more than to help people. To cure the sick, comfort the dying and give people a better chance at a longer, happier life. If the fates could be so callous as to have drawn his name out of the proverbial hat, Steph shouldn't be surprised that hers had come out too. She was no one, nothing. She had no grand aspirations or plans to try and make the world a better place. Until the last few months, Steph had barely given much thought to her future, she didn't have the time. Every waking moment was spent trying to find enough money and food just to survive to the next day. Planning for the future had always seemed impossible. Steph was just a waitress, scrambling to get by day to day on a meagre wage, with no real education behind her and very few prospects. If someone like Tom had ended up with their head on the chopping block, why shouldn't someone like her too?

Not for the first time since she had received her alert, thoughts of running ran through Steph's mind. She could throw a few items of clothing in a bag, and a couple of her precious books and just start walking, see how far she could get before the authorities caught up with her. The thought was incredibly tempting, but entirely unrealistic. Steph had no idea how to fend for herself on the streets. She wasn't resourceful like Crystal, wasn't well built and strong like Jose at work or even clever like Tony, and she didn't have a penny to her name. Steph knew that there was just as much chance of her tripping over her own feet and breaking her leg or starving to death in some huge field in the countryside as there was that she would find a safe place of refuge. Besides, the Cull Enforcement Agency had made it very clear that anyone who didn't show up for their execution would be tracked down and killed anyway. Every evening for the last week when Steph had caught snippets of the news at work or projected onto the high rise buildings in town, she had seen footage of C.E.A agents going from house to house, kicking down doors and dragging out people who had failed to turn up to their population control centres at the appointed date and time. Steph had watched in horror as grainy bodycam footage had shown screaming men and women being dragged from their homes without so much as a chance to say goodbye to the loved ones that they were leaving behind, before being bundled into sleek black cars, never to be seen again.

Why prolong the inevitable? Why put her friends and family through the distress of having agents knocking on their doors and questioning them about Steph's whereabouts, possibly even arresting them if the agents thought for one minute that they were helping to conceal her. Steph couldn't bear the idea of someone she cared about being arrested and potentially facing the death penalty all because she was too scared to face up to the hand that life had dealt her.

Shaking her head to try to rid her mind of such depressing thoughts, Steph focused on counting the different shades of red and orange emitted by the slowly setting sun far off in the distance. Have sunsets always been this beautiful? She wondered, or was it just because she knew that this was the last one she would ever have the chance to truly take in that was making it seem so magical?

There was no point in dwelling on the things she could not change. All Steph could do now was try and fortify herself for the next couple of days and attempt to work out how she was going to find the courage to walk through the doors of that centre and allow a stranger to pump poison into her veins without screaming at the top of her lungs and making a fool of herself.

Chapter Thirty-Five

Initially, Steph didn't notice the sound of the dried grass crunching under the sole of someone's shoe behind her, so engrossed was she in watching the setting sun. It wasn't until she felt the bench depress slightly as the unknown person lent a hand onto the backrest next to her that she realised that she was no longer alone.

"Steph?" a familiar voice called over her shoulder, and Steph could swear she felt her heart physically skip a beat.

Dragging her gaze from the peaceful sunset, Steph turned slightly on the seat and looked up into the same pair of stunning green eyes that she had found herself dreaming of more and more lately and forced herself to find a smile for the man behind her. She had very much wanted to be alone tonight, to allow herself to get lost in her own thoughts and prepare herself for the things to come, but if there was anyone else she knew who could understand how she was feeling at the moment, it was Tom. She couldn't remember a time when she had ever been disappointed to see him and this evening was no different.

"Hey, Tom." She said, her voice cracking slightly due to her not having uttered a word since earlier this afternoon when she said goodbye to Crystal at their flat and headed out for her evening walk after an early dinner.

"Here to watch the sunset?" Tom asked her.

"Yeah, I thought I should, you know, before Monday," Steph admitted, not seeing the point in trying to disguise her motives from him when it was highly likely that his were the same.

"Great minds think alike, I guess. Or perhaps damned minds." Tom replied, and Steph thought she could hear a trickle of frustration cutting through his words.

"Do you mind if I sit? Will I disturb you?" Tom asked, starting to edge his way around the bench.

When he left home this evening, he had been determined that this was something he wanted to do alone. Watch one last sunset whilst he still could, enjoy the peace and quiet and solitude and try and prepare himself for what was to come. However, when he had seen the familiar brunette sitting gazing down the hill, seemingly lost in a world of her own, he had felt drawn to her somehow.

Probably because of all the people that Tom knew, Steph was the only one who could truly understand what he was going through at the moment he realised as Steph nodded at him and he took a seat on the bench beside her. Tom's family and the few friends he had told about his alert had been doing their best to comfort him over the past few weeks. However, none of them truly understood, and he couldn't bear

the pity-filled looks on their faces whenever they saw him.
It didn't even matter if the subject of the culls came up or not. He knew that it was the only thing that the people he came in contact with could think about each and every time that they saw him. Tom knew, as well as he knew that the setting sun on the horizon would rise again tomorrow, that they all felt sorry for him and that not one of them knew what on earth to say to him anymore.
There was no light chit-chat about work or hobbies. No conversations about upcoming summer plans or making arrangements to hang out. There was just the perpetual cloud of his imminent death hanging over all of their heads. So much so that Tom had pretty much stopped bothering to hang out with his friends at all anymore. He hadn't joined them for their weekly pool game at the local pub in over three weeks. It was just too difficult to hold his tongue as they all let him win every game he played as though it would somehow improve his situation and all clamoured to pay for his drinks in case it was the last opportunity they had to do so. Tom hated it when they all suddenly went deadly silent whenever he rejoined them after a trip to the bathroom because they feared whatever future plans they were discussing might be too painful for him to hear. It made him feel like an outcast. As though he were already dead, just a ghost walking among them. It was easier to stay home.
Well, almost. Home was just a different version of the same thing, really. His brother could barely manage to be in the same room with him anymore and tended to suddenly have urgent homework that he had to do or a shower he had to take right that second as soon as Tom walked in the room. Not knowing what to say and acting as though Tom were already gone by distancing himself from him as much as possible. His baby sister simply stared at him with wide, watery eyes every time he saw her. Her tiny hands shaking as she wrung them in her lap, trying to hide her distress from the brother she had idolised all her life. Their mother, on the other hand, was still living in a dream world where she thought that Tom was somehow going to be handed a reprieve at the eleventh hour and hadn't even begun to process what was about to happen to him. Tom honestly wasn't sure if that was better or worse than seeing her break down and cry again. And his dad? Well, Jack Walker was so exhausted, so traumatised from working at the population control centre that he barely managed to keep his eyes open through the family dinners that their mother insisted on preparing every night, which lately, had always consisted of Tom's favourite dishes from his childhood.
When he caught Steph's gaze, Tom saw none of the pity that he was so used to having reflected back at him shining from her hazel eyes. She

didn't look at him as though he were a dead man walking or as though she needed to tread carefully so as to not upset him. She just looked like Steph. The woman who had trained him when he first started working behind the bar and who, more recently, had served him in the restaurant, always greeting him with a smile and remembering how he liked his steak cooked no matter how long it had been since he'd been in there for dinner.

"Kind of cliché, isn't it?" Tom said, breaking the silence after a few moments, and Steph raised an eyebrow at him questioningly. "Two people whose lives are about to end spending their final Saturday night watching a sunset." Tom clarified for her.
"Yes, I suppose it is." Steph smiled back, and once again, Tom was amazed by her ability to appear so calm as her voice didn't waiver.
"How are you dealing with all this so well?" He blurted out without really thinking whether he had any right to ask her such a personal question. It's not as though they were close or had any contact with one another outside of the restaurant that he visited every few weeks.
"Huh?" Steph asked, turning to face him, her eyes wide in surprise.
"I mean, look at you, sitting here calmly watching the sunset, managing to smile for a near stranger. Aren't you angry?" He asked incredulously.
Steph sighed deeply as she considered Tom's question, twisting her hands in her lap as she tried to put her thoughts into order before responding.
"Angry? No, Tom, I'm not angry." She began, watching his expression closely as she spoke. "I'm frustrated, hurt, sad, and more terrified than I ever knew it was possible to be. But I'm not angry. Not anymore."
"That's crap!" Tom shouted, jumping to his feet and beginning to pace in front of the bench, partially blocking Steph's view of the last few rays of the rapidly setting sun behind him.
"You're not angry that some computer somewhere, programmed by someone you've never met, in a place that you've never even been to, spat out your name out of all the millions it could have chosen and decided that you had to die?" Tom shouted, his frustration getting the better of him. "You aren't pissed off that on Monday morning, you and I have to hand over our lives to the government so that other people might have a chance to live a little longer? 'Might' being the important word there, as no one actually knows if these culls will make the slightest bit of difference. Maybe it's all too little too late. Maybe no amount of government-sanctioned murder can save humanity now! Maybe we've already caused too much damage to the planet, and all any of us can do is enjoy whatever time we have left before it all comes to an end?" He ranted, dragging his fingers through his too-long hair and

tugging at the roots as he paced back and forth in front of the bench, finally allowing some of the frustration that he had been feeling for weeks now to escape from him as the last rays of the setting sun dipped below the horizon.

Chapter Thirty-Six

Steph stared up at Tom with wide eyes. In utter disbelief as he paced before her, wondering where on earth he had been hiding all this anger. She had always thought of him as an incredibly well-composed person, not someone who was likely to lose their temper in public and start ranting about the world's injustices to someone he barely knew. It took her a moment to take it all in, and she had barely started to compose a response in her mind before Tom began speaking again.
"How aren't you angry that you have to say goodbye to your family? Your friends? That you have to walk out of your house on Monday and never see them again? That you've got to give up on all your dreams and everything you've ever worked for!" Tom's voice was reaching fever pitch now, his face reddening with each step he took as he vented his frustrations at the one person he felt he could be honest with. The one person who he thought would be able to understand how he felt.
"What good would it do for me to be angry, Tom? It won't change anything! Getting worked up and shouting at the top of my lungs about how it isn't fair isn't going to stop me from having to walk into that place any more than it is you! I guess I prefer to not spend my last few days in this world being angry. I'd rather try and be grateful." Steph said in a soothing voice, trying to calm him down.
"Grateful? What the hell is there to be grateful for?" Tom spat back, pausing his frantic steps for a moment to look at her in utter confusion.
"A thousand things!" Steph shouted, raising her voice to compete with his. "For starters, how about the fact that you're not the one who has to say goodbye to any of your family or friends? They are the ones who have to say goodbye to *you* and mourn *you*. Knowing all the while that there is nothing that they can do to change your situation, and then live with that long after you are gone. I wouldn't want to be in their shoes! I'm grateful that none of my immediate family or close friends got an alert. That none of them will have to go through what we will. Most of all, I am beyond grateful that they will get to live on and hopeful that the culls will allow them to do that in a more comfortable and sustainable way than they have been able to up until now." Steph said passionately, pausing to take a breath.
"I'm grateful that I will get to walk into that centre on Monday morning, knowing that I am at least trying to help make this world a better place. Probably in a more significant way than I would manage if I lived another fifty years! You might be right, and it might be too late. Maybe it won't help at all, but surely if there's even a chance, if there is even the remotest possibility that me surrendering my life might help other people to continue to live theirs, that's a chance worth taking?" She

finished.

Tom had stopped pacing now and instead stared down at the deep brown eyes of the waitress he had worked with, laughed with, sang with, and bored with his dreams for the future. The longer he looked at her, the more he replayed her words in his mind, the more Tom realised that not once in all that time had he ever really known her at all. With just a few sentences, she had made him see she was three times the person he could ever hope to be. Even with all of his hopes and aspirations of helping people through his chosen career, he had never been that selfless, that willing to give up everything for a load of people he had never met. Tom liked to think of himself as a good man, the kind of man that would go out of his way to help others and to make their lives better, but Steph? Steph was willing to lay down her life for them, and she wasn't even angry about it.

Swallowing the lump he could feel rising at the back of his throat, Tom retook his seat on the bench and rested his elbows on his knees, cradling his head in his hands as he stared down at the sun-bleached dirt beneath his feet in the last few moments of sunlight, cursing his temper and his harshly spoken words.

"I'm sorry." He mumbled to the ground, unable to look up and meet Steph's eyes.

"Don't be." Steph shrugged. "I didn't say that there was anything wrong with being angry, or that you don't have any right to be. In your shoes, I would probably be much more pissed off than I am. But then, I was never going to amount to much anyways. It's not as much of a big deal to me, I guess." Steph admitted, wanting to offer Tom some kind of comfort as she could see how much her words had bothered him.

"I don't deserve to live any more than anyone else does, Steph," Tom said quietly. "But yeah, I'm angry. I wish I weren't! I wish I could be calm and composed like you and walk into that place with my head held high, but I just don't know how to be. I don't know how to stop being so damn pissed off." He admitted, clenching his teeth to try and hold in his temper.

"Calm and composed? You think I'm calm and composed?" Steph asked incredulously, and something in the tone of her voice caused Tom to finally meet her eyes.

"Tom, I'm terrified! Every night for weeks now, I've had this recurring nightmare where I get to the front of the queue at the centre and just fall apart and start sobbing. Begging them to let me go until they finally have to carry me kicking and screaming into that God-forsaken place. I can't even begin to describe how scared I am and how hard this has all been. But I know that if I fall apart now, that will be it. I won't be able to put myself together again. And there are people in my life that I don't want to see me like that. Well, just one person, really, but still, I won't allow myself to become a blubbering mess and cause more pain for her. What you see as composure is nothing more than a carefully conceived act to try and keep myself in one piece!" Steph told him, her voice quivering over the words as tears pricked the backs of her eyes. Don't cry. Don't cry. She repeated in her mind, trying desperately not to embarrass herself any further in front of the man she had once hoped would become more than just someone she used to work with.

"I've been having nightmares too," Tom admitted, suddenly wanting to comfort the woman beside him and let her know that she wasn't alone in all of this, that someone else understood. "I don't know how I'm going to find the strength to walk in there. Into that place. The last thing I want to do is embarrass my family and the people I am leaving behind by causing some huge scene."

"What if..." Steph began but cut herself off mid-sentence.

"What if what?" Tom probed.

"Nothing, it was stupid, don't worry."

"Steph, I just threw a tantrum worthy of a five-year-old in a public park, and you're worried about sounding stupid? Just tell me what you were going to say." Tom pushed, curious now.

"I was going to suggest that maybe, well, what if we went together, on Monday, I mean. We could meet in the queue and try to keep each other strong?" Steph finally managed to reply.

So much for being better off on my own. She thought to herself as she waited for Tom to respond, unsure whether she wanted him to decline her offer or not. The reasons she had given Crystal for not wanting her to come to the centre with her rang in her ears as she sat on the bench, and whilst Steph knew that they were as true now as they had been when she had said them to her best friend, something in Tom's expression, in the way he looked so dejected and scared, had forced the offer out of her lips before she'd had time to really think it through. As much as Steph knew that she would be stronger on her own than with Crystal, she also knew that she could not stand in that queue worrying about Tom the entire time. Wondering if he had managed to hold himself together, if he had already gone inside before her or if he was still lingering outside on the street after she struggled through the doors. Wondering if he was dead already before she'd even stepped inside. Steph could be strong alone, yes. But she knew she could also be stronger for him if he needed her to be.

"I'd like that, Steph. Thank you." Tom replied, and when she saw what she thought was the ghost of a smile flutter over his full pink lips, Steph knew that she had made the right choice.

Chapter Thirty-Seven

As the sky above Tom and Steph's heads darkened, fading from the reds of the sunset to a deep purple and then eventually to a foreboding black peppered with tiny yellow pin-prick-sized stars shimmering back at them in the moonlight, the silence between them dragged on.
The only sound in the park was that of the animals that still managed to make their homes in the tall trees waking up for the night and starting to scurry around in search of food or water. Steph sat contentedly, listening to the nature around her coming to life and trying her best to enjoy the peace that the serene scene provided her. She could still feel the tension rolling off Tom in waves though, almost believing she could reach out and touch it because it was so palpable and she began to rack her brains for something, anything that might lighten the mood a little. She knew that it was probably a long shot, that with their impending doom so close at hand now, the chances of either one of them being able to overcome their dark thoughts and actually feel something close to happiness for more than a few fleeting moments was a long shot but, she would never forgive herself if she didn't try. Above all things, Steph knew that she had always been a people pleaser. She couldn't bear to see those that she cared about in pain and had embarrassed herself on more occasions than she cared to remember trying to cheer them up. So why change that now? On her penultimate night on earth. Might as well go out with an embarrassing bang, she thought to herself.
"Dum. Dum-dum dum, dum-dum dum." Steph began to hum quietly, gradually increasing her volume as Tom turned to face her, eyebrows raised high on his forehead and a curious expression on his tired face as he tried to work out what on earth she was doing.
"Dum. Dum-dum dum, dum-dum dum." She repeated, more loudly this time, before reaching her hands out in front of her and tapping them against her thighs, finding the rhythm and thumping out a drum beat which was the familiar introduction to one of the songs that they had spent countless evenings singing behind the bar together at the top of their lungs what felt like a lifetime ago now.
It took Tom longer than he cared to admit to catch on to what Steph was doing, he was so focused on using all of his energy trying to keep his anger at bay that he wasn't even really paying much attention to her at first. However, as she began pretty much assaulting her own legs, using them as her own personal drum kit and making the rickety bench beneath them start to shudder in protest at the sudden movement, he felt the unfamiliar sensation of a smile tugging at the corner of his lips. It took two repetitions of the introduction to the old classic AC DC rock song, 'Back in Black', before Tom couldn't help himself anymore. On

the third round, he began to sing along to Steph's backing track horribly off key and probably out of time, but he couldn't find the energy to care.

"Back in black, I hit the sack. I've been too long. I'm glad to be back. Yes, I'm, let loose from the noose that's kept me hanging about." Tom began, becoming bolder and bolder with each line. By the time he reached the chorus, Steph was singing along with him, still hammering away at her thighs, which Tom was sure must be red raw under her thin blue jeans by now, but he couldn't find it in himself to try and halt her enthusiasm. He was enjoying the moment of unabashed stupidity far too much.

Steph squealed in an almost childlike manner when Tom suddenly jumped onto his feet and plucked an imaginary air guitar from nowhere. He began strumming away into the night on an instrument only he could see as they continued to sing away together. A pair of kids in their early twenties without a care in the world. That's what they must look like to the other people walking through the park this balmy Saturday night, he mused. Perhaps a girl and a guy out on their first date, or maybe two old friends getting lost in the music and forgetting the troubles of the world around them, which seemed to grow more significant by the minute.

When the song came to an end, with a final few vigorous slaps to her thighs from Steph and an extended air guitar solo from Tom, Steph found herself blushing profusely as an elderly couple walking a huge German shepherd on a path nearby that she hadn't noticed until now, raised their hands and began to clap politely, both smiling down at the young pair as Steph bent her head in embarrassment. Tom, on the other hand, felt no such shame and turned to face the couple, taking an exaggerated bow and tipping an invisible hat on his head, as imaginary as the guitar he had just been strumming, all with a huge smile plastered across his face and his eyes sparkling in the light of the full moon that now shone brightly over their heads. The sound of laughter caught Steph's attention, and she finally glanced up to see the old man chuckling happily at the sight of them, and she sighed. Well, at least I made someone laugh. She thought to herself.

"Thank you. Damn, I needed that." Tom chuckled, taking a seat back on the bench beside her. "It feels like all I've done lately is think about this death sentence I have hanging over my head. I can't remember the last time I lost myself in a song like that, or even just enjoyed myself for a few minutes."

"Mission accomplished then," Steph announced. "I just wanted to take your mind off things. Even if just for a moment."

"You certainly did that. Do you have any other tricks up these short sleeves of yours to stop me from going crazy tonight, then, Miss

Moore?" Tom asked, stretching out and tugging lightly at the hem of Steph's T-shirt sleeve.

He could already feel the all-too-familiar cloud of despair starting to descend upon him, and he was desperate to hold it back just a little longer. Tom was also feeling guilty, knowing that he should really be getting home. That his mother would be worrying about him and that his empty place at the dinner table this evening would have already caused her more pain than he wanted. As much as he loved her, loved all his family, right now, Tom needed to be a little selfish, and he thought that he deserved that on what would be his last ever Saturday night.

"Hmm. Let me think." Steph said, placing a finger to her lips in an exaggerated pose of contemplation and spinning to face him on the bench, hiking up her legs and crossing them beneath her on the wooden slats as Tom watched her intently.

"How about. Instead of us sitting here dwelling on what the future holds for us, we look back into our pasts for a moment? Tell me a good memory. Any memory, the first one that pops into your head that makes you happy." Steph suggested, folding her hands under her chin and staring up at Tom, waiting for him to oblige her. Unsure anymore if her attempts at distraction were more for him or for her.

"A good memory, huh?" Tom said, racking his brains for a story to tell her.

He had never really been much of a storyteller, preferring to read books or watch movies and allow other people to transport him into their worlds rather than try and bring them into his. Something in the hopeful expression on Steph's face and the curious look in her deep eyes staring up at him patiently made him want to please her though, to repay the favour she had just done him in distracting him for a few minutes. When, after a few moments, a memory came to him, he knew that he wouldn't be able to do it justice, not really, he wouldn't be able to paint the picture well enough for Steph to feel like she was seeing it through his eyes or feeling what he felt that day, but Tom figured he'd give it his best shot anyways.

"Alright, so it was about ten years ago, I think. I was around thirteen or fourteen, something like that. Me and my family were on our annual holiday to Greece. Every year when I was a kid, my parents would drag us back to this tiny little island called Alonnisos, the same island they met on by chance when they were both vacationing there with their parents when they were teenagers. Anyway, we're on this island, staying at the same old resort, and we've been there for nearly two weeks. During that time, we've done basically nothing as a family. My younger brother and sister had enrolled in the kid's club at the hotel and spent all their time there doing arts and crafts and learning strange Greek party dances. My mother had pretty much moved into the spa. I'm pretty sure she was trying to pay them enough money to refurbish the entire place by booking herself in for every treatment they offered at least twice. And my dad, well, he spent most of those two weeks closeted away in the hotel room on his laptop. Working on some presentation or another that he was hoping would get him the promotion he was so desperate for." Tom began

"And where were you?" Steph asked him

"Anywhere they weren't, pretty much. Honestly, I spent most of my time doing what most boys that age do, following around a pretty girl." Tom admitted with a wink, and he could have sworn he saw a flash of something like jealousy or perhaps even anger cross over Steph's features as he spoke. Must have just been a trick of the light, he convinced himself after a moment's pause, carrying on with his story before she could ask any more questions.

"The day before we were due to fly home, my mother, having run out of treatments to try, decided in her infinite wisdom that we should do something together, as a family, and went off and hired us a boat for the day. Nothing grand or anything, just a little speed boat with enough room for the five of us to clamber aboard and go and explore the surrounding Aegean Sea."

"That sounds lovely," Steph said honestly, wishing her family had ever been able to afford such luxuries.

Even before the world went to hell and flights became something only the rich and celebrities could afford, her family had never been well-off enough to go on foreign holidays. They had to make do with ten days in a caravan in Devon most summers, where they spent the majority of their time hiding away from torrential rain storms, which seemed to somehow always decide to hit the west country whenever they ventured near it. I was cursed even then, Steph thought as Tom continued his story.

"In theory, it was sure. In reality, though, my dad, the well-educated doctor, had never attempted to drive a boat once in his life, so it wasn't exactly the day out that my mother had hoped for. My little sister got sick from dad's abysmal attempts to control the boat and spent most of the trip with her head in a bucket, and mum spent the entire time berating my dad for not taking better care of us. It was during one such argument while we were perilously close to a cove that my dad turned to shout more directly at her over the sound of the roaring waves and, in the process, crashed the boat into a nearby bunch of rocks."

"He didn't!" Steph exclaimed.

"Yep. Not only did he crash it, but he basically tore a hole in the side of the thing bigger than the bucket that Emily had been puking in all day. The boat started taking on water, flooding the engine and leaving us stranded. There was a radio on it, and we called for help, eventually managing to get around the language barrier and explain the trouble we were in. But it was getting dark by that point, and they said they couldn't send anyone to get us until first light due to the shallow waters around the cove, which were filled with, you guessed it, sharp and dangerous rocks." Tom continued giving Steph an exasperated look.

"So, what did you do?" Steph asked, enthralled by his tale.

"The only thing we could do. We packed up our few meagre supplies and waded through the water until we reached dry land, which thankfully wasn't all that far away, which I was grateful for as they made me carry my sister on my back, seeing as how she couldn't swim and was still unsteady on her feet from having been so sick. We ended up having to spend the night there, in this sort of cave, I guess, which was more just a hollow that had been cut out of the rocks by the tide. All huddled together under the one and only blanket that we'd thought to bring with us and eating half-stale sandwiches which my mother had acquired from the hotel before we'd set off that morning."

"God, that sounds... horrible! I thought I asked you to tell me a good memory?" Steph said, confused. She couldn't work out why *this* was the memory that Tom had decided to share with her. It didn't sound particularly happy, and she was sure he must have some more pleasant ones that he could have chosen instead.

"You did, and I am," Tom told her confidently, turning to face her on the bench and giving her his full attention. "You see, we might have been stuck in a cave in the middle of nowhere for the night with extraordinarily little to eat and only that one blanket between the five of us, but we were together. For the first time that trip, we were all in one place, with no laptops, no spas, no kids' entertainment, nothing. Just each other. And it turned out to be one of the best nights of my life. I remember after everyone else had fallen asleep, I was asking my dad what had made him want to become a doctor and why he had chosen a career that took him away from his family and took up so much of his time? He told me that all he ever wanted was to help people, that he wanted his life to have meant something. He felt that if he managed to save just one person, someone's child, someone's father, then all the time he was away from his own family was worth it. That was the night I decided to become a doctor." Tom finished, smiling fondly as he remembered the memory.

"That's beautiful. What your father said, I mean. You guys sound remarkably similar." Steph said.

"Hardly." Tom scoffed. "Other than our chosen profession, my dad and

I are like chalk and cheese. The other reason why that memory is special to me is because it was the last time I can remember my dad talking to me without a look of disappointment in his eyes. He disagrees with me working for the national health service."

"I remember you telling me. You probably won't remember, but I asked you once, back when we were working behind the bar, why it was that you wanted to be a doctor. And you told me then that your father disapproved of the choices you were making." Steph said quietly, embarrassed to admit that she recalled that conversation from so long ago. The truth was though, she remembered nearly every conversation they had ever had as clearly as if it had happened yesterday.

"You remember that?" Tom asked incredulously. He could barely remember what he'd had for dinner last week, let alone the specifics of a random conversation shared during a shift at work years ago. He was amazed that someone he had thought about so little in the last few years, unless she was standing before him taking his dinner order, had bothered to remember something he had said in such detail.

"Yeah, I mean, you were so passionate in the way that you spoke about wanting to help people that night, so earnest and sincere, I don't think I could have forgotten it if I tried," Steph admitted, averting her eyes from his and looking out over the hilltop down into the town which was now shrouded in darkness. Only the few still open businesses and a couple of the larger houses on the outskirts of town were illuminated by electric lights, which seemed to pierce the darkness with their intensity. Needing to change the subject and get the attention off of herself before her face went any redder than she could already feel that it was, Steph asked, "Tell me, what happened with the girl?"

"Haha!" Tom laughed, a booming sound so loud that it seemed to echo off the surrounding trees and shake the bench beneath them. "I was supposed to meet up with her that night, the night we got stuck in the cave because we were both flying home the next day..."

"You missed your chance?" Steph asked, unsure if she was pleased or disappointed for him.

"That night I did, yeah. But the next day, when we were back at the hotel, and I was supposed to be packing up my stuff, I snuck out of my room and went to find her. She was in the car park with her family, waiting for their taxi to the airport. So I walked up behind her, grabbed her hand, pulled her behind one of those massive wheelie bins by the side of the hotel, and kissed her. She was the first girl I ever kissed." Tom admitted, unsure why he was telling Steph all of this. He had never once told anyone, not even his family or closest friends, that he had snuck off to steal a kiss from the girl he'd spent two weeks following around like a puppy before they had left the island. Tom thought it was a secret that he'd take with him to the grave. Well, It's not like I'm far off, he thought sarcastically.

"Did you ever see her again?" Steph couldn't help asking. She didn't mean to intrude or force a confidence where Tom wasn't ready to give one, but she couldn't seem to stop herself.

"Nope. We were meant to meet up again the next year at the same resort, but then the price of flights started going up, and dad got the promotion, but it meant he was working even more, so that was the last time we ever went to Alonnisos. I never saw her again."

The pair sat in silence for a few moments, mulling over the memory that Tom had shared, until another question picked at Steph's mind. Once again, she couldn't stop herself from prying.

"Do you think maybe that's why you and your dad don't get on? Because really, deep down, you're so similar? I mean, it sounds like you both want the same things. To help people, to make the world a better place. You may have different ideas about how to go about it, but the end goal is the same." She asked.

"Maybe. I don't know. Up until a few weeks ago, I'd have said my dad didn't see me as anything other than a disappointment. But now..." Tom trailed off, unsure if he was ready to tell Steph about his dad's recent change of heart.

"Now what? I mean, you don't have to tell me if you don't want to, but what could it hurt? It's not like I'm going to have time to gossip about it with anyone before Monday." Steph said with a forced giggle, trying to find the lightness in their conversation again but also enjoying this new intimacy between them and the fact that Tom seemed to be opening up to her, despite it being far too late to matter now.

"He took a job at the population control centre," Tom admitted so quietly that for a moment, he was worried that his words would get carried away on the soft breeze that was whistling through the park and that Steph wouldn't hear them at all. But his fears were unfounded. When he glanced up at Steph, he could see that she had heard him by the sight of her wide-open jaw, which had fallen slack in shock at his words. "That was my reaction as well, at first. Turns out, though, that in his own way, he only did it to try and help me. He said that he was there when I came into the world, and he wants to be there when I leave it as well, and he knew it's the only way he'd be able to be."

"Wow." Was all Steph could manage to say.

Her own parents hadn't even bothered to make the trip up to see her before her end-of-life date, and here was Tom's supposedly estranged father taking a job at possibly the worst place in the world on the off chance that he could somehow manage to be with his son when he was put to death. Swallowing hard, Steph felt tears prickling at the backs of her eyes. She quickly pushed them away before they had the chance to fall and embarrass her any further tonight.

"Yeah. Wow." Tom echoed as they both returned their gazes to the moon and stars above them, lost in their own thoughts.

Chapter Thirty-Eight

Doctor Lincoln Mahoney was alone in his office, pacing back and forth and internally debating with himself once again as to whether he was making the right decision. He had gone back and forth so many times in the last few hours that he had managed to give himself a pounding headache from arguing with himself, making things even more difficult and debilitating his ability to think clearly, something the older man usually prided himself on being able to do in almost any situation. Shaking his head in an attempt to clear some of the pain lingering at his temples, Mahoney rubbed his eyes with the back of his hand and squared his shoulders, finally coming to terms with his choice. He would just go along and see what it was all about. If he disagreed with what was said, he was under no obligation to stay, Mahoney thought as he made his way out of his office. Pausing briefly by the receptionist's desk out in the waiting room as he strolled as casually as he could towards the hospital's main entrance.

"I'll be taking my lunch hour outside of the hospital today, Anne. Please leave any important messages on my desk." He told the stout woman who was gaping at him like a fish. Yes, it was unusual for Mahoney to do anything other than eat a sandwich at his desk during the working day, but really, there was no need for her to look quite so surprised. He was as entitled to a proper lunch break as anyone else, not that he would be getting that today.

Mahoney could still feel the stunned receptionist's eyes boring into his back as he stepped outside and sucked in a lungful of clean, fresh air, well as clean as the air got around here anyways and quickened his pace. He only had an hour to get to his destination, learn what he could and return to the hospital, and the doctor knew that he couldn't afford to lose any time.

Mahoney had been surprised when he received the invitation to today's meeting from an unknown source. It seemed to come entirely out of the blue and was wholly unexpected. Whilst Mahoney had made no particular effort to conceal his distaste of the culls, not to mention the way that they were being handled by the Cull Enforcement Agency, he had not realised that his opinions were public enough knowledge to lead someone to believe that he would be interested in attempting to do anything to stop what was going on in the world either.

The note had appeared on his desk two days ago. Scribbled in thick black ink on the back of a torn-off piece of light blue paper which seemed to have someone's shopping list inscribed on its other side. It had been hidden amongst the piles of paperwork, prescription pads and assorted paraphernalia that often littered the doctor's desk. Had he not been intently searching for a particular piece of paper of a similar size on which he had jotted down the telephone number of a colleague in Paediatrics whose opinion he had wanted on one of his patients, he probably wouldn't have noticed it at all. It would have been thrown out in the trash when the cleaners arrived, or worse yet, seen by the wrong person and gotten him into all sorts of trouble even though Mahoney had not personally requested the invitation or to his knowledge, done anything to imply that he wished to receive it.

By nature, Doctor Mahoney was not a paranoid man, especially now that he was well past the point of middle age. He imagined that very few people gave him a second thought or paid much attention to him at all as he went about his daily business. However, today was different and much more was at stake. As he strode along the pavement away from the hospital and through the sun-drenched streets towards the outskirts of town, he couldn't help but continually sneak a glance over his shoulder to ensure that he was not being followed.

Every crunch of gravel in his vicinity, every tree that rustled in the midday breeze drew his attention, forcing him to prick up his ears and ascertain that wherever the noise was emitting from was of no consequence to him before he allowed himself to relax again. It wouldn't do to have anyone see him making this journey or discovering his destination. If Doctor Mahoney so much as had an inkling that he was being watched, he would turn back and try to make it appear as though he had just decided to take a stroll before returning to his office and the sea of patients waiting for him to treat them back at the hospital. Much to his relief, as Mahoney approached the street whose name had been scrawled on the blue note, he was very much alone. He was confident that no one had attempted to accompany him on his afternoon jaunt and heard nothing except the occasional chirping of a friendly bird overhead or the sound of a car driving past on the busier roads to the south as he entered the run-down old shopping centre and breathed a sigh of relief. The centre had been closed for several years now and seemed deserted as he followed the directions which had been drawn in a crude map on the message that he had received. So deserted in fact that Mahoney began to wonder if perhaps he had come to the wrong place or perhaps gotten the time wrong, surely he couldn't be the only person attending this meeting?

"Password." The gruff voice belonging to a burly man in his mid-fifties with a thick beard asked when Mahoney finally reached his destination, slightly out of breath and sweating into his shirt. He hadn't got the wrong place after all it seemed.

"Professor Peter Jones." Doctor Mahoney said clearly, easily remembering the name of the head of the C.E.A, which had been scribbled next to the map on his note as the password that would gain him entry to the meeting with a sly smile. Only a group like this would think to use their adversaries name as their password, he thought to himself as the burly man nodded and pushed open the door in front of him, gesturing for Mahoney to step inside.

It was eerily quiet in the large, disused room, which, from the mannequins scattered about haphazardly and the few remaining empty racks, appeared to have once been a clothes store. People of all ages, sexes and races almost entirely filled the space, but few seemed to be conversing. They perched on the edges of old countertops or on low plastic benches, which Mahoney recognised as the kind that people used to sit on to try on shoes when he was a much younger man and shopping for pleasure was something that ordinary people had the time, and the finances to do. The sheer amount of people startled him at first, not because he did not believe that this many people would be against the culls, but because he had not realised that so many would be brave enough - or stupid enough, depending on your point of view, to put themselves in danger of losing their very lives in order to support the opposition.

Mahoney knew all too well that if this place were to be raided, if the police or the C.E.A got wind of this gathering and stormed the store this very instant, then the authorities would be perfectly within their rights and the law to shoot every person here on sight without question, and the very thought caused a shudder to run down his spine. Once again, he questioned his reasoning for coming here today. Wondering if this was just a foolish old man's last-ditch attempt to make a difference in a world that he was soon to leave, and whether any number of people could ever be enough to fight back against such a global initiative. Mahoney kept a neutral expression firmly in place on his somewhat withered features as he walked towards the back wall of the room and found a space between the groups of people lingering there to rest his aching body against the cracking plaster.

"Good afternoon, folks. I know we all have other places that we need to be. I'm sorry to have dragged you away from your jobs and homes this fine Sunday lunchtime. As I'm sure you can appreciate, it's important that these meetings be held in utter secrecy and we have to pick our times carefully. After curfew, there's much more chance of them sniffing us out than there is in the middle of the day." A tall, bald man said confidently from a raised platform at the front of the store, which Mahoney realised was nothing more than several old wooden pallets stacked precariously on top of one another. Although the man didn't have a microphone, his voice carried easily to Mahoney's place at the back of the room, helped along no doubt by the utter silence that had fallen over the crowd the moment the man had taken to the makeshift stage.

"To those of you who haven't been to a meeting before, there's a few things you should know right from the start so that there's no confusion. We aren't what the media are trying to make us out to be. We aren't rebels trying to cause havoc in the streets or destroy the few businesses that are still operating, nor are we a bunch of idiots committing mindless acts of violence or destruction, so if that's why you're here, feel free to show yourselves out." The man said, nodding towards the doors to Mahoney's left and pausing his speech momentarily to let his eyes wander around the room to see if anyone would take him up on his offer. Not a single soul moved an inch.

"All we are is a group of like-minded people who want to see an end to this barbaric scheme that those in power have decided is the only way to save our species. We do not believe that the only way for the human race to survive is to kill off millions of innocent people and impose heartless laws which condemn the least healthy of our population to certain death from diseases which they could live with for years with the right treatment. Nor do we believe that the government has a right to tell us how many children we can have and start sterilising us as though we're nothing more than livestock. We intend to fight, and die if need be, to try and save those whose names were spat out by some computer halfway across the world and sentenced to death for no greater crime than the fact that they were born into a broken world." The man continued in a clear, deep voice which seemed to boom across the store and bounce off the walls behind Mahoney's head.

"Sadly, as many of you are already aware, our attempt to raid the population control centre on Bleecker avenue last weekend and liberate any survivors inside failed, many of our members were arrested and are now being held at detention centres around town waiting to be charged. We are hopeful that our brothers and sisters in arms will be liberated in time. But even if they are not, we will continue honouring them by fighting for the cause they believed in so strongly."

That was what happened last weekend, then. Mahoney realised, putting together the pieces of gossip that he had heard at the hospital with the man's words. That's why they've suddenly increased the security at the centre so much. He couldn't help but notice each morning as he'd arrived for work this week, that the number of guards standing outside of the population control centre had at least trebled since they first opened. Initially, Mahoney had thought it just a precautionary measure, due to the unrest that he had seen so much of in the news. It seemed that was an incorrect assumption if what this man was saying was true.

"We've asked you all to come here today to let you know that the next action we plan to take will happen at o-two-hundred hours this coming Tuesday morning. As usual, the exact location will not be disclosed to anyone but group leaders. Each person here, upon exiting, will be handed the name of a street on which, if they choose to take part in our next mission, they can report to by no later than midnight on Monday. There you will find a group leader who will escort you to the mission's location at the appointed time. As always, we recommend wearing dark clothing and covering your face as much as possible. Please bring any weapons you see fit, but be aware that we take no responsibility for you being caught with such items about your person. As many of you have no doubt noticed, I haven't introduced myself by name today, and there's an incredibly good reason for that. We can't have any of you running off and reporting us, now, can we? Anonymity protects us all." The man said, and the crowd let out a small chorus of low chuckles. "Every man and woman here should know that it's their choice whether or not to attend. No one will think less of you if you choose not to, but if you do attend, we cannot promise your safety or that you won't be arrested by Jones's thugs and subjected to the full force of the law." Doctor Mahoney noticed a few people turn their heads to talk in hushed whispers to those around them at this declaration, but he was unsure why. Surely these people had realised when they arrived here this afternoon, or even before then, that there was no honour amongst thieves? Once they were out on the streets, it would be every man for himself.

"That's it for today, folks. You'll be asked to leave in groups of no more than seven, so we can be sure we don't draw unnecessary attention to ourselves. You'll be given your meet-up address on your way out. Until tomorrow night. Stay safe, and remember, we all have the Right to Life." The man who Mahoney assumed was the leader of the R.T.L rebels finished, and the crowd in the room erupted into cheers and applause at his words.

Having stayed near the exit for the duration of the meeting, Doctor Mahoney found himself amongst the first to be ushered out by the same burly bearded man who had let him in, along with half a dozen other people of varying ages. As promised, as they made their way through the oversized double doors, each of them was handed a small slip of folded coloured paper, which Mahoney hastily placed into his pocket and out of sight as he rapidly made his way down the long corridor of empty shops on the ground floor of the shopping centre.

Doctor Mahoney had not yet decided if he planned to attend tomorrow night's 'action' as the balding man had called it, the idea of dragging his tired old body out of bed in the middle of the night to go and walk the streets armed with a makeshift weapon didn't exactly fill him with enthusiasm. However, at the same time, a small voice somewhere in the back of his mind kept whispering to him, "Father, give us the courage to change what must be altered." The second verse of the Serenity prayer, which he had spoken to poor Thomas all those weeks ago now when he had first discovered that the young man, his protege, the boy that he had so much faith in, who he truly believed could do good in this world was to be put to death on the government's orders.

Granted, Mahoney had left that line out when he had recited the prayer to Tom, not wanting to give the boy false bravado or encourage him to behave in one way or another. His was a choice that every man had to make for himself. As much as Mahoney had guided his young apprentice as best as he could since he was assigned to him at the hospital, Mahoney was a firm believer in allowing moral decisions like this one to be made without pressure from outside sources.

The journey back to the hospital seemed much shorter than the one he had made to the meeting place on the edge of town. Probably because I was not looking over my shoulder the whole time, Mahoney thought to himself as he stepped through the automatic doors and flashed Anne, a cheerful smile.

"Any messages?" He asked her, not slowing as he strode past her desk towards his office.

"On your desk as requested, Doctor Mahoney," Anne told the senior doctor, still a little shocked that for the first time in the five years that she had worked here, the old man had ventured out of the hospital during working hours.

Mahoney acknowledged her answer with a quick nod as he pushed open the door, which read 'Staff only' that would lead him back to his office and to another afternoon of looking into the pained eyes of those he was unlikely to be able to save and dwelling on the next decision that he now had to make.

Chapter Thirty-Nine

Tom's final patient of the day slouched their way slowly out of his office shortly after six o'clock, limping slightly on the sprained ankle that Tom had just finished putting a support on to, A job that was usually the responsibilities of the nursing staff, but seeing as it was his very last shift at the hospital, Tom had decided to take on the task himself. Something that he had instantly regretted the moment the patient had removed his sock to reveal a rather smelly foot and Tom had been forced to breathe steadily through his mouth as he helped the elderly gentleman into the support, desperately trying not to gag on the stench. .

The moment the door closed behind the man, Tom felt the familiar wave of despair and hopelessness crash down upon his shoulders. That's it. He thought to himself. The last patient I will ever treat. In a few minutes, I will walk out of this room and out of the hospital for the very last time.

He had spent the entire day desperately trying to keep busy, seeing more patients in his eight-hour shift than he thought he had ever managed to before. Giving each and every one of them his full attention in an attempt to distract himself from the dark thoughts that plagued his mind. Tomorrow morning he would take the same route that he had every working day for the past year as usual, only this time, instead of heading into the familiar white-washed walls of the hospital, surrounded by the smell of disinfectant and the hoards of people waiting to be treated, Tom would instead join the queue on the opposite side of the road, the queue which would end in his death.

His mother had begged him not to come in to work today, as he had known she would. She had been pleading with him for weeks already to give up his position at the hospital and spend what little time remained to him at home with her and his siblings, building memories, but Tom just couldn't do that. He had spent the last six years of his life training to become a doctor. It was his dream. The thing that had kept him going night after night when the world around him seemed so incredibly hopeless, and Tom's mind had been set on spending as much time as he possibly could doing the vocation that he had been called to as a spotty teenager and that he loved so very much before it was too late.

Looking around the sparsely decorated office, Tom tried to take a mental picture of it in his mind to hold on to tomorrow. He had saved lives in this room. Cared for the sick and consoled the dying. Those were the memories that he wanted to be front and centre in his mind tomorrow when he walked into the building across the road. Memories of the people he had helped, the lives he had changed. Memories which would remind him that, although his life may have only been a short one, it was one during which he had managed to make at least a slight difference to the world around him.

The fading mint green paint on the walls, which he had always despised, finding it a cold and unwelcoming colour, suddenly felt comforting and safe. The stacks of paperwork on his desk no longer felt overwhelming and tedious, but like a security blanket that he wanted nothing more than to wrap around his slumped shoulders and lose himself in for the rest of the night.

That wasn't an option, though. Tom knew that. It would break what remained of his mother's fragile heart if he didn't arrive home in time for dinner tonight. And so, the paperwork would be left for his replacement, whomever that would be. They would have to take on the tasks that he had been unable to finish. They would have to sit in the rickety old desk chair with the one wobbly wheel and try to remain balanced and professional as patient after patient entered this room. Tomorrow this office would belong to them. Tom would be just a memory.

A knock at his door pulled Tom harshly from his thoughts and he called for the person to enter, wondering if Anne, the middle-aged receptionist, had forgotten that Tom's shift ended at six and had sent him another patient by mistake. A part of him couldn't help but hope that she had, he almost relished the idea of prolonging his last day just a little longer, anything to hold off what was to come for just another few minutes.

When the door swung open, creaking on its hinges and protesting at the movement, instead of a weary patient awaiting his help, Tom saw the familiar face of Doctor Mahoney as his mentor stepped into the room and closed the door behind him.

"Doctor Mahoney." Tom greeted the man, trying to force a welcoming smile onto his lips but failing miserably.

"Thomas, I'm sorry to disturb you. It is not my wish to hold you up, I am sure your parents are eagerly awaiting your return this evening, but I would like to talk to you briefly if you don't mind." Doctor Mahoney said in a tired voice, sounding as exhausted as Tom felt.

"Sure." Tom acquiesced, gesturing to Mahoney to take a seat and slumping back down into his own chair.

"I know that you are probably dreading the goodbyes which you will have to subject yourself to throughout the course of this evening and tomorrow, and I will, therefore, not force another upon you now. However, I want to remind you of a conversation that you and I had some weeks ago before you leave tonight." Mahoney began, and Tom frowned, trying to figure out which conversation his old mentor was referring to specifically.

"After discovering that you had received an alert, I attempted to make it clear to you that if you should ever require my help or assistance, you would be more than welcome to come to me. At any time. And I wish to reiterate that to you tonight, on the eve of your appointment. I do not wish to put ideas into your mind or encourage you to act against your conscience in any way. That being said, should you find yourself in a situation that you have not planned for, I want you to know that it would be my honour to assist you." Mahoney said cryptically.

Doctor Mahoney himself was not even sure what it was that he was offering to young Thomas at that moment. A place of refuge perhaps? Should Tom decide not to appear at his appointed time at the population control centre tomorrow? A shoulder to cry on throughout the night tonight should the young man require it? Mahoney didn't know that there was anything that he could possibly do to help the poor boy now, for that was all that he was, in truth, a boy. Barely starting out in life. Still, the old Doctor knew that he would never be able to forgive himself if he did not make sure that Thomas knew that he could go to him for anything that he might need.

"Thank you," Tom said quietly after several heartbeats of silence. "There is one thing you could do for me, actually." He continued after a moment,

"Of course, Thomas."

Shuffling through the stacks of paperwork on his desk, Tom struggled to find the notes he was searching for, eventually locating them at the bottom of the pile and smoothing them out with his hand before passing them to Doctor Mahoney.

"This young girl came in a few weeks ago with severe asthma. Her mother bought her back in today, and her condition isn't improving at all. I think she needs to be admitted, but when I tried to find a bed for her earlier today, I was told that there weren't any available." Tom said, and Mahoney nodded solemnly, all too used to being told there was no room left at the proverbial inn.

"Anyways, I'd be grateful if you could maybe try and see if you can get her in somehow. Even if it's just for a few days. I don't think she'll survive much longer out there." Tom said, glancing out of the small, discoloured window at the back of his office as he spoke.

"Ah, Thomas, always thinking of others. Right up until the end." Doctor Mahoney said with a smile. "It would be my pleasure to assist the young lady. I will see that she receives the care that she needs." He added.

"Thank you, Doctor Mahoney. Not just for this but for everything. I wouldn't be the man that I am today if it weren't for you." Tom sputtered, unable to meet the other man's eyes which were now shining brightly under the harsh fluorescent lighting in his office with unshed tears.

"No, no, Thomas, thank you. Thank you for reminding this old man that there are still good people in this world. That there is hope." Mahoney managed to reply as he stood from his chair and reached out a withered old hand towards Tom. Tom shook his mentor's hand firmly, trying to pour all the gratitude that he felt towards him into that one action before, without another word, Doctor Mahoney turned and left the room. Leaving Tom alone once more.

Chapter Forty

Monday mornings are invariably the hardest of the week, endless bands over the years had written songs lamenting their very existence. It was always the one day when it is harder to get out of bed than any other, when every task ahead seemed insurmountable, when all anyone wants to do is to remain hiding under the covers, in a warm and safe cocoon and pretend that the world outside does not exist.
The sun that shone through the thin, moth-eaten curtains in Steph and Crystal's flat casting a ray of glittering light over their bedspread just seemed to be adding insult to injury this morning. Surely it should know better than to rise so bright and full of life today of all days? Shouldn't thick grey clouds be covering its view of the world beneath it on a day that is destined to be so terrible? How could it bear to show its face? Steph wondered as she pushed back the covers and slowly slid out of bed as carefully as she could in an attempt not to wake Crystal, who still slept soundly beside her.
Steph didn't blame her friend; it wasn't her fault that Steph hadn't managed more than an hour or two's worth of sleep all night. Even that had been a restless sleep from which Steph had awoken with a jolt as the nightmare she was experiencing became too much for her brain to contend with. She had startled awake, a thin sheen of sweat coating her body as she struggled to catch her breath and rid herself of the images which had flickered behind her closed eyelids almost an hour ago now. She and Crystal had already stayed up into the small hours as it was, talking and reminiscing about happier times. Carefully avoiding any and all conversation topics about the future or even today's events, and enjoying the very last hours that they got to spend in one another's company before Steph had to make the long walk in the morning sunshine to the population control centre to surrender herself to be culled.
Creeping around the small studio flat, Steph gathered together the few meagre belongings which she was permitted to take with her to the centre and shoved them into the oversized paper bag that the two girls typically used to carry what little shopping they could afford to buy from the store home in. Every crunch and crinkle of the paper made her cringe and she was sure that before long, her best friend and roommate would be woken by the sounds which seemed incredibly loud in the silent room. But even after Steph had finished filling the bag, had tied her hair into a tight ponytail and pulled on her best pair of jeans and her favourite T-shirt, Crystal hadn't stirred.
Glancing at the government-issued watch on her slim wrist, Steph swallowed heavily as she flicked open the message which had appeared

at one minute past midnight last night and which she had read over and over again as the night drew on and she lay staring at the ceiling, willing sleep to overtake her.

Stephanie Moore. Your end-of-life date has arrived. Please report to the population control centre on Bleecker Avenue no later than 9am. Thank you for your sacrifice.

As if you gave me any choice in the matter. Steph muttered to her reflection in the tarnished mirror that hung on her bathroom wall which had a sizable crack in the top right-hand corner, trying to not let the nausea swarming in her empty stomach from overtaking her senses. She could not recall having ever been so terrified, at least in a few hours, it will all be over, she murmured to herself as mournful thoughts invaded her mind..

This is the last time she would ever stand in this bathroom. The last time she would ever brush her teeth in this sink. The last time she would ever curse when she caught her toe on the broken tile to the left of the toilet like she had done nearly every single time that she had walked in here barefoot since she moved in five years ago causing it to have a permanent purple bruise which shone back at her in the sunlight.

How had the time passed so quickly? Steph wondered, it seemed like just yesterday she had packed up her belongings and moved out of her childhood home and into the small studio, how could her short life already be over?

Making her way back into the bedroom, Steph gazed down at the misshapen lump hidden under the covers on the bed which was her best friend. Watching as Crystal huffed out a small puff of air through her plump lips before rolling over to her side with a slight moan. Steph knew that she should wake her, that Crystal would want to say goodbye to her before she left this morning, but she just couldn't bring herself to do it.

What could she possibly say to the woman who was more like family to her than any of her blood relatives? How could Steph find the words to tell Crystal how much she meant to her, how much she had changed her life for the better? How could she find the courage to walk out the door with Crystal staring after her with tears streaming down her rich ebony skin?

With one last longing look around the small room which had been her only refuge since her parents had moved away, Steph sighed in resignation, picked up the paper bag, careful not to rustle the material too much, and crept to the front door with tears tumbling onto her face which she didn't take the time to bother wiping away. Locking the door behind her, Steph quietly posted her key back through the letterbox and placed her palm flat against the wooden surface, just below the small brass numbers that hung slightly askew which indicated which flat she lived in, no, that she *had* lived in, and murmured against the wood, "Goodbye Crystal. I love you."

Chapter Forty-One

Tom stretched out his arms and ran his fingertips lightly over the soft bedding beneath him, yawning widely as his alarm blared from the bedside table next to him. He vaguely remembered seeing the luminous numbers tick by until the small hours last night and still lying awake long after the sun had begun to rise, casting strange shadows across the walls of his bedroom. If he had to guess, Tom would have estimated that he had managed to sneak in a couple of twenty-minute naps throughout the entire course of the night, and each of those had been quickly interrupted by yet another nightmare. Nightmares that were becoming all too familiar to him now and which no longer woke him in a cold sweat as he was just too used to the images which flashed behind his closed eyelids in the darkness, but they did still disturb his sleep.
It wasn't that Tom had somehow overcome his fear of what was to come today or the horrors that the nightmares held, but he had become used to carrying it with him. He was past the point of being able to feel the pain and fear that had accompanied the nightmares for the past few months and instead felt numb when they startled him awake. It was too late now. There was nothing that he or anyone else could do to change what was about to happen to him. All Tom could hope was that the numbness that he felt continued, that it stayed with him as he took the long walk to the population control centre this morning with his father and as he stood in line with the countless others destined to step through those doors today and meet their fate.
Tom dragged himself out of bed, stopping briefly to look at the mess of brown hair splayed across the pillow next to where he had just been lying. His morning routine of lifting the heavy dumbbell weights that sat in the corner of his room and stretching out his muscles seemed pointless now, but he couldn't help but do it anyway. Needing the comfort that such a long-standing tradition brought to him this morning. Tom needed to treat today like any other, to keep things as normal as possible if he had any hope of getting through what was to come.
His little sister Emily had knocked so quietly on his bedroom door last night that, at first, Tom had thought he had imagined the sound before she has slowly inched into his room and had tiptoed across the floor, wrapped in a thin pink blanket that Tom remembered her having had since she was a baby, and without a word, had clambered into the bed next to him. Tom hadn't said anything to her either. What was there to say? They both knew why she was there.
Emily needed to be near him while she still could, needed to spend as much time with him as possible before it was too late and as much as Tom had craved solitude in his final, restless hours, he hadn't had the

heart to ask her to leave.

Emily had fallen asleep quickly, clutching his outstretched hand under the covers and whimpering quietly into the darkness next to him as he had laid wide awake, unable to shut off his brain, staring up at the ceiling and cursing himself for spending his last night this way. His dad had tried to encourage him to sit in the study with him last night after their mother had fallen asleep on the sofa in front of some movie or another that they had only been half-watching, but Tom had declined. He and Jack Walker had managed to find some kind of peace in their relationship over the last few weeks, sure. Still, Tom didn't want to tempt fate by pushing things too far, and he feared that, in his anger and frustration at what was to happen to him today, he would have ended up saying something that he might regret. Something which he would no longer have the time to make up for or to take back.

He was sure that other people who were destined to appear at the centre today would have spent last night on this earth doing something more memorable. Perhaps getting completely wasted one last time with their friends or making love all night to their partner, but not Tom. He had spent his last night in much the same way that he had spent countless others throughout his life, waiting for an appropriate time to excuse himself from his parents' company before disappearing to the quiet and solitude of his room.

Tom showered and dressed quickly, somehow managing not to wake Emily even when he accidentally stubbed his toe on his chest of drawers and let out a flurry of expletives before he could stop himself. That girl could sleep through an earthquake, he thought, envying her. After picking up the backpack his mother had packed for him as if he were still a little boy and slinging it over his shoulder, he took one last look at the room that had belonged to him for his whole life before heading downstairs to the kitchen.

"I made you breakfast." His mother said in a quiet voice when he entered the room, tears already streaming down her face silently as she busied herself buttering toast and placing a fried egg on Tom's plate.

"Thanks, mum," Tom said, attempting to smile as she placed his plate on the table in front of him. The last thing he wanted to do right now was attempt to eat anything. He already felt sick to his stomach and he was sure that anything he forced down his throat would only make a reappearance again in an hour or so, maybe less. Tom couldn't bear to disappoint the woman who had fed him every day of his life though, and so he picked up his knife and fork and cut himself a small slice, placing it into his mouth and barely tasting it as he chewed methodically on the too-hot egg.

"Tom!" a frightened, high-pitched voice screamed from the hallway before Emily bounded into the kitchen and straight over to his side, throwing her arms around him and nearly upsetting the glass of water his mother had just placed on the table in the process.

"I thought you'd already left and that I had missed my chance to say goodbye." She sobbed into his shoulder.

"What? You thought I'd leave without saying goodbye to my favourite little sister? Not a chance." Tom replied, trying his best to keep his tone light. If there was anyone he could be strong for, that he *had* to be strong for, it was Emily. He never had been able to deal with seeing her cry.

"I'm your only sister." Emily spluttered through her tears, finally releasing him so that she could wipe her running nose on the sleeve of her pyjamas.

"Oh right, I forgot." Tom joked as Emily pulled up a chair and positioned herself as close to him as she could manage.

"We'll need to leave in about thirty minutes." Jack Walker interrupted them, pushing around the untouched breakfast on his own plate as he spoke.

Today was going to be the worst day of his existence, the most challenging day that Jack would ever have to live through, and the last thing that he was interested in doing this morning was lining his stomach with anything other than the strong black coffee that he so desperately needed after not sleeping a wink last night. Between his wife waking to sob on his shoulder frequently and his own dark thoughts, Jack had not managed so much as a moment of sleep. His tired mind needed as much caffeine as he could manage to consume if he had any chance of being able to function properly today.

Tom nodded at his dad from across the table, fully aware of how little time he had left in this house with his mother and siblings before he would have to leave it for the final time without Jack Walker's reminder. At least he wouldn't have to make the long walk to the centre alone, he thought. One step at a time. That was how he would get through today. Never looking too far ahead or dwelling on what was to come.

Step one was finishing as much of the breakfast his mother had lovingly prepared as he could manage. Step two would be more problematic. How was he supposed to say goodbye to them? He had spent a large portion of his restless night trying to come up with the right words to say to each of them and failing miserably. There was no guidebook for this, no hints in the end-of-life kit that the Cull Enforcement Agency had so kindly sent out to himself and others like him to direct him in the best way to get closure for both him and his family before he walked out of their lives for the last time.

"Tom? Can I talk to you for a minute?" Mark's cracking voice called from the doorway; Tom hadn't even noticed him come downstairs.
"Sure." Tom agreed a little too quickly, glad for any excuse to not have to try and force down any more of his breakfast and pushed his chair away from the table, standing up. "I won't be long." He reassured Emily, who was looking up at him with wide, wet eyes from her place by his side, and the young girl nodded dejectedly.
"Look, I don't want to do the whole family goodbye thing. You and I both know that mum is just going to cry through the entire time, and no ones going to be able to actually say what they want to say. So, I wanted to talk to you alone." Mark said, sounding much more mature than his sixteen years, and Tom nodded in understanding.
"I just wanted to say, I know I've not really been around much these last few weeks. It's not because I don't care or anything, just that I didn't know what to say. We were supposed to grow old together, you know? You were meant to teach me about girls, give a toast at my wedding. It's taken a bit of time for me to get my head around it all, but I think I've figured out what I need to say now. I want to say that I'm happy to have been your brother. I've learned a lot from you, you know. Things I don't even think you've realised you've taught me. And I'm grateful I've had someone so strong and so selfless to look up to. Also, don't worry about Em. It's gonna be hard on her, sure, but I'll look after her, I promise. I'll make sure that she's alright." Mark said quickly, finally performing the speech that he had spent most of the last few days rehearsing in the mirror in his bedroom to its intended audience.
Mark knew that his brother loved him, but he knew that of all of them, it would be Emily that Tom would be worrying about the most, especially after how she'd been behaving the last couple of weeks. So, he had figured the best thing he could do for his big brother now was to reassure him that he'd look after her, give him one less thing to worry about.
"Thanks, Mark. I'm grateful to have had you as a brother, too, even if you have been annoying since the day you were born. I wouldn't have changed you for anyone else." Tom told his younger sibling, throwing an arm around his shoulder and pulling him to his side.
"And Tom?"
"Yeah, buddy?"
"I'm really sorry that you have to do this," Mark muttered, looking down at his shuffling feet as he whispered the words to the carpet beneath him.
"I know you are. I'm sorry too. Sorry, I won't be around to do all those things with you, but I know you're gonna make me proud, right?" Tom said, looking into Mark's eyes when his brother finally raised his gaze

from the floor, eyes which were so very like his own.
"I'll try."
"I know you will," Tom reassured him, patting him on the shoulder once before leaving the room and his baby brother for the final time.

Chapter Forty-Two

"And how are you going to stop me, Jack, hmm? Are you going to lock me in the house? Why should you be the only one who gets to go with him?" Tom's mother shouted ferociously at her husband over the kitchen counter as he stared her down, willing her to see sense and listen to him for once.

Marion Walker very rarely got angry or raised her voice to anyone, but on the few and far between occasions that she did, it was as though she stored it up for years and suddenly allowed all her frustration to explode out of her at once, which was exactly what Jack was being confronted with now.

"We talked about this! Because Emily and Mark need you here, Marion. Do you think I want to walk into that place with my eldest child today? Do you think I am looking forward to it, gaining some sick satisfaction from taking this away from you?" Jack retorted, trying in vain not to raise his voice.

"I could at least walk with you to the centre; I could stand in the queue and get those last few precious moments with my boy before..." Marion pushed, before her words failed her. All the fight went out of her as quickly as it had appeared and she lost the ability to finish her sentence.

"Marion, please. Can't you see that I am trying to protect you? I need you to trust me. You don't want your last memory of Tom being him walking through those doors. You need to stay here with the children and remember him in this house, the house that we bought him home from the hospital to all those years ago. Remember him laughing, sitting in this very kitchen while you taught him his ABCs and read him stories. Remember the good times, Marion and let me take care of the rest." Jack pleaded with his wife, his eyes boring into hers as he tried to make her see, to make her understand that all he was trying to do was protect her.

The last thing that she or any mother needed was to go to that place, to see the long lines of broken men and women who were all someone's daughter, someone's son, awaiting their fate. She would break down, Jack knew that she would and if she were honest with herself, Marion would admit that she knew it as well. Jack wouldn't be in a position to take care of her, he would already be inside the centre, waiting for his son to walk in and meet his end. He couldn't worry about them both being out there. Not today. Today was about Tom. The whole reason Jack had taken this job, a position that was destroying him, carving a dark hole into his soul that he didn't think he would ever be able to fill, was to be there for his boy. He wasn't about to let anything jeopardise that now, not even his beloved wife.

"I'm sorry, Marion. But I'm going to have to insist. I need you to stay here." Jack begged, reaching across the counter and taking one of her small hands in his, noticing that he could feel the bones protruding through her skin. She had lost so much weight over the last few months. He sincerely hoped that after today, once she could start grieving properly, that things might get better. Honestly though, he didn't know how any of them would ever be the same again.

Marion stared up at her husband with tears glistening in her tired eyes. She knew in her heart that he was right, that the best thing that she could do was to remain here with her younger children and trust Jack to look after Tom as much as possible, but that didn't mean that her heart wasn't breaking at the very idea of watching her eldest child walk out of the door never to return again. He was Marion's firstborn, the one who had made her a mother, the child she had named in her mind years before she had even met Jack, let alone fallen pregnant. She had harboured so many dreams for him, so many aspirations for what he would become, and today, all those dreams would come to an abrupt end.

"Dad's right, mum," Tom said as he walked back into the kitchen, having lingered in the hallway and listened to their conversation. "I need you to stay here. Please?" He said in a quiet voice. He didn't want to guilt trip her into doing what he asked, seeing it as some kind of last request, but he'd play that card if he had to. The last thing Tom could cope with today was having his mother break down in the street outside the centre, there was no way he'd be able to walk inside if she were there beside him.

"But you shouldn't spend your last hours standing alone in that queue. You should have someone with you!" Marion cried, the tears falling freely down her face now, all composure lost.

"I won't be alone, mum. I'm meeting a friend there. You remember Mark told us about the waitress from the restaurant where I used to work who he witnessed get an alert? Well, it turns out we have the same birthday, which means we also have the same end-of-life day. We're going to queue together." Tom told his mum and watched as she attempted to regain control of herself.

"See, he won't be alone. Not for a minute. I promise, Marion." Jack told his wife.

Slumping down into a nearby chair, Marion admitted defeat. She knew there was nothing more she could say or do to try and convince them, and the last thing she wanted was for Tom's final moments in this house to be consumed by arguments.

"I should get your brother and sister. It's nearly time to leave." Jack said, glancing down at his watch before heading out of the kitchen.

Tom stood in the hallway, his backpack hiked up high on his shoulder, staring into the faces of the family that he knew he had spent most of his life taking for granted. Sure, they weren't perfect, but they were his, and he loved them more than he'd ever be able to put into words. He just wished that he had taken more time to try and show them that whilst he could.

"Well, this is it then," Jack said, reaching his son's side and standing as straight and tall as he could manage, attempting to put on a strong façade for his wife and children despite the deep, bone-crushing pain reverberating through his body.

"No! We must have more time! It's not enough time!" Emily wailed, launching herself forwards and throwing her arms around Tom's waist, burying her head into his chest as she began to sob.

"Sshh Em. It's okay. Everything's going to be okay. Mark is going to take care of you, alright? I need you to be strong now." Tom tried to console her.

It was taking every ounce of strength that he possessed not to break down, too. Every molecule of his body wanted nothing more than to cling to her for dear life and just stay here, safe in his home. For a moment, he seriously considered doing just that. Let them come and find me, he thought to himself. Why should I make it easy for them? Before he could make any rash decisions, Mark appeared before him and prised Emily out of his arms, taking her in his own and backing away from Tom with a look of steely determination in his eyes. No, I can't do that, Tom thought. I can't let them down. I can't embarrass them like that. What if the Cull Enforcement Agents come for me, and they find Mark instead? What if mum does something stupid trying to protect me and gets hurt? I have to be strong, he realised and squared his shoulders.

"I know I haven't said it enough, but I love you. All of you. Very much. Take care of one another." He told his family, looking each one in the eyes in turn before his mum reached out and took his hands in hers.

"I am so immensely proud of the man you have become, Thomas. And I love you too. More than you will ever know." Marion said, embracing him one last time as her heart broke. She would never know how she found the strength at that moment to step back from her eldest son and let him go, it was the hardest thing she would ever have to do in her lifetime, but somehow she did.

Tom took one last longing look at his family, standing in the small hallway of their home, his sister still clinging on to Mark for dear life and their mother standing behind them both, her fingers digging into Mark's thin shoulders, causing him to wince, and then he turned and pulled open the front door and walked out into the stifling morning air for the last time.

Chapter Forty-Three

The familiar walk to Bleecker avenue seemed shorter to Tom today than it had on any of the other countless occasions that he had made it over the last year when he had been heading to work. It felt as though time itself was conspiring against him, speeding up somehow just to make Tom feel as though he had even less time left than he genuinely did. The cracked pavement, boarded-up buildings, and crowds of homeless people that he passed every day on his way to the hospital seemed to fly past him in a blur as he and Jack Walker trudged along in silence, both wishing that they could think of something profound to say, something which might make today a little easier but, ultimately neither man had been able to come up with anything.

They were still a few streets away from the centre when Tom first began to notice the multitudes of other people around him heading in the same direction. Some walked alone, their heads bowed and their shoulders slumped as they dragged their feet beneath them. Tom could swear he could see the effort it was taking on their drawn features to continue putting one foot in front of the other and to not turn and run in the opposite direction and he couldn't help but wonder if his own face carried the same resigned expression. Others walked in small groups, clutching the outstretched hand of the person nearest them for comfort or had their arm wrapped tightly around a loved one at their side. No matter whether they were alone or not, all of the people Tom looked at had one thing in common, other than their destination, of course, every single person was utterly silent.

With the exception of the occasional muffled sob or whimper, the only sound that filled the streets was that of footsteps as the crowd walked down the long winding road. No one was making conversation, no one was attempting any small talk whatsoever, most people weren't even looking at one another. They just stared resolutely ahead of them. It was eerily quiet as the meandering cavalcade of people made their way along the roads, and the silence somehow made things feel all the bleaker. It seemed as though none of them had anything to say in their final hours, or perhaps, like Tom and Jack, they just couldn't seem to think of the *right* thing to say and so chose to say nothing at all.

Jack desperately searched his tired mind for some words of comfort to offer his son as the end of the long queue outside of the population control centre came into view, snaking down the street all the way to the corner, where the old boarded up newsagents sat abandoned, as he had seen it do every day since he had taken his position there. No matter how much he racked his brains, nothing that sprang to mind seemed to be quite good enough. It felt to Jack as though all the words in the English language that he had learned in his nearly fifty years of life had somehow abandoned him at this moment when he needed them the most. All that was left were the most basic of pleasantries or comments on the weather, which he couldn't bear to utter.

Cursing himself for the multitude of times he had failed the young man beside him over the years as he did it yet again, Jack came to a halt a little way back from the end of the line and turned to face Tom, forcing himself to look into the eyes of the child that had, for so long, been the one that he held out the most hope for, the one that he could see the most of himself in and had subsequently put the most pressure on and began to speak.

"I'm afraid this is where I have to leave you, Tom. My shift starts shortly." Jack said in a low voice, not wanting the crowds of people around him to hear his almost whispered words and realise that he worked there for fear that they might turn on him or alert the always present crowd of protestors across the street to his presence before he could reach the relative safety of the centre. Safe for me, he thought to himself, but not for Tom or so many others. "I will see you inside, I have arranged to be stationed on the floor which you will be taken to today, and I will be waiting for you. As I promised your mother, you won't be alone, son."

"Thanks, dad," Tom mumbled, feeling the heavy weight of his father's firm hand resting on his shoulder.

"You're meeting your friend here?" Jack asked, needing to reassure himself that he wasn't leaving Tom to stand out here on his own all morning, knowing how long it took them to process each new arrival and that it would be hours before his son entered the centre and Jack saw him again.

"Stephanie, yes, I'm supposed to be, although I don't know how I am going to find her in this lot," Tom admitted, raising his arm to gesture at the long queue of people ahead of him and wondering why he hadn't thought to arrange a specific meeting place with Steph. What if he couldn't find her? What if she thought he had abandoned her at the last minute and left her to queue alone?

"Alright, well, I guess this is it for now, then, Thomas. I will see you again shortly." Jack said, a lump rising in his throat as he patted his son on the shoulder once more and realised that this would be the last time he got to speak to him as a free man, outside in the sunlight.

"Yeah, see you, dad," Tom replied. Unable to tear his eyes from the man that raised him as he walked away,

Tom stood silently and watched as his father stepped out into the centre of the road, not bothering to even check if there were any cars around as the street was nearly always empty of traffic, and strode along the tarmac past the long line of the damned waiting on the pavement beside him without so much as glancing over at them once. It's like we're already dead. Tom thought to himself, even my own father is already treating us as though we aren't here.

Tom knew that his spiteful thoughts were unfair, that it was understandable that after weeks of working at this horrible place, Jack had realised that he had to behave this way just to get through his days. If Tom were honest with himself, he knew that if he were in his fathers position, he would do the same.

He's doing this for me. Tom reminded himself. He's spending his working hours in absolute hell, participating in things that no doctor should ever have to so much as witness, let alone take part in, for me. I shouldn't be spending what remains of my time judging him for how he needs to behave in order to get through it. Tom took a deep breath, turned away from the empty road, and slowly began to join the crowds of people shuffling their way forward into the long queue.

When Steph arrived on Bleecker avenue, she was startled by the sheer amount of people crowding along the winding pavement outside the centre. There seemed to be even more people here today than there had been when she and Crystal had visited a few weeks ago. Perhaps they're trying to get through the cullings more quickly, she thought to herself, scanning the long line of people huddled together by the dilapidated buildings, squinting her eyes into the bright sunlight in an attempt to see if she could spot Tom's chocolate brown curls in amongst the throngs of people.

As her tired eyes finally reached the end of the queue, she saw him. Standing with his shoulders hunched, Tom's hands were tucked deep into the pockets of his black jeans, his messy hair falling to his forehead as he focused on the ground beneath his shuffling feet. Breathing a sigh of relief at the sight of his familiar face, Steph squeezed past the other cull victims waiting on the pavement until she reached his side.

"Steph! I wasn't sure you'd find me. There's so many people here." Tom said when he saw the petite girl approaching him, feeling the tight knot in his stomach loosen somewhat now that he was no longer alone.

"Me neither, but here I am," Steph replied in a forlorn voice.

Tom hadn't expected his ex-colleague to be in a particularly good mood this morning. He certainly wasn't himself. Still, the dark circles surrounding her bloodshot eyes gave him pause as he looked down at her.

"Are you okay? Stupid question, I know, considering where we are right now, but you look..."

"Awful." Steph finished for him, self-consciously tucking a strand of hair which had escaped her tightly bound ponytail behind her ear. "I know. Tom, I think I've made a terrible mistake." She admitted feeling tears welling again in her eyes and marvelling that she had any fluid left in her after spending the entire walk to the centre crying.

Tom stood awkwardly for a moment, unsure what to do. In any normal situation, he would try and comfort the woman before him, tell her that everything would be okay and that he was sure that whatever mistake she felt she had made could be rectified. Those words would be meaningless today though, and they both knew it. Any chance they had had to make amends had ended when they stepped out of their homes this morning.

"Do you want to talk about it?" Tom asked her quietly as the queue shuffled forwards and the pair took a shaky step closer to the population control centre, which was growing ever closer.

"I... I..." Steph began, unable to stop the tears from falling now and cursing herself for the mistake which had been weighing heavily on her shoulders the whole way here. "I didn't say goodbye." She managed to finish, feeling the ache in her chest grow exponentially and wanting nothing more than to collapse onto the ground and sob her heart out.

"What? To who? Your parents?" Tom asked, shooting her a confused look.

A small, humourless laugh escaped Steph's chest, which caused Tom to look more incredulously at her.

"No, not them. We said our goodbyes. To Crystal. I didn't say goodbye to Crystal. She was sleeping when I left this morning, and I thought it was for the best. I thought it would be easier for us both to not have to put ourselves through that. But I had barely managed to reach the end of my road before I realised I was wrong. That I had made a huge mistake. Only it was too late. I didn't have time to go back. She's my best friend in the world, and I didn't say goodbye to her! I should have woken her up! I should have told her how much I love her, how much she means to me. And now, now I'll never be able to." Steph said quickly, the words tumbling over one another as she rushed to push them past her trembling lips.

Standing beside this woman who he barely knew, not really, and staring into her waterlogged brown eyes, Tom was suddenly struck by an overwhelming instinct to protect her. He wasn't sure entirely where it had come from. The only other time he could recall feeling this way was when he had watched his little sister Emily cry. He couldn't stop himself from reaching out and wrapping an arm around Steph's thin shoulders, feeling her vibrating next to him as she tried to compose herself and regain control of her emotions.

Tom couldn't imagine how he would be feeling in her position right now. There weren't many people he had felt the need to say goodbye to outside of his family. However, he could see from the look on Steph's face that she was very much regretting her decision.

"What if she never forgives me?" Steph whispered quietly into Tom's shoulder. Her words muffled as she spoke them into the fabric of his T-shirt.

"She will. Of course, she will. And I'm sure she knows how much you care about her without you having to tell her." Tom tried to reassure her. He remembered Crystal vaguely from his trips to the restaurant. She was hard to miss with her larger-than-life personality and a loud booming laugh that he'd often heard wafting across the tables while he'd been eating his steaks. "I'm sure that she'll realise that you were only doing what you thought was best for her, for both of you, and yeah, she'll probably be sad that she didn't get to say goodbye to you too, but she'll understand Steph, just like you would if the situation were reversed." Tom continued, and Steph sniffed audibly, pulling a crumpled tissue from the pocket of her jeans and blowing her nose.

Usually, Tom would have been uncomfortable standing on a public street, surrounded by strangers, as a woman cried on his shoulder. Today though, it didn't seem to embarrass him the same way that it might have done a few weeks ago. Perhaps it was the fact that he knew that in a few hours, nothing would matter anymore. Not what people thought of him and not who had overheard this conversation or witnessed Steph's distress. Nothing about him at all would matter. He would no longer exist.

Or maybe it was simply because he knew that the majority of the people surrounding them were not long for this world either and had bigger things to worry about. After all, most of them were crying too.

When the queue started to shuffle forwards again a few minutes later, Tom lowered his arm from around Steph's shoulders. She felt a cool breeze replace the warming touch of his skin against hers as he stepped away from her, and she instantly wished he hadn't removed his arm, which bothered Steph more than she cared to admit. The last thing she should be doing right now was focusing on how nice it felt to have his strong arm wrapped around her or how comforting the smell of vanilla and musk that flowed from his skin was. It had been a long time since Steph had been comforted by a man, years in fact, and she hadn't realised how much she had craved it until now. She mentally added that to the seemingly never-ending list of regrets in her mind which she would never have the chance to try and correct.

Maybe in another life, they could have had a chance, or perhaps if Steph hadn't been so shy and too scared to tell him how she felt about him on

one of the many times that their paths had crossed in the last couple of years, they could have scraped a few months together, a year maybe? Perhaps then she would have had the opportunity to feel more of his embraces and to breathe in other parts of him. But it was too late now. Just like it was too late for her to go back and say goodbye to Crystal, she thought to herself, and another tear rolled down her cheek.
Tom didn't even think about it before he reached out and took Steph's hand in his, entwining her small fingers between his own and squeezing them gently. The action was more of a reflex than an actual decision that he had to make. At that moment, he knew she needed him, and if he was being honest with himself, he needed her too.

Chapter Forty-Four

The morning seemed to pass by more quickly than usual, just like the walk to the centre had this morning, the sun rose higher and higher in the sky until it shone directly down over the heads of the people in line on the pavement where there wasn't even the smallest area of shadow that they could hide in to escape some of the heat.
Tom cursed himself for not thinking to bring more than one bottle of water as beads of sweat gathered on his forehead and his mouth felt as though he had shoved it full of sand. He and Steph had been standing out on the pavement for nearly three hours now, shuffling along slowly on trembling legs every five minutes or so when the line moved forwards as another person was admitted to the centre.
Part of Tom wished he had gotten here earlier and been nearer the front of the queue. The waiting was almost unbearable, it gave him too much time to think and his mind was conjuring up ever darker images of what lay beyond the doors of the centre ahead of him as he stood still clutching Steph's hand.
They had made some small talk over the time they had been standing here, just the odd pleasantry which sounded hollow and fake to them both before they lapsed into silence again. On several occasions, Steph's tears had returned, despite her best efforts to keep control of her emotions, and she had lamented aloud yet again that she hadn't taken the time to say goodbye to Crystal until even she was sick of hearing herself repeat the same thing. Tom had found himself momentarily distracted from his own concerns as he tried to comfort her. It seemed that he had found another person who drew a strength he didn't know that he had to the surface, someone who forced him to push aside his own worries and put their wellbeing first. As much as he didn't want Steph to suffer, he couldn't help but selfishly feel grateful to her for her sadness, which kept his own at bay.
They could see the front of the queue now, and the doors to the population control centre through the handful of people who still remained ahead of them in line, and Steph craned her neck to get a better look at what was ahead of them. A formidable-looking man in his thirties sat behind a square white plastic table on the pavement, just outside of the small courtyard which led into the centre, with a pile of paperwork on his makeshift desk and a small electronic tablet in his hands. Steph couldn't make out his words from where she was standing but she watched, entranced, as the woman at the front of the queue, an elderly lady who was propped up on a wooden cane, handed the man her laminated cull card, which he examined for a moment before returning it to her.

"What do you think will happen? When we get in there, I mean?" Steph asked Tom in a fear-filled voice.

"Honestly? I don't know. I would imagine we'll be taken to some kind of holding area until it's our turn." Tom guessed.

"Your father didn't tell you anything? Didn't give you any clues as to what we can expect?" Steph pressed him. She wasn't sure that she believed that, surely with his dad working as one of the senior doctors at the centre, Tom must have some idea of what awaited them.

"I didn't ask," Tom admitted. "I was worried he'd only say something which would make me more afraid, so I didn't ask, and he didn't tell me." He said, glancing apologetically down at Steph.

He could see from the look in her eyes that she was the kind of person for whom there was nothing scarier than the unknown, and at that moment, he wished he had something more useful to tell her, so he squeezed her hand again. "I'm sorry."

"Don't be. You did what you thought was right. Just like I did with Crystal." Steph told him, feeling the ache in her chest start to grow once more. Try as she might, she had been unable to think of anything but her best friend all morning, picturing her waking up to find Steph gone without so much as having left a note. A note! That was it!

"Do you think maybe they'll have writing equipment in there? I could write a note for Crystal and put it in with my belongings to explain why I didn't wake her up this morning and apologise?" Steph asked, her voice suddenly more animated than it had been all day at this unexpected idea, and Tom shrugged.

"I don't know, but I could ask my dad when we get inside? See if he could find a pen and paper for you. But, I don't think you're going to need one..." Tom said cryptically, and Steph raised her eyebrows at him as he nodded his head slightly towards something over her shoulder, indicating that she should turn around.

Steph spun on her heels so quickly that she almost lost her balance, and Tom had to reach out and grab her elbow to steady her as Crystal's voice rang out across the street, and the busty, dark skinned woman strode towards them, looking furious.

"Stephanie Elizabeth Moore!" Crystal shouted, and several heads in the queue turned to look at her as she closed the distance between herself and Steph, who looked utterly mortified.

 "How dare you leave without saying goodbye to me? What the hell were you thinking! Did you think I'd let you get away with that? That after everything we've been through together, I wouldn't come and find your skinny arse and force a damn goodbye out of you?"

Steph didn't know whether to be horrified or thrilled as she watched her best friend barrelling towards her, chest puffed out and looking so angry that Steph almost imagined she could see smoke coming out of Crystal's ears, and the conflicting emotions battled inside of her as she tried to respond.

"I..." She began, but her larger-than-life best friend cut her off before she could utter another word.

"I know, I know, you thought it was for the best. You were only doing it to protect me. I've heard it all before, so save it. Do you have any idea how scared I was when I woke up and saw that you were gone? Look! I rushed out the door so fast that I'm not even wearing matching shoes!" Crystal yelled, pointing down at her feet, and Tom couldn't help the laugh that slipped past his lips when he saw that she was indeed wearing two totally different coloured shoes. One jet black and one mint green with scuffs on the toes.

"Think that's funny, do you, Tom? What the hell are you doing here anyway? I thought you told me you wanted to do this alone, Steph?" Crystal asked, no longer yelling now but sounding incredibly hurt as she took in the scene before her. Although she wouldn't have thought it possible just ten minutes ago, Steph suddenly felt even more guilty than she had done all day as she looked into her best friend's distressed features.

"Don't be angry with Tom, Crystal, please. Not today. It's not his fault." Steph managed to stutter before Tom stepped in to try and explain.

"Stephanie and I have the same birthday and the same end-of-life day. I'm being culled here today too." He said, trying to keep his voice as steady as he could.

"Oh. I see. Well then, I guess that makes it alright that you're here, but it still doesn't explain why you left without saying goodbye to me, Steph. Me, your best friend!" Crystal stammered, tears welling in her eyes as the profound sadness and confusion she felt rose above her anger and threatened to overwhelm her despite her attempts to keep it inside. Crystal had always been much more comfortable being angry than upset, and part of her wished that her rage would overtake her again so that she wouldn't have to feel this deep, mind-numbing pain.

"I know. I'm sorry! Believe me, I am! I've never been so happy to see anyone in my entire life Crystal. I knew I'd made a huge mistake from the moment I left this morning, but it was too late to take it back. I've spent all day falling apart on Tom here and telling him what a colossal idiot I am!" Steph half sobbed, half-shouted back at her friend.

"She really has." Tom nodded in agreement, watching Crystal's dark eyes soften as she took in their words.

"I'm so sorry, Crystal." Steph whimpered quietly.

"So you should be. Now come here and give me the goodbye that I deserve." Crystal ordered, reaching out and wrapping her arms around

Steph's small frame. Tom stepped back slightly to give them space and watched on in silence as the two girls sobbed in one another's arms and the queue shuffled forwards once more.

Chapter Forty-Five

"Name?" The somewhat stern-looking man behind the desk barked as Tom and Steph finally reached the front of the seemingly never-ending queue of people they had been standing in all morning and Tom begrudgingly stepped forwards.
"Thomas Walker."
"Cull card?" the man asked in a bored, uninterested voice without raising his eyes and Tom handed over the credit card-sized piece of laminated plastic which he had put in his back pocket before he had left home this morning.
"Thomas Walker. Walker… Why do I know that name?" the guard asked.
"Erm, I don't know, it's a pretty common name," Tom replied with a shrug, suddenly grateful for the blistering heat which had been causing him to sweat all morning as the dampness increased on his forehead in apprehension.
Tom didn't know exactly how things worked here, but he was pretty sure that if the wrong person got wind of the fact that his father was one of the senior doctors at the centre, they could make trouble for both him and Jack. The last thing that Tom wanted was for his dad to have gone through all of this, all these weeks of working in this terrible place so that he could be with Tom when his time came, to end up being for nothing if someone decided that him being here at the same time as Tom was breaking some sort of rule. After all, people over the age of fourteen were not allowed to be accompanied to their end-of-life appointments, and Tom had passed that age many years ago.
The guard in front of him furrowed his thick eyebrows as he finally met Tom's eyes, searching his face intently as though he were trying to work out where he knew him from before shaking his head and handing Tom back his cull card.
"Report to floor six for processing. Next!" The guard called, dismissing Tom without another glance and looking over his shoulder towards Steph, who was standing just behind him.
"Is it okay if I just wait here for a minute for my friend?" Tom asked, gesturing towards Steph, who he noticed, was shaking like a leaf and shifting her weight from one foot to another in agitation.
"No, it's not okay. Everyone goes in alone. Sixth floor." The man said in a tone clearly intended to halt any further pleas on Tom's part.
Tom shot another fleeting glance over his shoulder and watched as all of the colour drained from Steph's features. Her face, which had been flushed from the hours that they had spent standing in the sun, suddenly went from a rosy pink to ghostly white in a matter of seconds. Turning

back to the guard, Tom took a step to his left, away from the desk, to allow Steph to approach but made no further move towards the centre. Crossing his arms over his chest, he stood and waited, determined to stand his ground.

"I thought I told you to go inside?" The guard asked, though the question was clearly rhetorical. Completely ignoring Steph, who was now standing in front of the table, still trembling from head to toe and looking as though she might pass out at any moment as she fished around in her bag for her identification, causing the sound of rustling paper to fill the air around them.

"What are you going to do? Kill me? I will go inside as instructed in just one minute *with* my friend." Tom said stubbornly, staring the man down, and he could have sworn he saw the corner of Steph's lips twitch up in gratitude.

As much as Tom was terrified about walking through those doors, as much as he wanted to put the moment off for as long as possible, steal a few more precious seconds out here in the fresh air as a free man, able to look up at the sky above him and feel the breeze rippling across his face, his little show of defiance actually had nothing to do with himself at all. The protective instinct which had kicked in earlier today when Steph first began to cry had returned with full force. He couldn't stand the idea of leaving her out here alone, even for a moment. He was honestly concerned that if he didn't help her through the doors, she wouldn't make it inside at all. Or at least not without assistance in the form of one of the men milling around in their bland brown jackets. Tom wouldn't allow her to go through that, not when he had the power to prevent it.

"I'd watch that smart mouth of yours if I were you." The guard replied, snatching Steph's cull card out of her hand and marking her name off on his tablet.

"Stephanie Moore. Report to the sixth floor. It seems you have an escort. From the looks of you, it's probably for the best. Don't want to spoil the doctor's fun by having you expire out here on the pavement now, do we?" The man said, his voice dripping with sarcasm as he flashed Steph a toothy grin.

Steph's face fell as she took in the man's callous words, amazed that anyone could be so heartless. He was one of the last people on this earth she would ever speak to, and here he was, talking to her as though she were some kind of animal, not worth his time or empathy. It wasn't as though she had done anything to deserve this, like she had committed some heinous crime, the retribution for which was to be her death. She was just an ordinary young woman, sentenced to this horrible fate by a computer programme; she didn't deserve his hatred.

Before Steph could attempt to respond to the man's harsh words, her view of him was partially obscured by Tom's broad shoulders as he stepped towards the desk, slamming his hands down on the shining white plastic and making the whole thing shake violently as he stared furiously at the man.

"What did you say to her? How can you be so cruel? She's a human being, for god's sake! We're all human beings!" He shouted into the man's face, all his weight pushing down onto the desk before him, and his muscles coiled tightly, ready to attack. Tom wasn't a violent man. He much preferred to heal people than to hurt them, yet something about the dismissive tone in which the guard had spoken and the fact that his emotions were already so heightened today triggered something inside of him that he had rarely felt before in his twenty-three years of life. Pure rage.

"I said you better help the little lady inside Romeo before a strong gust of wind knocks her over. Now get out of my face before you say something even more stupid than you already have." The man said coldly, rising out of his chair to tower over Tom. The guard had to be at least six and a half feet tall. His well-built frame had been somewhat obscured as he sat behind his desk, but Tom couldn't pretend it wasn't intimidating now that he was standing at his full height.

"Not until you apologise," Tom ordered. Straightening up to look the man in the eyes as best he could despite their height difference.

"Ha! Why? I didn't say anything that wasn't true. I suggest you get your arse inside unless you want to be the one taking a win away from the doctors. Not that I wouldn't enjoy having that pleasure myself." The man said, twitching aside his vest to reveal a holstered gun.

"Tom, it's okay. Let's just go. He's not worth it." Steph pleaded with him, tugging on Tom's elbow and trying to prise him away from the desk. She could feel the eyes of the few people that remained in the line behind them boring into their backs as the confrontation continued and noticed that they had also attracted the attention of the two guards standing by the doors to the centre who were now having a whispered conversation to one and other, glancing back and forth between Tom and the man behind the desk, clearly trying to decide whether or not to intervene.

"Please, Tom?" Steph asked again, her voice coming out as little more than a whisper as she slid her hand into his, just like he had done with hers earlier and squeezed it lightly.

"It's people like you that should have to walk through those doors. Not us. People like us shouldn't have to be sacrificed so that the likes of you can live on." Tom said venomously, barely managing to contain his anger.

The only thing that was stopping him from punching the man squarely on his bulbous nose was the feel of Steph's small clammy hand grasping onto his. If he got carted off now to be disciplined in some manner or another by the guards, then this whole protest would have been for nothing, as Steph would end up having to walk into the centre alone. So he tried to get his temper in check.

Steph forced herself to step forward, tugging Tom along with her as she made her way towards the cobblestone pathway which led through the courtyard to the centre's main doors. As much as every bone in her body was willing her, no *begging* her to turn and run as far away from this place as she possibly could, she knew that if she didn't get Tom away from the guard soon, the situation was only going to get worse. She didn't want him to spend the last few hours, or however long remained of his life, being angry, especially not because of her. She hoped that perhaps once the guard was out of sight, she might be able to calm him down a little. If she could just get her own emotions in check for long enough to do so.

"Thank you for your sacrifice." The man behind the desk called out behind them, determined to get the last word, and Tom saw red. The thin thread that had been holding him back until now pulled tautly and snapped like a flimsy branch under his foot as he wrenched his hand out from Steph's grip and whirled around. He closed the distance between himself and the guard in just a few strides of his long legs, grabbing the collar of his hi-vis vest and yanking the man, who had just retaken his seat, back to his feet.

"Say that again!" Tom growled, spit flying through his clenched teeth and landing on the guard's face just inches away from his own.

"I said. Thank you for your sacrifice." The man repeated, and as his face split into a huge grin, Tom loosened his grip on his vest and freed his right hand, rearing back and snapping it forward towards the guard's smirking face. The satisfying impact he expected to feel never came. Instead, he felt the vice-like grip of the guard's thick hand as it closed around his own, squeezing his clenched fist until Tom could feel the bones rubbing together under his skin and he was sure something was about to break.

"Tut, tut tut. That was a dumb move, Romeo." The guard chastised him, using his grip on Tom's hand to shove him away. Tom stumbled back on the uneven pavement, losing his balance and crashing onto the hard ground. Steph was at his side in moments, her small, shaking hand on his shoulder, trying to ascertain if he was hurt as the guard continued to stare down at them. She noticed that the eyes of every person waiting in the line were firmly fixed upon the scene now, looking over at them with a mixture of respect and fear on their faces as they wondered what would happen next.

Tom had barely managed to struggle onto his knees before he felt another hand wrap around his bicep, a much larger one this time, with a grip so firm that it made him wince. He glanced up to see another of the security guards, one of the pair that had been watching the exchange from the doorway behind him, pulling him to his feet as Steph backed away, her face impossibly paler than it had been just a few moments ago.

I'm making this worse. Tom realised, suddenly having a moment of clarity as he looked into Steph's terrified face and all of his anger rushed out of him as though someone had thrown a bucket of ice cold water over his overheated skin.

"Inside. Now." The guard holding his arm growled, pushing Tom forwards and manoeuvring him back up the cobblestone pathway with Steph rushing along behind them. Tom didn't attempt to resist the man, knowing it was pointless. The sound of the guard behind the table laughing maniacally as he was forcefully directed towards the large wooden double doors to the centre grated on his nerves as he continued to stumble forwards.

Chapter Forty-Six

Steph had imagined a thousand different versions of how she would react to walking into the centre today. She had pictured herself being utterly hysterical, screaming and shouting as someone manhandled her inside. She had even imagined herself passing out or throwing up as she crossed the threshold as fear overtook her. In even the worst of her nightmares though, she had never imagined that she would be scurrying through the doors behind a guard dragging Tom after he had attempted to defend her honour.
Perhaps she should be grateful for the argument which had occurred and the guard's callous words towards her. At least it had stopped Steph from getting too worked up and had forced her out of the almost catatonic state that she was nearing when she reached the desk to present herself and brought her back into the present with a crash. Now Steph could feel nothing but guilt and she wasn't entirely sure which feeling was worse.
She felt guilty that she hadn't been able to be stronger, hadn't been able to keep herself together and not put Tom in the position where he felt he couldn't leave her side even for a moment. She felt guilty that his last few minutes of breathing free air had been spent in an argument and almost a fistfight. Most of all, Steph felt guilty that she had suggested that they queue together in the first place. If she had just let Tom come alone as he had planned, then he wouldn't be limping slightly on his right ankle, which she was guessing he had hurt when he fell to the ground. Nor would he have angry red finger marks encircling his muscular left arm, which she was sure were bound to leave nasty bruises.
"You going to cause any more trouble?" The guard asked Tom, dragging him to a stop in the middle of a large, almost empty room with only a few chairs scattered around it. Two flights of rickety old-looking wooden staircases stood flanking the opposite end of the room, and an ancient looking coffee machine sat on a stool in the far corner. There was what looked to be an old elevator between the two staircases, but the dulled metal of the double doors was taped off with a stripe of bright red tape, indicating that it was not in service.
"No, sir." Tom managed to say, keeping his voice as level as possible as he rubbed at the spot on his arm, which the guard had thankfully now let go of.
"Good. Get out of my sight." The guard said, jerking his head towards the set of staircases to his left and folding his arms across his chest.
"Tom?" Steph called to the man beside her in a small voice when he didn't move after a moment or two.

It took all of the willpower that Tom could muster to turn away from the guard without another word , ignore the man's attitude and flash Steph what he hoped was a reassuring smile as he turned and retook her hand, relishing the comfort of her soft skin against his and drawing strength from her.

"Let's go." He said and led the way towards the back of the room.

They climbed the stairs in silence, each lost in their own thoughts as they trudged up flight after flight, pausing briefly to check the laminated black numbers stuck to doors on each floor until they eventually spotted the large number six shining back at them in the dim light of the darkened stairwell. Tom reached out his free hand and pushed on the door's surface, expecting to feel some resistance, but it swung open easily, revealing a small thin room with doors at each either and a high receptionist's booth directly in front of them, behind which sat a pretty blonde who looked eerily similar to many of the women that Tom had dated over the last few months.

"Name and cull card, please." The woman said, smiling broadly at them and revealing a set of perfectly straight and unnaturally white teeth behind her red lipstick.

Stephanie reached into the paper bag clutched in her hand and pulled out her cull card, holding it between shaking fingers for a moment before losing her grip and dropping it. She watched as the small object tumbled end over end towards the linoleum floor beneath her feet in slow motion, landing face up, leaving the photograph of her younger self printed on it smiling up at her from the ground and Steph felt a shiver run down her spine as she gazed at the image. Had she ever truly been that happy? She must have been on occasion she supposed, but right now, it was hard to remember what being happy even felt like, all Steph had been able to feel for weeks was fear..

"I've got it," Tom said, bending down to scoop up the card and handing it to the receptionist along with his own.

"Thomas Walker, please make your way through the door to the left for processing." The receptionist said, still smiling up at them as though they were simply here for a nice day out. "Stephanie Moore? The same through the door to the right."

"We can't go together?" Stephanie asked, her voice wavering as she spoke.

"I'm afraid not, hon. Processing has to be done by gender. But you'll be reunited soon enough in the dorms." The receptionist said in a cheery voice.

What is with the people who work here? Tom wondered to himself as he placed Steph's card back into her bag, not trusting her to be able to keep hold of it if he placed it directly in her hand. Either they are obnoxious, rude and uncaring, or they are so falsely sickeningly sweet that it makes your teeth hurt. Do none of them realise where they work? What goes on here? He asked himself, shoving his card into his pocket and turning to face Steph.

"I'm sure it won't take long; I'll see you on the other side, Okay?" He said, trying to keep his tone light, but his own apprehension was starting to slip past his defences. Until now, the need to be strong for the woman in front of him had kept Tom from dwelling too much on what was going to happen when they entered the centre. He wasn't honestly sure if he'd be able to hold himself together once he left her side and had no one to distract him, but it didn't seem they had any choice.

"Okay." Steph managed, swallowing the lump in her throat and staring up into Tom's green eyes, trying to remember every detail of them. The fluorescent lights shining harshly down from the ceiling above them distorted their colour somewhat, making them suddenly look more ocean blue than the clear green that she found so comforting and so she averted her gaze. It wasn't that she didn't believe the smiling receptionist's words that they would be reunited in the dorms in no time exactly, but something in Steph's gut was warning her that anything could go wrong between now and then.

What if, after processing, someone decreed that one or the other of them had been sent to the wrong floor? What if Tom's dad came and ushered him off somewhere to spend time with him whilst he still could, and Steph was left alone? Could she do this without him? Leaving Crystal outside had been hard enough. Forcing her friend to leave before they reached the front of the queue so she wouldn't have to see the pain in her eyes as she walked into the centre had nearly broken Steph's heart, still she knew it had been for the best, and for once, Crystal had barely protested. Simply giving Steph one last hug, squeezing her so tightly that she almost couldn't breathe, before telling her that she loved her more than anything, that she would forever be grateful to have met her, and that she was more sorry than she could say for what was about to happen, before rushing off back down the street so quickly that Steph had lost sight of her thick black hair much sooner than she had wanted to.

Steph didn't expect to have anything like as emotional a goodbye with Tom, she wasn't that naive. Crystal was her best friend, her sister for all intents and purposes. Saying goodbye to her had been physically painful and she barely knew Tom, not really, but whether their final goodbye was destined to be a simple whispered word or a more heartfelt moment, Steph wasn't ready for it to happen just yet. She needed more time.

She watched as Tom turned away from her and walked towards a tall,

stark white door at the opposite end of the hallway, limping heavily on his injured ankle and hoped that it wouldn't be the last time that she saw him. Steph took a deep breath and tried to compose herself as best as she could as she stared after him. Watching as he pulled open the door and glanced back at her, his lips pulling into a thin line as he nodded his head in her direction once as their eyes met before he stepped over the threshold and out of sight, the door swinging silently closed behind him.
"Miss? The door to your right, please." The receptionist prompted her, and Steph snapped out of her daze, finally willing her feet to move underneath her and carry her towards her own door, wondering what exactly she would be faced with once she got inside.

Chapter Forty-Seven

Stepping through the door felt like walking into another world to Steph, the freshly painted white walls, which had been her only surroundings since she entered the population control centre, were long gone. There were no fresh flowers up here like there were in the newly mown courtyard downstairs. The illusion, it seemed, was no longer needed. The government had made some effort to ensure that the public-facing areas of the centre were as pristine as possible, inviting even, but once you got inside, into the true belly of the beast, into the rooms only the condemned and the handful of staff that worked here ever got to see, the illusion was no longer necessary.

The low ceilings above Steph triggered a mild case of claustrophobia which she hadn't realised she suffered from until that very moment, they looked so unstable to her tired eyes that she felt sure they were going to tumble onto her head and crush her at any minute, appearing almost smoke or fire damaged as they loomed above her, grey and discoloured. Steph tried in vain to recall what this building had been used for before it had become the population control centre, but she could not remember. It had been years since it had been in use, so chances were that any damage that had been caused was down to the squatters that would have no doubt used it for shelter in the cold winter months she reasoned. The walls on either side of the slim corridor were no better than the ceiling above her. Covered in nothing more than flaking plaster, some of which had fallen to the ground and was getting caught on the soles of her shoes as she willed her feet to continue moving forwards on the cracked, dirt covered tiles beneath her.

The only light in the hallway emitted from a stuttering fluorescent strip above her head which had clearly seen better days and created a muted strobe-like effect as it flickered in the windowless space, making Steph feel slightly off balance. As she stumbled along, focussing on her feet to ensure she didn't trip over any debris, the realisation that she was walking to her death suddenly hit Steph like a ton of bricks, and she found herself unable to move any further.

Coming to a standstill in the middle of the corridor, she turned and pressed her back up against the wall, placing her hands on her knees as she bent over and tried to suck as much of the stale air surrounding her through gritted teeth as she could as a sense of panic overwhelmed her and her vision began to blur. She had known before now what awaited her inside this building, but seeing her rundown surroundings, which more resembled a haunted house than the hospital set-up she had expected, and how little care had been taken really made it hit home for her at that moment that she was nothing, no one. That she did not mean anything at all to these people, they would do little to make her last living moments in any way comfortable, and it chilled her to the bone. Her head swam as she stood, desperately trying to compose herself and wishing more than anything that Tom's strong hand was still holding hers and that they hadn't been separated. Steph wondered for a moment if he had been greeted by the same sight when he'd stepped through his door on the other side of the building, if he were, even now, mirroring her own position, doubled over and desperately trying to keep his breakfast down in his own hallway. She hoped for his sake that he was doing better than she was.

Steph allowed herself to the count of ten to pull herself together, forcing herself to breathe in through her nose, and out through her mouth slowly and steadily until her heart rate returned to a more normal rhythm. The sooner I get through this, the sooner I will be with Tom again. Steph reminded herself, repeating the mantra in her head until she felt stable enough to put one foot in front of the other and continue down the hall towards yet another door, a more intimidating one this time which was the colour of mud with a single round brass handle in its centre looming in front of her.

She knew that she shouldn't be clinging on to Tom so much, that she should be able to find the strength within herself to get through this without having to rely on him or anyone else. She had always been independent and had been taking care of herself for years now since her parents moved away, she couldn't expect Tom to protect her from what was to come. Try as she might though, Steph couldn't help herself from grasping onto the one thing that was making this situation slightly more manageable for her and she decided to forgive herself for this minor lapse in judgement. Right now, I have to take anything I can get, she thought to herself as she straightened her shoulders and reached out and grabbed the door handle with a shaking hand.

Chapter Forty-Eight

Tom kept his head down focusing on the ground as he walked as quickly as he could manage across the broken terracotta tiles that littered the floor of the hallway before him. Trying desperately not to focus on his surroundings or allow himself to get into his own head, he powered forward and attempted to ignore the throbbing in his injured ankle and the pounding in his chest. After standing in the heat all morning and his altercation with the guard, Tom was exhausted. All he wanted to do was sit down somewhere with a cool glass of water and try to rest, but he doubted he'd be given that opportunity anytime soon. Wrapping his hand around the tarnished brass doorknob on the door at the opposite end of the corridor, Tom pulled it open, cringing slightly as a high-pitched noise emitted from the rusted old hinges, drawing the gaze of every person in the room as he stepped inside. Four men stood in the ample space in front of him, which was in slightly better condition than the rundown corridor he had just traversed, but not by much. At least this room had a window, he thought to himself as he looked around for any sign of his father, but Jack Walker was nowhere to be seen.

"Cull card." The man closest to him demanded, stretching out his hand and displaying dirt-encrusted fingernails to Tom as he waited impatiently, tapping one foot on the ground.

"Thomas Walker." The man said, giving Tom's card a cursory glance and reading his name from it without meeting his eyes. "Place your bag on the table and follow me," he instructed, gesturing to a stained wooden table off to his left, behind which stood another employee who looked equally bored.

Pulling off his backpack, Tom did as he was asked and watched as the employee ripped it open with more force than was necessary and turned it upside down, tipping the few meagre belongings which Tom had been permitted to bring with him on to the surface of the table without a care in the world for their fragility or worth. Tom had to bite his tongue to stop himself from protesting as he watched the two photos of his family that his mum had packed so carefully fall to the floor. Deciding that there was nothing to gain by getting himself into another argument, Tom wearily turned and walked over to the first man who was already on the other side of the room, waiting by a plastic screen with his arms folded across his chest.

"Take off all your clothes and put them in this." The man said, thrusting a clear plastic bag into Tom's hands. "I'll be in to check you over in a minute, so don't take all day about it."

A strip search. Excellent, just what today was missing. As if this place

weren't already degrading enough, Tom thought as he stepped behind the thin screen made of flimsy paper-like material and began to undress. He didn't think it was providing him much privacy from the other people out in the room, so he did his best to keep his back to them as he pulled his clothes off and shoved them unceremoniously into the bag, hoping he'd be allowed to put them back on again soon. He heard the creaking door he had just come through open and close out in the room behind him, followed quickly by the frightened voice of a seemingly young man by the sound of things, apologising for being unable to find his cull card. Moments later, the man who had accompanied Tom to the screen suddenly appeared in front of him, and Tom hurriedly covered himself with his hands, trying to retain some small amount of dignity.
"None of that. Raise your hands and turn around. Slowly." The man said, sounding exasperated. Did none of these people have any compassion? Tom wondered as he begrudgingly complied, his face growing hot from embarrassment as the man brazenly stared at his naked body.
Snatching up the clear bag Tom had put his clothes into, the man shook it once in his fist.
"Got anything in here that you shouldn't have, boy? Anything that's going to hurt me?" The man asked, staring at Tom seriously.
"No. Just my clothes and my cull card." Tom told him, trying to disguise his annoyance at being referred to as 'boy' as he hurriedly covered himself again. Surely the man had just seen more than enough of him to prove that Tom was a man
"Wait here." The man said, leaving Tom alone again behind the screen, naked this time and shivering slightly in the cold, damp room.
Thankfully, he wasn't gone long and returned just a few moments later..
"Alright, you can get dressed again." The man told him, tossing the bag which contained Tom's clothes to the floor by his feet. Tom scooped it up quickly and got dressed at top speed, relishing the feel of the fabric against his chilled skin and desperate to get out of this room now.
The man didn't speak again as he waited for Tom to get dressed. He stood in a corner by the exit to the screen, picking at the dirt under his fingernails, until Tom crunched up the now-empty plastic bag in his hand and regained his attention. With a jerk of his head, the man indicated that Tom should follow him. So he fell into step and returned to the main room, where another man handed him back his backpack, with the zipper still undone and his belongings haphazardly shoved back inside. Tom noticed that the photos of his family had at least been retrieved from the floor. However, they were now slightly bent as they sat on top of the spare T-Shirt that his mother had packed for him, which had also been scrunched up and he winced, remembering his

mum taking the time to iron it perfectly and carefully fold it before placing it into his bag the day before.

The man that Tom followed didn't bother to slow his stride to allow Tom a moment to close his bag or even to put it back on his shoulder. Tom struggled behind him on his sore ankle, trying to keep up as best as he could, clutching his backpack in one hand and frantically trying to pull the zipper closed with the other as they got closer to yet another door off to one side of the room.

"Put your index finger on the mark." The man said gruffly, thrusting an electronic tablet in Tom's direction before pulling open the door behind him once Tom had done as he'd asked. "You'll wait in here until your name is called." The man advised him.

"And how long is that likely to be?" Tom asked, knowing full well that the man was unlikely to give him a straight answer but trying his luck nonetheless.

"How longs a piece of string?" The man responded with a smirk. "As long as it takes. Could be a few minutes, could be a few days."

"Great. Thanks for your help." Tom said sarcastically and, taking a deep breath, stepped through the doorway.

Chapter Forty-Nine

The first thing that hit him was the smell. A musty odour hung in the air so thick that Tom almost imagined he could see it floating around in front of him. The scent was a potent mixture of unwashed bodies and the sheer fact that there were too many people congregating in the room before him with no ventilation that he could see on such a hot day. Although, as Tom couldn't see any form of heating apparatus on the bare plaster walls either, perhaps he should be grateful that his end-of-life date hadn't fallen in the dead of winter. At least he wouldn't end up freezing to death, he thought as he scrunched up his nose in disgust and hovered by the doorway, taking in the scene before him and trying to see if he could spot Steph or his dad maybe, amongst the crowd of people.

The second thing that Tom noticed was the noise. Gone was the near silence from the queue line outside, where the only sounds to be heard were the occasional muffled whisper or stifled sob, it had been replaced with the frustrated chatter of a large number of people who were clearly pissed off from the tones of their voices, if not damn well angry. Some of the room's occupants laid on their backs on paper-thin mattresses, which were all the protection they had been provided from the hard metal two-storey bedsteads positioned far too close to one another for comfort. Others milled around by the walls of the large room, talking in loud voices, and a small group stood by a door to the far end, which had the word 'toilet' engraved onto its front.

No matter their positions though, every person in the room had one thing in common, all of them were conversing, venting their disgust at the situation in which they found themselves and Tom felt as though the tension in the room could be cut with a knife. For the first time, he fully understood why the guards insisted on searching everyone so thoroughly as they entered. If anyone had managed to get weapons in here, he was sure that a riot would have broken out by now.

Unlike the processing area that he had just passed through, which had been segregated by sex, the dorm, as the receptionist had called it, was full of both men and women of all varying ages and ethnicities, and as Tom made his way deeper into the room he almost collided with an elderly lady supporting herself on a wooden cane whom he recognised from the queue outside.

"Careful there, deary, you don't want to take me out before my time. Wouldn't want to spoil their fun." The woman said to him in a cheery voice, smiling to reveal shiny gums and missing teeth and nodding in the direction of two people in long white lab coats, the kind that Tom had worn to work every day for months, standing in a far corner of the

room by a door marked 'staff only'.
Tom let his eyes wander over to the two doctors and took what felt like his first deep breath in hours as he saw the familiar figure of Jack Walker standing by the side of a short, Asian woman with a severe countenance and stepped forwards, intending to approach his dad. He had barely managed one step on his injured ankle when Jack's eyes snapped up as if sensing that he was being watched and he shook his head minutely as he met Tom's gaze, warning him that now was not a good time.
Not wanting to cause any trouble for his father or betray the fact that they knew one another to Jack's colleague, Tom walked to the nearest set of empty bunk beds pressed against the wall and slung his bag down on the mattress, perching on the edge and planting his feet on the dirty floor. At that moment, Tom wanted nothing more than to press himself against the wall behind his bunk and make himself as small as possible, to try and disappear from the prying eyes of the groups of people around him, but he couldn't. He needed to stay visible and keep an eye out for Steph. What was taking her so long? He wondered as he stared over at the adjacent door to the one that he had entered the dorm through, assuming that would be where the women would come from, waiting as quietly as he could for her recognisable face to appear and willing his hands to stop trembling.

"Marcus Webber?" Jack Walker called out into the dormitory, raising his voice to be heard over the sea of chattering and trying to stop himself from looking over at his son. All he wanted to do was rush over to his side and remain there until such time as Tom's name was called, grasping every possible moment with his eldest as he could before it was too late. No matter how much he wanted that though, Jack knew that he couldn't right now, there were too many people paying attention to him, not to mention Doctor Lee standing by his side, and he didn't want to jeopardise his chances of being able to accompany Tom into the sterile cubicles that hid behind the very wall on which the bed his son had picked out was pressed up against by drawing attention to their relationship as soon as Tom arrived.
A stout man in ripped trousers who was wearing shoes with holes in the toes stumbled towards Jack, his shoulders pushed back in a show of defiance or perhaps false bravado as he walked. Jack purposefully avoided making eye contact with him, he knew it was unfair to dehumanise these poor men and women even more, yet it was the only way he could maintain some distance from the people he was employed to put to death. Their faces still swam through his mind each and every night as he lay in the darkness, pitifully attempting to snatch a few

hour's sleep before the whole process started again as it was. At least this way, he couldn't picture the fear and sadness shining in their eyes.
"I'm Marcus." The man said in a clear voice as he reached Jack and Doctor Lee.
"Please collect your belongings and come with us." Doctor Lee said, her voice utterly devoid of any compassion, and Jack noticed, not for the first time, that she didn't seem to have any issue with looking directly into their patients eyes.

"Steph!" Tom called out when he finally saw her appear through the tall brown door several minutes later, noticing that she looked even paler than before if that were possible.
Steph tried her best to force a smile onto her features as she headed towards Tom, but she had a horrible feeling that it would appear to him more like a grimace. The humiliating strip search in the processing area had robbed her of what little composure she had left, and Steph was sure that if she didn't sit down soon, she'd end up collapsing.
"Are you okay?" Tom asked, his voice full of concern as he shuffled over on the mattress to make room for her to sit down. "Sorry, I couldn't find two beds close to one another." He added, suddenly feeling embarrassed that he was sitting on a bed with a woman that he barely knew.
"Don't worry about it. I'm just glad to sit down for a minute," Steph said, sounding exhausted as she placed her crumpled paper bag, which now had a large rip in the side after being roughly handled by a woman in processing, onto the mattress next to her and laid her head against the wall behind her, pulling her legs up onto the bed.
"You mean you weren't given the five-star treatment in processing?" Tom asked, feigning shock as he raised a hand to his heart. "No champagne? No massage? Remind me to write a strongly worded complaint to the Cull Enforcement Agency. Bleecker avenue population control centre, three out of ten. Delightful exterior but shocking customer service." He joked, and to his surprise, Steph actually played along, a little colour returning to her features as she replied.
"Well, the champagne they did offer was really only that cheap knock-off fizzy wine that tastes like washing-up liquid and I couldn't lower myself to consume that, so I had to refuse. And when I got undressed for the massage, this woman just stood and stared at me, and I most certainly ended up more tense than I was before I went in. So I'd actually say that three out of ten is generous. Not to mention that I requested a private sleeping area." Steph said in as serious a voice as she could manage, feeling her heart lighten just a little at the conversation. "You should get right on to that complaint." She added,

smiling over at Tom seated on the bed next to her, his tall frame somewhat bent over in the small space.
"I'll do that the moment we check out." Tom smiled back, grateful for once to have been able to distract Steph for a change but unsure how long he'd be able to keep up his jovial tone.

Chapter Fifty

"Marcus Webber, you will now be put to death by lethal injection in accordance with the cull laws set out in the indiscriminate agreement. Do you have anything you would like to say before your injection is administered?" Jack Walker asked the trembling man lying on the hospital bed before him, repeating the same few lines that he had uttered more times than he cared to remember as the nurse behind him busied herself preparing the syringe which contained the light blue liquid that he would soon plunge into Mr Webber's vein, which would stop his heart in about thirty seconds.
Jack knew that some of his colleagues, like Doctor Lee, who he was not sure had a single ounce of compassion in that tiny body of hers, relished this moment. They wholeheartedly believed that in putting these people to death, they were saving humanity and that they actually felt good about the work being done here. Some of the doctors even kept a tally of how many people they had personally administered injections to, like some sick scorecard which they would compare at the end of the day to see who had managed to murder more people on that particular shift. It made Jack sick.
Since starting work at the centre, Jack had done his best to keep himself to himself, even sitting alone in the small staff area to eat the meals that his wife packed for him each day as he listened to the animated chatter of his colleagues around him, never once joining in, and repeating to himself over and over again that he was here for Tom. Just for Tom. And that if this was what he had to suffer through in order to be with his eldest son in his last moments on this earth, then so be it.

Marcus's eyes flitted back and forth around the room, dancing from the walls to the ceiling, to the nurse, before finally settling on Doctor Walker's face just long enough to shake his head dumbly in response to the man's question. What was the point in giving some poignant final speech when no one was here to listen to it except for a couple of strangers in lab coats? It's not as though anyone would make a note of his words and send them out into the world, and Marcus didn't have any family who would care to listen to them anyway. Most of the people that he knew on the streets where he had lived for the past five years since he had lost his job and, shortly thereafter, his home, were nothing more than acquaintances, people to share food scavenged from a nearby rubbish bin with or perhaps a joint, or a can of beer on the rare occasions when they managed to get a hold of such things.
They didn't know or care enough about him to be concerned about what his last conscious thoughts were before he was culled. Come to think of

it, Marcus wasn't even sure if he'd mentioned to many of them that his name had been called up, let alone that his date was today. He wondered idly who would take his coveted spot outside the grocery store where he slept almost every night, where the owners would leave the red and white checked awning open in wet weather in an attempt to keep him and any guests he might invite into his makeshift home out of the rain.

Now that he was here, more terrified than he could ever recall having been in his life before, Marcus wished that he had made more of an effort to form some kind of real human connection out there in the world that he would never set foot in again. That there had been someone worth taking the time to say a proper goodbye to, someone who would miss him, and not for the first time, he cursed the fact that he hadn't even been able to come up with anyone to nominate to collect whatever remained of his body after he was dead. Maybe the lottery computer had made the right choice when it spat out his name. It's not as though he was contributing to society in any way.

Laying flat on his back, staring up into the stoic face of the doctor, Marcus realised it wouldn't have mattered if he had. Whether there were a hundred people out in the world who cared about him or none, he'd still have ended up in this situation. Lying here entirely alone.

Following the doctor and the tall nurse who accompanied him into this cramped room that smelled strongly of disinfectant had been the most difficult thing Marcus had ever had to do. He had managed to keep himself together for the journey to the centre two days ago on what was supposed to have been his end-of-life date. He had somehow stayed sane for the forty-two hours and thirty-five minutes – not that he'd been counting or anything, that he had waited in that overcrowded, stinking dormitory despite barely managing to scrape more than a couple of hours of sleep the entire time. But the minute he'd heard his name called by the doctor, standing by the door marked 'staff only', which he'd seen countless people be taken through over the time he'd been at the centre but had only ever seen the doctors return from, he'd suddenly barely been able to stand.

Marcus's mouth had gone bone dry, and he was convinced that if he tried to utter more than a word or two, he would bring up the meagre excuse for a meal that he had been served earlier today, and that was the last thing that he wanted.

He wanted to leave this world with a little bit of his pride intact. He wanted to be strong. He was doing this for the good of the planet, to save humanity, wasn't that what they had been told? And he wouldn't lay here and cry like a baby about it. He'd take it like a man.

The nurse handed Doctor Walker the long syringe filled to the brim with the solution that would stop the man on the bed's heart, and watched as the doctor depressed the plunger and a little of the liquid sprayed from the tip into the air.

"The solution will take around thirty seconds to stop your heart. You may feel some slight discomfort, but it will not be painful." Jack told the man before him as he searched his arm for a vein. Eventually, locating one that hadn't already been blown out by drugs and would accept his needle, slowly pushing the tip into his skin as gently as he could and saying in a low voice so that his colleague wouldn't catch his whispered words to the dying man, "I'm so sorry Marcus. Rest easy" As he pushed down the plunger and watched intently as the light blue liquid disappeared into Marcus's body.

"Marcus Webber, time of death three fifty-four pm, July twentieth, twenty-fifty-three."

Chapter Fifty-One

"How much longer do you think we'll be here?" Steph asked Tom, her tired voice betraying the exhaustion she felt as she sat on the hard mattress beside him with her arms tightly wrapped around her knees, which were tucked up under her chin.

"I don't know. But I heard those guys over there saying that they've been here for nearly two days."

"Two days?!" Steph repeated, shock colouring her voice. "I know the end-of-life letters said we could be kept here for a few days, but I figured that was just them covering their backs in case something happened. I didn't think they actually meant it."

"Me either. Honestly, there have been nights when my dad hasn't gotten home until long after I'm in bed, so I assumed that things were taking a bit longer than they'd hoped, but three days seems excessive. They'll have to at least feed us at some point, right? If they're going to keep us here that long?" Tom said, his stomach growling, and he wished he'd managed to force down a bit more of the breakfast that his mum had made for him that morning.

It was already nearly six in the evening and the only refreshment that had been offered since Tom and Steph had arrived in the centre was a few sips of metallic-tasting water from the bathroom sink, where they had filled the water bottles which had been given to them when they were processed. As much as he could barely believe that he'd be able to keep anything more substantial down, Tom was starving.

"I'm going to ask one of those guys over there if they know when we can expect to get some food," Tom told Steph, rising from the bed, but she stretched out a hand and grabbed hold of his wrist, restraining him as she stared up at him wide-eyed.

"I don't think that's such a good idea," Steph said. The group of men who stood a few feet away from their cramped bunk bed didn't look like the sort who would welcome questions from strangers as they all stood with their hands in their pockets, their heads bowed, deep in conversation.

"It'll be fine, don't worry. I'll be back in a minute, okay?" Tom tried to reassure her, gently prising her fingers from his arm.

"Excuse me? Hi, sorry to interrupt you." Tom began when he reached the group of four men leaning against the metal frames of a pair of nearby bunks. "I was just wondering if you knew whether or not we're likely to get any food tonight?" he asked as the man nearest to him, a heavy-set, muscular guy in his late twenties with a shaved head and several tattoos turned to him, looking him up and down once before answering.

"Yeah, normally they bring food around seven. Or at least, what they consider to be food." The man said in a rough voice.

"Great. Thanks." Tom said, turning to return to Steph, but another, much heavier hand on his arm restrained him this time before he could limp more than a couple of steps.

"What did you do to your leg?" The man asked him curiously.

"I erm, I had a disagreement with one of the guards outside. Let's just say that I lost." Tom told him, not seeing the point in hiding his little altercation from the stranger before him and too exhausted to devise a plausible lie.

"Really? Hmm. Maybe you'll be more useful than I thought." The man said, rubbing the stubble on his chin with his free hand. "Do me a favour? No matter how much the food they bring disgusts you, try and eat as much of it as you can, alright? You'll need your strength later." He finished, releasing Tom's arm from his grip as the three other men around him chuckled lightly.

Tom had no idea what they could possibly be talking about. What use could he be to anyone at this point when at any minute, he could be ushered through the 'staff only' door, never to be seen again? And what strength could he need? How much strength did it take to lie on a table? Other than mental strength of course, which Tom was sure he was going to need a bucket load of, but Tom was sure from the look in the other man's eye that was not what he was referring to.

Not wanting to spend any more time lingering with these men, who honestly gave him an uneasy feeling in his stomach as they all continued to smirk at his confusion, Tom decided not to ask any more questions and, after quickly thanking them again, made his way back over to Steph's side, sitting down heavily on the bed and propping his sore ankle on the frame to try and relieve some of the pressure on it.

"So, what did they say?" Steph asked the moment Tom had gotten comfortable

"Not much. Apparently. We'll be given food around seven." Tom told her, furrowing his brows as he debated whether or not to tell her the rest of the details from his brief conversation with the four men. After deliberating a moment, Tom shook his head slightly, deciding against divulging anything further. What was the point? He reasoned to himself. He had no idea what the men were talking about in the first place, so he wouldn't be able to explain it properly, and besides, Steph was already scared enough without worrying about some nonsense that the group of wild-looking men had spouted at Tom, especially when she had already tried to prevent him from going to speak to them in the first place.

"Not too long now, then," Steph said, glancing at the clock on the room's far wall, which read six forty-five.

"I wouldn't get your hopes up too much. From what those guys said, I don't think we should expect a lot." Tom warned Steph.

The pair lapsed into silence again as they reclined on the mattress, both lost in their thoughts as they allowed their eyes to wander around the room. Steph's attention was primarily taken by a pair of elderly ladies on the bunk opposite them, who were chattering and showing each other photos of children whom Steph assumed were their grandkids, as though they had intentionally met here for a good old chat instead of being drafted up in the cull.

Steph envied them. The two women had to be in their eighties at least. They had both lived long and hopefully happy lives. It was evident from the photos that they had families and children who had gone on to have their own babies. They had created legacies to leave behind them, people to carry on their family names and traditions long after they were gone. They had achieved all of the things that Steph had once dreamed of for herself. She couldn't help but feel cheated as she sat watching them chatter away, wondering why they had deserved to live for so long, and she didn't.

Steph imagined herself and Crystal sitting in their places, as hunched over little old ladies with grey hair and liver spots covering their hands, and suddenly and without warning, Steph felt an emotion bubbling up in her that she had managed to suppress for the last few months, like a white-hot burning poker igniting in her chest, it's fire spreading out slowly throughout her entire body until she thought she would explode as sheer rage engulfed her.

Chapter Fifty-Two

Tom couldn't seem to stop himself from stealing glances over at the somewhat dishevelled group of men who he had approached earlier, who were now standing near a small crowd which had gathered by a plain brown door at the back of the room, where Tom assumed their food would appear from shortly given that it was the only door left that he didn't know what was behind. In complete contrast to most of the people in the room, the men seemed... Happy? Excited? Yes, excited, that was the right word, Tom thought to himself as he strained his ears to try and hear what they were saying to one another, but he was too far away. There were too many other people talking around him for him to be able to make out their words from his place on the bed.

The men shifted on their feet animatedly as they talked, gesturing cheerily, until one of them, much to Tom's amazement, suddenly threw back his head and laughed. A loud cackling sound that reverberated around the room and caught the attention of many of the other people crammed into the space, who turned their heads towards the sound, their faces were a mixture of confusion and shock as they took in the scene before them. What could they possibly have to be laughing about? Tom wondered, as he was sure many others around him did too.

At any moment, any one of them could hear their name called, possibly in Tom's own father's deep voice, and they would be ushered through the 'staff only' door, never to be seen again. How on earth could they possibly find anything funny right now?

Tom was so lost in the scene unfolding at the other end of the room that he failed to notice Steph's sudden change in mood for several minutes, it wasn't until she suddenly jumped off of the bed and started to pace back and forth across the small metre or so wide space between their bunk and the next, that she drew his attention away from the group of men and he turned to look at her stricken face.

"Steph?" He called to her in a concerned voice, watching as she thrust her hands over her head, disturbing her tightly bound ponytail. Her skin, which had been so pale all day, was suddenly flushed pink, and her narrowed eyes were focused on the floor before her as she walked, not acknowledging that Tom had spoken to her at all. It was as if she hadn't even heard him.

"Steph? Are you alright?" Tom asked again, pulling his sore ankle down from the bed frame and sitting on the edge of the mattress looking up at her.

"No. No, Tom, I'm not alright." Steph said, her voice so full of anger that, for a moment, Tom was utterly taken aback.

Up until now, he had seen a myriad of emotions pour out of the woman before him. He'd seen her be strong that night in the park when she'd got him singing in an attempt to calm him down. He'd seen her guilt-ridden over not saying goodbye to Crystal, seen her hysterical and scared. He'd seen the pure joy and love on her face when her best friend had unexpectedly joined them as they'd reached the front of the queue outside. Conversely, the pure, unfiltered sadness which had covered Steph's features as Crystal had walked away from them for the last time. But this? The look on Steph's face now was a new one on him and something he'd not expected from her. Tom had assumed that if either of them was going to get mad, no, furious, he corrected himself taking in her appearance again and realising that 'mad' didn't even come close to describing how Steph looked right now, that it would be him. Not her.

"Why did I even come here?" Steph asked no one in particular as she resumed her frantic pacing, trying desperately to find an outlet for the overpowering emotions she could feel coursing through her veins. "I could have just run. I'm sure plenty of other people did. I'm sure a whole lot of people didn't turn up to their appointments today and for days before then, too, weeks probably. And you know what? They were right not to!" She continued, her voice rising as she continued to ramble. "What right do the government have to lock us up like this? To confine us all to this stinking room, just waiting until god-knows-when for our names to be called so that we can be murdered? Is that what I voted for? Is that what anyone here voted for when they elected these people? What gives them the right!" Steph ranted, and several heads turned in her direction, but she didn't care.

"I should have run. I could have gone to my parents maybe, or further. Gotten to the coast somehow, found a boat, made it to France, and just disappeared into the countryside. I should never have come here."

Pulling himself up on tired legs, Tom placed a hand on each of Steph's shoulders, stopping her in her tracks and forcing her to face him, but she continued to stare resolutely down at the ground.

"Ssh shh. It's okay, Steph, please, you've got to relax. Getting upset like this isn't going to help." Tom tried to calm her,

"So? Nothing can help me now, Tom, don't you see! Nothing can help any of us. So why the hell shouldn't I get angry! That's the one thing they can't take away from me, how I feel! Not until they put that needle in me!" Steph almost growled.

Her words were quieter now, too quiet, Tom realised, her anger had turned into fury, and she could barely even manage to force out what she wanted to say, so powerful were the emotions consuming her.

Having spent more time than he cared to remember trying to console his patients during his time working at the hospital, some of whom would get understandably angry when they were told that despite their failing health, there were just no beds to be had at the facility and that they would have to leave, even if they knew that there was no chance of them surviving without treatment. Tom had had patients scream and shout at him, call him every name under the sun, even throw things when he had turned away their sick children with nothing more than a prescription that he knew wouldn't be enough to cure them and the suggestion of them trying to get more food. He was no stranger to anger, but this was different. How could he possibly try and calm Steph when, deep down, he felt just as furious as she did?

"You're right. They can't. They can't take away how you feel, and you have every right to feel the way that you do. God, Steph, I'm angry too! So fucking angry! But I don't want you to spend your last few hours, or however long we have left feeling that way. I don't want you to give them the satisfaction of turning you into someone you're not. You didn't run because you're a good person Steph. You've always been a good person, and you knew that if you ran, you'd put the people around you at risk, your friends, your work colleagues, Crystal. You came here today for the same reasons that I did, to keep the people you love safe and to prevent anyone else from having to take your place." Tom said in a firm voice

"Why me Tom? I mean, why us? Why don't we deserve to grow old and grey like them?" Steph asked him, finally raising her head to meet his concerned gaze and nodding toward the two women on the bed opposite them, who had paused their happy chit-chat to watch the exchange.

"I don't know," Tom said quietly, wishing he had a better answer to give her.

"Because the world is a cruel, cruel place. You envy me for the life I've lived, and I don't blame you." One of the women chimed in.

Steph recognised her as the same lady she had seen with the cane outside the centre this morning, stubbornly standing as straight as her crooked frame would allow as she handed over her cull card to the rude guard.

"But let me tell you something, I wasn't done living. Not yet. I wanted to see my grandkids get married. I wanted to spend my last few years living peacefully with the man I've loved for sixty-one years. Dammit, I just wanted to see another Christmas. Yet here I am, just like you. No matter how many years you've lived, young lady, I can assure you, it'll never feel like enough. You'll always want more." The woman finished sagely.

Her words weren't intended to be unkind. That was clear from her tone and the small smile that played on her chapped lips as she spoke. They were just honest. Raw and painful, but at their core, honest and Steph realised that she was right. That Steph didn't deserve to live any more than the frail old woman, and her anger quickly faded into guilt for her harsh words.

"I'm sorry," Steph whispered.

"Don't be sorry, darling. Don't be angry." The woman said, reaching out and placing both of her tiny, withered hands over one of Steph's, clasping it firmly. "Be brave. Keep your head held high, and when your time comes, don't give them even one of your tears. Remember that they're the ones who have to live with what they've done. They're the ones who have to carry on knowing that they're only here because they murdered us."

Chapter Fifty-Three

When Steph's eyes flickered open, it took a few moments for her to recognise the dank room around her and recall where she was. The room had grown dark in the time that she had been sleeping, and only two insignificant bare bulbs remained lit over by the bathrooms, casting strangely elongated shadows from the bunks across the floor. Pushing herself up on her elbows into a sitting position, Steph stretched her legs off the edge of the mattress and pointed her toes, trying to ease some of the tightness in her muscles from falling asleep curled into a small ball. It was then that she noticed that Tom was no longer on the bed with her. Craning her neck around the side of her bunk, Steph squinted at the round clock on the far wall. It was nearly two o'clock in the morning. How long have I been asleep? She wondered to herself. Probing her mind, she recalled laying down on the too-hard mattress shortly after finishing the meal that had been provided for them and curling up under the thin mud-brown coloured blanket that she had been given, which was full of holes. She wasn't sure exactly what the non-descript soup-like substance that they had been served for dinner was, nor what the floating yellowish chunks inside of it had been and even if she had known, the smell coming off the steaming bowl that she had been handed would have been enough to put her off of tucking in. However, after some urging from Tom, she forced herself to consume as much of it as she could, despite not believing anything he said about needing to keep her strength up. What could she possibly need strength for now? Perhaps it would be better to allow herself to wither away on this brick of a mattress so that when they came for her, when someone stepped out of the door that she had seen many people walk through tonight but only doctors in stark white lab coats return from, and called her name, she would be too weak to resist what they were about to do to her. Steph remembered reminiscing with Tom about their days working together behind the bar, recalling some of their old regulars and a few staff members who had long since left fondly as they attempted to take their minds off of where they were and what was shortly to happen to them after they had forced down their dinner. She guessed she must have fallen asleep to the sound of Tom's comforting velvety voice sometime after then, the emotions of the day and pure exhaustion after sleeping so fitfully for so long getting the better of her.
Steph fumbled around the thin blanket on the bed, searching out the water bottle which she had refilled shortly before they had eaten with the chemical-tasting water from the bathrooms, wanting to quench her dry throat and rid her mouth of the taste of the soup, which was still lingering around her gums. I should have brushed my teeth after we ate.

She thought to herself, roaming her hands around in the semi-darkness, trying to locate the paper bag which contained her belongings into which she had placed the small toothbrush, toothpaste and bar of soap that she had been given earlier this afternoon in processing.
Eventually, Steph's fingers closed around the items she was looking for. She carefully withdrew them one by one as quietly as possible, not wanting to disturb the two elderly women on the bunk opposite her, who were both fast asleep, sitting upright side by side on the bed, emitting small puffs of air through their open mouths with their own blanket draped over both of their legs. Standing softly, Steph tiptoed between the long rows of bunk beds towards the bathrooms, trying not to focus too much on any of the people cocooned inside them but finding herself unable to resist sneaking a look at each of their faces as she passed.
It's like driving past a car crash on a motorway, she thought to herself. As much as you knew you shouldn't look, that there was a high chance that you would see something you didn't want to and regret it later, you couldn't seem to stop yourself at the moment. Every single one of the faces Steph caught a glimpse of in the muted-light of the room belonged to a condemned person. Someone who would shortly take their last breaths, and she knew that their pale, drawn faces would linger in her mind until her own time came, yet still, she looked, unable to stop herself. .
When Steph reached the ladies' room, she pushed open the door and, thankfully, found it deserted. A wave of relief crashed over her as she found the solitude she craved under the harsh fluorescent lighting that flickered above her head and reflected off the discoloured tiles on the walls. As much as Steph was grateful to Tom for trying to keep her calm and distracted all day, right now, she needed a few moments alone.
Just a few moments to try and resign herself to the fact that this was probably going to be her last night on earth and to try and come to terms with that fact so that she didn't get angry and start throwing another tantrum and embarrass herself again like she had earlier.
Twisting the stiff, tarnished tap, Steph watched as the water first began to drip, then sputter and then eventually steadily stream from the faucet before splashing some of the cooling liquid on her overheated skin. She tried her best to ignore the tingling sensation that the water left on her face as she squeezed some toothpaste from the tiny tube she had been given on to her toothbrush and began to scrub away the disgusting taste in her mouth.

Chapter Fifty-Four

"Do you know how much longer it will be?" Tom asked his dad as they stood together in the semi-darkness of a cramped storage room, surrounded by tall shelves full of vials of light blue medication and boxes of syringes along with other medical equipment on all sides. Nice place for a chat, dad, he thought to himself as he glanced around at the drugs, which were most certainly going to be used to kill him sooner rather than later.

It wasn't that Tom was eager for his name to be called and his life ended, however the waiting around was starting to get to him. Every time one of the doctors appeared from behind the 'staff only' door, Tom's heart began to race against his ribcage and he felt as though he couldn't drag enough air into his lungs. The familiar white lab coats which had been his constant companion for the last couple of years at work had now become a symbol of fear so potent that Tom didn't know how much longer he could stand it.

"I'm afraid I don't know, son. I know we're running behind; however, we are only given the next five people's names at a time. All I can tell you at the moment is that your name is not amongst those, but more than that, I just don't know. It could be tonight, tomorrow; it might be the day after. I'm sorry, I truly wish I had more information for you, but they don't tell us very much at all. They say it is for security purposes, but honestly, I believe that they are just trying to ensure that we know our places and that we remember that we have no power here." Jack whispered, keeping his voice low to ensure they wouldn't be heard by anyone who happened to pass by the storeroom, which had been the only place that he could think of to bring Tom tonight.

Most of the other staff members had long since left the centre for the night, heading home to their families, where they would try to forget about the horrors they had seen that day, but that wasn't an option for Jack. Not tonight. When his shift had ended at seven o'clock, he had shrugged off his lab coat, leaving it slung over the arm of one of the chairs in the staff room and picked up his tablet, pretending to be deeply engrossed in reading a recently published medical study as his colleagues had said their goodbyes. It had taken longer for them to leave than he had hoped. Some issue or another with one of the crematoriums had caused several of the higher-ups to have to hang around later than usual and Jack hadn't managed to sneak back into the dormitories and retrieve Tom until now, to spend what little time he could with his son before it was too late.

Jack couldn't go home tonight, perhaps not tomorrow night either. He knew that he wouldn't set one single foot outside of the centre the entire time that Tom was still breathing inside of it. He could not go home to his wife and his two other children until he could tell them that Tom was now at peace and he couldn't bear the thought of leaving Tom alone in this place.

Until Jack could return the few meagre belongings that his son had brought to the centre with him to their rightful place in his childhood bedroom, a place that he knew would become a shrine to the young man who stood before him under the muted light from the torch that he had retrieved from a toolbox left behind in the staffroom to light his way with this evening, he would stay right here.

Jack wouldn't leave the centre until after Tom had been culled, and when he did, he had already vowed that he would never again return. They could find someone else to murder innocent people. Jack had already put himself through more days in this dreadful place than he wanted to remember.

"It's not as though I'm in a hurry," Tom said, forcing a laugh from his dry throat, which came out as more of a sarcastic bark. "It's just, the longer I sit around in that dorm, the more time I have to think, you know. And the weaker I feel."

"You aren't weak, son. You could never be. You've always been one of the strongest people that I know. And the most stubborn. No matter how many times I've tried to convince you to follow the path that I had in mind for you, you've always known what you wanted and stuck to your resolve, never wavering in your decisions. It's one of the things that I admire about you the most." Jack said honestly, a lump rising in his throat as he spoke. He knew it was far too late for him to admit these thoughts to Tom, when nothing could be changed. Jack should have realised all this sooner. When it could have made a difference, when he still had time to try and repair their fractured relationship, but even though that was no longer an option, he didn't want his eldest child going to his death without knowing how proud of him Jack truly was.

"That might have been nice to know a little earlier, dad," Tom said, raising an eyebrow at his father's words. "I've spent most of my adult life convinced you thought I was an idiot."

"I did." Jack chuckled, raising a hand to cover his mouth and stifle the sound, "I still think you'd have had a much easier time of it if you had agreed to come and work at my hospital with me. Not to mention that you would have been better compensated. That doesn't mean I wasn't proud of you for standing up for yourself and doing what was right for you, no matter who tried to dissuade you. Even when that person was me."

Tom found himself laughing lightly at his father's words, more out of shock than actual amusement. Why did it take such a horrible situation for them to finally speak to one another like this? As adults? As equals? Why couldn't they have found a way to overcome their differences long ago?

"You've only got yourself to blame, you know that, right? It's not like I inherited my stubbornness from mum." Tom said, his laughter dying instantly on his lips as he pictured his mother sitting at home alone, waiting for Jack to return and tell her that their son was gone.

Before Jack could respond to his son's words with anything more than a solemn nod, a thunderous noise reverberated through the storage room. Sending boxes of syringes and vials of medication tumbling from the shelves around them and onto the floor, where the glass bottles shattered into a thousand tiny sparkling shards reflecting in the torchlight. Caught off guard, Tom stumbled backwards and reached out a hand, pressing it heavily against the wall beside him, trying his best to keep his balance as the whole building seemed to quiver beneath his feet, his eyes locked on to his fathers as he watched Jack do the same thing on the other side of the room.

The deafening noises seemed to bounce off the walls around them, careening into Tom from every direction. Although they couldn't have lasted for more than a few seconds, to Tom, it felt like an age passed before the ringing in his ears began to dim and he started to make out the sounds of voices frantically screaming out to one another from back in the dormitory.

"Steph." He whispered to himself, and without so much as glancing back at his dad, Tom wrenched open the door and headed out into the hallway as fast as his injured ankle could carry him. He had to get back to the dorms. He had to find her. A wave of guilt crashed over him as he cursed himself for leaving her alone in the first place. What was I thinking? He scolded himself with a shake of his head as he stumbled down the hallway. .

Chapter Fifty-Five

The scream that escaped Steph's lips as she fell to the floor was drowned out instantly by the crashing of plaster crumbling from the walls around her and tumbling to the ground. She felt a large, jagged piece smash into her forehead, blurring her vision for a moment as she tried to figure out what the hell was going on. Lifting her arms over her head, Steph curled into a ball on the hard, cold tiles beneath her in an attempt to protect herself from sustaining any more injuries as debris continued to fall and clouds of dust seeped into her lungs, making her cough. Steph sucked in short sharp breaths through her nose and desperately tried to stop imagining herself being buried alive as the vibrations continued and deep, booming noises echoed all around her. When the noises stopped at last, Steph could not convince herself to move from her cocooned position on the ground or even to open her eyes. Trembling from head to toe, she lay in shock, waiting for the next blow and willing her heart rate to return to normal. The next sounds that she heard were not those of destruction, but of fear. Pure, unfiltered fear and sheer chaos erupting from the frightened mouths of the people that she had left sleeping in the dorms as they all shouted over one another, trying to figure out what had happened, whilst others, who she assumed had been injured, cried out for help.
Scrambling to her knees, Steph placed a palm carefully on the floor and pushed herself to her feet, taking in the destruction around her as she did so. The bathroom hadn't exactly been in the best condition when she had arrived but now it looked like a battlefield. Only a handful of the discoloured tiles had stayed secured to the walls, the rest having smashed to the floor, taking large chunks of plaster along with them and leaving deep crevasses in the brickwork. Two of the doors to the stalls had come off their hinges and now hung precariously at rather odd angles and the sink, which she had been standing at just a few moments ago brushing her teeth, sported a long crack down one side and looked as though it may split open at any moment.
The mirror above the sink had somehow miraculously survived. Although it was now covered in a thick layer of beige dust and as Steph gazed at her reflection, she could clearly see the bright red blood trickling from a cut above her right eyebrow and the large angry welt forming around it. "Dammit." She hissed as she raised her fingers to the wound, probing it gently and wincing in pain. She was dimly aware of other injuries on her body, but she knew she didn't have time to concern herself with those now, she had to get out of here, she had to find Tom. Hastily scooping up her few belongings and shoving them into the pockets of her jeans, Steph made her way quickly to the bathroom door.

Suddenly no longer concerned for her own well-being but terrified for his. What if he'd been injured? If the devastation in the tiny bathroom was this bad, how bad was it out in the dorms?

"What the hell?" Steph muttered to herself, stifling a cough as she tugged on the bathroom door handle, increasing her force as it remained stubbornly closed before her, barely so much as registering the fact that she was trying to move it at all. A trickle of cold sweat began to slide down

Steph's forehead as she used all of her strength to try and force it open, pushing one foot against the wall to try to gain some leverage, but no matter how hard she tried, the door refused to budge.

I'm trapped. Steph realised as fear coursed through her, and she began to pummel the wood in front of her with her fists, taking as deep a breath as she could manage in the dust-filled air and screaming out at the top of her lungs. "Help! Somebody help me!" As she prayed that her hoarse wails could be heard over the cacophony in the dorms and that someone would come to her rescue.

Tom's eyes burned as he hurried down the hall, and he felt trickles of liquid run down his cheeks as the thick black smoke that clung to the air around him irritated them and made them water. He felt the substance which seemed to be part smoke, part dust from the crumbling walls around him, start to seep into his lungs as he heaved in gulps of air and began to cough as he half ran, half stumbled along, wondering what on earth had happened, and more importantly, whether or not it was over.

"Son, wait!" Jack cried, grabbing Tom's elbow harshly just before he rounded the corner at the end of the hallway. "You have to get out of here now." He told him insistently, digging his free hand into his pocket.

Jack had suspected that something like this might happen sooner rather than later. However, he hadn't dared to hope it would coincide with Tom being at the centre, too much hope could be a dangerous thing. Now that it was happening however, now that there was a chance, he knew that they had no time to lose and that he had to get his son out of here right now.

"What? Get out? Dad, what's going on?" Tom asked, bewildered, as Jack yanked him towards a small, cracked window and pointed down towards the street by way of explanation.

The sight outside of the population control centre stopped Tom dead in his tracks, no longer even bothering to try and fight against his fathers too tight grip on his arm, where Jack's fingers were pressing on the bruises that the security guard who had dragged him into the centre earlier had left on his skin, causing them to throb. Ignoring the pain,

Tom stared out of the window in utter disbelief at the chaos unfolding on the street beneath him.

"The Right to Life rebels. Tom, that's them, I'm sure of it. They tried to attack the centre before, and they failed, but tonight, well, tonight, it seems that they have come better prepared. You must get out of here, Tom, whilst you still can! Please, son. Here, take these." Jack said frantically, shoving the torch, a set of keys and his wallet into Tom's shaking hands. "There's a few hundred pounds in there, enough to get you moving at least. And you can withdraw the rest from my savings at the first cashpoint you see. But make sure to do it as close to the centre as possible and then dump the wallet. Don't give them any chance of being able to track you. Head for the country, or the coast perhaps, and lay low. You're a smart boy. Live off the land, stay out of the cities and away from populated areas."

"What, dad? I can't just leave! They'll know you helped me! It won't take long for them to realise I'm your son. Besides, what even makes you think I could get out? We're six floors up! No doubt the C.E.A will be here long before I can reach the exit." Tom replied, still unable to take his eyes off the swarms of people on the street below him. There's got to be five or six hundred of them down there, he realised as his eyes roved over the black-covered bodies illuminated under the streetlamps. He watched in amazement as one of the rebels lifted a thin burning piece of wood to a small black device in another's hand, lighting a fuse that dangled from the end of it. Tom's eyes widened in shock as the man holding the device reared back, pulling his arm as far behind him as he could before shooting it forwards and releasing the object clutched in his fist straight towards the population control centre's lower floors. Within seconds the sound of another explosion, so similar to the one he had heard just moments ago, ripped through the air and the building shook violently, causing the light fixtures above Tom to rattle unsettlingly.

Bombs. They're throwing bombs. Tom realised, and he prayed that there weren't too many people housed on the lower floors where the rebels were aiming.

"Don't worry about me. I'll be fine. You just get yourself out of here! The keys will open the rear door of the centre, don't try and get out of the main entrance, not with all those people out there. There's a forest behind the centre which goes on for miles. Just get yourself in there and keep running!" Jack insisted, shouting now to be heard over the sounds of the crowds outside and the screams coming from inside this very building where he was sure that all hell was breaking loose.

Glancing over his shoulder, Jack saw the familiar unfriendly face of one of the security guards who always prowled the centre at night appear

from the staff room at the other end of the smoke-filled corridor and begin charging in their direction. He knew he had to get Tom out of here right now. If the guard caught him, he'd no doubt try to restrain Tom or perhaps shut him in one of the secure rooms where the cullings took place until the C.E.A arrived or the rebels outside dispersed, and that would be that. Tom would be trapped here. Any chance of him managing to escape would be gone.
Not caring at that moment for his own safety or for what might happen to him, Jack grabbed Tom's arm again and pushed him around the corner out of sight of the security guard who was approaching rapidly, his heavy footfalls echoing along the corridor getting louder by the minute.
"I can't just leave you here, dad," Tom shouted at his father as he stumbled along, unsure if the moisture in his eyes was from the smoke or the overwhelming emotions that he could feel bubbling up inside him. He thought he was going to have more time, enough time at least, to say a proper goodbye to the man that had raised him. There were so many things that he still wanted to say! No, that he *needed* to say. But it seemed his time had run out.
"You can. You can and you will." Jack said stubbornly.
Accepting that his father was right, that it was now or never, Tom reached out his arms and gave his dad the only goodbye he could now in these frantic moments. Jack pulled his son tightly to his chest, his thick arms encircling Toms shoulders as he struggled to hold back his own emotions as they embraced for what was not only the first time in years, but probably the last time that they ever would before he stepped back, taking one last moment to look into the startling green eyes that were so like his own.
"I love you, son. Now go. Go!" he ordered, pushing Tom back toward the dorms.

Chapter Fifty-Six

"Alright, lads, showtime," David shouted as he sprung from his bunk nimbly despite his bulky six-foot-four frame. He was more than ready for action, having been waiting eagerly for this moment since he first entered the centre two days ago. Thrusting a large, calloused hand underneath the mattress, he pulled out a long shard of plastic which he had snapped off the tray on which his dinner had been handed to him the night before and which he had subsequently spent most of today carefully sharpening against the bare floors when no one was paying any attention to him until its tip was as lethal as any knife would be. Straightening up, he listened to the reassuring sounds of the other men in his team doing the same thing as he caught the eye of Paul, one of his colleagues for this operation in the next bunk and gave him a reassuring nod. They were ready. More than ready.

The first explosion had hit at precisely two am. Exactly as he had been told it would, and David had been laying on his bunk wide awake for hours, staring up at the clock opposite his bed, just willing the minutes to tick by faster as the people around him finally succumbed to sleep. As he could have predicted, the entire room around him had descended into chaos within seconds of the first bomb being thrown, and the noise, even now, was deafening. People were screaming, calling out in fear and confusion as they were awoken from sleep by the noise of the explosions and the vibrations of their metal bedsteads beneath them and were now all starting to rush towards the doors through which they had first entered the dormitories. It made sense, David figured, that was the only way out that they knew, it was how they had gotten into the centre, so it was the most logical way to escape again. Only David and the handful of others in his group who had been planted here specifically to participate in tonight's action knew better. The doors which led back into processing were one way. They only opened inwards, towards the dorms. Once you were through, there was no going back. The only way out was through the staff area.

Forcing his way through the throngs of hysterical people darting this way and that in the semi-darkness, David felt his team fall into step behind him as he stormed down the rows of bunk beds towards the door marked 'staff only', pausing for only a moment to check that his group was all with him, ready and armed before he reached out and grabbed the metal handle.

"Woah!" David sprang back as the door before him swung open, adopting a fighting stance and raising his makeshift weapon, ready to attack whatever staff member was in front of him until he saw the familiar face of the young guy who had approached him earlier and asked when they could expect to receive dinner. His drawn face as white as snow except for what looked to be ash streaked here and there across his defined features.

"Jesus, kid, I nearly stabbed you. What were you doing back there?" David demanded, suspicious now as he looked down into the man's bright green eyes. None of the condemned people that had passed through this door in the two days that he had been here had ever returned, the only people who went through these doors were the staff and those on their way to be culled. So what was this guy up to?

"Nothing. I mean, it doesn't matter. Just get out of my way!" Tom shouted back at the man as he tried to shove past him, barging into his shoulder as he barrelled through the doorway. Tom didn't have time to be polite or make idle chit chat with the man who he'd spoken to earlier or his band of friends standing behind him. He needed to find Steph. I should never have left her, he scolded himself yet again as he continued to push past the men standing in his way.

"You're going the wrong way! The only way out is back this way!" David called after Tom as he regained his balance, unable to help himself. Something about the young guy drew David to him, and honestly, the kid looked like he could probably handle himself in a fight if it came to it. David wouldn't have minded having another person backing him up tonight but Tom didn't stop or even acknowledge his words, so David couldn't be sure if the kid had heard him as he continued to stare after him.

"Let him go, David. We don't have time for this. The others will get in eventually, and they'll get everyone else out, but for that to happen, we've got to get downstairs and get the doors open." Matthew, one of David's group and a friend whom he had known since childhood, said from over his shoulder, shouting to be heard over the volume of voices still frantically yelling in the dormitory and tugging on David's arm, preventing him from trying to follow Tom back into the dorms.

David knew that Matthew was right. This plan had been in motion for weeks now, months maybe, and he couldn't be the one to ruin it. It was too important. He knew it had taken an awful lot of effort to get his name, along with those of the other six men around him, onto the cull list and into the centre this week when they weren't supposed to be here, when their names had never been drawn in the so-called lottery. That there were hundreds, possibly a thousand people outside the centre right now, putting their lives and the lives of their families in jeopardy to try and liberate the people who had been unjustly sent here to be murdered and that he had to stick to the plan. He couldn't go chasing after some random guy just because he felt bad that he was going the wrong way, no matter how curious he was about him.

"Come on," David said, resigning to leaving the boy to fend for himself and turning back to the still-open door. "Let's go."

Chapter Fifty-Seven

"Steph? Stephanie Moore?" Tom shouted between coughs when he finally got back into the dormitory. It felt like it had been hours since he had left it, since he had spotted his fathers tired looking face peeking out from behind the staff-only door with a torch in his hand and had left Steph sleeping on the bunk they were sharing and gone to talk to Jack. He hadn't even thought to wake her, to tell her where he was going so that she wouldn't worry if she woke up and found him gone, because he hadn't anticipated being away for more than a few minutes and because, well, she just looked so damn peaceful. For the first time since they had arrived at the centre, Steph's rapid breathing had fallen into a steady pattern, her cheeks weren't flushed with anger, and no tears streamed from her closed eyelids and Tom hadn't been able to bring himself to disturb her. He had just left, tiptoeing across the room as carefully as he could manage and slipping through the small crack in the doorway and out to his father.

I should have woken her. Tom scolded himself as he shouldered his way through the crowds of people darting around the room. He hadn't gotten more than half a dozen steps inside when he was suddenly knocked from his feet by another shockwave which caused the ground beneath him to shudder violently and caught him so off guard that he careened straight into the post of the nearest bunk, jarring his shoulder on the metal frame painfully as he crashed into it.

"Please! Please help us!" a frightened voice called out to him from the bottom bunk, and Tom ducked his head down to look at its owner as the room continued to shake around him and screams fell on his ears from every direction.

Laying on the bed, her head resting in the lap of a guy in his twenties with a buzz cut, was a frail young woman who couldn't have even been out of her teens. Blood was pouring from a wound on her head, and one of her arms lay at an awkward angle, clearly broken. Shit. Tom thought, his eyes darting around the room, still searching for Steph. He didn't have time for this. He had to find her, but the doctor inside of him, the man who had trained and dreamed of nothing more than helping people for as long as he could remember, couldn't walk away from the bleeding woman.

"Please." The man pleaded again, his wide eyes staring up at Tom as he cradled the woman, desperate for help.

"Shit," Tom said again exasperatedly, only out loud this time, as the shuddering around him stopped, he was able to make his way around the bed, crouching on the floor and reaching out a hand to check the woman's pulse.

"What happened?" He asked the man who had called out to him, who he could see was barely a man at all now that he was closer to him and the torch he still clutched in one hand was shining its beam across the guy's face.
"We were on the top bunk, and then everything started shaking, and she fell. What's going on? Is it an earthquake?" The kid asked him, stuttering slightly as he spoke.
"No. Not an earthquake." Tom told him as he examined the wound on the back of the woman's head. "What's your name?" He asked the boy.
"Terry. I'm Terry. And this is Sarah. My sister."
"Terry, I need clean water and something to make a sling out of." He continued.
"I can get water from the bathrooms. Here, take this." The boy said, pulling the button-down shirt he wore from his shoulders and handing it to Tom before extricating himself from underneath his sister carefully.
Tom continued to examine his patient while waiting for the boy to return with the water, but he couldn't stop himself from scanning the room every few moments, hoping to catch a glimpse of Steph. Where the hell is she? He wondered.

"Help!! Somebody help me!!" Steph screamed as loudly as she could, still banging her fists against the hard wooden bathroom door just like she had been doing for at least the last five minutes. Two more explosions had gone off in the time that she had been trapped in here. Both times she had hoped against hope that one of them would knock the door free from its rusted hinges as the first one had done to the doors on the stalls so that she could get out, but no such luck.
The main door was much sturdier than the flimsy pieces of plywood that sat in the stall door frames and it seemed utterly determined to continue blocking Stephs exit no matter what she did. There was a small window at the opposite end of the bathroom, and she had considered for a moment, trying to smash the glass and squeeze through it. Until she remembered that she was six floors up that is, and that even if she could get out of the window, the chances of her surviving a fall like that were slim, so she had resumed her pounding.
Surely someone would have to hear her soon. Someone would find a way to get the door open and free her? Wouldn't they? She wondered as her heartbeat rapidly in her chest and her anxiety increased.
"Is someone in there?" A male voice called through the wood, and Steph nearly fainted from sheer relief at the sound.
"Yes! Yes, I'm in here! I'm trapped. Can you try and open the door?" She cried
"Yeah, erm, stand back." The voice said timidly, and moments later,

Steph heard a heavy thud as something, his foot, she assumed, connected with the wood. The door shuddered in its frame for a moment but then returned to its previous position.

"Harder! You need to hit it harder!" She shouted to the stranger, willing him to try again.

"I can't, I... I…" Terry stuttered, unsure what to do. He needed to get back to his bunk, to his sister who had been so badly injured and give the man that was helping her the water he'd just fetched from the men's room. He couldn't bear to be away from her for any longer than he had to be, his sister was all that he had now.

When both of them received alerts within two days of one another a couple of months ago, it had hit their parents hard. Especially their mother. She couldn't stand the idea of watching both of her children march off to the population control centre to be culled. Let alone contemplate the idea of living on without them after they were gone. So, one night, when everyone had been sleeping, she'd climbed into the bathtub and taken a razor blade to her wrists.

Their father had found her the next morning, and it was the first time Terry had ever seen his old man cry. Attracted by the wails emitting from the bathroom, Terry had stood in the doorway and watched in disbelief as his dad had lifted his mother's lifeless naked body from the bright red water that filled the porcelain tub and cradled her tightly to his chest as he begged and pleaded with her to open her eyes.

Nothing had been the same after that. His dad, angry and grieving for the woman he loved, could barely stand to look at either of his children or to be in the house that reminded him so much of his wife of fifteen years and had started coming home less and less until he just stopped coming back altogether. Then, it had been just Terry and Sarah. Fending for themselves, awaiting their end-of-life dates.

Taking a deep breath Terry took a few steps back from the door and fortified himself to make one last attempt to knock it down. Just one more try, he told himself. Then I'll get back to Sarah.

"Stand back!" He shouted again before racing forwards, barrelling into the door with as much force as he could muster and shoving his shoulder into the wood. The impact made him wince, and he heard a slight crack as part of the door splintered where his shoulder had connected with it, but it didn't swing open as he had hoped that it would.

"I'm sorry! I'll get help!" Terry shouted through the door, knowing there was no way he could break it down on his own and resigning himself to getting someone else to come and help him free the woman trapped behind it.

"No, no, you have to help me! You can do it. I know you can! Just try one more time!" Steph pleaded with the stranger, leaning her sore head

on the door, her breaths coming thick and fast now as she started to panic. He couldn't let her leave. What if he never came back? What if no one else heard her screams and she remained trapped here?
"I'm sorry." The voice repeated, but more quietly now and a single tear slipped from Steph's tightly closed eyelids as she heard his footsteps retreating from the bathroom.

Chapter Fifty-Eight

How much longer was the kid going to be? Tom wondered to himself, his anxiety mounting as he perched on the edge of the bed next to the young woman who was still unconscious. He needed to find Steph, they had to get out of here. Tom had no idea how long it would be until the Cull Enforcement Agency arrived en-masse to secure the building, but he guessed that it wouldn't take them long to send in the troops and he couldn't risk losing his only chance to escape.

When the boy, Terry, finally reappeared by his side, red-faced and huffing great puffs of air from his lips as he wordlessly handed Tom a full bottle of water, Tom sighed in relief. Just a few more minutes, I'll just wash out her cut, and then they'll have to fend for themselves, like everyone else here. He thought to himself as he took the bottle and wet the corner of a blanket. Not the most hygienic option, but short of taking the shirt off his own back, it was the only one Tom had right now.

Every chance he could, Tom stole a moment to check over his shoulder and around the dormitory for any signs of Steph. Twice now he thought he had heard her voice calling out for help, but no matter how much he scanned the room, he couldn't see any sign of her.

"Is she going to be okay?" Terry asked Tom in a frightened voice, and, as agitated as he was with this whole situation, Tom couldn't help feeling for the kid. He couldn't have been more than twenty or so, and the fear in his voice was clear for anyone to hear. Tom couldn't even begin to imagine how he would feel if it were his sister lying unconscious in this place. Just picturing Emily having to walk through the doors to the centre made him sick to his stomach, let alone lying here with a head wound in the middle of all this chaos and destruction.

"I think so. Her pulse is steady and strong, but her arm is definitely broken. She probably passed out from the shock. When she wakes up, if she's slurring her words at all or complaining of double vision, then she might have a concussion." Tom told Terry, slipping easily back into his doctor's role despite the unusual circumstances.

"How do you know all that? Are you some kind of doctor or something?" Terry asked. He'd finally caught his breath after his exertions trying to break down the bathroom door and was now curious about the kind stranger who was gently cleaning the cut on his sister's head.

"Something like that," Tom admitted, unsure what else to say.

Normally in a situation like this, he'd tell the boy what to do if his sister did appear concussed when she regained consciousness and he'd advise taking her to the emergency room to have her arm set and plastered, but what use would that advice be now? It's not like the kid could carry his sister down six flights of stairs, past the crowds of rebels outside and over to the hospital across the street. They would have no choice but to stay here, and that meant that both the boy and his sister would more than likely be dead within days. Anything Tom might suggest would just be pointless, empty words.

When Tom was satisfied that he had done all he could for the young woman, he jumped to his feet and started to walk away from the bed, darting his head left and right, still searching for Steph in the jumble of people rushing here and there in the dormitory.

"Wait! There's someone trapped back there in the bathrooms. I tried to help her, but I couldn't get the door open. I promised her I would get help and come back." Terry called after him, and Tom felt his shoulders slump as he turned back to face him. Seriously, this kid just needed to leave him alone. Tom couldn't take responsibility for everyone in the dormitory, there had to be two hundred people in here. He had to prioritise, and right now, his priority was to find Steph.

"Sorry, Terry, but I've gotta go. My friend is missing. You'll have to get someone else to help you this time." Tom said, feeling the guilt weighing heavily on his chest already but knowing he had no choice as he watched the boy's face fall.

"Okay. I'll do that. And Mr? Thank you." Terry said, and the ghost of a smile slipped across his features.

Chapter Fifty-Nine

When the explosions finally stopped and a couple of minutes had passed since the building last reverberated beneath her feet, Steph sucked in a sigh of relief. Pacing up and down the small bathroom, she weighed her options as she tried not to slip on the debris-covered floor and injure herself any more than she already had. The pounding in her forehead resembled a marching band drummer keeping time, and Steph was pretty sure she had bruised, if not cracked, at least one rib if the stabbing pain in her side was any indication.
Not that it matters, she thought. It's not like the medics here will see my injuries and give me a reprieve, it's not as though they are going to care if the person they murder is in one piece or not.
She needed a plan. By her estimations, it had been over ten minutes since the boy with the frightened voice had given up trying to knock the door down and left her stuck here alone. It seemed highly unlikely to her that he was going to return, so she would have to devise another plan of action. The way Steph saw it, she had two choices. Either she could continue pacing up and down the bathroom until her legs gave out or her anxiety got the best of her and she crumpled to the floor and curled into a ball until another explosion hit and killed her, or someone magically came to her rescue, which seemed unlikely. Or she could find a way to open the goddamn door and get out of here herself.
Springing into action, Steph started to look around the room for something, anything that she might be able to use to pry the door from its frame or perhaps take it off its hinges. The hinges! That was it, she realised, and not wanting to waste another moment, she dropped to her knees and started searching through the cracked tiles on the floor. There had to be something here that was small enough, sharp enough, she reasoned as she searched through the debris, pricking her hands-on splintered pieces of porcelain in the process. Eventually, Steph managed to locate a two-inch-long tile shard which had broken off into a point at one end. Yes, this might just work! She thought as she jumped back to her feet and rushed towards the door. Positioning the tile, she slipped its broken edge into the groove on the head of one of the screws holding the door in place and began to twist.

"Stephanie! Stephanie Moore! Dammit, Steph, answer me!" Tom shouted as he ran down the rows of bunkbeds frantically searching for her. There were only four logical answers that Tom could come up with for why Steph wasn't answering him, for why he couldn't find her even in amongst all this chaos. The first answer was quickly disproven by a quick glance in the direction of the two stark white doors which led through to the processing area which they had entered through earlier today, where a large group of people were intently pulling at the metal handles, trying desperately to pry the doors open with no success and getting more frustrated by the minute from the looks of the expressions on their dust covered faces.

Alright, so she hadn't gone through that way then, if those doors were firmly shut.. Tom deduced. That left option two, the staff-only door he had returned through after talking to his dad. But that seemed unlikely. Even when he'd been helping the young boy and his sister, he had only been a couple of bunks away from that door. Surely he'd have seen Steph if she had passed him? Or she would have seen him and stopped? The third option to explain Steph's disappearance wasn't one he could bear to even contemplate right now, that she had been hurt or perhaps even killed in the blasts and was lying under one of the piles of rubble that littered the floor all around the dormitory. No. That can't be what's happened, Tom tried to reassure himself as he rounded the next row of bunks and shook his head, trying to rid his mind of the dark images gathering there.

That only left one other place that she could be. The bathrooms. Shit! Tom thought as he hastened his movements, heading back towards the other end of the room. Terry had said there was a woman trapped in the bathroom who needed help! What if that was Steph? What if she were hurt and he'd spent all this time running around searching for her for nothing when he could have just done as Terry had asked and gone to the bathrooms to help whoever was trapped in there straight away? Trying to banish the guilt from his mind, knowing that it would do him no good now, Tom raced down the last row of bunks as fast as he could, barging past stragglers who were still standing idly by their beds, looking lost and confused and Ignoring pleas for help from others who had visible injuries. He even jumped over what was either a dead or unconscious body on the floor, he couldn't be sure as he hadn't taken the time to stop and check. Tom was a man on a mission and made his way as quickly as possible towards the wooden doors at the far end of the dormitory.

Chapter Sixty

David kept his back pressed firmly up against the wall as he crept along the long corridor behind the staff doorway, feeling the peeling plaster crumbling behind his shoulders with each step that he took as he pulled the images of the plans of the building which he had studied for weeks before heading to the centre to the forefront of his mind and tried to get his bearings. Take the first left, then the staff room will be the third door on the right, he muttered quietly to himself as he made his way down the hallway.

The darkness was almost absolute in the thin corridor. Only a faint light shone from a distant, partially open doorway at the other end of the passage, casting shadows across the damaged floor and making it difficult for David to see anything in his immediate vicinity. A double-edged sword, he thought to himself. He might not be able to see if anyone were in front of him, but equally, they wouldn't be able to make out him and his team lurking in the darkness either.

Approaching the corner, a faint sound no louder than a gust of wind attracted his attention in the near silence in the corridor and David held up a clenched fist, signalling for the rest of his group to come to a stop as he flattened himself against the wall, trying to keep his breathing as quiet and as even as possible whilst his heart beat frantically as he waited in the darkness.

The adrenaline coursing through his veins was all too familiar to him, David had been in this situation many times in many different countries all over the world, and his experience wrapped around him like a warm, comforting blanket, settling over his shoulders and filling him with a sense of calm. He barely had to think about his actions, barely had to focus on anything more than taking his next breath, knowing that instinct would take care of the rest. After all is said and done, aren't we all animals? I'm just another animal stalking my prey, David thought as another sound, closer this time, only a few feet away, caught his attention and he inched forwards, craning his head around the nearby corner and squinting his eyes down the passage.

He heard the speeding bullet flying through the air before the sound of the shot even registered in his ears, hastily fired from his prey's gun. The man wasn't aiming at him specifically, he had just fired a warning shot into the dark, more designed to deter anyone approaching than to actually hit them and the bullet didn't even come close to colliding with David or any of his team. Instead, it crashed into the opposite wall with a sickening crack as it buried itself deep into the plaster, sending clouds of white powdery dust into the air. Despite the shooter's misplaced aim, the shot and the flash from the gun barrel as it spat out the speeding projectile were enough to tell David where his quarry was and he rushed forwards before the sound of the gunshot had even finished echoing down the hall, his makeshift weapon held high in the air in front of him and the sound of another pair of footsteps, Matthew's he guessed, following close by on his heels.

David's instincts didn't disappoint him, as he knew they wouldn't. The sharp piece of plastic slid into the man's neck as though he were made of butter. Penetrating deep into the fragile skin and causing warm liquid to spurt over David's hand as he yanked his weapon free before plunging it into the man's neck again. Raising his free hand, David slapped it across the guy's mouth to stifle the screams he was pitifully trying to force past his lips and felt more sticky wetness congeal on his palm as the man coughed up mouthfuls of blood between gasping breaths.

When David withdrew his weapon for the third time, he felt the man begin to slump and he quickly repositioned himself to catch him as he started to fall towards the ground, supporting the bulk of his weight and lowering him to the floor with the help of Matthew, who had just appeared by his side, as quietly as possible.

"Do you think anyone heard that?" Matthew asked in a hushed whisper, his face barely visible in the darkness even though he stood just inches from David.

"Let's not stick around to find out. Come on, the staff room is just down here." David replied equally quietly as he signalled for the rest of the team to follow and continued down the hall.

Chapter Sixty-One

One down. Two to go. Steph thought to herself when she finally managed to extract the pair of screws from the hinge on the door nearest the ceiling. Dropping them to the floor, she paused momentarily to wipe the sweat from her brow and allowed herself to settle her feet flat on the floor below her. Having been standing on her tiptoes for the best part of ten minutes whilst she wrestled the annoying metal object from the door, the backs of her calves were screaming at her for a break. Her hands ached from gripping the shard of tile that she had foraged from the mess on the ground, and tiny specks of blood trickled down her palm from where the object had bitten into her skin.
This is going to take forever, she realised as she stared helplessly at the three remaining hinges before her. Any hopes she had harboured of the boy with the frightened voice returning with help to rescue her had long since vanished from her mind as she worked. The only thoughts that clouded her anxious mind now were that of her own predicament, and of Tom.
Where had he disappeared to when she had been sleeping? Why hadn't he come looking for her? She wondered as she started to work the thin edge of the tile into the crevasse in the next screw head and began to turn it. Was he trapped somewhere as well? Or, had the doctors decided to carry on the cullings throughout the night? Had he not been by her side on the bed when she awoke because, behind as they were, the staff had summoned him and taken him off to be killed? No, surely if that had been the case, he would have woken her up, would have told her what was happening. He would have said goodbye. Wouldn't he?
Panic began to overwhelm Steph again as she worked. On more than one occasion, she nearly dropped the slippery ceramic tile in her hand as her palms grew sweatier and trembled as her heart raced. She couldn't allow herself to think this way, not if she wanted to have any chance of getting out of here alive, she had to concentrate on the task at hand. Steph couldn't help the bubble of laughter that rose in her dry throat as she continued to wrestle with the screw. Yes, better concentrate on getting out of here in one piece so that I can be killed by the nice injection, she giggled to herself, realising the absurdity of her thoughts. Perhaps she was going mad, or perhaps her head injury had been more severe than she had thought. Ordinary people didn't laugh over thoughts of their impending death.
Pull yourself together, Steph scolded herself, blinking firmly twice and refocusing on her task. As soon as she got this door off, she could search for Tom. If he were trapped, too, then she could help him, if he were injured, she could try and care for him, but if she didn't get out of

here... Well, that was another thought she couldn't afford to have right now.

Tom's heart pounded in his chest as he covered the last few feet to the bathrooms, ignoring the throbbing pain in his ankle as he stumbled along. It was quieter down this end of the dorms now, only a handful of people still lingered near the bare lightbulbs, which swayed in front of the doors, illuminating his way. They seemed to him like frightened moths, too scared to move away from the only source of light nearby. Some were sitting in silence against the walls, their legs pulled up tightly to their chests as they rocked back and forth, whether in shock or pain, Tom did not know. It took all the willpower he possessed not to stop and check on every person that he passed as he made his way to the door, it wasn't in his nature to ignore people in need of help, but he knew that he didn't have the time.

If it was Steph trapped in the bathroom, who knew what state she was in. The explosions had caused masses of devastation in the vast open-plan dormitory, he could only imagine how severely damaged the tiny bathrooms would be, and he couldn't waste another minute getting to them.

Skidding to a stop before the door, Tom took a deep, dust-filled breath and called out "Hello? Is anyone in there?" at the top of his lungs.

"Tom?" Steph cried, tears of joy filling her eyes at the sound of his voice booming through the wood before her.

"Steph!! Steph, is that you? I've been looking everywhere for you. Are you okay?" Tom asked her frantically as the knot that had been sitting in his stomach since he returned to the dorms finally started to loosen at the sound of her voice. He had found her, at last.

"Yes, I'm okay. Are you?" Steph asked him, desperate for reassurance that he wasn't hurt.

Tom couldn't help but chuckle slightly at her absurd question. No one in this building was okay right now, not really. However, she was the one trapped in the damn bathroom with all this chaos going on around them, not him, and yet here she was, only worrying about everyone else, something which was becoming more evident to Tom by the minute was a well-ingrained personality trait.

"I'm fine. We need to get you out of there." He called back, and Steph breathed a huge sigh of relief. Thank goodness he's alright, she thought as her shoulders slumped and she felt her heart rate begin to steady for the first time since the initial explosion.

"The door's jammed. I've managed to unscrew one of the hinges, and I'm working on another, but maybe you can find a way to knock it loose?" Steph asked, unsure she had the strength left to finish her task.

"Stand back!" Tom shouted, backing up slightly before ramming his shoulder into the wood. He felt the soft muscle of his shoulder depress at the impact and tried to ignore the pain that shot through his arm, studying the door as it shuddered against its frame for a moment or two. To his dismay, it did no more than that.

Shit. He thought, there's no way I can break this down alone. Twisting around, Tom surveyed his surroundings, trying to see if there was anyone nearby who he could ask to help him, but the only people within his immediate area were the ones rocking against the walls, and they wouldn't be of any help. Then he saw it, sitting on the floor just a few metres away, glinting up at him in the muted light from the bulb above his head, a large steel bar which had once been part of a bunk bed but had broken clean off in one of the explosions and now lay abandoned on the floor.

Racing across the concrete, Tom stooped and grabbed at the bar, yanking it up and stumbling slightly under the weight. Yes, this should work, he reassured himself as he headed back to Steph.

"I'm going to try something. Get as far back from the door as you can!" Tom called to Steph, and she immediately did as she was told, backing herself up against the far wall of the bathroom under the small window and crouching into a ball.

"Okay, I'm ready!" She shouted back to Tom.

Within seconds a deafening boom echoed around the small bathroom as something heavy and metallic from the sounds of it connected with the wooden door. Steph listened as it rhythmically connected with the surface repeatedly, as though it were on a pendulum and felt herself flinch in time with each metallic clang. Eventually, after several hits, came the reassuring sound of wood splintering as the door began to cave in under the force of the blows.

"That's it! Keep doing that!" Steph screamed at the top of her lungs, unsure that Tom could hear her over the noise but determined to try and encourage him as much as possible, not wanting him to give up.

Ignoring the sweat that trickled down his forehead and the deep ache in his injured ankle, Tom continued to barge his makeshift battering ram into the solid wood before him repeatedly in a steady rhythm. Any minute now, he thought to himself. Any minute now, it will open. Just keep going. Tom told himself, ignoring the pain in his tired arms.

He didn't think he'd ever heard a more welcome sound than the one the door made as it finally submitted to his volley of attacks and crashed to the ground before him a few minutes later. The loud, booming echoes made the people sitting by the walls snap out of their reverie for a moment, raising their heads and looking wide-eyed towards him, but Tom didn't care.

He couldn't take his eyes off the woman behind the door. "Steph." He breathed in relief, rushing forwards and reaching out a hand to help her to climb over the thick wood spawled between them. Steph scrambled up from her position crouched against the far wall of the bathroom and stumbled forwards, her outstretched hand closing around Toms and clasping onto it for dear life as she clambered through the door frame clumsily, her feet slipping on the highly polished wood. Tom cringed as he felt the half-dried blood on her palms crush into his own, cracking against his dry skin as Steph gripped his hand too tightly and made her way through the door frame. He had thought she was lying before when she said she was okay. Now he had proof.

Steph had barely managed to take a single step back inside the dorms before she felt Tom's hand tugging her underneath the bare lightbulb, which swung precariously from a thin cord above their heads. She watched in confusion as he released her, only to grab both her wrists and hold her hands out, palms up, under the yellowish glow, examining them closely as he furrowed his forehead.

"I'm fine." She reassured him, trying to tug her hands out of his tight grip, but Tom held fast.

"Really? So, I guess none of the blood on your hands is yours, huh? How about the lump on your head? That's nothing either, I suppose?" Tom half scolded, half-joked as he let go of one of Steph's hands and stepped closer to her, diminishing the space between them to nothing more than a few inches as he placed a finger under her chin and tilted her head back in order to examine the large cut over her eyebrow.

"I could be worse. I think I got off pretty lightly considering." Steph replied, looking over her shoulder into the remnants of the bathroom. Much worse, she added silently to herself with a slight shudder. Her breath hitched in her throat as she turned back to Tom and caught his gaze. His eyes were shimmering in the light above them, the obvious concern in their depths was as clear as a bright summer's day as his fingertips brushed over the welt on her forehead so gently that she almost wondered if she imagined it.

This close, she could almost count the beads of sweat gathering on his tightened forehead and she could feel every puff of air he expelled through his tightly pursed lips as he continued to examine her. She could even smell the faintest hint of the aftershave he always wore clinging to his skin and it took everything in her not to whimper out loud in disappointment when he released her, stepping back and appraising her as he spoke.

"You don't feel dizzy or sick at all?" Tom asked, trying to judge if Steph had a concussion. The wound on her head looked reasonably superficial, it could do with cleaning up, but he didn't think it was severe, yet, he couldn't help but ask his usual questions.

"No," Steph said stubbornly, straightening up to her full height in defiance and instantly wishing that she hadn't as a searing pain shot through her ribs, she curled her arm around her chest in a knee-jerk reaction, trying to hold herself together.

"What? What is it?" Tom asked anxiously, stepping forwards again and reaching out towards Steph in alarm.

"It's nothing. I think I did something to my ribs when I fell during the first bomb. Those were bombs going off, weren't they?" Steph asked as the events of the last half an hour came flooding back to her, and she felt herself begin to tremble again in fear.

Tom couldn't decide if Steph was trying to change the subject or whether she had only just thought to voice the question about the explosions now that she was out of the bathroom, but he didn't want to let her off that easily. All his instincts were screaming at him to take her to one of the still-standing nearby bunks and insist that she allow him to examine her properly and deduce the severity of her injuries before they went any further. Still, as she gazed up at him wide-eyed and pale, he found himself unable to help answering her.

"Yes, they were bombs. The Right To Life group is outside. I saw them. They were throwing some sort of homemade devices at the building, and they all had weapons." He admitted.

"They're trying to save us?" Steph asked in a small voice, so quiet that Tom found himself reading the words from her lips more than actually hearing them.

"Something like that. I don't know if they'll be successful or how much time we have, but we need to get out of here."

"Out?" Steph echoed dumbly, not understanding. "Surely, if they're breaking in, we should just wait here? They'll fight their way inside or whatever and help us to get out safely?" She suggested hopefully, but Tom wasn't so sure.

"Perhaps. Or perhaps they'll be stopped before they get this far. Perhaps they won't get in at all. We can't rely on them. The best chance we have is to try and get ourselves out. It might be the *only* chance we have." Tom told her, and he watched as her eyes fluttered closed.

Steph stood silently for a moment, seemingly absorbing his words as she pulled long, deep gulps of air into her lungs. The action clearly pained her, and Tom ached to examine her again, but as though she sensed his need, Steph raised a hand between them, asking him for a moment, which it nearly killed him to give her. They didn't have time.

Steph knew that Tom was getting impatient now. She could feel the anxiety pouring off of him and hear the agitation in his quick sharp breaths and the shuffling of his feet on the dust-covered floor as he waited for her to open her eyes but she did her best to tune him out. She needed this time, needed a few moments to compose herself if she had any chance of being able to follow his plan, she had to get her own fear under control and steel herself for what they were about to attempt. Just a few more seconds, she thought before she finally opened her eyes, staring up at Tom with a newfound resolve.

Tom was astounded by what he saw as he continued to look down at the woman before him. In just the minute or so that she had remained motionless, she had somehow managed to go from being a frightened, trembling mess who could barely breathe without flinching, to a resigned and ready woman with a fiery look of determination shining out from behind her deep brown eyes. He couldn't help but admire her at that moment. Admire her, and envy her strength.

"Okay. Let's go." Steph said confidently, and Tom gritted his teeth and turned back towards the staff entrance.

Chapter Sixty-Two

It was eerily quiet back in the staff area and Tom couldn't help but cringe every time he took a step, fearing that the sound of his boots echoing down the halls would draw unwanted attention. He tried to make as little noise as possible as he snuck down the hallways in the near complete darkness with Steph close behind him, breathing heavily and making the odd whimpering sound, clearly still in pain..
Occasionally one of the lights overhead flickered against the blackness, illuminating the long corridor for a moment as the fluorescents, which must have been damaged in the explosions, made a valiant attempt to stutter back to life. The effect reminded Tom more of a strobe light than anything else, as the lights flashed in the darkness. As he continued along the corridor, his mind flashed back to images of the haunted houses that had used similar lighting which he had visited when he was a child and his parents had taken him and his brother and sister to a fairground as a rare treat. He squinted his eyes against the flashing which was starting to make his head ache as he gripped tightly onto Steph's hand and pulled her along the debris-covered floor.
It was difficult to get his bearings in this light, even with the flashes from above him, Tom was fairly sure they were headed in the right direction, but he couldn't help but wish he'd remembered to grab the torch again before they headed down here. Cursing under his breath for leaving it abandoned on the floor by the bathroom, he ploughed forward, hoping their destination would appear soon. Tom knew that he needed to get Steph back to the storage room where he was talking to his dad earlier so that he could examine, and hopefully treat, some of her wounds before they tried to go any further. He still wasn't sure how much damage had been caused to her slim body, but he knew they wouldn't be able to seek medical attention once they got out of here. No doubt their faces and those of any other people lucky enough to escape this god-awful place would be sent out in bulletins to the population's watches the moment the C.E.A regained control of the centre and they would be plastered in technicolour onto the sides of the enormous buildings in town, which were so often used to broadcast news bulletins. Tom and Steph would become wanted criminals whose faces would be far too recognisable for them to be able to seek out any kind of assistance from anyone. Glancing down at his bare wrist, Tom lamented the fact that his own watch was taken from him when he was in processing. It might have come in handy when they got out of here. *If* we get out of here, he corrected himself, realising that they still had a long way to go yet. There were six floors to fight their way through, no doubt most of them crawling with C.E.A agents, police and even the

R.T.L by now. Tom knew that it wouldn't be easy, and it's not like either he nor Steph had any experience in a situation like this one, but what other choice did they have?

Taking another cautious step forward, Tom felt the tip of his boot connect with something on the floor. Something reasonably sturdy but with a little give to it, enough that his boot sunk slightly into the object before he could pull his foot back. What the hell? He wondered and felt his eyebrows furrowing on his forehead. Bending his knees, Tom gently released Steph's hand from his own and slowly reached out into the darkness in front of him, connecting with the object just as the lights overhead flickered again, illuminating the gory sight and he recoiled, wishing that they hadn't.

Steph could not contain the squeal that edged past her lips as the body strewn across the floor came into view. The high-pitched sound seemed to bounce off the walls around them as it escaped her, making Tom cringe. She quickly slapped a hand across her mouth to try and stifle the sound, hoping no one had heard it as her breaths came thick and fast against her sore ribs.

The man's lifeless eyes stare up at her as the corridor lights up once again and Steph gets a clear view of a large pool of blood surrounding what she can only describe as a corpse in front of her and it makes her stomach turn. Covering her mouth, she takes a frightened step backwards, pressing herself against the wall and trying desperately not to throw up. Steph had never seen anything like the man lying prone on the floor before her, and honestly, she could have gone her whole life without ever seeing it.

Occasionally she had been unlucky enough to stumble past a deceased person on the streets near her home, but most of them just looked as though they were sleeping. Propped up against a wall or in the doorway of an abandoned shop with their heads dipped towards their no longer moving chests and their eyes closed. The few that she had been unlucky enough to see never had any signs of injury to them, no pools of deep red beneath their frail bodies or seeping through their clothing, and certainly no gaping holes in their necks and so Steph had always been able to convince herself that they were just sleeping and banish the images from her mind. The man lying on the ground before her now would not be as easy to forget.

"Sssh. It's okay. Just don't look at it, alright?" Tom said gently, trying to soothe her. It was clear that there was nothing that he could do for the man on the ground. He straightened back up, reached out to wrap an arm around Steph's shaking shoulders, and pulled her tightly to his side, trying to block the man from her sight. He wished the lights would give up already, the effect of them flickering above the body only added to the macabre scene and the last thing he needed was Steph passing out on him in the middle of their escape attempt. They'd already come up against too many obstacles and wasted too much time as it was.

Steph turned her head and buried her face into Tom's warm chest as he began to edge them past the body, having to push the feet out of the way to clear enough space for them to get by. The sight on the ground, whilst disturbing, wasn't exactly new to Tom, although he was more used to seeing things like that in the hospital than prostrate on the floor at his feet in a darkened corridor, he was sure it was far more upsetting to Steph than it was to him. Truthfully, he was just thankful to not recognise the man. For a single heart-stopping moment, he had feared that he was about to discover his father's lifeless body when he had crouched down to examine it. The relief that flooded through him at the sight of the muddy brown uniform that all of the security here seemed to wear was palpable.

Tom couldn't be sure if the dead man was the same guard his dad had rushed off to intercept so that he could get away earlier though and he couldn't help but wonder if his father had been caught up in the altercation. Had he been hurt too but perhaps managed to get away? Was his father, even now, bleeding on the floor in another part of the centre? A thousand questions raced through his tired mind as he stared down at the man on the ground with the deep puncture wounds in his neck, and a surge of guilt ran through him. Should he have stayed with his father instead of going back to find Steph?

"Who would do that to somebody else?" Steph whispered into Tom's ear in the darkness, her voice so full of fear that he tightened his hold around her slim frame in an attempt to reassure her.

He found himself not wanting to answer her question. He had a good idea of who must have done this, the same group of guys she had asked him not to speak to earlier this evening, whom he had run into again when he was returning to the dorms. It seemed that her instinct had been right about them from the start. Female intuition, perhaps he should have listened to her. The men were clearly trouble. Tom hadn't noticed anyone else venturing through the staff doorway and given that the men had all been brandishing what had appeared to be homemade weapons when he last saw them, they seemed a pretty safe bet to have been the culprits of the bloody scene before him now.

Chapter Sixty-Three

A sigh of relief escaped Tom's tightly pursed lips and he felt his shoulders relax slightly when he rounded a familiar corner by the cracked window, which he and his father had stared out of earlier in disbelief at the crowds outside and spotted the storage room. The door hung slightly ajar on its hinges, and a faint light shone through the crack. That'll make things easier, he thought as he quickened his pace, grateful for an excuse not to answer Steph's question.
"This is it. In here." He stated, tugging the door open just enough for Steph to slip inside.
The sound of cracking glass pulled Steph up short after only a few steps into the cramped storage room, and she jumped back, lurching into Tom's chest in the process as she raised her foot in alarm. Glancing down, she saw the remnants of what looked to be several glass vials scattered across the floor, surrounded by a liquid which she assumed had once been inside of them, glinting in the muted light coming from a single bare bulb that hung from the ceiling and Tom felt her shudder slightly against him as she connected the dots.
"Is that the..." Steph began to question but cut herself off midway through the thought. Deciding that, actually, she didn't really want to know if the bottles she had just crushed once contained the poison that she had been expecting to have plunged into her veins today.
She surveyed the rest of the small room around her, taking in the tall metal shelving units pressed up against the walls, stacked high with various medical equipment, and tiptoeing around the piles of debris on the floor as she made her way further inside, allowing Tom to pull the door closed behind them as best as he could as he followed her in.
"Okay, let me see," Tom mumbled as he started to rifle through the shelves. Among the more deadly medicines he had noticed earlier, he was sure he had also seen some simpler first aid supplies. Gauze and bandages, plasters and creams, and although he couldn't for the life of him work out why they would be needed in a place like this, right now, he was grateful to whoever had thought to fully stock the room as he took in Steph's head wound under the light and saw just how deep it really was.
Grabbing a box of cotton balls and some antiseptic, Tom gestured for Steph to raise her chin. He cleaned up the cut on her head as softly as he could, feeling her wince under his fingers from the sting of the antiseptic as he rubbed it against her skin.
"Where were you? Earlier, when I woke up? You were gone." Steph said quietly, sounding almost disappointed in him as she looked up at Tom with wide eyes.

"With my dad," Tom answered in an equally low voice. "He brought me in here before, well before everything happened. We were just talking, spending what time together we could, you know? And then the bombs started going off. He grasped what was going on much more quickly than I did. Apparently, this isn't the first time the Right To Life group has tried to attack the centre, and he told me I needed to get out of here. To use the explosions as cover and find a way out of this place and into hiding. He told me to run and went off to go and distract a security guard coming our way." He continued, frowning as he placed thin, steri strips across Steph's cut, closing the wound as best as he could without stitches and wondering again what had become of his father. Had he managed to get out of the centre? Was he trapped somewhere or hiding perhaps from the man with the shaved head and his band of goons with their makeshift weapons?

Tom debated for a moment going in search of him after he'd finished patching up Steph, but he knew his father wouldn't want him to. They both knew that Tom's best chance at getting out, at getting past the R.T.L, who were no doubt already storming the building, was to be just another cull victim. If he were seen with one of the doctors, he would instantly be assumed to be a member of staff and judging by the state of the man in the hallway, Tom didn't think that the Right To Life rebels would show him any mercy if they presumed that he worked here.

"Why didn't you?" Steph asked as Tom stepped back to examine his work on her cut.

"Why didn't I what?" he asked, raising an eyebrow at her in confusion.

"Why didn't you do what your dad said? Why didn't you run?" Steph clarified.

As grateful as she was that Tom had found her and gotten her out of the bathroom, she couldn't help but wonder why he had returned to the dorms at all and not just headed straight for the exit. She wasn't sure that she would have had the strength to do what he did when the chance to escape was so close at hand.

"I came back for you," Tom admitted in a small voice, surprised at how embarrassed he was to admit this to her and feeling his cheeks flush with heat.

"Oh." Was all Steph could think to say as she stared up into his green eyes. They were standing just inches apart now, and she could feel Tom's breath fanning across her face as he exhaled. If I just leaned a tiny bit forwards, I could kiss him. She thought to herself, knowing full well that she would never have the courage to do such a thing but allowing the fantasy to take her mind off her injuries and the pain she felt for a moment.

"Does it hurt anywhere else?" Tom asked, pulling her out of her thoughts and back to the present.

"My ribs," Steph admitted shyly, wincing as Tom reached out his large hands and placed one on either side of her torso, just below her breasts, gently probing at her ribcage with the pads of his fingers.

"Here?" He asked as his fingers brushed over the very spot which was causing her so much pain. Steph sucked in a breath through gritted teeth and nodded vehemently as a sharp pain coursed through her chest.

"At least one is cracked. Maybe two." Tom told her, and as he removed his hands from her to grab another box of supplies from the shelf, Steph internally scolded herself for her reaction as she felt her face fall in disappointment. Not because her ribs were cracked, she had already assumed as much. Her response was much more pathetic than that. She felt bereft, almost to the point of tears, that he had removed his hands from her. It was a stupid reaction to have at the best of times but right now? When they were standing in a storage room trying to patch up her wounds before attempting to escape the building where they had thought they would die today? In which they still might? It was such a ridiculous thing to be upset about that she laughed out loud at her own stupidity.

Tom raised a questioning eyebrow at Steph as she began to giggle before raising a finger to his lips to quieten her. He wasn't sure exactly what she could possibly find funny right now. Perhaps her head wound was worse than he thought? Regardless, he couldn't afford someone hearing her peals of laughter and seeking them out. They needed to avoid attracting anyone's attention, whether it be staff, the R.T.L or even another 'patient' as the doctors here so delightfully called them. They couldn't take the chance of anyone else slowing them down, and they'd wasted too much time as it was.

Carefully, he lifted the hem of Steph's top to expose the damaged rib he had felt so he could bandage it. He felt a slight jolt of electricity shoot through his fingertips as they brushed along the soft skin of her taut stomach and he pulled his hands back slightly, not meeting her eyes and preventing any further contact between them as the strange sensation fluttered through him. What was that about? He wondered as Steph took over holding her top up, and Tom began to wrap a large bandage around her.

Trying to control herself and stop laughing, Steph thought over Tom's plan and his intention for them to escape and began to feel an uneasy sensation bubbling in her stomach. She took in Tom's appearance and noted his ashen face streaked with dirt, his bloodshot, tired eyes and his injured ankle, which she could see he was trying to keep his weight off as best as he could as he tended to her wounds and sighed, unsure if making a run for it was their best course of action, given the state that they were both in. Perhaps waiting for the Right to Life group to reach them would be better? Surely, they would, and then they could leave with them and go into hiding somewhere?

"Are you sure that we shouldn't wait?" She asked Tom, breaking the silence between them, and he stopped filling his pockets with medical supplies from the shelves to shoot her a quizzical look. "I mean, if the R.T.L group are breaking into the centre, perhaps they have a plan, a way to shelter the survivors once they've gotten us out? Maybe it would be better for us to wait for them rather than trying to go on the run? Look at us, Tom. We're hardly in the best state to be roaming the countryside alone. And besides, neither one of us are used to having to rough it . We probably wouldn't get more than a few miles before we got caught." Steph suggested, wringing her hands nervously between them.

Tom couldn't pretend that the same thought hadn't crossed his mind. Hadn't he said basically the same thing to his father just a little while ago? But he had had time to think since then, time to weigh up their options, and he was sure he had made the right choice.

"I don't think that's the best idea, Steph. We have no idea what the rebels are planning. For all we know, they'd help us get out and then leave us to it. If they manage to free everyone, we'd be too large a group to go unnoticed for long. We'd end up back in here, or someplace worse even, within hours. I think we're better off taking our chances on our own." He told Steph.

Deciding not to bring up the fact that, having seen the rebels outside in action, he wasn't entirely convinced that they could be trusted, she didn't need more to worry about right now.

"What about all the other people back in the dorms, Tom? Are we just going to leave them? Run out the door and not look back or give them another thought?" Steph pushed, her voice getting louder now as passion overtook her.

She recalled the sleeping faces she had tried not to look at as she had made her way to the bathroom earlier, remembering the sweet little old ladies sharing their blanket on the bed across from them. Could she really just abandon them?

"Steph, look, we can't save everyone," Tom told her, running a hand through his messy curls as he spoke. "I wish that it weren't this way. Really I do. But we have to prioritise. Right now, we're going to have to learn to be selfish, to put ourselves first if we want to stand a chance at surviving."

"If that's how you really feel, then why did you come back for me?" Steph asked the man before her, getting agitated now.

"That's different! Those people back there, they're strangers, Steph. I can't help them. But you... Well, you, I couldn't leave behind." Tom admitted.

It was the best that he could manage. If he was being honest with himself, he didn't know exactly why he had returned to the dormitories determined to locate Steph. It had been his first instinct the moment that the bombs had hit, as though some unseen force had been pushing him along, propelling him back to the dorms before he'd even really given the matter much thought. He knew that he wouldn't have been able to face himself in the mirror if he had left her there alone, but he couldn't really put his finger on why and he knew that now was not the time to spend searching his soul for the answer.

"Maybe you should have," Steph mumbled so quietly that Tom almost didn't hear her.

"What? Why?" He asked

"Because Tom, look at me!" Steph almost shouted in response, managing to contain herself at the very last moment and keep her voice at what she hoped was a reasonable volume. "I've got at least one cracked rib, maybe more, and a head wound. I'm only going to slow you down. You'd be better off on your own." She admitted, her voice cracking over the words as she spoke.

Exasperated, Tom placed his arms firmly on Steph's shoulders as he looked deep into her dark eyes, shimmering up at him, full of unshed tears.

"I'm not leaving you, Steph. You hear me? We're going to get out of here. Together." He told her firmly.

Steph stared up at him for several moments, the air between them thick with all the things they were leaving unsaid, but she knew now was not the time for arguments. She could see in Tom's eyes that he was determined, that there was no way she was going to be able to convince him to leave her behind and that she was only going to waste more time if she insisted on arguing with him. So she hung her head, resigning herself to his plan as she nodded slightly.

"Good. I'm glad we got that straightened out. Now, any other injuries I need to look at?" Tom asked, his expression turning serious as he waited for her response. Steph wondered if this was the face his patients were used to seeing when they visited him at the hospital across the street. His kindness and concern still shone through in his eyes, but he looked more professional somehow, more detached as he waited for her to answer. She shook her head as she responded to him.

"Nope, well, a few bruises, I'm sure, and the cuts on my hands, but nothing to worry about." She clarified.

Tom had forgotten about the scrapes on her hands, but he didn't think they were severe enough to require much attention. The most serious of her injuries had been taken care of now, and that would have to do. They had to get moving. He averted his eyes as Steph rearranged her clothing, pulling her top back into place and exposing the edge of her white bra in the process and tried to focus his mind on something else. He hadn't heard any more explosions since before they reached the staff area, and he didn't think that was a good sign. It probably meant that the R.T.L had caused enough damage to the outer walls to gain entry to the centre and he wasn't sure how much time they had left before this place descended into complete mayhem, if it hadn't already.

"So, how do we get out of here? Back through processing?" Steph asked, conscious that they needed to get moving.

Tom had already risked his chance at freedom, his very life in fact, to come and find her, and now here they were wasting more time cleaning up her wounds. She would never be able to live with herself if Tom's acts of kindness cost him his one chance to escape.

"No, not back that way. Dad said the best way out was through the staff area and out of the back door on the ground floor. He gave me these." Tom told her, fishing the keys his father had handed him out of his pocket and brandishing them at her, watching her eyes widen in surprise. "And he gave me his wallet as well and told me to withdraw some cash at the first cash machine we see, then dump it and head for the countryside to get as far away from here as we can."

"Won't he get in trouble for helping us?" Steph asked, her voice laced with concern. Tom was once again struck by her ability to always worry about other people before herself, even now.

"Maybe. If they find out who he is." Tom admitted. "I just have to hope they don't," he added.

Steph yearned to reach out to him then, to wrap her arms around him and comfort him the way he had done when she had been the one in need of reassurance several times today, but before she could move to do so, Tom was turning towards the door.

Wrapping his fingers around the handle, Tom looked over his shoulder deep into Steph's eyes.

"Ready?" He asked and then watched in amazement as, once again, the small, shy and fragile woman in front of him closed her eyes momentarily to steel herself for what was to come, opening them to reveal a whole other person as she nodded resolutely and came up close behind him.

"Ready." She said in a low voice. And Tom pulled open the door.

Chapter Sixty-Four

Even before Captain Williams' watch crackled to life as he drove along the quiet, almost deserted streets tonight, making his usual rounds to ensure that curfew was being adhered to, he had already known that something was very wrong.
It was too quiet out here, way too quiet. The groups of homeless people who usually prowled the streets after dark, trying to score drugs or perhaps scrounge up some food from the bins of nearby restaurants for their hungry families were nowhere to be seen. Occasionally Williams had caught sight of the odd frail-looking woman ambling down a side road with a child or two in tow, but for the most part, the streets were empty. It had been unnerving him since he'd started his shift tonight, and the announcement over the crackling device had just confirmed his suspicions.
The moment he had heard the words 'Bleeker Avenue,' Williams had stomped his foot down hard on the accelerator, almost flattening it to the floor as he raced down the quiet roads towards the population control centre.
He had been waiting for this, everyone in his department had. Tensions had been growing between the so-called 'Right To Life group' and the Cull Enforcement Agency for weeks now and he had known it was only a matter of time before the rebels made another attempt at storming the centre after he had foiled their plans the last time. He just hadn't expected it to be so soon or so destructive.
"They're detonating homemade bombs to try and gain access to the centre. Early approximate number of rebels is around three hundred. Full body armour will be required, and the use of live ammunition is permitted." The distorted voice of his Lieutenant had spoken through the speaker on his watch, and Williams internally praised himself for never leaving home without his bulletproof uniform firmly in place and his guns cleaned and loaded.
Williams tore through the streets as fast as he dared, weaving in and out of lanes to overtake his colleagues who were the only other people out on the roads tonight, some of whom either didn't appreciate the seriousness of the situation or just weren't in a hurry to join in the fight. Cowards. Or worse, sympathisers. Williams thought to himself as he sped past yet another meandering vehicle. They were only two streets away now, and he wound down his window, pricking up his ears and listening to the chaos he was about to drive into.
The sounds of shouts and chants filled the night air and whistled through the open window and into his vehicle, replacing the previous silence instantly and even drowning out the engine and Williams felt the

tension in the car increase as his three team members all stiffened in their seats, preparing themselves for what was to come. This isn't going to be like last time, Williams realised as the shouts grew louder and were punctuated by a substantial booming explosion that echoed off the buildings around him and sent a plume of smoke into the air behind the row of houses to his left. This wasn't just a few dozen disgruntled and disorganised rebels trying to cause havoc. This time they were organised. This time they had a plan. Williams steeled himself as best as he could as he continued driving down the road and tried to formulate one of his own.

Despite his Lieutenant's warning that there were somewhere in the region of three hundred rebels at the population control centre, nothing could have prepared Williams' for what he saw as he skidded to a halt behind a blockade of C.E.A vehicles and yanked on his handbrake, not even bothering to take the keys from his ignition as his eyes widened whilst he took in the sight before him. Three hundred was a low estimate.

The entire road before him was full of people, all clad from head to toe in black, some with balaclavas or scarves pulled up high around their faces but some wearing nothing more than the rags that they had been living in on the streets for god knows how long. They all had one thing in common though, they all wore the same furious and determined expressions as they faced the centre holding makeshift weapons in their hands. From his vantage point, Williams couldn't see a single C.E.A employee in the crowd but wisps of smoke and bright orange and yellow flames were clearly visible through the cracked walls of the centre. Despite the smoke and chaos before him, William's could see a gaping hole in the building right where he was sure the doors had once stood. Shit. They're already inside. He realised as he tugged on his car door handle and stepped out into the warm night air.

"Williams!" the familiar voice of his Lieutenant called and Williams jerked his head toward the sound and began moving forwards between the rows of cars, his team close on his heels.

"How many are we?" He asked as soon as he was close enough for Armitage to hear him over the cacophony of voices filling the night air and the sounds of people scrambling over one another towards the building.

"Barely a hundred. More are on their way." Armitage replied tersely Yeah, but they won't get here soon enough at the speed they were going, Williams thought as he surveyed the scene before him and remembered the number of C.E.A vehicles he had passed on his way here. Ignoring the temptation to inform Lieutenant Armitage of what he had seen, Williams' squared his shoulders.

"Orders?" He asked.

"We need to disperse this crowd. I've got men over at the hospital getting any civilians off the streets. The last thing we need is for this to turn into a bloodbath with innocents caught in the crossfire. The press would have a field day with that." Armitage said, and Williams' nodded his head in agreement.

"As soon as I get the all-clear, we'll advance. Clear a path to the centre and disperse as many rebels as possible. Try not to use lethal force unless necessary, but our main objective is to secure the centre. We can't let the Cudos escape, or we'll end up with a full-scale man-hunt on our hands." Armitage barked, beads of sweat trickling down his forehead as he used the colloquial term that had first popped up in the media a few months ago as a nickname for the people whose names had been called up in the culls and had been adopted by the population at large.

Williams' gritted his teeth in frustration. He didn't want to wait, the longer they stood here watching, not engaging the rebels, the more confident they would become and the more damage they would cause. His hand strayed to the belt of grenades he wore and his fingers twitched at their edges, wanting nothing more than to start pulling pins and releasing clouds of toxic gas into the air to begin subduing the Right To Life rebels before him. Somehow, he resisted, Williams prided himself on being a good soldier. If his superior had decided that they should wait, then he would follow orders, no matter how much it rankled him.

Chapter Sixty-Five

Holding up a hand in the air, Tom came to a stop at the bottom of the staircase that he and Steph had been traversing and felt her stumble slightly as she hurried to copy his actions. A large black number three was displayed on a wooden door to his left, and to his right, the stairs continued downwards. Tom knew which way they had to go, the trouble was, he could also hear what awaited them.

"What should we do?" Steph asked in a low voice, standing on her tiptoes and whispering the words directly into Tom's ear from her place on the higher stair above him. She, too, had quickly noticed the raised voices, crashes and screams emitting from below them and she was struggling to keep her composure as she debated their options.

Either they could keep going down, towards the back door as Tom's father had instructed them to do, hoping they could escape the notice of whoever was on the floor below them or perhaps somehow blend in with the crowd. Or they could try and find another way, another staircase or perhaps a fire escape that might lead them in the same direction but avoid the crowds, time, however, was not on their side and Steph was very aware of that fact, whatever they were going to do, they needed to do it fast. The sound of sirens outside the centre had become more frequent since they left the sixth floor and she was certain that they signalled the arrival of the police and, quite probably, the C.E.A as well. It would only be a matter of time before the authorities entered the centre and tried to regain control, that much she was sure of, and they needed to be out of here before that happened.

"We have to get downstairs. There's no other option." Tom told her quietly, but his words were interrupted by a loud banging coming from behind the door to his left, and suddenly, Steph had an idea.

"What if we open it? There's got to be other people like us in there, right? If we let them out, perhaps we can hide in the crowd. Safety in numbers?" She suggested, and after deliberating momentarily, Tom nodded in agreement. It was the best idea they had right now.

"Will your dad's keys open the door?" Steph asked and watched as Tom pulled the small bunch from his pocket and jangled them in his hand.

"Let's find out." He said, striding quickly towards the door.

The pounding reverberated through the wood frantically as they drew nearer. Tom could almost feel it in the depths of his chest, the way that you did when you stood too close to a speaker with the bass turned to full in a nightclub. His heart seemed to beat in time with the fists hammering against the doors, and he struggled to grasp the keys in his shaking hands as he started trying each one in the lock.

He didn't have to try for long. The third key on the chain was longer than the rest, with a lengthy silver handle and only a few prongs sticking out at its end, a skeleton key. Designed to be carried by cleaners no doubt so that they could enter each area of the centre without having to fish around for the right key. It slid easily into the lock, and Tom heard a faint click over the sounds of the pounding as he began to turn it, pushing the door forwards and stepping back at the same time so that he wouldn't get trampled by the people he was sure were about to storm out of it.

The crowd surged the instant they realised that the door was no longer blocking their exit, beginning to squeeze through the gap Tom had made for them before it was more than a few inches in width and scrambling over one another in their haste to try and escape. Steph felt herself being pushed back against the wall behind her as one of Tom's muscular arms shot out into her stomach, jolting her ribs and causing a sharp pain to flow through her body as she pressed herself against the crumbling plaster. Tom quickly positioned his entire body in front of her, shielding her from the frantic group pouring out of the third-floor dormitory.

Steph was once again surprised by the sheer number of people being held in the dormitory on this floor. She had, somewhat naively, assumed that her own dorm upstairs had been an anomaly, that there couldn't be that many people being kept prisoner on each of the seven floors of the centre, but judging by the never-ending stream of people pouring out of the door, she had been very wrong.

"Come on!" Tom said the moment he spotted a break in the crowd of people and reached back to grasp Steph's hand tightly in his own. The last thing he wanted was for them to get separated. He couldn't stand the idea of having to go and search for her again, so he held on tightly as he pulled her forwards and into the crowd who were now descending the next set of stairs at a rapid pace.

Rounding the corner at the bottom of the first flight, Tom could just about make out the landing on the floor beneath them and the matching wooden door at the end of it emblazoned with the number two over the heads of the people in front of him who were all pushing and shoving one another in their haste to get down the stairs. He felt people jostling into his shoulders as he tried to stand his ground, tugging Steph behind him and feeling her warm breath on the back of his neck as she tried her best to keep up. Someone on his right fell as they descended, unable to keep their footing under the mounting pressure of the wall of people behind them and Tom ached to stop and assist them, but he knew he didn't have time. Remembering what he had said to Steph earlier in the storeroom, he ploughed forwards. They had to prioritise, and right now, his only priority was getting her the hell out of here in one piece.

Steph did her best to keep her legs moving under her as Tom propelled them through the crowd, feeling the hands of strangers grabbing at her clothing for balance as they struggled to stay on their feet and doing her best to ignore the pleas for help that she could hear being uttered from the lips of those who had fallen or been trapped by the fast-moving crowd. She focused her eyes on a small freckle at the base of Tom's hairline, which became partially obscured by his brown curls as they bounced against his neck as he pounded down the stairs, trying desperately to block out everything and everyone else. Prioritise. She repeated to herself over and over as she clung on for dear life to Tom's outstretched hand and pushed every other thought out of her mind. Right up until the arm twisted around her waist.
"Tom!" Steph screamed as she felt her feet leave the floor, and her hand was ripped from his. The vice-like grip around her chest constricted her injured ribs and restricted her ability to breathe through the white-hot pain that the pressure caused. Steph had no idea who had lifted her or why, she couldn't even get enough space to turn her head to see who was spinning her around. It felt as though the action took hours as the whitewashed walls around her blurred into one and Steph fought against a wave of dizziness before she was tossed aside like a discarded piece of rubbish. Hurtling face first into the people behind her whose expressions turned first to shock and then to fear in the seconds before she crashed into them, sending them all tumbling to the floor like dominoes.
"Steph!" Tom shouted, twisting his head around in the confined space to try and look over his shoulder but finding himself being carried along by the crowd despite his best efforts. "Stephanie!" He shouted again when he didn't get a reply and, planting his feet firmly on the ground, wincing as his twisted ankle throbbed beneath him, Tom squared his shoulders and did his best to make himself immovable as he forced his body to rotate in the small space on the staircase.
There was no sign of Steph behind him, no wisp of brown hair or flash of the blue hooded top she'd been wearing all day to guide him, but he knew that she had to be there. Craning his neck, he could see that there was a pile of people on the ground back towards the top of the staircase, all attempting to stagger to their feet as scores of bodies pushed into them from behind, scrambling over them as they tried to surge forwards and towards freedom. Shit, he thought to himself as he started shoving at the man directly in front of him, pushing him far enough to one side that he could squeeze past.
Steph could hear Tom calling out her name over the sound of the footsteps, grunts and shouts that filled her ears and she tried to suck in a breath to respond, but something was restricting her, stopping her from

filling her tired lungs with the air she so desperately needed. Looking down, Steph saw that a woman, probably not much older than herself, was strewn across her chest, lying flat on her stomach and not moving an inch. Dammit. She thought to herself as she tried to free her arms from under the obstruction, pushing at the woman with all her might until she finally rolled off her and tumbled down to the next stair. Guilt coursed through her veins as she watched, but Steph knew she didn't have time for this. She couldn't stop and see if the woman was okay. She had to get up, to find Tom and get out of here.

Chapter Sixty-Six

"Tom!" Steph shouted the moment she caught her breath. Wincing against the pain in her ribs, she screamed his name with all the force she could muster and tried desperately to get to her feet, but it was useless. Though the crowd above her had slowed remarkably, going from a steady stream of pounding feet to a slow trickle, people were still crashing into her as they tried to get past her and the others who had fallen when she had landed on them. Every time Steph got one of her feet under her, she found herself knocked to the ground again almost instantly.

Searching the scene in front of her, Steph squinted her eyes against the bright lights as her gaze flickered from one person to the next until, finally, she saw the pair of determined green eyes storming towards her. She watched in fascination and just a little bit of awe as Tom barrelled through the crowds, pushing people out of his way in his haste to get to her, his expression turning to pure relief when he finally spotted her on the ground.

Thank God. Tom thought to himself as he pushed past the last person between him and Steph and took the final stairs two at a time to reach her. He hadn't realised how far the crowd's momentum had carried him until he had tried to turn back and found himself on the second floor's landing. It had taken him much longer than he had hoped to retrace his steps and images of finding Steph unconscious or worse assaulted his mind with every passing second and filled him with dread. But here she was, awake and alert, and he was so incredibly grateful, he just hoped she wasn't too badly hurt as he stared into her frightened features.

Steph clasped her fingers around Tom's wrist the moment his arm was close enough, feeling him do the same to hers as he pulled her to her feet. A searing pain shot through her chest again at the jerking movement, but she pushed it aside, focusing instead on his pleading eyes boring down on her, looking full of relief. The moment she was on her feet, Tom released her and pulled her into his arms, holding her tightly to his chest as the last few stragglers that Steph had knocked over stumbled to their feet and dodged around them and down the stairs, avoiding the unmoving bodies that lie prone on the floor before them.

Letting her eyes flutter closed, Steph buried her head in Tom's chest and listened to the reassuring sound of his strong heartbeat pounding against her cheek as he held her close to him, allowing herself just this one moment of peace. She knew they should be moving and that they didn't have time for this, but she couldn't find it in herself to care. Right now, she needed this, needed him. She had been waiting for him to embrace her this way for years now, and she intended to enjoy this moment no matter how fleeting it was or how much danger they were in.

The relief that Tom felt as he gathered Steph's shaking body into his arms and cradled her against his chest was immense, more powerful than he had felt in a long time. He dipped his head into her hair and inhaled deeply as she clung to him, struggling to catch her breath and trying to calm his own racing heart as he reassured himself that she was alright. It was foolish, he knew, to be standing here embracing her this way when chaos was breaking out all around them, but he needed this. They needed this.

Tom felt the vibrations beneath his feet before he heard the explosion that crashed through the air a few seconds later as he held Steph and with quick reflexes, he stretched out an arm to the side and grabbed hold of the bannister, steadying them both as Steph continued to cling to him, trying desperately to keep her balance as the echoes of the explosion filled their ears and chunks of plaster began tumbling from the walls.

The moment the sounds died out and the floor beneath them stopped shaking, Steph turned her head towards Tom's, meeting his eyes and straightening herself as she took a step back before placing her hand firmly back in his.

"Let's go." She said, and within moments, they were hurtling back down the stairs.

Chapter Sixty-Seven

Crouching behind the bumper of an old abandoned Ford which had seemingly been discarded a few buildings down from the population control centre with smashed windows and a significant dent in the passenger side door, Williams raised the automatic weapon in his hand. He positioned the heavy butt against his shoulder, bracing the gun as he peered through the scope. The swirls of thick grey smoke that permeated the air, along with the dark protective goggles he wore, obscured his view somewhat and yet he smirked slightly, knowing that he wouldn't need to take careful aim to accomplish his goal. Not yet... Not yet... he whispered to himself, knowing that for his actions to have the maximum effect, he had to make sure that he waited until the opportune moment.

A large group of rebels were rushing in his direction towards the rest of his team, who were approaching behind him from the south, doing their best to attract the crowd's attention and draw them closer to Williams' location. Although the rebels were armed, most of their weapons would require close contact to be effective and so they offered little threat at this range as they charged forwards brandishing knives and long planks of splintered wood in their raised arms, clearly hoping for a fight. Well, they're not going to get one. Williams thought to himself as the group closed in and he depressed the trigger on his gun.

A spray of bullets flew through the air instantly, catching the charging rebels off guard. They began to stumble as Williams' aim proved true, and the bullets lodged in their lower limbs. He had chosen to incapacitate as many as possible rather than shooting to kill, wanting the satisfaction of seeing these ingrates carted off to jail cells once this was all over, not being put into coffins. Despite Armitage's orders that they were permitted to use lethal force if necessary to regain control of the area, Williams did not like the idea of standing as judge, jury and executioner over these people. He would rather leave their fate in the hands of the law of the land and the government in which he believed so fiercely.

Within moments, the charging crowd was cut in half and the few who remained on upright and who were not clutching at one limb or another, crying out in pain, whipped their heads back and forth in a frenzy as the bullets sprayed around them, trying to seek out their source, but Williams' had chosen his hiding place well. Even the lights from the fires littering the wide street and the centre itself couldn't reach him here, hiding in the shadows. Bullet casings littered the ground at his feet, bouncing off his raised knee as he continued to fire indiscriminately into the rebels until, at last, his ammunition ran out, and he tossed his weapon to the ground.

Williams was on his feet in seconds, pulling his sidearm from its holster and charging forwards, emerging from the darkness and startling the rebels closest to him, who shrank back in fear as he towered over them with his six-foot-four frame. Williams' knew that he was an intimidating sight at the best of times, tonight though, in full riot gear with a gun in his hand and a scowl across his weathered features, he was confident that he looked even more menacing than usual as he barrelled into the remaining crowd.

Crossing his right arm across his chest, Williams fired a single shot into the kneecap of a woman approaching him from the left, whose long, flowing blonde hair splayed out behind her as she ran towards him with a small kitchen knife in her hand, and then spinning quickly, he turned to fire again at a man in a black balaclava approaching directly in front of him. A fist darted out towards him, a ring on its middle finger glinting in the firelight and catching his attention just in time for him to drop to his knees, causing its owner to hit nothing but air as Williams brought his left hand up in a powerful uppercut that connected with the man's gut as he toppled forwards, his momentum carrying him directly into Williams' space and he shoved the man away.

The rebel staggered backwards; the wind knocked out of him. Clutching at his stomach as he attempted to catch his breath, he tripped over the fallen body of one of his comrades who screamed out in pain into the night air as the weight of the first man landed squarely on top of him, pinning him to the hard, unyielding ground. The rebels are more organised this time, and they certainly have the numbers. They did not have the expertise to win in hand-to-hand combat though, Williams knew, grateful once again for the years of training he had received in his time in the army as another man approached him, fists raised, bouncing on the balls of his feet like a boxer about to take the ring.

The temptation to simply shoot the man and move along was high, and William's finger itched against the trigger of his gun but he was conscious of his limited ammunition. He didn't want to waste any more bullets than he had to, instead, as the rebel lurched towards him and started his attack, Williams raised the arm in which he held his weapon, spinning his gun deftly on his finger and whipping the man across his temple with the steel butt of the revolver. The sickening crunch of the man's skull as it fractured pierced the night air, seeming louder to Williams than even the cries of the injured rebels lying on the ground clutching their wounds as the man fell to the floor to join them, unconscious.

The rest of William's team had reached him now and he could sense them all around him, engaging in similar battles of their own, swinging their fists and firing their weapons into the raging crowd, taking down more and more rebels with every move they made. A second unit approached from the north and effectively boxed in the R.T.L between the centre, the hospital and the agents on Williams side of the fray and he couldn't help the smile he felt tugging at his lips as he took in the frightened expressions on the rebel's faces as several of them turned and began to flee, weaving through small gaps in the cars or down dank alleyways and out of sight. That's right, you cowards, run. Run home and hide. I'll be knocking on your door soon enough, he thought as a fist connected with the side of his helmet.

Williams had just one objective at this point. Only one goal in mind; to gain entry to the centre. Whilst he understood that Lieutenant Armitage's main concern was minimising civilian casualties, Williams had his own agenda. He was sure that the press would have much more to say about a mass breakout from the population control centre than they would about a few people being caught in the crossfire during a rebel attack. Hundreds of Cudos on the run would make international news. It would be broadcast by high-definition holograms emerging from the wrists of every citizen over the age of ten all over the world. The C.E.A, the government of the United Kingdom, and the entire bloody country would become a laughing stock.

Having spent the best years of his life fighting for the country into which he had been born, Williams' had no intention of allowing that to happen. No, he wouldn't let a bunch of misguided fools damage his beloved country's reputation or disrupt the cull process in which he believed so strongly. He had to secure the centre as quickly and efficiently as possible, at any cost.

The building drew closer with every shot that he fired and every punch that he threw and Williams could already feel the blistering heat from the fires raging on the front lawn against his exposed cheeks. It would only be a few minutes now, perhaps less, until he reached his destination. Adrenaline sang in his veins at the thought as he raised his head and charged forwards with his second-in-command hot on his heels.

They reached the low gate at the same moment, kicking aside the splintered pieces of wood which were all that remained of it as it hung precariously on one hinge and blew slightly in the wind. Williams heard the man beside him curse as he took in the sight before them. A group of rebels, probably twenty across and three rows deep, stood arm in arm across the gaping hole that they had blown in the centre's front wall. Blocking the only entrance.

"Get down!" Williams shouted, dropping to his knees behind the brick wall that surrounded the previously well-manicured garden which sat in front of the centre, which was now almost all aflame, sending twisting sparks of red and orange into the sky and casting eerie shadows across the rebels faces as they stood patiently, waiting to be challenged. Yanking a small cylindrical object from his belt, Williams tore out the pin and heaved it over his shoulder towards them before he curled into a ball and threw his arms over his head. The explosion rocketed through the air around them, shaking the very ground beneath their feet as the grenade detonated. Knocking the rebels to the ground in some parts of the line and utterly decimating those in others who had been too close to the grenade when it went off.

A wet smack emitted from the pavement beside him and Williams turned his head to see the remains of a severed arm lying on the concrete, blood and tissue seeping from its end and he couldn't help but cringe away slightly from the grisly sight. Pushing the image from his mind, Williams sprang to his feet, his ears still ringing from the detonation and faced the centre as the rest of his team joined him, locking eyes with those of an elderly woman standing just inside the gaping hole. She had to be at least seventy, perhaps older, judging by her sparkling white hair and the deep lines set in her forehead and she leaned heavily on a cane at her side as she peered around the rubble. Her wet eyes shone with tears in the firelight as she glanced from the remains of her would-be saviours burning where they had fallen in the courtyard, and William's dark glasses before stubbornly raising her right hand and extending her middle finger into the air towards him. Ballsy old bird. Williams thought as he chuckled under his breath. Good on her.

Sensing that this might be their last chance to escape, several of the Cudos who had been cowering behind the protective rebel line in the centre started to scramble forwards and out into the night, struggling to climb over the rubble left from the multiple explosions and past the fallen bodies of the rebels. A few of the braver ones tore the makeshift weapons from the hands of the dead and dying and surged forwards, screaming battle cries at the top of their lungs which would be heard for miles around the sleeping city tonight. Too late, Williams mused. They should have run long before now whilst they still had a chance.

Brawling rebels still littered the street behind him, battling uselessly against the C.E.A and the police, more of whom were arriving by the minute. Williams' knew that it was over, even if the rebels hadn't figured it out yet. The C.E.A had won this battle, although the real war was still to come. The Cudos had to be rounded up and returned, and the centre must be secured.

"Forward!" He cried, his bass-filled voice easily carrying to the ears of his colleagues who, as one, began to jump over the low red brick wall and into the fires and carnage in the small garden before them. Ignoring the scattered, dismembered body parts and the flames licking at their heels, the C.E.A agents surged forwards as one. Quickly taking down the remaining rebels and Cudos before them and tossing them out of their way. The battle cries that had so recently filled the air were soon replaced by the whimpering voices and pitiful sobs emitting from the injured, the burning, and the dying all around him, but Williams paid them no attention.

Jumping over a prone corpse in front of him who starred up into the star-filled sky with lifeless eyes, Williams ran as fast as he could manage in his heavy gear towards the centre, ripping the empty cartridge from his weapon and tossing it to the floor as he moved before slapping a new one in its place. He dodged fists, kicks, and even a flaming torch which he only just managed to duck beneath as he tore forwards, feeling the heat from the fire licking at his cheeks as he passed. But eventually, he made it to the opening in the wall and flung himself inside.

Chapter Sixty-Eight

Despite the roar of the rebels and the crackling of the fires that licked at the sides of the building, Tom heard the man's voice loud and clear as he shouted, "Get down!" at the top of his lungs. Whilst he had no idea who had given the order or why, there was an authority to the voice which made the hairs on the back of Tom's neck stand on end and something in his gut tell him to obey.

Steph and Tom had just reached the top of the final flight of stairs, the one which would lead them to the lobby and hopefully to freedom when the man's voice cut through the air and choosing not to second guess his instincts, Tom instantly dropped to the ground, flattening himself against the concrete surface and, dragging a disorientated and out of breath Steph, who was still clinging tightly to his hand down with him. Stumbling and losing her balance at the sudden movement, Steph felt her feet slide out from under her as she began to fall, crashing to the ground beside Tom in an ungainly heap.

Tom reached out and wrapped his arm around her, pulling her tightly to him and pushing her head into his chest as the desperate need to protect her overwhelmed him once more. Just in time, too. He barely had time to register the warmth of her breath on the exposed skin of his collarbone in the seconds before the explosion hit and he saw a bright ball of yellow and orange flames erupt somewhere on the floor below them, the brightness of which forced him to close his eyes as he felt a brush of heat rush passed him.

Tom tried to keep them both steady as the floor beneath them began to shake, and lumps of plaster and debris tumbled on their heads as the very walls around them began to crack and crumble and he ducked his head down on top of Steph's just in time to escape being cut by a shower of breaking glass as the small window high up on the wall behind them shattered into a thousand tiny pieces and scattered across the floor.

The dizziness returned to Steph's aching head as she clutched onto Tom's vibrating body and felt her teeth rattle in her skull. Her cracked ribs were constricted by the pressure of Tom's arm curled tightly around her and a new wave of white-hot pain shot through her body as it jerked in his embrace and the sounds of the explosion and chaos finally began to die out, leaving an unsettling quiet in their wake.

She raised her head slowly, peering down the long staircase and into the lobby below where she could just about make out scores of people clambering through a jagged hole where she was sure the centres doors had stood this morning, and into what looked from this distance, through the haze of dust and smoke, to be a sea of fire that reached as far as her tired eyes could see.

"We have to get to the staff exit," Tom told Steph firmly as he scrambled to his feet, reaching out a hand to help her do the same. "I think it's towards the back of the building." He added, remembering his father's earlier words of warning about not trying to get out of the front door and through the rebels.

It felt like a lifetime ago now that he had been standing up on the sixth floor with his dad even though, logically, Tom knew that little more than an hour could have passed since the first explosion hit and he wondered once again what had become of Jack as he took in the scene before him,

His eyes burned in their sockets, whether from sheer exhaustion or from the plumes of smoke that seemed to be penetrating every molecule of air in front of them, Tom did not know so raised a hand to rub at them furiously anyways, trying to clear his disorientation.

"How are we supposed to get through all of that?" Steph asked, gesturing towards the crowds of people who still lingered in the vast lobby along with the piles of debris, overturned tables and the small fires which seemed to have ignited in every available space.

"However we can. Just, whatever you do, do not let go of my hand, okay?" Tom replied, entwining his fingers with hers again and giving them a reassuring squeeze before he took his first step down the stairs.

Chapter Sixty-Nine

The Cudo's remaining inside of the building scattered in every direction like frightened children the moment that Williams and his team crossed the threshold of the lobby, holding their guns aloft and trying to make their voices heard over the sounds of the crackling fires and the footsteps rushing left and right across the wooden floors as they announced themselves.

"Cull Enforcement Agency! Everybody stop where you are and put your hands in the air! Now!" Williams shouted into the chaos before him, unsurprisingly, only a few people half-heartedly complied. Slowly coming to a standstill and looking at him wide-eyed as they raised their hands above their heads in fear, the rest, mostly the rebels, ignored him entirely.

At least they're easily distinguishable from each other, Williams thought to himself as he grabbed the arm of the person closest to him, a rebel no doubt judging by his black clothing and the thick scarf twisted around his face. This man had come prepared and ready to fight, unlike the Cudos, who were easy to spot, with shocked, almost traumatised expressions on their pale faces and most of them wearing a selection of different colours with flashes of every colour in the rainbow glinting in the light from the blazing fires.

After securing the man he had grabbed and handing him off to one of his colleagues, Williams paused for a moment, bouncing on the balls of his feet as he debated which direction to head in first. The decision was made easier for him as a torrent of shattering glass exploded from somewhere to his left, where a group of people had heaved one of the heavy tables from the ground and thrown it with all their might at one of the windows that fronted the centre. He knew that all the windows on the lower floors had been boarded up by wooden panels outside and that it would take the group at least a minute or two to get through them and Williams was also well aware that getting to them through the crowds of frightened people and preventing their escape wouldn't be easy so he had a little time.

"Mackenzie, Smith, Rogers, to the right. Peters, Bartram? You start securing people over there." Williams shouted, barking orders at his colleagues behind him and pointing in the direction of an old-fashioned and no doubt long out-of-use metal radiator along a side wall. Yes, they could use that, he realised as he turned back to face the second team who had just arrived through the cavernous hole in the building behind him.

"You lot, stay here. Protect this exit. Do not at any cost let anyone get outside!" He yelled into their faces, satisfied when they obeyed his order without question and formed a human barrier in front of the exit, much like the rebels had done.

It wouldn't be enough though, Williams could see that the C.E.A were still outnumbered by at least five to one. He just had to hope that more reinforcements arrived soon and do the best that he could in the meantime. Leaving his colleagues to carry out their assigned tasks, Williams turned and raced towards the group by the smashed window, crunching glass under his heavy boots as he dashed towards them. Most of the Cudos between him and the window scattered as he approached, some rushing towards the back of the building and others up the tall staircases which flanked the room, but Williams' didn't have time to worry about them right now. There was no way out up the stairs, that much he was sure of, but he couldn't allow the rebels to create another exit to flee through down here. He knew they didn't have the manpower to cover another hole in the wall and so he surged forwards, barging his shoulder into anyone who was stupid enough to try and get in his way. A few feet away from the window, he lunged, using his momentum to carry him across the remaining space and grabbed onto the heel of a man who was balancing on the window ledge. The man gripped the top of the frame with bleeding hands, no doubt cut by shards of glass that lingered there as he frantically pulled his leg back in preparation to kick out at the wooden boards blocking his exit, but Williams was faster. Twisting the man's ankle forcefully, he pulled him backwards, knocking him off balance and wrenching him from the frame. The man, taken entirely off guard by Williams' actions, lost his precarious grip on the ledge and began to fall, one leg extended behind him at an awkward angle, face first towards the windowsill.

The foot in his hand began to tremble and Williams glanced up in time to see that the man, a Cudo judging by his light, torn clothing, had been speared through the eye by a thick piece of triangular-shaped glass still clinging to the edge of the frame. Spatters of shockingly red blood flew from the wound, landing on the shocked faces of the rest of the group who had, just moments ago, been so intent on escaping, several of whom began to scream in terror. They stared at the window for several heartbeats, taking in the gory sight and Williams before them, who was still clutching the dying man's foot even as his gurgles grew weaker and his body began to go limp before they dispersed, turning and running as fast as they could in the opposite direction and away from him.

Chapter Seventy

Steph stopped dead in her tracks at the bottom of the stairs, unable to tear her eyes away from the sight on the dark wooden floor before her illuminated by the flickering glow of a nearby fire. She sucked in a breath through her teeth, and her hand went slack in Tom's grip as she stared down at the familiar face on the ground. It was twisted at an awkward angle, and its features were contorted in a pained expression, even in death. The emotionless grey eyes of the old woman with whom she had been speaking earlier, the woman who had told her that no matter how old you are, you're never ready to relinquish your life, stared back at her. Steph had to swallow down the bile rising rapidly in her throat.
"Steph, come on!" Tom shouted from somewhere by her side, and although she could hear his words and feel his hand tugging against her own, she couldn't bring herself to move. She couldn't look away from the woman on the ground, whose wooden cane lay prone beside her. Who would do such a thing to a defenceless old lady? Steph thought to herself as tears began rolling freely down her cheeks. She wouldn't have been able to put up much of a fight, surely, they could have restrained her? Taken her back upstairs and locked her in one of the dorms? But no, these monsters with a badge, dressed head to toe in dark armour which would protect them even from the worst of weapons, had chosen to end this poor woman's life. One of them had twisted her neck until it sat almost at a ninety-degree angle from her shoulders and tossed her lifeless body to the ground as though she were nothing more than a piece of rubbish. Not a wife, a mother, a grandmother. Not someone's best friend. They had treated her as though she were a criminal for the simple act of trying to save her own life.
"Steph, we have to go!" Tom shouted again, trying desperately to get her attention as he whirled to face her. Following her gaze, he too stared down at the body on the floor, and his stomach turned in anguish as he took in the sight. He knew that the old woman didn't deserve that, that no one did, however, there was nothing that they could do for her now. She was at peace, and they were wasting precious time, they had to get out of here.
Tom's fingers bit into the soft flesh of Steph's thin shoulders as he reached out and turned her to face him, dragging her around on unsteady feet and breaking her connection with the woman on the ground as he bent his knees and looked her straight in the eyes.
"Steph, I'm sorry, I know this is upsetting, but we have to move. Unless we want to join her, we have to get out of here now!" He said forcefully, trying to get through to Steph and break her from her trance.

Steph blinked at the man before her once, then twice, trying to clear the image of the elderly lady from her vision and take in his words which sounded muffled to her ears, as though she were underwater. On the third blink, she succeeded, and the room around her suddenly snapped back into focus, as did Tom as he shouted at her again.

"We. Have. To. Go!" He stated, emphasising each word as he spoke, agitation rolling off him in waves as he spotted yet another contingent of the C.E.A storming through the hole in the wall and ploughing into the crowd in the lobby.

Steph didn't resist this time when he took her hand in his and pulled her forward into the horde behind him. Tightening her grip on his fingers, she kept as close to Tom's broad back as she could manage, almost tripping over his feet in her haste to keep up as he weaved them through the mob, changing direction so fast and so frequently that it made her aching head spin.

They dodged past rebels engaged in fistfights with uniform-clad C.E.A agents, past swinging lumps of burning wood and other projectiles being hurled across the room. They ducked as someone threw a chair in their direction and felt the hairs on the back of their necks stand on end as the object flew just inches above their heads, displacing the air around them. The one thing they didn't dare to do was slow down. Their progress was slow, too slow, Tom knew. They weren't even a third of the way across the vast lobby yet and he still couldn't make out the staff exit at the other end of the room through the crowd. He just had to hope that they were going the right way.

A deafeningly loud crash reverberated through Tom's ears, and he craned his neck over his shoulder in the direction it had come from, squinting his eyes against the smoke, he watched as a massive crowd of people surged toward him from what had previously been a window and was now little more than a hole in the wall. Tom felt bile rise in the back of his throat as he spotted an impaled man hanging limply by his head which was covered in blood on the windowsill, being buffeted from side to side as people scrambled over his body and out of the newly formed exit. For a moment, Tom debated turning back and exiting the building that way, wondering if it would be quicker, but a quick scan of the nearby area changed his mind.

More and more law enforcement were piling through the gap in the wall now and into the centre, throwing punches left and right as they went. Some even fired their guns at point-blank range into the backs of the fleeing Cudos, indiscriminately taking them down one by one. Tom was sure he had seen a smirk on one officer's face as they had watched the body of a middle-aged woman tumble to the ground. They're enjoying this, he realised, and his stomach churned again.

So caught up was Tom in the chaos by the window that the force of the blow hit him out of nowhere whilst his head was still turned towards the disturbance on the other side of the room. His head jerked violently from the impact as a pair of hands closed around his throat, and he pitifully tried to gulp in as much air as he could. Instinctually he raised his own hands to try and loosen the grip that the C.E.A agents' had around his neck, attempting to fight the agent off and dropping Steph's hand in the process.

Stumbling backwards on shaky legs as he wrestled with his attacker, Tom felt himself collide with someone behind him and heard a dull thud as they hit the floor. Steph. Realisation dawned on him, and his body ached to turn and help her, to get her up off the floor before she was trampled by the horde of people who were now all turning back towards the front of the lobby, trying to reach the open window, but the agent's hands around his neck prevented any such action.

The edges of Tom's vision began to blur as his oxygen supply was depleted, and some instinct that he hadn't known he possessed until that very moment kicked in. He raised his leg sharply, swiping it backwards and aiming a kick at the man's kneecap. The agent instantly dropped his hands in shock, releasing Tom from his vice-like grip as his knee buckled out from under him and Tom threw two punches in quick succession into the agent's shocked face, watching in satisfaction as the man finally lost his fight with gravity and plummeted to the floor, his helmet bouncing off the hard wood with a loud smack. Struggling to regain his composure, the agent placed his palms on the floor and began pushing himself up as he furiously narrowed his eyes at Tom.

The agent had just about managed to force his body into a sitting position when it happened. The tall man with the shaved head who Tom had spoken to earlier came out of nowhere, diving between Tom and the C.E.A officer and straddling his legs, effectively pinning him in place. Sucking in a deep breath, the agent's eyes went wide as he took in the long shard of sharpened plastic in the man's hand, which was already stained with someone else's blood. Time seemed to slow as the agent stared in utter horror at the black-clad assassin atop of him, who raised his fist into the air before plunging the knife in his hand directly into the agent's exposed neck.

Tom had no idea where the man had come from or why on earth he had chosen to jump in and effectively save Tom's life, but he suddenly felt incredibly guilty for his thoughts towards the skinhead and his friends from earlier when he had decided that Steph had been right and that they were nothing but trouble. He wanted to say something, to thank him, maybe? But by the time Tom had registered what had happened, the bald man was already on his feet, rushing away from Tom and back into the crowd. The long piece of sharpened plastic in his hand dripped with the blood of this, his most recent kill, as he glanced over his shoulder to Tom and winked at him before disappearing into the crowd.

Chapter Seventy-One

Steph's scream sliced through the air penetrating the ears of everyone around her, ripping Tom's attention away from the retreating skinhead and causing many others around them to turn their heads in her direction at once, just in time to see her be yanked from the floor by her ponytail. The pain was excruciating, unlike anything she had ever felt. She scrambled to get her feet underneath her and redistribute her weight as strands of hair were ripped from her scalp.
"Steph!" Tom cried, spinning on the spot to face her as quickly as he could and cursing himself for not helping her sooner as he took in the scene before him and a shudder ran down his back.
The man holding her was at least a foot taller than Steph, perhaps more, and three times her size. His thick arm splayed across her neck, obscuring half her chest as it pressed down on her, and Tom watched in horror as her face began to turn red as she struggled against his grip.
"Let her go!" Tom shouted at the man, who was clearly a C.E.A officer judging by his uniform. The agent stared him down, not relinquishing his grip or saying a word as he looked at Tom through his dark goggles.

Williams had seen Vincent and the boy in front of him fighting from his position several feet away as he had handed off another secured Cudo to one of the other officers nearby to take over to the group that they had already secured to the radiator, and he had acted instantly. Pushing his way through the crowd, he ran as fast as he could manage to get to his old friend only to have to stand there in horror and watch as the man who Williams considered to be more of a brother than anything else, a man who he had served in the army with for eight years before they had joined the Cull Enforcement Agency, a man with a wife and two young children at home and his whole life ahead of him, was stabbed mercilessly in the neck.
There was nothing that Williams could do, the weapon had slid straight into Vincent's throat as though it were made of butter, and his attacker had clearly known what he was doing. He hadn't aimed directly for an artery through the side of his neck like they did in the movies, no doubt knowing that the muscle there was too tough for his makeshift blade to penetrate. He had aimed his blow straight for the larynx, then twisted the sharp object and tore it to the side, effectively slitting Vincent's throat and severing the carotid artery. He was dead before his head even hit the ground.
Standing frozen a few feet away, Williams weighed up his options. As much as every bone in his body ached to chase after the murderer, to pin him down and beat him to a bloody pulp, he knew that the chances

of him catching him were slim. Within seconds of committing his
crime, the man had jumped up and disappeared into the sea of people
ahead of him and Williams didn't have time to waste trying to find him
again and so he settled for taking his anger out on the guy that Vincent
had initially been grappling with.
Stepping forwards towards the dark-haired man whilst his back was still
to him, preparing to strike, Williams had almost tripped over the girl on
the floor, who he hadn't noticed until that very moment. She was staring
up at the man with the dark chocolate curls desperately, reaching out her
hands to try and grab at the back of his trousers as she tried to get up
from the floor, and Williams had sensed an opportunity.
Slipping his hand into the woman's hair, he had wound her long
ponytail around his wrist and tugged harshly, dragging her to her feet.
She had screamed of course, but then that was the point, he wanted to
get the man's attention, and now it seemed he had it.
"Let her go!" Tom begged him again, and Williams let a low,
humourless chuckle escape his lips.
"I don't think so, Cudo. I take it she means something to you? She your
girlfriend? Your friend?" He asked Tom in a menacing voice, and Tom
nodded slowly. "Yeah, well, he was *my* friend," Williams said,
gesturing behind Tom with his free hand to Vincent's blood-covered
body on the floor. "What's that old saying, an eye for an eye?" he
finished threateningly.
Tom's blood turned to ice in his veins as he took in the man's words,
and his tired mind scrambled to devise a plan to free Steph from her
attacker's grasp. Tom knew he wouldn't stand a chance against the agent
before him if it came down to a fight, and the best option he had was to
try and reason with the man.
"I'm sorry. Truly. He didn't deserve what happened." Tom said quietly,
"But it wasn't her fault. If you want to punish someone for that, punish
me, not her." He added, hearing the desperation in his own voice as he
spoke.
Steph's eyes widened as she took in Tom's words, and she redoubled her
efforts to free herself from the agent's vice-like grip. Thrashing around
as much as she could manage and clawing at the arm around her neck
with her nails, but the man behind her barely even seemed to notice,
paying no attention to her at all as he continued to stare over her head at
Tom.
"An interesting idea. But this isn't a negotiation. You're both under
arrest for crimes against humanity, the punishment for which, I am sure
you know, is death." Williams sneered. His top lip curled up in disgust
as he spoke. Hadn't he resolved just half an hour ago not to use lethal
force on these degenerates? And now here he was, threatening the life

of not one but two of them.

Logically he knew that his actions were wrong, that this wasn't who he was. That murdering a woman in cold blood, even a Cudo who should have been dead within a few days anyways, was not the right thing to do, that he should take her over to the radiator and chain her up with the others and then return for the guy. Hell, he might even come with us if I ask him nicely, he seems to be determined to protect her, Williams thought to himself.

As his concentration divided, his grip on the struggling woman in his arms slipped, and Steph made her move. Raising her right foot from the ground, she stamped backwards as hard as she could into the agent's shin the moment that his hold on her loosened. Then, pushing all her weight into his body, she twisted and turned her head as she bent her knees, sliding out from under his arm. She felt the man grabbing at her jumper as she lunged forwards towards Tom, who grabbed her hand and started to pull her as hard as he could, tearing her away from the officer and creating a few feet of distance between them.

Williams' lunged then, leaning forwards with his arm outstretched grasping towards the girl, his fingers closed around the soft material of the top she wore and he tightened his grip and pulled, attempting to drag her back to him but the girl was too quick. Within seconds, she had entirely shrugged off the garment and was dashing away from him. As his momentum carried him forwards, Williams found himself tripping over his feet as he tried to keep his balance and fell forward to the floor, with nothing to show for his efforts other than her blue hooded sweatshirt in his hand.

Grabbing Steph's hand again now that she had shrugged out of her hoodie, Tom redoubled his movements, forcing his feet to move as fast as they could beneath him despite his injured ankle, and practically dragging her along behind him. Very few people are still lingering at the back of the lobby now, most had made their way to the smashed window and the large hole at the front of the building and were grappling with the C.E.A agents and police officers there as they desperately tried to escape, so, mercifully, their progress was much less impeded than it had been earlier.

They covered the ground quickly, both gasping for breath as Tom struggled to pull the set of keys free from the pocket of his jeans with his free hand, not slowing for a moment as the staff exit door in front of him loomed ever closer. Just a few more feet, he thought to himself as he felt the skeleton key slide in between his fingers.

Propping himself up on his hands, Williams forced himself into a rudimentary push-up position and planted his feet on the floor as he watched the two figures darting away from him. Ha. Idiots. He thought to himself, they've got nowhere to go. Scrambling to his feet, he tossed aside the blue hoodie still clutched in his hand and straightened his back, wincing at the pain in his leg from where the girl had kicked him and started forwards, not even bothering to run, there was no need. The pair were headed straight towards a dead end.

It took him a moment to see it through the smoky air in front of him, the tall wooden door with the words' *staff only exit'* emblazoned on the front, but as it came into focus Williams' cursed loudly and pounded forwards, his heavy boots slamming against the floor with every step that he took but even then, he knew that he would be too late.

It took Tom three attempts to slide the long silver key into the small lock, Steph panting and pleading with him to hurry at his side the entire time. After what felt like an eternity but in reality couldn't have been more than a few seconds, Tom heard the reassuring click of the mechanism disengaging. His whole body sagged in relief as he pushed the door wide open, and a wisp of fresh air danced across his face.

"Go!" He shouted, shoving Steph through the exit as soon as there was enough space before flinging himself through the gap after her.

He could hear the thudding of the agents' boots getting louder as he closed the distance between them, calling out to them to stop, but he ignored the man's orders. He didn't even stop long enough to close the door behind him as he stepped into the cool night air and ran, hand in hand with Steph, as fast as he could into the darkness.

End of book one.

The Escape

Book two in The Cull book series is now available on Amazon in paperback, on kindle and FREE to read with Kindle unlimited. Grab your copy today to follow more of Steph and Tom's story as they attempt to flee from the death sentences hanging over their heads.

Book three coming soon!

Follow me on social media for more updates

You can find @thecullbookseries on X, TikTok and Instagram

Acknowledgments

Growing up I've often heard the phrase 'it takes a village' to describe bringing up children. Well I don't have any children of my own, (I am fairly sure my cats don't really count!) but I can certainly tell you that this old adage applies just as well to writing a book. Without the unending support of my nearest and dearest, I could never have completed this story and I wanted to take a moment to thank them here.

To my Kristien, where to even begin? You have been here from the very first day I decided to try my hand at writing, which seems like a lifetime ago now. You helped me to work through the half-remembered parts of a dream I had in order to turn it into the story that this has become. From reading along chapter by chapter as I have written this book, to helping me come up with character names, plot twists, cover ideas and being a never ending source of encouragement, you have always been on hand to help. Despite calling myself a writer, I cannot quite come up with the words to express how much having you by my side throughout this whole process has helped me. I truly would never have been able to write this book, or any other without you and I am eternally grateful.

Tim, for a long time now you have encouraged me to pursue this thing called writing, which I never saw as more than a hobby. Pushing me steadily to continue, praising me much more than I deserved for every little milestone I hit, and encouraging me to continue when imposter syndrome hit me so hard that I couldn't see the point anymore. You even took my little story to the other side of the world and 'worked' through your holiday editing it for me so it was ready to publish in time and I am incredibly grateful. Thank you.

To Karryn, Eileen, Suus, Lyndz, all my other ladies, thank you for taking the time to be my sounding boards, for all your advice and for supporting me through this venture. And last but not least, to my mum, Maxine and sister, Lisa, your support means more than you'll ever know.

Thank you all. Here's to the next one!

Printed in Great Britain
by Amazon